THE MISFITS OF COPPER COUNTY

MAY ARCHER

Cover Art: Natasha Snow Designs
Editing: One Love Editing
Proofreading: Jodi Duggan

All the good bits are theirs, and any mistakes are my own!

THE MISFITS OF COPPER COUNTY

**When you burn down your contractor's home…
and kind of, accidentally invite him to move
into yours.**

First things first, that fire was a fluke. A tragic, completely
unintentional byproduct of high emotions, an ill-timed
backyard grilling… and one very shirtless man.

I only meant to confront Brewer—my maddeningly stoic
contractor—about a few *small* concerns with the renovation
of my historic money pit.

Instead, I got distracted by his muscles (who grills shirtless
in February, I ask you?), I tripped over my words—and my
feet—and… well, my carefully-ordered life went up in
flames.

Suddenly, Brewer's living in my attic, his dainty teacups are
in my cabinet, his slobbery dog is all up in my business, and

I find myself renovating my whole future just as surely as Brewer's renovating my home.

Copper County was never my endgame. Once I finish writing my article, I'm off on my next assignment. But between late night conversations, sledgehammer therapy sessions, and solving the Jam Cupboard Mystery (it's a real thing, I promise), I'm starting to think we're building something neither of us expected.

Because the more I learn about Brewer, the more I realize I'm not the only misfit in Copper County. And that maybe it's time I stop chasing other people's truths... and start writing my own.

CHAPTER ONE

Let's get one thing straight: I never meant to burn Brewer Barnum's home to the ground, okay?

In fact, I'd woken up that morning in my half-renovated house on the shores of beautiful Copper Lake feeling pretty fucking chill.

Optimistic.

Possibly even... cheerful.

I'd stared out at the snow-covered trees and the lake while I'd sipped my coffee, thinking this was the kind of easy Sunday morning I'd signed up for last fall when I'd left the city, moved to this little town in the middle of nowhere, and bought a fixer-upper a few doors down from my sister.

While sipping, I hadn't felt the urge to glare at the flooring and paint cans stacked where my dining table should be.

I hadn't cast a single guilty glance at the ripped-out ceiling in the living room.

I hadn't spent even a moment perseverating on the fact that Brewer Barnum—my unfairly tall, disturbingly sexy nemesis—would be showing up the next morning with his giant tool belt and his long-suffering sighs and his I-know-better-than-you-Delaney attitude.

In fact, for once, I hadn't thought of Brewer at all.

It had been lovely.

Then a weather alert for Copper County had popped up on my phone with the words WINTER STORM WARNING in big red letters, and my whole day had gone to shit.

There were many scenarios in which a man like me would enjoy "getting 6 to 9 inches" on a Tuesday night.

A blizzard was not one of them.

Especially not when the remains of the last winter storm still lingered in my driveway. And especially-especially not when Brewer's dry, almost-definitely-judgmental "Guess I'll just... shovel you out myself, then, if I want a place to unload my truck?" was fresh in my memory.

Just the thought of him using that disapproving tone while looking down at me with those clear blue eyes that crinkled at the corners sent an unwelcome heat through my body.

By which I meant the heat of *fury*.

Of outrage at the *injustice*.

Obviously.

As a responsible adult, I owned my mistakes, and I really should have shoveled my driveway or paid someone to do it. But in my defense, shoveling wasn't a thing I'd had to worry about back in the city. So not-a-thing, in fact, I didn't own a shovel.

Which, I realized with slow-dawning horror, was something I needed to rectify.

Today.

At the store.

Where the Coppertians were.

I drained my coffee cup and sighed deeply.

Was it more than a little lowering that I, Delaney Monroe, the award-winning journalist who'd once sweet-talked his way into a classified government facility in São Paulo without speaking a word of Portuguese, was actively dreading a trip to a small-town hardware store?

Yes, thank you for asking. Yes, it was.

But something about this town made me feel like I was twelve years old again—the runt of the Monroe litter, standing on the sidelines while my hockey-star siblings glided effortlessly through their lives.

I hypothesized that whatever recessive gene manifested in broad shoulders and the ability to see a puck without tripping over it also gave a person the ability to smile at ridiculousness without the need to point it out and correct it. Which meant my siblings had tragically terrible scores on standardized tests but were almost universally beloved.

Meanwhile, I had been blessed with different genes. Genes that made me small and smart and nimble and brilliant at ferreting out a good story... but slightly less competent with things like changing tires and, you know, having interpersonal relationships.

Trade-offs, right?

Despite what some people assumed, I was more than satisfied with the genes I'd gotten... but it did make things tricky, considering the most ridiculous humans in the universe existed in Copper County, New York. And unlike the refugee camps and political hotspots I'd found myself in over the years, where I could deal with whatever conditions I had to in order to get the story, Copper County was home now. The place where I was supposed to feel comfortable.

Repressing a sigh, I rinsed my cup and set it in the

drainer, then forced myself to walk directly to my car and drive to town because that was what responsible adults did...

And because I knew if I didn't get this errand done immediately, I'd spend the rest of the day thinking up compelling reasons to remain snowbound until spring.

But my responsible adultness fizzled once I'd parked my Audi in a diagonal parking spot outside the hardware store. Instead of going inside like a normal human, I tapped my thumbs on the steering wheel and watched the people go by.

My phone buzzed with a text from my editor.

MARJORIE

Call tomorrow morning to discuss Empire
Ridge story? I have exciting news!

As I typed out an affirmative reply, some of the tension left my shoulders.

At least my career was the one area of my life where I knew exactly what I was doing... mostly because, unlike Brewer Fucking Barnum, *Marjorie* never "adjusted" my renovation plans without asking. *Marjorie* would never change the bathroom tile I'd selected or complain that the sliding door I wanted to add to my walk-in closet would compromise the flow of the house, despite having zero evidence beyond "experience" to explain this assertion. And *Marjorie* never took smug satisfaction in proving me wrong at every turn, nodding at me with a little half smile that screamed, "I'm humoring you," unlike certain enormous people.

In fact, *Marjorie* was as excited about this story as I was. Possibly even more excited. She'd called it "career defining" when I'd sent her transcripts of my initial interview with

Anthony Harmon and said the corruption whistleblower angle gave it an extra punch publications were looking for.

I stretched my neck from side to side as I watched a child skip happily into one of the snowbanks lining the street while their mother sighed in exasperation and rolled her eyes.

I imagined my sister would have roughly the same reaction if she saw me sitting here now. I could hear her voice in my head saying, *Try getting out there and actually talking to your neighbors, Delaney. You'll fit right in! You'll see!*

Then again, Tam had the aforementioned Broad-Shouldered Gene. She loved the people of this town, and they loved her. Also, she was naive enough to insist that Brewer was just being *thorough* whenever I voiced a complaint about him and that he treated all of his clients the same way. So, really, what did Tam know?

I could *talk* to people all day long. Fitting in with them was different.

And, anyway, I was halfway convinced that the people of Copper County—with the possible exceptions of my sister and my friend Jasper, who had, not coincidentally, both grown up far from here—weren't actually *people* at all but some sort of mutant golden-retriever-human hybrid. Hyper-friendly and eager and possibly rabid.

The first day I'd ventured to town to run errands last fall, the lady at the Books n' More had spent fifteen minutes telling me about her nephew who "also didn't play sports but turned out just fine" while I purchased stamps. Three different people had invited me to join their book clubs. And six people I'd never met had given me unsolicited advice about which contractor—Brewer Barnum, naturally —I should hire for my renovation.

I'd concluded that some people were just meant to live

in small towns. They thrived in tight-knit communities that were alllll the way up in each other's business. They liked talking slow and walking slower. They relished the in-jokes and the weird-as-fuck rituals. They *fit*.

And then there was me. A man who had to psych himself up to buy a shovel.

So, you might rightly ask, why the hell did I move here? Excellent question, really. Top-notch.

In some ways, it was a little like the story I'd been working on. A simple guy—ambitious, for sure, but earnest enough—had made a choice for what he'd thought were all the right reasons and had instead found himself caught up in something bigger and more complex than he'd imagined.

In my case, the big, complex thing just happened to be this weirdly friendly town.

"Stop being such a baby, Monroe," I muttered. "And buy a damn shovel."

I forced myself out of the car, slammed the door, and resolutely headed for the store—

"Hey, there!" A parka-clad woman popped out at me from behind one of the decorative trees along Weaver Street.

"*Gahh!*" I jerked back, bumping my hip against my car's side mirror.

"You're Delaney!" Before I recovered my balance, parka-lady waved a stack of flyers in my face that made the crystalline air even colder. "I'm Janice! Janice Plum. Have you heard about the O'Leary-Copper County Council for Historical Happenings' Candle-Making Symposium and Dipping Demonstration this afternoon?"

My heart thundered in my chest. In Kuala Lumpur two years ago, someone had jumped out at me when I was exiting a vehicle, but that incident had involved a nasty parang with a ten-inch blade and a teenager who'd taken all my money. This ambush—from a middle-aged woman in a knitted hat with pom-poms—should not have triggered the same fight-or-flight response, but my body didn't seem to understand that.

"Come dip your wick from two to four!" Janice continued, undeterred by my wide-eyed silence.

"No." Annoyed by the jump scare—mostly annoyed at myself because my pulse was racing—I gave her a wide berth as I headed for the sidewalk. "My wick's perfectly fine as it is, Janice."

"But... you didn't even take a flyer. Everyone takes a flyer." Her pout was audible. "It's rude not to."

I could practically feel Tam judging me from across town. *You're not in the city anymore. Here, you don't have to lock your doors, but you do need to make an effort to engage.*

Fine, then. I'd try to engage.

I turned and looked at parka-woman seriously, trying to ignore how my heart was still hammering in my chest. "Has it occurred to you, Janice, that what's really rude is accosting a man with the desiccated remains of dead trees..."

She frowned down at her flyers.

"... while he's running a lifesaving errand to the hardware store?"

Janice blinked. "Lifesaving? Are you okay?"

"Oh, yes," I said. "I am perfectly fine. But I engaged a contractor to renovate my house, Janice. A contractor whose ego is as massive as he is, which is saying something since he's six-foot-twenty. And he's already working my very last nerve. My plans for my primary bathroom? Scrapped. My instructions to replace my creaky hardwoods with something modern and sustainable? Ignored. My specific request that the paneling in my office should be painted white since walnut stain would make the space feel like I was working in a freaking catacomb? Literally scoffed at."

A strong gust of wind whistled down Weaver Street, making the pom-poms on Janice's hat dance. She clutched her flyers tighter. "But—"

"And," I continued, "if I don't have a shovel on Wednesday morning to clean the snow, the man will sigh at me like I'm incompetent, Janice. He won't be able to help himself. He will roll his eyes. He'll give a little snort that's just low enough to make it seem plausible that he thought I wouldn't hear it, though he absolutely knows I can hear it. And because I am actually very competent, there will be a murder in this town." I leaned toward her and lowered my voice. "Do you want there to be a murder, Janice?"

I hadn't meant to say that much or be quite so abrupt, and I felt a little bad when Janice's eyes went wide and shiny... until I realized she wasn't upset so much as *awestruck*.

"But you... you don't mean... you can't be talking about... Brewer?"

I pinched the bridge of my nose with cold fingers. *Oh, here we go.*

"Because Brewer's awesome," Janice breathed. "He's, like, a renovation genius. He's never had a single unhappy client. And he's so handsome! And his voice is so pleasant. And gosh, he's so nice! When my father's hot water heater burst while I had the flu, Brewer went to his house and changed it out for him at cost, and—"

"Yes, yes, and he helps little old ladies cross the street while simultaneously rescuing kittens from mine shafts, ending global famines, and single-handedly saving the environment," I finished. "I know."

"Oh, wow." Janice clasped the flyers to her bosom. "I hadn't heard that, about the kittens. But I totally believe it."

A noise not unlike the whistle of a teakettle escaped me.

I might not be able to make Janice see the light about Brewer—if I couldn't change *Tam's* mind, I had zero chance with someone I wasn't related to—but I could set her right about some things, at least.

"Janice." I forced a smile. "I bet most of the people who take your flyers don't actually show up."

She seemed startled. "Well, people are busy—"

"People are statistically more likely to do something when they want to do it, when they choose it, rather than when it is foisted upon them. Read 'The Art of Choosing' by Sheena Iyengar and thank me later."

"But—"

"You need to make people come to you, Janice. Maybe make a visual splash of some kind. Wear a historical costume, for example. People are suckers for a hoop skirt, am I right? But for God's sake, change the name of the event to something you can say in one breath, like..." I tapped my lip. "Wicked Fun Candle-making, for example. That's a banger."

Janice stared at me, mouth open and face blank, like I'd whacked her with a stick.

See, this was what happened when I engaged. No matter how helpful my suggestions, people here just looked at me like I was speaking an alien language.

"You have a good day now," I said, smiling a little harder. Then I bleeped the locks on my car and headed for O'Leary Hardware.

"Sir! Excuse us, sir!" Some adorable little girls in scout

uniforms stopped me outside the store and shook a coffee can in my direction. The few coins inside jingled. "Would you like to donate to the Shoemaker Day Career Fair our troop is organizing?"

I glanced from the girls to their chaperone, a dad holding a coffee cup in one hand and a phone playing sports commentary in the other.

It was on the tip of my tongue to ask him if I'd heard right—Shoemaker Day? Were we encouraging shoemaking as a career choice in this economy?—but I heard Tam's voice in my head and kept my mouth shut

Small towns are all about helping each other out, but you don't have to be Dictator Delaney about it. Your opinions aren't always helpful.

I pictured my newborn niece standing here one day, her own plea for... Jesus, shoemaking funds?... and eagerly awaiting a response. Would I want her to get a clipped "No, thanks," or would I want the man to have a little consideration for her feelings?

"Sure. I'll donate," I said, realizing my smile wasn't quite so forced as I pulled out my phone. "What's your Venmo?"

"Oh, um." The girls looked from me to the dad and back. "We don't have that."

I tried to stifle my irritation, but how was I supposed to hold back from giving an opinion when I encountered such a grievous lack of good leadership, I ask you?

"You don't take Venmo? Or any cash app?" I addressed this to the man, who'd finally glanced up from his phone. "Did you know a recent study by the Federal Reserve found that fifty-four percent of people don't carry cash on them? You could be getting twice as many donations if you took them electronically."

The guy blinked.

With a sigh, I pulled out the emergency $20 I kept tucked into my phone case and stuffed it in the coffee can. "Here," I told the girls. "Good luck with your... shoes or whatever."

The inside of the hardware store was boiling hot and crowded—two of my least favorite things—and the big display under the "Snow Shovels!" sign was incomprehensibly empty. Was I too late? Had they sold out?

The answer came when I decided the most expedient way to ask was to get in the checkout line—a line that was moving slower than a taxi in Midtown at rush hour since Hen, the white-haired proprietor, felt the need to chat with every single customer while he rang up their purchases.

"No snow this week," I heard him say with confidence. He did a little jig behind the counter like one of those puppets that flail when you pull its string. "See that? M'bad leg always feels achy when there's a storm coming, but spry means dry! Gonna be cold, though. My feet are itching like nobody's business."

Several people nodded seriously.

I glanced at my phone, confirming that, indeed, the National Weather Service was still warning about significant snowfall. But apparently, even when trained meteorologists were predicting a big storm, the local populace took their weather cues from an octogenarian with foot rot.

Am I the only one who finds this beyond bizarre? Really? Just me?

Sweat prickled on the back of my neck, and I unbuttoned my jacket.

I hadn't realized just how... Copper County... this town was when I'd come here on visits. I'd been seduced by the scenery, charmed by the slower pace, pleasantly surprised by the diversity. I'd thought it was just another town, and I could be as happy here as I was anywhere else. It wasn't until after I'd signed on the dotted line that I learned how wrong I'd been.

And, if I was being honest, that hadn't been my only fuckup in recent memory.

Against my will, I remembered the autumn day I'd walked into the little bakery across the street for my first meeting with the contractor Tam and all her friends recommended.

I'd been armed with inspiration photos, a firm renovation budget, and a take-charge attitude—a requirement when you were a person of slightly below statistically average height dealing with a power-tool bro so you could make it clear you weren't the sort of person to be trifled with.

But then Brewer had stood up (and up, and up) to greet me with a smile and a "Delaney, right?"

His eyes had crinkled at the corners when he smiled—a genuine smile that reached all the way to those eyes, making the room feel suddenly warmer—and when he'd stretched out one ginormous paw, I'd been mesmerized by his calloused fingers and broad palm. I'd had the mortifying thought that I wanted those fingers to touch more than just my hand.

I'd managed to mumble out something about "inspired by industrial spaces" and "clean lines," but I couldn't have told you what else I said. My brain had short-circuited the moment he'd said my name in that deep, woodsmoke voice, and my very last coherent thought had taken a sabbatical when he'd accidentally brushed his knee against mine under the table.

Brewer had spent the next hour patiently going through

my plans, asking questions and offering suggestions in that low rumble that felt like velvet sliding across my skin. Meanwhile, I'd fixated on how the afternoon light caught the golden-brown highlights in his hair and how his forearms flexed when he reached for his mug of coffee—which he took with cream and sugar, no fucks given, like he'd never heard of calories or was too enlightened and real to care about bullshit like that.

A voice in my head had sighed, *Tam and everyone were right! You can trust this guy, Delaney.* And I'd listened.

Pro tip, friends: Never sign legally binding contracts while lust-drunk on a man who looks like he could bench-press your car with one hand while making you a soufflé with the other. It won't end well.

It wasn't until our first real meeting at the house a week later that I realized the voice in my "head" actually belonged to my penis. My dick was a notoriously bad judge of character (see also: every one of my exes), and since Brewer was out-of-my-league gorgeous and probably straight, he was exactly the kind of guy it would point me toward... especially since I'd been in the middle—or, as it turned out, closer to the *beginning*—of a months-long dry spell.

That day, Brewer had shown up to my house in a stupidly tight henley that accentuated his stupidly firm muscles and a tool belt that accentuated his stupidly trim hips, examined my bathroom plans, and suggested—no, *announced*—several changes.

That was when I'd discovered two things: one, my initial dick-straction had blinded me to the fact that Brewer Barnum was the most infuriatingly stubborn, arrogant, my-way-or-the-highway builder in North America... and two,

I'd signed a contract giving him far more "design approval" authority than I ever should have agreed to.

Those crinkly smile-eyes? A tactical weapon.

The attentive listening? Just gathering ammunition.

The competent hands? Well... I had nothing to say about those since they were admittedly very competent... at building things *and* at driving me absolutely insane.

But since that fucking contract appeared to be legally binding, whether I liked it or not—and I *didn't*—I was still very much...

"Brewer's client, right?" a voice said.

I turned my head and found an older gentleman in a plaid scarf smiling at me. In his arms, he held a tiny, trembling dog with puffy hair, bulging eyes, and a face that suggested it was just as appalled to see me as I was to see it.

Beneath the arm of my cashmere blend coat, four small, decades-old puncture marks throbbed, reminding me of their presence.

I leaned away. "Delaney," I said stiffly. "And yes. Technically."

The dog let out a sharp, high-pitched yip that made my blood curdle as he lunged toward me.

"Admiral Barkington," the man admonished, tightening his grip. "Hush." To me, he added, "Don't be afraid. For the Admiral, barking's a sign of friendship."

Affronted, I lifted my chin. "I'm not *afraid*..."

A fear of dogs—especially small and harmless ones—would be foolish. Everyone knew that.

The creature was one-twentieth my size and had no opposable thumbs.

He hadn't taken a dozen Intro to Krav Maga classes a few years ago and nailed not only the technique but also the hot instructor.

"...I'm justifiably cautious," I concluded firmly. "There's a difference."

"Of course." The man beamed. "The Admiral is a very discerning judge of character, too."

The dog and I shared a dubious look.

"I expect he likes you because you smell like Brewer," he went on. "The Admiral's loved Brewer since their first meeting, you know."

"Figures," I muttered.

He scratched at the dog's fluffy head fondly. "You're Tam Monroe's brother, aren't you?" the man went on. "The one who doesn't play hockey?"

His words were enough to distract me from the small demon he carried.

"The one who's a journalist," I corrected.

Anyone who'd come from a family like mine knew there was a difference between being a Monroe followed by an asterisk (the *not-a-hockey-player Monroe*) and being something you'd made yourself. Something you were proud of.

"Hey, Delaney!" Hen called, a tease in his voice. "Hurry up, kiddo. I can't keep waitin' on ya all day."

I huffed and stepped around the Admiral in a wide circle with a nod of farewell to his owner.

Hen's eyes twinkled merrily as I approached. "Bet I know why you're here. You're here because you need..."

"A snow shovel," I said.

"Your vanity," he finished. Then he cocked his head in dismay. "You don't have a snow shovel?"

"No, I... wait." I did a mental one-eighty, forgetting about snow shovels and impending storms, about meddling Coppertians in general and one very large one in particular. "Are you talking about the bathroom vanity I ordered? It came in early?"

Giddy excitement and relief flooded me. I hadn't realized how much I needed a win today until Hen provided one.

"Yep. Truck dropped it off yesterday," he confirmed. "I was gonna call Brewer tomorrow to come get it with a couple of those helpers of his. It's a big ol' thing."

"And it arrived in one piece?" I asked. "The cement slab top? The metal bottom with the—"

"Clunky feet?" He nodded. "Looks a little rusted, if you ask me, but—"

I waved a hand. "That's intentional. It's industrial chic."

"If you say so."

"Do you know what this means, Hen?" I braced both hands on the counter and leaned toward him. "This means the downstairs bathroom can be finished soon! Maybe even this week. One more project done."

One step closer to having the renovation over and Brewer out of my business forever.

I was ready to bust out a spry little jig of my own.

"You're my new favorite person," I gushed.

Hen laughed. "Glad to hear it. I was worried you'd still be sore over your kitchen cabinets, but—"

My happy bubble wobbled and popped. "Hang on. What's wrong with my kitchen cabinets?"

"Oh, I just meant how Brew had to put the kibosh on those fancy metal ones you originally wanted." Hen's mustache twitched like his lips were shrugging. "But you're better off with the custom ones he's gonna make you. I never heard of him doing custom cabinets for a client before." He stroked his mustache. "You're pretty lucky, huh?"

For a moment, I lost the ability to speak. The store around me and all the people in it disappeared into a white haze. A rushing sound, like the engine of a train heading right for me, filled my ears.

Whatever I was, it was far, far from *lucky*.

I swallowed. "Brewer canceled my cabinet order? The one I placed myself?"

"Well, yeah. He said he'd told you those cabinets wouldn't work with your house, and he didn't want you to waste your money. That's just Brewer's way." Hen sounded nearly as besotted as Janice-with-the-flyers. "It's why his clients love him so much, and... uh... Delaney? Kiddo, you look kinda... peaky."

Yes, no doubt I was.

Peaky was a natural result of a man's brain short-circuiting.

Brewer hadn't just ignored my input this time. He hadn't just tweaked things without consulting me. He'd canceled my damn cabinets. The ones I'd researched. I'd ordered. I'd paid for.

For months, I'd let him get away with his attitude—a purse of his lips at my fixture choices, a huff when I suggested a layout tweak—but somewhere along the way, my entire renovation had been hijacked by Brewer Barnum and his big hands, big shoulders, and bigger-than-life ego.

And it wasn't just the house. The past few months had been a slow, relentless stream of reminders that what I liked —hell, who I was—just didn't work around here. Despite Tam's endless lectures, I was never going to be a wick-dipping enthusiast or a leg-pain-meteorology guy, and I refused to try to change myself just to win anyone's approval.

That wasn't adapting; that was *losing*.

And I refused to lose, especially to Brewer Barnum.

I exhaled slowly and forced a pleasant, deadly polite

smile on my face. "Hen," I said, voice tight, "would you excuse me? I need to have a little chat with my contractor."

"Now, Delaney," Hen called after me. "Don't go off half-cocked—"

But he was too late. I was already fully cocked, and both barrels were aimed at a very large man in a very snug tool belt.

CHAPTER TWO

BREWER

Some days called for *Hamilton*. Others for *Rent*. Today was definitely a *Wicked* day.

As I flipped the burgers on my little grill under the awning I'd strung up between my camper and a tent pole I'd hammered into the ground, I hummed along with the soundtrack playing in my ears.

Then, as I gazed out over the acres of pastureland I'd bought a couple of years ago—my first half step toward permanence after five years spent drifting from job to job, learning how to improve my trade from anyone who'd teach me—I went ahead and belted out the chorus of "Defying Gravity" because I *could*.

Because there was no one around to hear me.

Sunday afternoons on my property were sacred—no interruptions, no phone calls, no clients freaking out at me because I refused to paint the gorgeous, original woodwork of their 1932 Arts-and-Crafts bungalow a cheap, overdone, *wrong* matte white.

This one day of the week was for relaxing. For grilling half-naked in the freezing cold after a workout, if I wanted to, since no one was around to judge except the lazy dog inside keeping my couch warm.

I knew the fine people of Copper County had been surprised I hadn't bought a place closer to Copper Lake or to the shops and restaurants of neighboring O'Leary. They'd come up with some wild explanations for my strange behavior, and thanks to my cousin Hayes, who'd lived in town less than a year but had already plugged himself firmly into the gossip matrix, I'd heard them all.

The guys who knew me best assumed this land was an investment and that I *liked* living in my turquoise-and-white camper... which was accurate.

Some folks thought I'd given away all of my possessions like a modern-day Thoreau, trying to "live deliberately"... which, as Hayes teased, just went to show those folks had never seen my teacup collection.

Others thought I lived out here in consideration of my neighbors so they wouldn't hear the banging as I renovated the trailer with my own two hands... which made me sound more altruistic than I deserved.

And at least one person—I had to imagine it was Janice Plum since no one else could've said it with a straight face—had suggested I might be a time-traveling philanthropist who gave away all my money to support various causes and did historically accurate renovations as an homage to my "actual timeline"... which kinda made me wonder what was in those novels Janice was always reading and whether I needed to check them out myself. You know, for research.

The truth, though, wasn't that deep: I simply liked being alone.

I liked that I didn't have to explain or justify myself here.

I liked that my home wasn't my father's sprawling,

hollow mansion and that every inch of it, however few there were, was mine.

My grandfather used to say that the spaces we inhabit shape us as much as we shape them, and I believed that. So until I was ready to claim a house as my own again—and to have that house claim me—my trailer in the middle of nowhere was the ideal situation.

My phone rang, cutting off my soundtrack and catapulting me out of my peaceful haze. *Hayes*, the screen said, and I sighed as I let it go to voicemail.

Sunday afternoons were sacred, even from the cousin I loved like a brother. Especially when that cousin had started mentioning my father every time we talked.

Last time, it had been, "Uncle Tony's been trying to get in touch with you." The time before that, "My mom says your dad wants to explain about all the business stuff. He didn't do what they say he did. Can't you just listen to him?"

Hayes didn't have all the facts—partly because my dad was a master at playing the victim, partly because Hayes was too young to remember the actual events—but he knew my problems with my dad were about more than his shady business practices. Hayes was trying to play peacemaker, as usual.

But that part of my life was over, and I'd moved on.

An icy breeze blew across the field, sending goose bumps shivering over my bare chest, but fuck it. If I wanted to freeze, it was nobody's business but mine.

"*Something has changed within me,*" I sang, flipping another burger with a spatula flick.

But before I could recapture the peace of my musical interlude, I recognized the sound of feet crunching on gravel. I turned to find that a silver Audi had, at some point, parked itself at an odd angle next to my truck, and a man was marching toward me, looking like a specter of doom. And not just any man, of course, but the man guaranteed to disrupt my peace like no one else on Earth.

Delaney Monroe.

My current client, the permanent pain in my ass... and the star of thoughts I should *not* be having about someone paying me to renovate their house, though my brain refused to get that memo.

His hands were clenched into fists as he stalked toward me like his feet were spring-loaded. His face was flushed, blue eyes crackling with anger behind those hot glasses he sometimes wore, and his long coat flapped around him in the breeze. His entire five-foot-eight frame vibrated with indignation.

Despite myself, I enjoyed the show. Delaney was never more gorgeous than when he was righteously pissed off. Fortunately (which was to say, really fucking *un*fortunately) for me, he seemed to be perpetually pissed off when we were together.

He didn't slow, and as he got closer, every nerve in my body went on alert—a physical reaction I'd come to associate exclusively with Delaney. It was like my body recognized a coming storm long before it broke—that electric feeling in the air that made the hairs on your arms stand up—only this particular storm was wrapped in a cashmere-blend coat that hugged surprisingly fit shoulders and had a mouth that seemed permanently set in a displeased line I couldn't stop thinking about softening.

"Brewer," he called, voice sharp enough to cut through whatever remained of my peaceful afternoon.

I pulled my earbuds free, pocketing them as I responded, "Delaney. Hey. What's—?"

"Don't *Hey, Delaney* me. You stole my cabinets." He jabbed a finger into my chest.

I blinked, as stunned by the contact as I was by the accusation. Had Delaney ever touched me before? The way my skin lit up at the touch suggested he hadn't. Sure as fuck not like this.

I let out an extremely eloquent "Huh?"

"Don't play innocent." Another jab landed against my bare chest, and the contact ricocheted through me. "I talked to Hen. I *know* you canceled my order."

"Oh, right." I couldn't help the half smile that tugged at my mouth. "That."

I'd known this conversation was coming; I just hadn't expected it to happen here, on my day off, while I was half-dressed and covered in grill smoke, with Delaney's hand—well, fingertip, but still—touching me.

"Yes, *that*," Delaney snapped. "The tiny matter of that multi-thousand-dollar purchase we discussed at length." His voice sharpened further. "I sent you an email. I linked the exact cabinets I wanted—salvaged metal, ridiculously expensive shipping, worth every penny—and followed up the next day. Do you remember what you said?"

I tilted my head slightly—trying to remember the precise conversation wasn't easy under the circumstances—but he barreled on before I could speak.

"I said, 'Did you see the cabinets I picked, Brewer?' And you nodded. And I said, 'And?' And you said"—he dropped his voice in what I assumed was an attempt to imitate my deeper tone—"'That style won't work in your house.' Remember?"

I nodded once. That, I remembered. I'd spent three hours that night researching period-appropriate alternatives that would actually fit his kitchen's dimensions without requiring us to move the gas line or strip the original plaster from the walls to square them up.

"And then *I* said," Delaney continued, "'I don't care what you think about my design choices, Brewer. You're a builder, not an interior designer. These cabinets are exactly what I want for my kitchen, and I'm going to order them today based on the dimensions in your plans.' Do you remember *that*?"

There was a beat of silence where the only sound was the rustle of the awning in the wind and the crackle of the fire in the grill. I looked down at where his finger was still pressed against my sternum, then back to his face. For one second, our eyes locked… and then he yanked his hand back like he'd been burned.

I found my gaze following his hand, noticing the way he flexed his fingers at his side, and wondered if he'd felt it, too —that strange charge that had sparked between us.

"I remember," I said finally, managing to keep my voice even.

"But you canceled the order anyway. In direct defiance of my instructions." He set his hands on his hips. "Admit it."

"Do you remember what *I* said?"

He rolled his eyes with such melodramatic flair it was almost impressive. "You said, 'Trust me, Delaney.'"

I nodded, watching his face carefully. Those three words seemed to be at the heart of our ongoing battle.

Trust was a funny word, I knew. Simple but not always easy. Some people, like my dad, expected it without doing a damn thing to earn it. But that was exactly why I'd spent years building a reputation where my word meant something, where clients *could* trust me to do right by their homes.

The fact that Delaney refused to, despite me giving my all to his renovation, felt personal. It hurt.

"And did you?" Annoyed as I was, I didn't raise my voice or attempt to get in his face. I'd learned as a kid that when you're bigger than average, it's a dick move to make someone else feel small. "I know what I'm doing, Delaney."

"Trust isn't something people fling around like Mardi Gras beads in my world, Brewer. How can I trust you when you go rogue constantly and never communicate? When you undermine me at every turn?"

"Undermine you," I scoffed. "I have never once—"

"Need I remind you that you and your tile guys turned my clean-lined bathroom into a goddamn mosaic Alhambra?"

"Because the tile you picked was meant for a much larger space with a freestanding shower. I gave you choices that *would* work—"

"Three different colors of the same tile is not *choices*. That's like telling a toddler they can have broccoli *or* spinach." He huffed, sounding exactly like that toddler.

I lifted an eyebrow, fighting wholly inappropriate amusement. "—and you admitted you liked it."

"I..." He hesitated, and I caught a flash of something cross his face. "That's not the point," he managed, jabbing my chest again. "Not the point at all."

"Isn't it?" I demanded. "Isn't that the *entire* point?"

I'd meant to sound firmer, more businesslike, not so damn breathless. But I found myself distracted by the warmth of his fingertip against my skin and the way his hair was slightly ruffled from what I assumed was his angry drive over. His cheeks were flushed pink with indignation, his blue eyes bright behind his glasses, and despite my growing irritation, I couldn't help but notice how goddamn attractive he was.

His finger rested against me for a second too long as his gaze slid from my face down to my bare shoulders, lingering for a moment on my chest before darting away.

Heat blossomed under my skin that had nothing to do with anger.

"I know what you're thinking," he said, and I blinked, wondering for a second if he'd caught me checking him out.

"You do?"

"Yes. And don't give me that look."

"What look?"

"The look that says you know better than I do! The look I've seen on your face a billion times. You don't know better than I do about *my* house, Brewer." Delaney's voice grew louder, more heated. "I might be... I might be *resigned* to the bathroom situation. Because the tiles and fixtures are objectively beautiful, even though they're not what I asked for—"

I rolled my eyes.

"Just like, through sheer luck," he went on, face bright red now, "I don't *despise* the creamy color you used in my bedroom, though I will remind you that I specifically asked for sleek white. And yes, I agreed that the refinished floors in the living room look nice, though I still maintain that the vinyl planking I picked out would have looked equally good *and* been more durable! Me agreeing doesn't mean you're right; it means I'm an incredibly *adaptable, easygoing person!*"

I stifled a laugh at the idea of Delaney being "easygoing" and restrained myself to a nod. How could he manage to sound so wronged while still agreeing that he liked the end result?

The man was a fucking porcupine, all bristles and quills

for no reason I could fathom. But—and this was the part that really got me—he was not the only prickly client I'd had over the years. So why the fuck did this one get under my skin so badly?

And when the fuck had I started thinking his quills were as hot as they were annoying?

This wasn't like me. I was a calm, steady person. Truly easygoing, the way Delaney claimed to be. I generally wasn't interested in confrontation, and I'd rather walk away from a situation than fight about it. If someone wasn't on board with that, I didn't let them get close enough to get under my skin. But something about this guy, this one particular guy, had burrowed in and stuck there. And it was driving me crazy.

I didn't get him, I didn't get my own reaction to him, and I didn't like it.

I caught a few muttered words as Delaney turned slightly away—something about "power trip" and "ego the size of a planet."

I bit the inside of my cheek.

If he only knew how much time I spent worrying about his house, how many extra hours I put in to make sure everything was perfect. How I'd driven to four different salvage yards trying to find period-appropriate doorknobs only to come up empty. How I'd spent evenings sketching kitchen cabinet designs that would give him the industrial look he wanted without compromising the house's character.

But Delaney had decided I was the enemy, and nothing I did seemed capable of changing that. And I shouldn't care as much as I did.

"The customer is always right, Brewer," he said, turning back to me. "That's literally *Contractor 101*. I hire you, you do what I tell you. Easy peasy. I shouldn't have to explain this."

"You really shouldn't." In fact, I wished he'd stop trying.

His eyes narrowed, and I could see something vulnerable flickering beneath the bluster. "I... I know what you're thinking."

"Again?" I lifted an eyebrow. "So weird how you think you can do that."

"You're thinking about that ridiculous contract I signed, aren't you? The design approval clause, the contractor oversight clause. You're thinking that means you're in charge. Well, it doesn't." Delaney lifted his chin. "That contract wouldn't hold up in court."

I regarded him steadily. The contract was completely standard and definitely enforceable, and I was pretty sure he knew it.

But that didn't stop him from continuing, "In fact, it should be voided completely since the work was supposed to be finished before I moved in, and it wasn't. So..." He trailed off meaningfully.

I glanced down at his hand on my chest again, and once more, he snatched his hand away guiltily... but not before we both caught sight of the angry red scar running across his index finger—the result of his ill-advised attempt to move an electrical outlet on his own. An attempt that had flooded his living room when the frozen pipe burst after he'd knocked out power to the thermostat.

Coming after he'd nearly set the place on fire trying to sand a door that was coated in oil-based stain, it was a miracle he hadn't seriously injured himself.

My jaw tightened at the memory of getting that panicked call in the middle of the night, of finding him standing in ankle-deep water, looking so defeated it had physically hurt to see.

"So," I agreed, keeping my voice neutral despite the memory.

His chin jutted out. "There's nothing in the contract that says I can't work on my own home. I was helping you move things along faster—"

"You were trying to get things done *your* way... even though I explained why it wouldn't work," I countered, my voice coming out gravelly since I was still caught in the memory of what might have happened. "You wouldn't listen. You just *had* to try to do it yourself—"

"Not because I wanted to," he insisted. "I'm fully aware that I'm not a DIY guy. That working with tools is not one of my natural gifts. That I wasn't... wasn't *built* for that. There's a reason I'm the only Monroe who can't change his own oil." He sniffed. "But you've driven me to DIY, Brewer. What else is a man supposed to do when his contractor can't seem to understand basic instructions?"

I shook my head, feeling my calm exterior starting to crack. "It's not about obedience! It's not about a power struggle. It's about safety. It's about getting your house done *right*. It's about... and please hear these words when I say them... about trusting the person you hired to do the job." I was closer to losing my cool than I'd been in years, and I hated that feeling. I blew out a breath and finished calmly, "I know what I'm doing, Delaney. Satisfaction guaranteed, remember?"

Delaney's nostrils flared, and for a second, I thought maybe this time he'd heard me...

But no.

"Or you could simply do what I tell you," he shot back. "In fact, I came here today to tell you exactly that. If you can't accept that I'm in charge, Brewer, then I'll need to find a contractor who can."

Against my will, his words brought me back to a different time, a different conversation.

I didn't ask for your opinion on the deal because I didn't have to, son. If you can't accept that I'm in charge, go be your own boss. See how easy it is when you're the one making the tough calls.

I'd taken my father at his word that day. I'd walked out of his office and out of his life. And I was a better man for it.

My grandfather's integrity had made our family business what it was, as much as his skill with historical renovations and community projects. But under my father's leadership, it had become something I barely recognized anymore. The "Claybourne deal"—such a clean, polite way to say "stabbing your son in the back"—had been the final straw.

But my father had been right about one thing: it wasn't easy being in charge.

This time, I wasn't walking away. I'd built a reputation —a perfect record of satisfied clients and beautiful renovations—and I wasn't going to let one ridiculous, unreasonable man ruin it.

My frustration crystallized into something harder and colder.

If Delaney wanted to be in charge so badly, I'd give him exactly what he wanted. No more suggestions. No more expertise. No more guidance. Just complete, unquestioning compliance.

Let him see how that worked out.

"You know what, Delaney? You're absolutely right." My voice was calm, almost pleasant, though my hands had balled into fists. "From now on, we'll do things your way. You're the boss."

He scowled for a second like he was about to argue with this, too. But his eyes caught on something behind me, and his anger morphed into wide-eyed blankness.

"B-brewer." Delaney's fingers clutched my elbow, the unexpected content sending a jolt of awareness through me. "Behind you."

Frowning, I glanced over my shoulder... only to find my Newfoundland sitting there looking really fucking proud of herself.

"Teeny." I shook my head disapprovingly, but I couldn't keep the fondness out of my voice. "What have I told you about opening the camper door on your own?"

Teeny ignored me and instead trotted toward us, tongue lolling, ready to greet our visitor.

"Stop!" Delaney shouted, backing up a step with both his hands outstretched. "Stop right there."

I faced him again, wondering what the hell was wrong with him. The man who'd gone toe-to-toe with me was gone, and suddenly, he was the guy who'd flooded his living room again. A man whose fundamental understanding of the universe seemed to have been upended.

"Calm down," I told him. I reached for his hand, but he took another step away. "Delaney—"

But I'd bet any amount of money Delaney couldn't even hear me. He was staring at my sweet dog like she was a monster ready for attack... rather than a slightly disobedient sweetheart with an inconvenient knack for opening doors.

For the record, I hadn't taught Teeny that party trick. I was pretty sure she'd learned it when her previous owners, a hard-of-hearing elderly couple I'd done work for years ago, kept forgetting to let her out of the house to do her business.

But like me, Teeny hadn't forgotten the things she'd learned when she was young.

Realizing I couldn't get through to Delaney, I made a grab for Teeny instead, but she scurried away from me like we were playing her favorite keep-away game. She made a beeline for Delaney...

And stuck her head in his crotch.

Delaney leapt backward like an acrobat. "No! *Shoo.*"

"Teeny," I groaned. "Sit." I grabbed her collar, ignoring her mournful whine. "Delaney, it's okay. She's not dangerous."

But once again, Delaney wasn't listening. With both eyes fixed on Teeny and his hands clasped protectively over his crotch, he continued backing away—

"Delaney, *stop!*" I shouted, letting go of the dog and moving toward him as I realized a second too late what was right behind him.

But it was definitely too late.

Delaney's foot caught on a rock, and he stumbled, crashing backward into the support pole that held up my makeshift awning. The tension lines that held it to the pole snapped free with a metallic twang, and before either of us could move, the canvas dropped on top of us...

And on the fucking grill.

Flames erupted instantly, licking up the fabric with terrifying speed.

Delaney yelped and jumped clear. Teeny let out a bark as she did the same.

Still underneath the tarp, I tried to grab it and yank it away from the fire, but it was still attached to the camper at two points, making it hard to maneuver.

Then, a gust of wind blew, inflating the material like a

burning parachute. It tore out of my grasp, sailed into the air… and landed directly on the roof of my camper.

"No," I heard Delaney whisper in horror. "*No.*"

For a split second, I froze as the fire quickly engulfed the only real home I'd known in years. Then training and instinct kicked in, and I moved into emergency mode.

I grabbed Delaney's arm and pulled him back to a safe distance. "Stay here," I ordered, and then I sprinted toward the camper door, Teeny at my heels.

I needed to get my emergency bag, a few of my grandfather's tools, my grandmother's treasured *Belles Pivoines* teacups, the box of photos—

Inside, smoke was already filling the small space, making my eyes burn and water. I grabbed the essentials as quickly as I could, tossing them outside in a pile. My lungs burned, but I pushed forward, pulling open cabinets and drawers, vaguely aware of Delaney still behind the camper, throwing hunks of old, icy snow on the roof like he and the flames were in a one-sided, useless snowball fight.

"Brewer?" I heard him call. "What are you doing? *Brewer!*"

I went back inside for another armload—this time, mostly dog supplies—and when I emerged, I saw him running toward me, face pale with panic. He caught my arm with a grip that was surprisingly strong for his size.

"Stop, Brewer. You can't." He pointed at the roof, which was already blackening. His voice was ragged with what sounded like genuine fear. "You can't go back in."

I hesitated, looking back at my home. It was small, but there was still so much of me inside—my music collection, my books, the quilt my grandmother had made.

Delaney was right, though. The roof was starting to buckle, and another minute inside could be dangerous.

I took one last look at the camper... then ran my hands through my hair and turned away, my stomach sick with shock and grief. Delaney was already on his phone, calling for help, his voice cracking as he gave directions to my remote property.

"They're coming," he told me when he hung up. "Brewer, I'm so... I didn't mean..."

I couldn't bring myself to respond. Teeny pressed against my leg, whimpering softly, and I placed a hand on her head as we watched the flames consume our home.

Beside me, Delaney stood in horrified silence, his earlier anger completely forgotten. I caught him muttering to himself, "Oh *God*. Oh *fuck—*"

Despite everything, a small part of me wanted to reassure him, but I couldn't find the words. Not yet. Not while watching everything I'd built burn to the ground.

By the time the fire truck arrived, it was too late to save the camper. The firefighters soaked everything down, but what remained was a dripping, charred shell of my home.

"Not safe to walk in there," one of the firefighters said, confirming what I already knew. "Not much left to salvage anyway. Sorry, Brew."

I nodded, keeping my face neutral. "Thanks, Gideon."

Teeny pressed harder against my leg, and I scratched behind her ears absently.

Gideon studied the wreckage. "What a freak accident." His brow furrowed. "How'd you say that pole came down, again?"

I hesitated but didn't look at Delaney. "Accident, like you said. Just glad everyone's safe."

Gideon nodded slowly, but his gaze shifted to Delaney.

"You look familiar." He held out a hand. "Gideon Mason."

"Delaney—" His voice cracked, from the smoke or from emotion, I couldn't tell. "Delaney Monroe. I'm new in town. Sort of. I'm—"

Gideon was already nodding. "Tam Monroe's brother..."

I could almost hear the words Gideon didn't say—*the one who doesn't play hockey*—and knew Delaney heard them, too, when his shoulders slumped slightly.

"Yeah," he whispered. "That's me."

"You got someplace to stay, Brew?" Gideon asked, ruffling Teeny's fur. "With your cousin, maybe?"

I shook my head. "Hayes is allergic, and he doesn't have the room." I shrugged. "I'll figure it out."

Gideon nodded. "I'd say a hotel, but the Crabapple doesn't take dogs, and the Scarlet Maple's pricy. Maybe a friend—?" Another firefighter called Gideon's name. "Shit, hang on," he said as he stepped away.

Delaney and I stood together under a spindly tree, inhaling frigid, smoke-tinged air. Though it was still early, the horizon was already turning sunset pink, and the temperature had dropped precipitously.

I tried to think about my options. I had money, but finding a place that would take Teeny on short notice would be challenging. I could probably crash with one of the guys who worked with me for a night or two—

"I know you can figure this out on your own, and you... you probably don't want my help right now," Delaney said suddenly, his voice cautious. "But I feel terrible."

I kept my eyes on the sky, not trusting myself to respond. The last thing I wanted was anyone's pity, especially his.

"The hotel Gideon mentioned would probably be a great idea," he continued. "If only it wasn't so expensive."

When I didn't reply, he swallowed audibly. "Look, I know you and I *aren't* friends, per se, especially after today, but I want to make sure you have a place to stay until you can figure out something permanent. There's snow coming, unless you trust Hen Lattimer's trick leg, and I... I'd like to help you out, if you'll let me."

I turned to look at him then, surprised by the genuine concern in his voice.

"Please?" he said, almost eagerly. "Neighbors helping neighbors is how small towns work, right? At least, that's what Tam says. It wouldn't have to be a big deal."

I studied him for a long moment. His glasses were smudged with soot, his expensive coat stained with smoke, his expression openly conflicted. For someone who'd been ready to throttle me an hour ago, he looked startlingly worried about my well-being.

"Delaney," I said carefully. "I meant what I told Gideon. It was an accident—"

"I know! I know. But I want to help," he blurted. "I need to. *Please* let me do this."

I inhaled deeply, considering. Staying with Delaney was less than ideal, and our contentious relationship was only one reason. The fact that I found a pissed-off Delaney insanely hot was a far more pressing one.

More than that, I'd just agreed to give him exactly what he wanted on the renovation—to be the boss, to have things his way. It would be hard enough to bite my tongue about choices I knew were wrong for his house and let him learn the hard way; doing it while sleeping under his roof would make it ten times harder.

But I didn't have a lot of options in the short term. If I told Hayes, he'd be worried. And, allergies or not, he'd guilt me into staying on the sofa in the one-bedroom apartment where he and his former frat bro lived like video-game-loving raccoons, awake all night and subsisting on trash.

It was the least peaceful option I could think of.

I shuddered and nodded once. "Yeah. Okay, then. If you're sure."

"Really?" Relief flooded his face. "I'm sure. I'm totally sure. So, why don't you get, um, T-teeny in your truck, and I'll help you grab your stuff, then we'll go get you set up." He started to turn.

I caught his arm, stopping him. His muscles tensed beneath my hand, and for a second, our eyes locked. "Delaney... thanks." I meant it sincerely, despite everything.

"No problem." He managed a small, teasing smile. "Thanks for agreeing, when I know that's your least favorite thing."

He was confusing the two of us, I was pretty sure, but I wasn't going to call him out when he was being so generous. "I'll keep Teeny out of your hair, okay? And I'll help out around the house. In fact, I insist on it."

"Help with..." He shook his head slightly. "You're already working on the house full-time."

"I meant doing household stuff. Shopping and laundry and shit. I'm not much of a cook, but I can clean." I managed a weak smile of my own. "Maybe you could make up a chore chart. You seem like a chore chart guy."

"I... I am, but..." He blinked several times. "Why would I ask you to—?"

Gideon approached, and I turned to greet him. "Are we all set here?"

"For now?" He nodded. "I'll have the report for your insurance company tomorrow. I'll call you."

"Great. Or you can find me at Delaney's place."

"Yeah?" Gideon's eyebrows rose slightly as he glanced between us. "You're staying there?"

I shrugged. "Delaney's idea."

Gideon nodded in approval as his eyes met Delaney's. "Nice of you to offer."

"Oh. Well. That's not... You see..." Delaney waved his hands aimlessly, then stopped. He swallowed audibly, panic dawning on his face like he was only belatedly processing what was happening.

I felt my smile fall.

Was he regretting his impulsive offer already? I probably should have jumped in to provide him with an out, but something in me—maybe exhaustion, maybe pettiness—decided to wait and see how he'd handle it.

After all, he'd said he didn't want my help or my expertise, right? He'd said he was the boss? He could figure it out.

"It's no problem," he finally said in a small voice. "It'll be great."

I wasn't sure which of us he was trying to convince.

I packed up the few possessions I'd managed to salvage, loaded Teeny into my truck, and followed Delaney's Audi back toward town.

The reality of the situation slowly sank in as we drove. My home was gone. Most of my possessions were gone. And I was about to move in temporarily with the prickliest, most difficult client I'd ever had. A man who seemed to view me as his personal nemesis. A man I couldn't stop thinking about.

This was either going to be a complete disaster or...

No, who was I kidding. It was definitely going to be a disaster.

Possibly the biggest one of my life.

CHAPTER THREE

DELANEY

KAK-WEEEEE!

I was sleep-working at my desk the following morning when a sound like a deranged cuckoo clock and an air-raid siren ripped through the house.

For a single, startled moment, I sat bolt upright in my chair and looked around in a panic, thinking it was a fire alarm and there'd been a second Delaney-involved blaze in twenty-four hours.

Then I remembered the hasty plan I'd concocted—the *delivery* I'd scheduled—and realized it was the doorbell. I jumped to my feet and hurried out into the hall before it could shriek again.

The man on my front stoop wore a purple baja hoodie, a green Kitchen Couriers cap, a pair of Birkenstocks over fuzzy socks, and a name tag that read KEL in block letters. More importantly, he carried a large, white bakery box that contained strawberry croissants from Fanaille—aka the single best food in New York or, possibly, the world.

"Good morning," I said politely, reaching for the box. "Thanks for the—"

Kel took a step back, taking my croissants with him. "Dude. *You're* Delaney Monroe?"

I frowned. "Doesn't it say my name on the order?"

"As in... Tam Monroe's brother?"

This again? I blew out a breath. I was running on zero sleep—a side effect, it turned out, of being jumped at by a flyer-bearing Coppertian, crotch-sniffed by a canine with dubious intentions, intimately involved in a home burning, and then saddled with the world's sexiest, bossiest contractor *and his dog* as houseguests.

I had no patience for this game.

"Yes," I said shortly, reaching for the box again.

Again, he kept it just out of reach. "The one who—?"

"The one who doesn't play hockey, who caused a small fire in his own home, and who may have contributed to the... the accidental destruction of Brewer's camper?" I asked defiantly. "Yes. Yes, to all of it. Now, can I *please* have my croissants?"

"Dude." Kel the delivery guy managed to insert a wealth of rebuke into the single syllable. "I was gonna say the guy who sent fourteen handwritten letters to the Kitchen Couriers corporate office asking them to extend our delivery area 'cause we *never* delivered out this far before you moved in."

"Oh." I paused, taken aback. "Well. Fourteen seems excessive. I don't recall there being quite that—"

"Fourteen," he assured me solemnly.

I cleared my throat, feeling my cheeks heat. There was no shame in strategically influencing corporate policy, was there? It wasn't a *crime* to enjoy croissants.

"I may have... taken the lead on an issue that affects the entire neighborhood, yes," I said stiffly. "Did you know, studies show small towns are one of the fastest-growing sectors for delivery expansion, especially in rural and exurban areas where populations are increasing?"

He frowned deeply. "I guess. But dude—"

"And you should also know that the revenue from expanding these markets often outweighs the initial cost of longer-range deliveries. Which, obviously, means more tips for you."

"Yeah, but like—"

"Have a nice day, Kel." I took the box from his hands with extreme dignity.

"Wait!" Kel called. "You didn't *actually* destroy Brewer's camper, did y—?"

I closed the door firmly, then leaned back against it and took a deep breath.

It was just after 7:00 a.m., and this morning was already so far off the rails I couldn't remember where the rails were supposed to be.

Then I headed to the kitchen to arrange my peace-offering breakfast.

Brief confession time: I hadn't actually intended to ask Brewer to stay with me after the fire. When I'd offered to help him out, I'd meant to *hellllp* pay for the overpriced hotel that accepted dogs, not to move him into my home.

It was bad enough for my equilibrium having the man in my home five days a week doing renovation work. Only a truly deranged person would volunteer to have their sexy nemesis in their house 24/7, sucking up all their oxygen and distracting them constantly, and I flattered myself that I wasn't quite that deranged.

At least not yet.

But something about Brewer's defeated expression yesterday and the sight of his belongings in a sad, soggy pile on the snow had tangled my words, and when he'd misunderstood my offer...

Well, I wasn't a monster, okay? Of course I'd brought Brewer and his dog to my house.

And of course I'd placed Brewer's antique teacup collection with the hand-painted peonies and gold-leaf trim —"I use them every day," he'd explained when I'd looked surprised, which had only raised more questions—in my kitchen cabinet.

And of course I'd agreed that Brewer could use a blow-up mattress in the attic above the garage—a space that was heated, insulated, and mostly empty—so he could keep Teeny contained, and I wouldn't have to give up my office to be his bedroom.

I'd even sort of consoled myself with the knowledge that I was doing a good deed and earning some Copper County karma points that might help me fit in better.

I'd forgotten, temporarily, what they said about good deeds not going unpunished.

Imagine, if you will, my mentally, physically, emotionally exhausted self, freshly showered, slathered in night cream, and clad in my favorite silk pajamas, as I'd finally crawled into my bed last night.

I'd made it through the harrowing events of the day, through a scrupulously polite pasta dinner I prepared, through the weirdly domestic scene of burly Brewer scrubbing dishes, and even through feeding time for the dog— which I'd observed from a great distance and which had sounded not unlike running a Dyson over a bed of rocks.

I'd wanted nothing more than to curl up and sleep.

So I'd burrowed my head into my pillow and lain there in the dark, practicing some yoga breathing I'd once learned on an overpriced retreat. I'd allowed all distracting thoughts of fires, and dogs, and the solid wall of Brewer's chest under my hand, and the charged moment when we'd both realized I was touching him to just float through my brain. I'd felt sleep reaching out her arms to claim me...

And then Brewer's deep voice had murmured something I couldn't quite make out, *right in my fucking ear*, sending an unwelcome zing of electricity to my balls and making my cock hard almost instantly.

My eyes had flashed open, and I'd blinked disorientedly into the darkness, my heart pounding a million miles an hour... but my room had been empty.

And then the voice had come again—a low, soothing chuckle that time, followed by the jingle of dog tags—and I'd realized what I must have blocked out when I'd helped Brewer tote all his stuff to the little attic over the garage.

Namely, that although Brewer's attic room was as far from mine as you could get in terms of walking distance—down and around the stairs, through the house, out the kitchen door to the little breezeway that led to the garage, and back up another staircase—it was also *right next to my fucking room* as the crow flew, so to speak.

To put it more succinctly, Brewer's bed was inches from mine, separated by a single, thin wall.

To say it took an hour for my cock to deflate would not be an exaggeration. Not when I'd spent that hour motionless in my bed, afraid to move or sigh or breathe too hard for fear *he* would hear *me*. Not when I'd spent the majority of that time listening to Brewer shift around on his mattress, murmur to the dog in soothing words I couldn't make out, and laugh at whatever she was doing in response.

And the torture hadn't ended there.

My alarm had gone off mere minutes after I managed to fall asleep, but I'd dressed and shuffled downstairs like a zombie to prep for my Zoom with Marjorie, only to collide —literally, *forcefully*—with the exact same wall of warm muscle I'd spent the night trying to forget.

"Whoa, careful." One of Brewer's big hands had wrapped around my biceps. The other had—no word of a lie—reached out to fix my glasses.

I'd mumbled something incoherent, partly because I was half-asleep but mostly because Brewer's hair was damp, and he was wearing nothing but low-slung sweatpants, and the droplets of water clinging to his chest made rainbow patterns in the early morning light, and he smelled like a combination of my sea-salt and bergamot bodywash and his own Brewer-scent of grass and sawdust.

"Steady now?" he'd asked in that same voice I'd heard all night.

My tongue tied itself into a knot, but my dick had no such qualms. Apparently, at some point the evening before, it had become the victim of an inadvertent Pavlovian experiment, and it rose now, thinking the sound of Brewer's voice meant it was *erection time*.

I'd squeaked out a mortifying "yes, thanks" that sounded shriller than a recording played at five times speed and scurried into my office.

But while Brewer had taken the dog for a walk, I'd paced around my office and had a stern talk with myself, which had mostly centered around a single mantra:

I cannot keep doing this.

Yes, Brewer was attractive. While I would never suggest I had a type—the very notion was crass, not to mention outdated—I could admit that I had a... a *propensity* toward finding large, muscled guys attractive.

But that didn't mean anything would come of it. I barely knew Brewer—our conversations had been limited to polite arguments about the house—but what I did know drove me insane. Like most big guys, Brewer didn't seem to respect someone smaller than him. And while that apparently wasn't a deal-breaker for my dick, it was for *me*.

I refused to spend days or weeks tiptoeing around my own home, which meant I needed to put our relationship back on better footing. No more fighting, no more chest touching, no more... Pavlovian dick response. We could be cordial coworkers, of a sort.

After pacing and perseverating for fifteen minutes on how best to accomplish this, I'd finally pulled open my Kitchen Couriers app and ordered croissants to be delivered.

Peace-offering croissants.

I blamed my sleeplessness for thinking this was a sound plan.

By the time I heard Brewer's boots hitting the steps as he came down from the attic after taking Teeny upstairs, I'd arranged the pastries on a plate, poured us each a coffee—Brewer's in one of his "everyday" china cups—and tried to channel my most professional, most rational, most focused self.

Then he stepped into the kitchen, muttered a surprised "Oh. Hey."... and just like that, the very air between us trembled and thickened.

At least, it did for me.

Brewer's broad shoulders stretched his T-shirt, and as he took a cautious step closer, I had the visceral sensation of my space shrinking and heat curling into the room. His scruff-darkened jaw—had I ever fixated on a man's jaw before? Did this mean I was a *jaw man* now?—scrambled my concentration.

A beat too late, I forced a bright smile. "Hey. Good morning."

Brewer's gaze flicked to the pastries, then back to me. His brows drew together in suspicion. "Did I miss something? Are you having guests over?"

"What? Oh. No, of course not. It's just breakfast." I slid his coffee toward him.

He didn't move except to raise one eyebrow. "I wasn't aware buying me breakfast was part of our agreement, boss."

I set my teeth together. Did the man not understand that the first rule of peace offerings was that you didn't *talk* about peace offerings?

"I didn't buy you breakfast, per se," I argued. "I just felt like eating croissants, that's all. Croissants are serotonin in a bakery box. Practically... practically medicine. And since you're staying here now, I bought you one, too."

His gaze dropped to the mountain of food—admittedly, I might have gone slightly overboard, but I'd had to assume a man his size ate as much as my brothers did—then back to me. One corner of his mouth hitched up. "Okay."

"It's not a big deal," I went on. "It's simple politeness and respect. It's... fair and right."

"I said okay, Delaney."

Brewer stepped closer—close enough that I could say for certain the heat coming off him had not been my imagination—and reached for his coffee cup. I got another burst of bergamot-and-Brewer that made my pulse stutter.

Fuck.

"Delaney?" Brewer waved a hand in front of my face, and I realized I'd spaced out for a second.

My face flushed. "Pardon?"

He lifted his cup. "I said *thanks*. You remembered I like

cream and sugar from when we were at the bakery that time?"

"Oh. Er. Yes?" My stomach flopped like a fish on a line, and I added, "That's also not a big deal. I have an excellent memory."

Brewer held my gaze for a beat longer than necessary, like he was still trying to figure me out. Then he took a sip of his coffee. His fingers—strong, calloused—curled around the cup. His throat moved as he swallowed. His tongue flicked out to catch a stray drop—

I tore my gaze away, mortified.

Delaney. For the love of tiny baby Jesus.

"So." I cleared my throat. "Great news! Hen told me yesterday that the vanity for the downstairs bathroom came in. So if you could go pick it up this morning—"

"Wait. You got a vanity for the downstairs bath?" Brewer's tone was neutral, but his gaze sharpened.

"Yes." I straightened my shoulders. "Problem?"

His shrug seemed forced as he reached for a croissant. "Of course not. It's your house."

"Yes. *Yes.*" I nodded once. "Hen said it's pretty heavy, so you might need some help getting it in. I'd go myself, but I, ah..."

Brewer ripped off a bite-sized piece of croissant with his teeth, then licked the crumbs from his lips, and I lost my train of thought. In fact, I lost all higher brain function. For a second, it was just me and his mouth in that kitchen.

"You?" Brewer prompted, his lips so shiny and full I had to grip the edge of the counter to stop myself from leaning in to discover exactly how they'd feel against mine.

"I, um..."

Brewer's jaw flexed as he chewed. His throat worked as he swallowed.

Mortified by how fucking *aware* I was of him, I reached for my own coffee mug—a task I'd performed since I was my infant niece's age, I was pretty sure—and misjudged the distance. Hot coffee sloshed over my hand.

"*Fuck!*" I cried, snatching my hand away and shaking it off.

"Shit, Delaney." Brewer instantly reached for my hand. "Did you get burned?"

"N-no!" I yanked my hand away. The only thing burning me was the hot, tight ball of embarrassed *want* in my stomach. Brewer touching me would only make it worse.

"Let me see—"

"I'm fine," I insisted. "What was I saying?"

With a sigh, Brewer stepped away. "You were explaining why you can't pick up the vanity yourself."

"Yes." I cleared my throat. "Right. Because I have a call. A work call. With my editor," I explained, wondering why I felt compelled to offer any explanation at all. "About the story I'm writing."

"The same one you've been working on for a while?" Brewer asked. "How's that going?"

I was sure he was only asking out of casual politeness, but I wondered if maybe it was the same kind of politeness that had made me order a whole box of croissants, so I stopped and considered his question before answering.

"It's going well. At least... I think so? It started out as a piece about corruption and bribery of some town officials— not *this* town, obviously," I added with an eye roll that made Brewer smile.

"It's... it's actually a bit of a departure from what I usually write," I went on. "A little less... sensational, I guess? But a whistleblower came to me directly a couple months ago and asked me to take a closer look at the situation. He claimed he got a raw deal, which in and of itself isn't that interesting—I mean, if I had a nickel for every person implicated in a scandal who swore they were innocent, I'd be the Nickel King of New York—"

Brewer laughed, a deep sound that vibrated through me.

I swallowed hard and continued. "—but my editor freaking loved the idea, and a bunch of news outlets are interested, and... honestly, something about the guy got to me. My gut is telling me he is a decent guy who got caught up in something bigger than he knew. That he made the best decision he could at the time and ended up paying the price. He wants redemption and a second chance. And I'm not sure my article will actually make things, you know..." I waved a hand.

"Fair and right?" Brewer quoted me with a little smile.

A startled laugh escaped me. "Yeah, that. But sometimes people feel like they don't have a voice. I like to think I give them one."

"That's a pretty idealistic goal." Brewer looked thoughtful for a moment. "Because justice is subjective, isn't it? Every villain is the hero of his own tale."

"Well... yes." The unexpected depth of his response caught me off guard. "That's... that's true. But it's not up to me to decide. I put the facts out there because everyone deserves to have their story told, especially the little guy."

Brewer cast off his serious expression and forced a smile. "Well, good luck with that, I guess. I'll call Hen about your vanity first thing. Maybe he can spare Theo Ross to help me, if Theo doesn't have art class."

I struggled to switch gears. "Oh. Yeah. Okay. And if you and Theo need to hire a couple other guys, too, that's fine. Please feel empowered to do that."

Brewer's eyes danced. "I will. Thank you, boss. But we're moving a vanity, not an armored car. It should be a two-man job at most, unless your vanity's made out of concrete or something." He chuckled lightly.

I bit my lip.

Brewer shut his eyes. "Delaney, tell me it's not made of concrete."

"It's not," I assured him. "Not... entirely. It's a custom concrete top on a metal base, and it's going to look *amazing*. It's industrial but rustic at the same time, and—"

"Please tell me you measured the space—"

"Brewer." I held up a hand. "I don't want to fight with you, but I would like to remind you once again that this is *my* house and that I'm not incompetent."

"I never said—"

"I've learned my lesson about trying to move electrical outlets or refinish doors, but I'm perfectly capable of reading the measurements you provided and ordering a vanity that fits. I understand inches and feet."

"It's not that simple," Brewer insisted. "That space is tricky. And because of the unexpected repairs to the living room and dining room—"

My neck heated at this unnecessary reminder of my fuckups.

"—and the cost of those metal cabinets I assume you still want for the kitchen—"

"I do." I lifted my chin. "In fact, I'd like you to reorder them today."

Brewer's nostrils flared. "—we can't do any reframing or move any of the plumbing if you want to stay on budget, so the vanity needs to fit perfectly—"

I folded my arms over my chest. "Since I'm the person who created the budget, I am very aware, which is why I made sure this vanity is exactly as long as the little alcove where the current vanity is. Pop that one out, pop this one in."

Brewer huffed out a breath. "Sure thing, *boss*," he said before draining his coffee, rinsing out his cup, and heading for the door.

Needless to say, nothing about the peace-offering croissants actually got us back on track. I spent the next few hours alternating between staring at the notes for my article and replaying our interaction, thinking of a million better ways I could have handled it. There'd been a moment in there where Brewer and I had actually had a conversation that wasn't ruined by my weird one-sided lust or his insistence that I didn't know how to manage my own house renovation, and I'd liked it.

At precisely ten o'clock, my laptop chimed with an incoming FaceTime call from my editor, and I accepted, smoothing my expression into something professional.

"Marjorie, thank fuck," I said. "Tell me about complex journalistic ethics and give me a deadline. I need normal right now."

Marjorie Levine laughed, the sound warm and gravelly from decades of forbidden cigarettes she still indulged in "only at Christmas and on deadline days"—which meant at least once a week. Her home office backdrop featured the same chaotic bookshelf I'd seen in our calls for years, manuscript pages tacked to a corkboard visible behind her head.

"Well, hello to you, too, sunshine," she said. "Oooh, loving the shelves behind you."

I turned to look at the dark wood shelves that gleamed in the winter sunshine and scowled. "Hmph. They would've been nicer painted white."

Marjorie wrinkled her nose. "You really think that would've been better?"

The truth was, I didn't know what I thought. The shelves looked good, I had to admit, but I'd wanted them white. I'd *asked* for them to be white. And Brewer had insisted white wouldn't work.

"Okay," Marjorie said when I didn't respond. "What's got your boxers in a twist?"

"Nothing." I sighed. "Everything."

"Oh, goody. How about you give it to me in twenty words or less," she teased, her brown-gray curls dancing.

I snorted. Marjorie was famous for saying if you couldn't pitch her a story in twenty words, she didn't want the rest.

I held up a hand and counted off on my fingers. "I accidentally burned down my contractor's camper, and now he and his dog are living with me." I pondered for a moment, then added, "And he's hot."

Marjorie's jaw dropped. "Sold. And I'm going to need a few more words, babe."

I shook my head. "I don't wanna get into it, really. Suffice it to say, things here are..." I waved toward the bookshelves. "...complicated. Let's talk about Empire Ridge instead."

"Tell me what you got." She sat back in her seat. "It goes without saying we need this one wrapped asap, houseguest or not."

A tremendous crash echoed down the hall, followed by a loud curse.

"What the hell was that?" Marjorie demanded, leaning closer to her screen like she might be able to peek around the corner of mine.

"My new bathroom vanity, pretty sure." I rubbed at my

neck. "I should go see what's happening. I hate to do this, but could we reschedule—?"

"No, wait! I want to know about your investigation. Did your whistleblower send over the financial stuff? Was it the smoking gun he claimed it was?" Her eyes practically sparkled with editorial excitement.

Meanwhile, more cursing and a burst of raucous laughter filtered down the hall.

"He did, and it looks promising... at least in terms of implicating Empire Ridge. It doesn't do much to clear Harmon's name, unfortunately. But I'll keep looking," I assured her. "This story matters."

"That's my star reporter." She beamed. "The editor at *Counterpoints* practically salivated when I pitched this, by the by. 'Whistleblower reveals corporate conspiracy to frame his family business'? It's everything their readers love. A redemption story for the little guy. Making the bad guys pay. And who better to uncover it all than a reporter who moved to a town just a couple of hours away?"

"No pressure or anything," I deadpanned.

She grinned. "You get those documents, write it up in trademark Monroe style, and... *mwah.*" She kissed her fingers exuberantly. "I can see the Avery Decker Award nomination now."

I laughed. "Wouldn't that be nice?"

"It *will* be nice," she corrected. "And..." She wiggled her eyebrows. "If you need another dangling carrot to motivate you, I've also got two more leads for your next big story. Door number one, tech billionaire buys previously uninhabited island near the Philippines to build eco-utopia but ends up destroying coral reefs and displacing fishermen. Or door number two, unexplained tourist deaths at an exclusive resort in Costa Rica. I'm guessing you'll go for the second one since you speak Spanish."

"I... I guess," I said. The truth was, neither of those stories gave me the usual rush of excitement I got at the prospect of uncovering some hidden truth, finding justice for the deserving, or giving people a voice. All I could think was *hot, humid, crowded.* "You know me, Marjorie. One story at a time, right?"

"I know, I know." She waved a hand. "But can you at least tell me—"

"Ow!" someone yelled from the hallway. "Watch the hand, asshole!"

"*Shit.* Gotta go, Marjorie!" I said, already rushing out of the office... and into a scene pulled from a home renovation disaster show.

Theo stood in the hallway while Brewer was crowded into the small opening of the bathroom. Between them stood my beautiful vanity, wedged into the doorway at an odd angle.

"Hey, Delaney," Theo said cheerfully, his blue eyes lighting when he spotted me.

Brewer's head snapped up, his eyes locked with mine, and electricity arced between us. His expression was carefully blank, but I could see the tension in his jaw.

Always that damn jaw.

"Hey, boss," he said, his forced pleasantness doing nothing to mask the I-told-you-so lurking beneath. "Having a *slight* issue with the install."

"Are you?" I crossed my arms, trying to project confidence rather than the sinking feeling of dread in my stomach. "I couldn't tell."

"Quick question. When you were ordering a vanity long enough to fit the space, did you also take into account the width of the opening and the depth of the vanity?" he asked.

"Yes. Pfft. Obviously. The width of the door is thirty inches, and the vanity is thirty inches—"

"Uh-huh. Was that with or without the custom cement counter that's been welded in place?" he shot back.

"With..." I began.

Brewer shook his head once.

"...out," I finished meekly. "*Fuck.*"

Brewer nodded. "That about sums it up. This thing is fucking enormous—"

"Hey! Don't shame the vanity for being girthy, Brew." Theo patted the countertop like its feelings might be hurt. "Some folks like 'em big. Right, Delaney?"

I narrowed my eyes, but Theo merely smiled back innocently.

"Girthy or not, can't you guys, like, maneuver it?" I asked Brewer.

He folded his arms over his chest, copying my stance. "Maneuver a thirty-four-inch vanity into a thirty-inch opening?"

"I mean, finesse it and guide it and move it around." I made a twisting motion with my hands to demonstrate. "Sometimes you can fit a big thing in a tight space if you find the right angle."

Theo coughed lightly. Brewer's cheeks reddened, and so did mine.

I tried glaring at Theo again, but he seemed to be inspecting the ceiling.

"We've tried that, and it doesn't work. Besides, the issue isn't just getting it in the... in the opening." Brewer glared angrily at Theo, though Theo hadn't said a word. "It's that the space isn't deep enough to accommodate it, even once we get it in."

"Actually, Brew," Theo began. "If properly motivated and with the right thrusting—"

"*Theo*," Brewer and I said in unison, and Theo grinned.

"The vanity sticks out from the wall about six inches too far," Brewer said impatiently, "and—

Theo opened his mouth.

"Theo Ross, if you say one word about six inches, I will call your mother!" After a pause, Brewer added, "Or Bennett."

Theo laughed. To me, he added, "Bennett's my partner. He owns the observatory house we live in across the lake. You'd like him, Delaney. He lived in New York for a while, like you did, and he's smart like you, too."

"Oh?" I blinked. "That's—"

Theo's smile turned a bit sly. "And he also likes 'em girthy."

"Theo," I said impatiently, "could you give us a minute to discuss this?"

"Sure." Theo waved a hand. "I'll just stand here. Feel free to—"

"*Theo*," Brewer snapped.

Theo gave us both a grin so full of mischief and good humor that I nearly smiled back. "Come to think of it, why don't I step outside?" His boots clomped cheerily out the front door, and he closed it with a *click*.

I met Brewer's gaze. "So, what would you suggest we do?"

"Me?" Brewer pressed one big hand to his big chest, and his eyes widened. "Oh, gosh, that's above my pay grade, Delaney. I mean, I'm not paid to have an opinion, right? 'Cause you're the boss?" He leaned against the wall. I tried not to notice the way sweat dampened a little curl of hair above his ear or the way his biceps muscles strained the fabric of his shirt.

I pinched the bridge of my nose. "Fine, then. What if you get rid of the door and put in a pocket door?"

For half a second, he almost looked impressed. Then he shrugged. "We could. Except reframing and moving the electrical would cost money, like I told you earlier."

I rubbed at my forehead, where my nagging headache had become a full-blown throbbing nightmare. "What if you—?"

Brewer's face softened, and he leaned toward me, bracing his hands on the vanity. "Do you care about it that deeply, Delaney? Is this vanity really so important when there are a million vanities you might like just as much that would actually fit this space?"

Brewer's reasonable, sympathetic tone was annoying. I didn't want him to be gentle or understanding. I wanted him to be smug and insufferable so I could maintain my righteous indignation.

Objectively, I knew he was right. But admitting he was right meant admitting I was *wrong*.

And after everything that had happened in the past twenty-four hours, after the disappointing conversation with Marjorie about my story...

I just didn't have it in me to be wrong again.

"What you're saying is that I'm stuck with whatever you think is best for my house after all." I sounded like a petulant child, and I hated that.

"No. What I'm saying is that you have options. Keep this—" Brewer kicked lightly at the vanity. "—and change the budget. Or keep the budget and change this. But Delaney... something's gotta give."

He was talking about the vanity, obviously, but when our eyes met and my breath caught, it felt like he was talking about something else. Something more.

I swallowed hard, watching how his chest rose and fell with each breath, how his pupils flared when our eyes locked. The room felt ten degrees hotter, my skin hypersensitive under his gaze.

For the first time, a startling thought crystallized in my mind: What if Brewer felt this too? What if that intensity in his eyes, the careful way he maintained his distance, wasn't just annoyance or professional frustration but something else entirely? The possibility sent a jolt of heat straight to my core.

"Trust me," he said softly.

I wanted to. Well, I *almost* wanted to. But I couldn't.

I looked away first and toyed with the corner of my glasses. "Show me some vanity options," I said imperiously. "*Real* options. Not three color variations of the thing you've already decided I should get."

Though I wasn't looking directly at Brewer, I'd swear I caught his lips curving into that sideways-hook smile for an instant, there and then gone.

"Okay," he said.

Before I could formulate a response, Theo poked his head back in.

"So, we returning Mr. Girthy?" His gaze darted between us. "Or do you two need more time alone?"

"No," Brewer said, his voice suddenly brisk and professional. "Delaney's decided to return the vanity, so let's get it back on the truck."

"Okey doke," Theo said easily. "I figured that might be the case, so I called Hen while I was waiting and told him what was up. Delaney, he said to tell you not to worry about getting your money back 'cause a buddy of his works for the manufacturer and owes him a favor. He'll make sure they take the vanity without any ridiculous restocking fees or whatever."

I blinked. "Wait, really? Hen called in a favor for me? Please tell him thank you."

Theo shrugged. "I will, but don't sweat it. He's got a million buddies who owe him a million favors—like, if there were a hardware mafia, he'd be the don of Western New York—and he likes you."

He did? I blinked again, this new information more surprising than the last, but before I could formulate a reply, Brewer said gruffly, "Vanity, Theo. Move it along," and then he and Theo got busy.

It turned out that unwedging a stuck vanity was trickier than wedging it in there had been. The process took twenty long minutes and involved plenty of swearing (from Brewer), sweating on the sidelines (from me), and at least one lube joke (from Theo), but they finally got the truck loaded and headed back to town.

And that night as I lay in bed, listening to Brewer singing something softly to Teeny on the far side of the wall, I thought there might be a metaphor in there somewhere about being stuck and fitting... about trust and croissants and *rightness*... and about the way my stomach fluttered at the prospect of sharing breakfast with Brewer again, even though the man drove me crazy.

But I fell asleep before I could figure out what it was.

CHAPTER FOUR

BREWER

I'D THOUGHT THE "GIRTHY" vanity incident on Monday would be the end of it. That my client would finally start to trust me so we could cohabitate in peace while I focused on finishing his renovation and finding a new place to live.

By Friday morning, I was forced to acknowledge that peace wasn't really an option when dealing with Delaney Monroe.

Delaney, who used a complex system of color-coded sticky notes for different purposes and had rearranged my grandmother's teacups on his kitchen shelf five times in six days to achieve the right "visual harmony."

Delaney, who I'd overheard speaking to his sister for six uninterrupted minutes about an article he'd read on the importance of baby-wearing, as Tam's expression had morphed from shock—*Delaney reads articles on baby-wearing?*—to offense—*Does he think I'm not meeting Tierney's "psycho-emotional needs"?*—to concern—*Is he still talking?*—to reluctant admiration—*Holy shit, he memorized fourteen sling-wrapping techniques?*—to fond amusement, while I'd nearly fallen off my ladder while repairing the living room ceiling and brained myself, trying not to laugh.

Delaney, who, it turned out, had strong views that there was *one* correct way of folding towels and spent forty-five minutes explaining to me why the subway tile pattern I'd suggested for the downstairs shower was "pedestrian"... before changing his mind an hour later and deciding it was "preferable, Brewer, please proceed."

Delaney, who apparently wore slithery green silk pajamas that had stopped me in my tracks when I'd spotted them peeking out of his hamper and which had spawned a dozen fantasies since.

Delaney, who toyed with his glasses, and stared at my chest in an abstracted way all the fucking time, and left me glass containers of food neatly labeled with my name when I'd started avoiding the kitchen during mealtimes to minimize how much time I could spend staring back at him.

Delaney, who was cranky and unexpectedly sweet, cocky, and anxious, like a double-sided puzzle I couldn't help trying to put together, who'd invaded my brain to the point where I'd had to jerk off in the attic this morning before getting to work—not a thing I'd had to do when working with other clients—and who was the primary source of the low-level tension I felt crackling in the air like—

"There's a big storm a-comin', Brewer!" Hen said gleefully. "Good thing Delaney's cabinets came in this morning, eh?"

I shook myself physically and mentally, realizing I'd been woolgathering in the middle of the hardware store— another thing I didn't think I'd ever been reduced to before Delaney.

"That's why I'm here," I agreed. "I did hear there might be flurries tonight, but—"

"Flurries." Hen scoffed. His chest puffed up. "You sound like my grandson. I keep telling Everett TV meteorologists don't understand the unique microclimate around here. My leg's been aching something fierce, so I'm saying we'll get a solid foot." He stroked his mustache thoughtfully. "Maybe more."

"Tell you what, Hen," said a voice behind me. "I'll bet you a coffee and a cheese danish at Fanaille we get less than three inches."

I turned to find Reed Sunday approaching with a smile, carrying a tub of spackle and an armload of paint rollers. He and his husband had bought a new house around the time Delaney had but were doing most of the renovations themselves. I was scheduled to work on their kitchen after I finished at Delaney's place.

Hen's eyes lit as he extended a hand for Reed to shake. "You're on, son. You bet against the leg at your own peril. I can taste that danish already."

Reed laughed as he set his purchases on the counter, and Hen began to ring him up.

"Best to be prepared, that's what I say!" Janice Plum breezed out of the Seasonal aisle carrying three huge bags of Ice Melt... and wearing what appeared to be a wicker cornucopia on her head, decorated with silk flowers and miniature plastic fruit. "Right, Brewer?"

I was momentarily so blinded by her... hat-thing I couldn't process her words. "Er. Y-yes. Definitely."

"Tricky for other folks to be prepared when *you're* buying out the store." Angela Ross, Theo's mom and the leader of the local gossip tree, came up behind her carrying a mop propped over her shoulder like a rifle.

"I'm buying for the *neighborhood*, Angela," Janice said primly. "Some folks from my book club have banded together to form THWAC—The Helpful Wintertime Association of Coppertians—to do snow removal for folks who need help." She threw her head back proudly.

When she did, a fake orange fell off her head, plopped on the floor, and rolled under Hen's counter.

For a moment, no one moved or spoke. Then Angela broke the silence. "Janice, honey, what on earth are you wearing?"

"Oh, this?" Janice tweaked a cluster of grapes dangling by her ear. "Why, it's a historic harvest crown. Obviously. In honor of the Council for Historical Happenings' Harvest Festivals Retrospective." Janice leaned toward me and added with a wink, "Tuesday night, 7:00 p.m., at the library." Then she straightened and said, "I decided this would be a... a visually striking way to draw attention to the event. Do you like it?"

Reed and I exchanged a glance, and I bit the inside of my cheek.

"It's definitely striking," I offered.

"Yes," Reed agreed. "I can say that I, personally, feel struck."

Hen stroked his mustache, I was pretty sure to hide his laughter.

Janice blushed and ducked her head slightly. "You're too sweet. To be honest, it was Delaney's idea," she admitted. "Delaney Monroe."

"*Delaney* told you to put a harvest on your head?" I demanded. I felt my cheeks go red. "I mean..."

"Not exactly. I gave him one of our event flyers the other day, and he suggested I might get more engagement if

I wore a historical costume. *He* suggested a hoop skirt, but hoop skirts are impractical—"

"Whereas fruit bonnets are the very soul of practicality," Angela cut in.

"Harvest. *Crown*." Janice narrowed her eyes at Angela. "Anyway, at first, I was a *bit* put out with Delaney. I mean, that's not the way we've ever done things at the Council. But... well, then Hardison's had a sale on craft notions, and I thought, 'Why not live a little, Janice? You didn't know you liked fig jam until Chris Sunday moved to town and put it on a charcuterie board.'" She gave Reed a knowing wink. "So here I am."

"Here you are," Hen agreed.

"And I've had no less than *thirteen people* approach me this morning to ask about our event!"

I nodded politely, though I was confident that hadn't been why they'd initially approached her.

"I'm sure Chris would be honored that his charcuterie played a role in this transformation," Reed said solemnly. "In fact, I can't wait to get home and tell him."

"Aw," Janice sighed. "You're such a delight, Reed Sunday."

"I'm gonna tell Chris *that*, too. Can you believe he once thought I was a grumpy bastard?" Reed grinned. "Speaking of which, I'd better get going before my beloved sends out a search party." He picked up his purchases and slapped my shoulder. "Hey, Brew, you should come with us to the Hive tonight. There's a local alt-country band playing. You're a country fan, right?"

I blinked. I wasn't sure where he'd gotten that idea since I was actually a lot more Lin-Manuel Miranda than Luke Bryan, but it didn't bother me, really. People made assumptions about me all the time—look how they'd explained to themselves why I chose to live so far out of town—and it was easier to just nod along and let it ride. No need to make people uncomfortable by explaining they were wrong.

If I got really introspective about it, I knew I let them believe what they wanted because it made things simpler for me, too. Because if they didn't really know the real me, they couldn't judge the real me, and I got to kinda coast along.

The truth was, though I liked Reed and most Coppertians a lot, I didn't feel close enough to any of them for it to matter whether they *truly* knew me or not. At some point, they might get something so wrong I'd need to correct them, but that hadn't happened yet.

"I like lots of things," I agreed, which wasn't a lie.

"So come out with us," Reed said. "Chris and I are going. And Jasper and Watt. You probably need to blow off steam after everything with your camper." He grimaced sympathetically.

Whatever he'd heard through town gossip, Reed didn't know the half of it. Losing the camper had been bad enough. Living with Delaney meant I was losing my mind, too.

Still, even if the original Broadway cast of *Rent* had been in town, it would have been a hard sell to get me to go out in a crowd with loud music playing. What I needed right now was peace, quiet, and solitude.

Not that I was likely to get any of those things when I was just a few feet from Delaney.

"I don't think so. If Hen's knee is right and that storm's coming..." I shrugged.

Reed smiled easily. "Well, we'll be there if you change your mind."

Since I was officially done with small talk for the day, I

simply nodded. Then, waving a goodbye to the ladies, I met Hen's eyes and followed him to the back room to collect Delaney's cabinets and get back to the work I loved.

Four cabinet doors, sixteen screws, and countless muttered profanities later, I was about ready to say *fuck it* to home renovation and see if the Foreign Legion was taking new recruits.

I stared at the metal cabinets leaning against Delaney's kitchen wall and tried to tamp down my frustration.

For three hours, I'd been wrestling with them—measuring, leveling, remeasuring, and cursing under my breath—and I'd managed to get a few of them hung... sort of. But the gap between the cabinet and the ancient wall was uneven—nearly an inch in some places—and would need to be caulked to hell and back. Even with shims, I couldn't get them perfectly level because on a house this old, the floors and walls weren't square.

I'd promised Delaney I'd give him exactly what he wanted, though—that I'd be the perfect, opinion-free contractor—so I kept fucking going.

I was tightening a particularly stubborn screw when my phone buzzed in my pocket. Startled, my hand slipped, and the screwdriver jammed into my palm.

"Son of a *bitch*!" I shook out my hand, a bruise already forming at the base of my thumb.

From the hallway came the faint sound of Delaney typing furiously on his laptop. He'd been holed up in his office all day with his headphones on—not that I was keeping track—working on his article or avoiding me. Probably both. But he didn't seem to have heard my outburst, at least.

I pulled out my phone to find a text from my cousin.

HAYES

Dinner and drinks tonight? You, me, Kel?

My first instinct was to refuse. I was tired, sore, and in a foul mood, and the last thing I wanted was to hang around with my much younger cousin and his frat-bro bestie.

But then I reminded myself that Hayes had moved to Copper County at least in part to be near me, despite my aunt giving him the hard sell to move back home to Southbourne. Since his arrival, I'd tried to see him every week, though it ended up being more like every other. We'd managed what he'd called a "Bros Weekend" at the lake last summer. But I'd barely talked to him the past week, though he'd texted several times to express his concern.

Was I getting to be like my father, putting work and all the mixed-up feelings that came with it ahead of my family?

The cabinet door I'd just installed swung open violently and smacked me in the shoulder.

"What the—?" I pushed it closed, and it immediately swung back open.

Because it wasn't plumb. Because these cabinets were never going to work right in this house.

Frustration boiled over into anger, all the hotter for me trying to push it down.

I could have made Delaney cabinets. Beautiful, custom ones. But he didn't want to talk about alternatives. He wanted his fucking metal cabinets that were dead wrong for the space.

And, I realized, I needed to get out of this house before I marched down the hall and shouted that to his face.

Instead, I texted my cousin back.

> Sounds good. Meet me at the Hive in 2 hours?

I left the cabinets exactly as they were and headed for the attic. I fed Teeny dinner, then took her for a longer walk than usual since I'd be leaving her alone for a few hours. Spending time with her made me feel slightly less like a volcano about to erupt as I headed downstairs for a shower.

But the sight of the old vanity I'd reinstalled in the bathroom—my *boss* hadn't made up his mind about a new style yet, despite me providing him with five choices that were all fairly similar to the *girthy* one—amped me up again.

This whole situation was my own fault, and I knew it. I'd agreed to do things Delaney's way, hoping it would teach him a lesson, but *I* was the one suffering the consequences. If anyone in town saw those cabinets, my reputation would be toast... which was why I'd begun including design clauses in my contracts to prevent this kind of disaster.

I stalked out of the bathroom with a towel around my waist and promptly collided with Delaney—still wearing his fucking noise-canceling headphones—in the hall. It was at least the fourth time we'd smacked into each other that way in the past week, and it did nothing to improve my mood.

"Oh!" Delaney jumped. One hand flew to his glasses while the other pulled off his headphones, and his eyes came to rest on my bare chest. "Sorry. I... I didn't hear you."

He looked tired—dark circles under his eyes, hair mussed like he'd been running his hands through it—and despite everything, it was on the tip of my tongue to ask if his article was going okay or if there was anything I could do. But I stopped myself.

If Delaney was trying to control the whole world and

holding on so tightly it looked like he was about to crack, that wasn't my problem.

I tightened my own hold on my towel and my patience. "No problem. I'm done for the day."

"You are? Awesome." His cheeks flushed with excitement that made my stomach tighten. "You were working in the kitchen, right? I can't wait to see what you've done. Tam's coming over to see the progress, and I was going to order pizza. If you want, I can—"

"I'm going out." I stepped around him.

Delaney blinked, clearly taken aback by my tone. "Okay. They're, uh, predicting flurries tonight, so—"

I didn't bother to share Hen's predictions. I could imagine how that conversation would go.

"Have a good night, Delaney. Enjoy your new cabinets."

I headed for the attic, telling myself the flash of hurt in his eyes was my imagination.

The Hive was packed when I arrived, the crowd spilling from the bar to the tables and country music blaring from speakers near a small stage where a band was playing.

I tugged at the collar of my new navy henley—one of the few items I'd purchased to replace my burned wardrobe —feeling oddly self-conscious as I scanned the room.

I stopped at the closest table to the door and greeted Reed, who offered me a ride home if I wanted to drink, and Chris, who was already a little glassy-eyed from the single beer in front of him and kept glancing up at his husband like Reed was some kind of superhero. They pointed out Jasper and Watt, who were standing at the bar, pressed together by the crowd, ostensibly grabbing a fresh round... but with Watt's hand tucked in Jasper's back pocket, it was pretty clear that wasn't the only grabbing on their minds.

When they invited me to join them while I waited for

Hayes, I hesitated, deeply regretting my choice to come out. Finding a spot in this crowd would be annoying, but for some reason, I didn't think I could handle being surrounded by loved-up couples tonight.

I was grateful when I spotted Hayes waving at me enthusiastically from a table he and Kel had already claimed at the back, and I could make my excuses.

"Brewski!" Hayes stood for a quick hug, his lanky frame rising above the crowd. Though my cousin was shorter than me by a good four inches, he wasn't exactly small, and with our matching eyes and similar jawlines, there was no mistaking we were family.

Kel, whose muscular frame always seemed weirdly disconnected from his ever-present Birkenstocks—like he was half gym trainer, half laid-back delivery driver—gave me a wave and an easygoing smile.

"You made it!" Hayes said. "I worried you'd bail."

I slid into the empty chair. "Said I'd come, didn't I?" I flagged down a server and ordered a local favorite beer. "Two Hayburners, please."

Hayes's eyebrows shot up, and he and Kel exchanged a look.

"Whoa," Kel said. "Save some for the rest of us."

Hayes smacked Kel's shoulder and laughed like Kel's comment had been hilarious in the extreme. "Or wait for the wings we ordered. You eaten yet?"

I hadn't, but when the beers arrived, I immediately took a long pull from the first. "I've had a day," I told them, "and Reed just offered me a ride home if I need one." I paused. "I mean, to Delaney's place. Not... not *home*."

Hayes leaned forward. "Yeah, how's that going? Staying at Delaney's, I mean?"

I took another long drink, and Hayes and Kel exchanged a look.

"You know, you could totes stay with us, Brew," Kel offered. "Hayes and I usually take turns on the pull-out and the actual bed, but we don't mind doubling up for a while if you need a spot to crash. You could play DragonBlood4 with us! We just started a tournament, but you could get in on it—"

"Don't worry about me. Let's talk about you," I interrupted. "How's work, Hayes? Still loving it?"

"Oh, shit, yeah." Hayes smiled eagerly. "Let me tell you about my new client!"

While I sipped my beers, Hayes launched into a long, detailed explanation of the app he was developing. I understood about half of it, and I was pretty sure Kel didn't understand much more, but he watched Hayes with a kind of appreciative fascination and hung on his every word, anyway.

Eventually, the two of them fell into their own conversation about the video game they'd been playing. I couldn't help noticing the easy rhythm they had, finishing each other's sentences, punctuating points with physical contact —a punch to the shoulder here, a headlock there.

Watching them dance around each other was arguably worse than being with the loved-up couples I'd left behind.

"Dude, you should have seen Kel's face when that dragon horde broke through," Hayes crowed, throwing an arm around Kel's neck and ruffling his hair. "Like a wittle baby seeing a clown."

"Fuck off, dude!" Kel shoved Hayes with a laugh, but his hand lingered on Hayes's shoulder. "You were the one who screamed like a child."

"Did not."

"You *so* did. And your face was doing that thing, too." Kel reached out to poke Hayes's cheek. "Where your tiny, baby dimple pops out, and—"

It was exhausting watching two people so clearly in denial, so completely oblivious to what was obvious to everyone else.

Between this and Delaney's stubborn refusal to see what was right in front of him with his damn house, it felt like I was surrounded by people determined to make life harder than it needed to be.

"Can you two cut it out or get a room?" I snapped.

The table went silent. Hayes and Kel jumped apart like they'd been scalded, both turning bright red.

"What the... what the hell, Brew?" Hayes's cheerful smile disappeared, and his eyes went stormy with anger. "Kel and I are just friends. You know that. Not cool."

Shit. I rubbed my face. "No. It really wasn't. I'm sorry. I'm being an asshole tonight."

Kel and Hayes exchanged a look that seemed to communicate a thousand things without words, and then Kel nodded and cleared his throat.

"I'm gonna let you guys talk while I, uh... bathroom." He jerked his thumb toward the far side of the bar, then slid out of his chair and disappeared into the crowd.

Hayes fixed me with a glare, all traces of his usual eager-puppy enthusiasm wiped away. "What the heck is wrong with you?"

I took another swig of beer and sighed. "I'm really sorry, Hayes. I'm in a mood, and I'm taking it out on the wrong person. *People.* I'll apologize to Kel again when he gets back. Maybe I shouldn't have come out at all."

Hayes's face softened. "No. Fuck. *I'm* sorry, bruh. You've had a shit week. The shittiest. Losing the camper, replacing all your stuff? Fucking sucks. No wonder you don't want to hear me and Kel goofing around." His mouth twisted to one side. "Have you had any luck with the insurance company?"

"They're getting me a quote by the end of next week, I think." I shrugged. "Which is fine since I haven't had time to look for a new camper yet anyway."

"But you still have the money you inherited from Grandpa, right? You could always buy a place. Or build your own—"

I shook my head. "I didn't inherit *money*, Hayes, I inherited a *home*. Grandpa's home. Or I was supposed to." My voice came out even more bitter than I'd expected. "Until the trustee fucking sold it."

Hayes bit his lip. "Uncle Tony sold it because they offered him a killer price. Double the market value! And I'm not saying that makes it okay, Brewer," he added quickly. "He should have known how much the house meant to you and that you wouldn't've sold it for a *billion* dollars. He fucked up huge. But he was trying to be a good trustee. To make solid financial decisions for you, you know? And it's not like he stole the money or anything. And it's too late to get the house back now, so don't you think—"

"Hayes." I sliced a hand through the air. "As I've told you the last ten times you've tried to bring this up, I don't want to hear about my father's claims that he was swindled or manipulated or whatever the fuck. I don't want to talk about him, period. Ever. End of story." I took a long pull of my beer and swallowed. "Especially when I'm already dealing with the world's bossiest, pickiest client."

Hayes frowned. "Wait, what's going on with Hot Delaney?"

I choked on my beer. "*Hot?*"

I mean, yes, the man was attractive. Very. But I didn't expect to hear my cousin say so.

"Uh, yeah. Anyone with eyes knows Delaney's hot. Obvi. But he also dated Jasper for a minute last fall, and Jasper used to be a model, which by definition means *Jasper's* hot. And everyone knows if you bang a hot person, that makes you hot, too. Therefore... Hot Delaney." He chewed his chicken. "It's science."

I shook my head. "This is the brain that graduated at the top of his class in college?" I demanded. Then I added, because I couldn't help myself, "Delaney banged Jasper?"

Hayes shrugged. "Man, IDK. I think they only dated once or twice 'cause Jasper was pretty hung up on Watt even then." He gave me a sappy smile that was coated in buffalo sauce. "Aren't Jasper and Watt, like, the cutest? Second-chance romance, am I right?"

"You've been spending too much time in Janice Plum's book club," I grumbled. "In fact, this entire town has."

"Hey." Hayes pointed his wing at me. "Don't knock romance, Brewer, or romance will knock *you*. But speaking of Hot Delaney..." Hayes glanced around the crowded bar. "Is he here tonight?"

"No."

"Why not?"

"I don't know, Hayes," I snapped. "Because no one invited him? Because he's always telling people what to do and doesn't think their ten years of expertise might be worth listening to?"

"Whoa." Hayes leaned back, his chicken forgotten. "I'm sensing feelings here, Brewski."

"Anger. Anger is the feeling." I finished the rest of my second beer and signaled the server for a fresh one. "And stop calling Delaney *hot*," I muttered. "His hotness is irrelevant."

"But you do agree he's hot?" Hayes prompted.

Kel returned at this moment, sliding carefully into his seat. He and Hayes exchanged another of those speaking glances, and then Hayes stood.

"I'm gonna grab more napkins," he announced, leaving me alone with Kel.

Like the two of them were fucking tag-teaming me. I didn't appreciate that.

An awkward silence fell.

"So." Kel summoned a smile. "You guys were talking about Hot Delaney, huh? Is it true he, ah, had something to do with your camper—"

"No," I said shortly.

"Oh, thank fuck." Kel sounded relieved. "I was afraid I'd have to dislike him on principle. Enemy of my best friend's cousin is my enemy," he said solemnly. "It's science."

I shook my head. He and Hayes clearly spent too much time together.

"The camper was an accident," I explained. "Delaney's a pain in the ass, but I don't blame him for that."

"A pain in the ass? Delaney?" Kel's face scrunched. "But Delaney seems so cool and thoughtful."

I deliberately didn't let myself think about the croissants and the coffee and the containers of leftovers with sticky notes.

I eyed Kel across the table. "How would you know?"

"Well, I don't *know*-know. But I'm a Kitchen Courier."

He gave me a sage nod. "You can tell a lot about a guy by the way he orders food."

I snorted. "That so? Tell me about Delaney, then." Fuck knew I needed some insights.

Kel sipped his beer thoughtfully. "He's a big tipper, for one thing. Especially when the weather's bad."

"Good," I muttered. "He can probably afford to be."

"Dude." Kel shot me a look of rebuke. "Not everyone values the time and effort of the people doing stuff for them, even if they can afford to, believe me. Delaney does. Give credit where it's due, my man."

I frowned. He had a point. A small one.

"*Annnnd* I know when Delaney ordered from the Burger Barn the other night, he Co-Couriered some fancy dog biscuits from the bakery, too." Kel watched me steadily. "Which was interesting since I didn't know he had a dog."

I blinked, remembering the container of dog treats that had been left on the stairs to the attic... along with another of Delaney's stickies. "He said they were delivered by mistake and I shouldn't let them go to waste."

Kel chuckled. "I was Courier of the Year last year, bro. I don't make mistakes."

A startled bark of laughter burst out of me, but I quickly controlled it. "Well... that was surprisingly nice of him," I admitted. I took another sip of beer and added pointedly, "Considering he hates my dog."

"Hates her? Sweet Teeny girl?" Kel shook his head. "Not possible."

I rolled my eyes. "He looks at her like she's a monster, and he won't listen when I try to explain she's harmless."

"Huh." Kel's brow lowered in a frown. "Wonder why?"

"Why?" I scoffed. "*Why?* Because—" I blinked.

"Because... I don't know why, exactly. Delaney didn't volunteer."

Kel's eyebrows winged up. "And you didn't ask?"

"I..." My body flushed hot. How could I explain the weird thing that happened whenever I tried talking to Delaney? The way my blood sizzled just from being in the same room with him and I felt the leash on my emotions slipping? The way I was trying to keep my distance so I could stay professional, and it wasn't fucking working? "No. He's my client. We don't have deep, meaningful discussions, nor should we."

"Hmm. Maybe Delaney's ex had a big dog, and he has negative associations. Oooh, or maybe something happened when he was a kid that scared him." Kel's fingers traced patterns in the condensation ring left by his beer. "Where'd he grow up, again? Outside the city, somewhere?"

"I..." I blinked. "I think so. Maybe." Though, I had to admit, I knew this mostly from hearing Coppertians talk about the Monroes, not because Delaney himself ever had.

"Wonder why he came to Copper County," Kel mused. "I mean, Tam and Lucas and their baby, yeah. But still. Moving here is, like, *extreme*-extreme, huh? 'Cause I remember Tam saying Delaney travels all over for work. That's gonna be way harder with him living all the way out here."

Kel didn't pose this as a question, but it came out as one anyway.

Once again, I shook my head. "He's my client. We're not friends." And because I felt attacked for some reason, I added, "He's bossy as fuck, and he wants everything his own way."

Kel opened his mouth, but I figured I already knew

what he was going to ask. I held up a hand. "No, I don't know *why* he's like that, Kel. And I don't care."

He pursed his lips. "Dude. I was gonna point out that Delaney seems like a guy who gets defensive when he feels like he's on the back foot. I mean, samesies." He pressed a finger against his own chest. "So, like, it's gotta be overwhelming, being in a new town, doing his big career stuff, *plus* living through a renovation." He sat back in his chair and regarded me steadily. "I was thinking that if you knew *why* Delaney acts the way he does, it might make it easier for you to see him as a human and not just a client and, like, deal with him more effectively. But what do I know?"

Sometimes I forgot that my cousin's frat-bro roommate had graduated college near the top of his class, too. He was an easygoing guy, but he was also a good listener... and he had a good point.

Was Delaney in over his head? I'd assumed his stubbornness was because he thought he was so much smarter than I was, even when it came to home restoration. But what if it wasn't? What if, by trying *not* to get to know him, to keep distance between us, I'd made the whole situation worse?

Hayes returned with napkins and a plate of mozzarella sticks. "What'd I miss?"

Kel reached for the platter and inhaled half a pound of fried cheese and marinara sauce in a single bite. "Oooh, fuck! Hot, hot, hot!" He took a giant swallow of beer and fanned his mouth. "We were talking about Delaney," he said, sounding like he was speaking around a burnt tongue. "And I was saying maybe the reason he's been a tough client is because he's overwhelmed. People who feel powerless lash out. That's Psych 101."

Hayes gave Kel a proud smile I wasn't sure the other man even noticed. "You say the best shit, Kel!"

"Aw. 'Fanks, bruh," Kel said, stuffing more burning mozzarella in his mouth.

"Do you think that could be part of his deal?" Hayes asked me. "It's not easy moving to a new town, especially a small one—"

"Look, can we drop this, please?" I begged. "I came out tonight specifically so I wouldn't have to think about him—I mean, this situation. Because I've been trying to avoid him —*it*—and it's not working."

"Disengagement." Hayes pulled a face. "Classic Brewer move."

I frowned. "Huh?"

"Someone or something hurts you or even just gets under your skin, and instead of talking it through, you push them away to protect yourself. Like with your dad." Hayes's blue eyes met mine.

The words stung like a slap. "These two situations aren't the same at all. One is my client, who I'm trying to maintain a professional relationship with, to the point where I came out tonight just so he wouldn't say something to set me off and I wouldn't say something I'd regret. The other is my father, who I *had* to cut off for my own sanity because he repeatedly refused to listen and made choices that affected me without giving a shit what I wanted..."

I trailed off. That actually sounded a whole lot like my issues with Delaney.

Fuck.

"Uh-huh." Hayes nodded seriously. "You know I love you and I'm on your side, always. But this thing with your dad—"

"Hayes," I ground out.

"Yeah, it's 'cause he's been blowing up my phone. Look, I know he hurt you. He destroyed Grandpa's legacy. *I get it.* But you literally changed your name, changed your phone number. You won't listen to his explanations—"

"I won't listen to his excuses," I shot back. "You don't know him the way I do, Hayes. It wasn't only about the house. That was just the final straw."

Hayes blew out a breath. "You're right. I don't. Because you don't talk about it with *me* either. You've set up a protective wall around this whole subject, and you try to pretend like it never happened."

Kel's jaw tightened, but he kept his mouth closed as he stared down at his beer. I ground my own teeth together, trying to keep from snapping at my cousin. Hadn't we already discussed this two too many times tonight? "I don't want to talk about it," I gritted out.

Hayes barked out a humorless laugh. "That's just it, though. You never want to talk about it. I'm not fucking fourteen anymore, Brewer. This is my family, and I'm caught in the middle. You avoid, avoid, avoid, and it's not cool. How would you feel if I refused to talk to you about important stuff?"

I blew out a breath. He was right. He wasn't a kid anymore. But still. It had been a damned day, and talking about my father wasn't going to make it any better.

I met Hayes's eyes. "Yeah, okay. I see your point. But can we not talk about it here and now?"

Hayes's shoulders dropped, and the edges of his lip quirked up. "Yeah, fair. But this time, I'm holding you to it. Disconnecting isn't a healthy way of dealing with issues. And the reasons why people do things matter. Everyone deserves to have their story told."

I froze. That was exactly what Delaney had said the other day.

And while Hayes was totally misguided when it came to my father, he was right that I hadn't listened to Delaney's story either. In fact, I hadn't really stopped to consider that he had one.

Delaney was so capable and put together I'd never stopped to consider *why* he was so stubborn or mistrustful, *why* he needed to be in control, *why* he needed to prove he knew better than I did when he clearly didn't.

I took a long sip of my beer, letting the realization wash over me. I'd been treating Delaney the same way I thought he was treating me—dismissing him without giving him the benefit of the doubt. And I really fucking hated what that said about me.

"Fuck," I muttered.

A group of people pushed open the door of the bar, laughing and stomping snow off their boots. "You guys, it's really coming down out there!" one of them shouted.

Hayes laughed. "Score one for Hen's leg. Snow day tomorrow?" he asked Kel. "You, me, Dragon's Blood?"

Kel gave him a stern look. "Bro. We're members of THWAC now. We got responsibilities."

Hayes groaned, but I barely paid attention.

A strange urgency gripped me. Delaney was home alone. What if the power went out? The house had come with a generator, but did he have any idea how to start it?

"I should go," I said, standing suddenly.

"But you only sat down an hour ago," Hayes protested.

"I know, but..." I gestured toward the door. "I should get home before it gets worse."

Hayes's expression shifted from confusion to understanding. "You're worried about Delaney."

"I'm not—" I started, then sighed. "Slightly, maybe. Yes. He's got a long, slippery driveway. And Teeny's there. And..."

Kel and Hayes exchanged another of those looks, and then Hayes rose and clapped me on the shoulder. "Go," he said. "We'll catch up tomorrow."

I said my goodbyes, but as I headed for the door, I overheard Kel muttering, "Dude, your cousin and Hot Delaney are totally gonna bone."

"One thousand percent fuck vibes," Hayes agreed. "And isn't it crazy how he doesn't even seem to see it?"

I shook my head. I needed to call Hayes tomorrow and set him right before he and the gossips could start rumors, but at the moment, I was too busy calculating how long it would take me to get home.

The cold air outside the bar made me briefly light-headed, and I sucked in a deep breath. But it wasn't until I took an unsteady step toward the crowded parking lot that I realized it wasn't just the cold. Those three beers on an empty stomach had hit harder than I'd realized.

"Hey!" Reed appeared beside me wearing just his sweater, despite the falling snow. "Ready to head out?"

I ran a hand through my hair, which was already damp. "Shit. I don't want you to have to leave—"

Reed smiled. "We're ready to go. At least I am. Chris is tipsy and making new friends—"

Chris appeared behind Reed and wound his arms around his husband's waist. He was pink-cheeked and looked a little silly wrapped up in a huge coat that couldn't possibly be his own.

"I had three beers, Brewer!" he announced proudly. Then he turned to his husband. "Oh, those ladies I was talking to were *so* nice. Do you think I should go back and invite them over for charcuterie—?"

"Not tonight." Reed grinned at his pouting husband. "Baby, I have seen what happens when you have multiple beers and talk to ladies at a bar. It's only a matter of time before tables get flipped." He pulled Chris under his arm. "Besides, we're driving Brewer home."

"Oooh." Chris's eyes lit up. "Is Delaney there? Do you think he might want to watch—"

"Nope," Reed interrupted. "I think you and I are going to have a *private* John Ruffian party. Just the two of us. I'm thinking Season 3, Episode 4."

The flush on Chris's cheeks deepened. "Oh, *heck yeah*," he breathed.

The drive back to Delaney's place was mostly quiet, except for Chris occasionally giggling in the front seat and once whispering something to Reed that I'd swear sounded like, "Remember the time you kidnapped me?" which made me wonder if I was drunk instead of just buzzing.

"Thanks for the ride," I said when they let me out at the end of Delaney's driveway.

"Anytime!" Chris chirped. "You can count on us."

As I trudged up the path to the front porch, snow was coming down heavier, and a cold wind was blowing off the lake. The house was dark except for a soft, firelight glow coming from the living room windows. I stamped my boots quietly and let myself in.

I wanted to check that the house was alright, I told myself, but didn't want to disturb Delaney if he'd gone to bed early or locked himself in his office.

But the moment I closed the door behind me, I heard Delaney's voice, slightly slurred and softer than usual, coming from the living room.

"You're not supposed to be here," he was saying. "But I won't tell Brewer if you don't."

I froze, my hand still on the doorknob.

Delaney wasn't alone? Was it... was it fucking *Jasper?* This was unlikely since he'd been back at the bar, cuddled up to his boyfriend, but the beer in my system made it hard to think clearly.

"Hey. I don't recall giving you permission to touch that." Delaney's tone was lower and more intimate—more unguarded—than I'd ever heard it. "But, God, you've got pretty eyes, don't you?"

Heat flooded my body, creeping up my neck, tightening in my gut. Who the hell was in there with him?

"You're actually kind of beautiful. Terrifyingly beautiful," Delaney continued, his voice dropping even lower.

My heart hammered against my ribs. Delaney had someone in there.

In the house where I was staying. While I was out.

Which was none of my business. None....

Except it sure as fuck felt like it was.

I took a step toward the doorway before stopping myself. Did I really want to see whatever the fuck was happening in there?

"I wish you and I could be... friends," Delaney whispered.

Friends? Was that what they called it?

Something hot and possessive clawed its way up my throat. I had no claim on Delaney—no right to care who he brought home. But the thought of him in there with someone else, in the soft firelight, while I'd been out thinking about him, worrying about him in the storm...

Before I could talk myself out of it, I strode the rest of

the way toward the living room, rounding the corner with enough force that I nearly stumbled.

"Delaney—" I began, but whatever I'd been about to say died in my throat.

Because Delaney was sprawled on his stomach in front of the fire, a mostly empty wine bottle on the hearth beside him.

He wore a pair of those damn silky pajama shorts—blue this time, I thought. Fucking blue—which were twenty times hotter when they were stretched across his ass and baring his toned, beautiful legs.

And he definitely wasn't alone.

CHAPTER FIVE

AFTER BREWER HAD STORMED off all shower-damp and angry, I'd barely had a chance to recover my equilibrium before my sister showed up.

"I think they're very... industrial. Very you." Tam's voice was carefully neutral as she examined my new cabinets while bouncing baby Tierney against her chest in a baby sling. The darkness outside the kitchen window made it feel much later than it was. Incredibly late. Probably bedtime. "But the important thing is how you feel. Obviously."

I swiped dust off one of the boxes stacked on the floor tiredly, more for something to do with my hands than because it would make a difference.

My kitchen was a disaster... and not simply because every surface was covered in construction dust, the refrigerator and pantry had been moved to the laundry room two days ago, my trash was mostly takeout boxes, and the space that should have been my sanctuary—where I'd imagined myself preparing elaborate meals while NPR played in the background—was now a chaotic war zone.

"Me? Oh, I love them!" I said, forcing enthusiasm into

my voice. "Love them. They're exactly what I wanted, so how could I not, right?"

As if sensing my lie, one shiny red cabinet door swung open with an ominous creak.

I closed it and gave it a proud little pat.

The second I removed my hand, it swung open again.

I groaned and rubbed a dusty hand over my forehead. "There might still be a few bugs to work out—"

"Oh my God, you hate them, too, don't you?" Tam said in a relieved rush. "Thank fuck. I thought I was going to have to get Lawson and Wells on FaceTime so we could stage a sibling intervention. Delaney, what were you thinking?"

From her chest, little Tierney was giving me the same expression her mother was—tiny eyebrows drawn together, rosebud mouth pursed in disapproval. It seemed the Monroe women were united against my decorating choices.

"I—" I began to argue, but Tam gave me a look that was pure no-nonsense sister—the same look she'd given me when I'd tried to convince her I hadn't taken her sparkly nail polish while *wearing* her sparkly nail polish—and I folded. "Fine. I admit it. They're awful. The red metal manifestation of my poor judgment. And they won't even sit right on the walls." I folded my arms over my chest. "But should you really be saying the f-word around my niece? Studies have shown—"

"Zzzt. Don't change the subject, Uncle Laney." Tam rubbed her three-month-old daughter's back in a soothing motion. "Lucas and I know Tierney's going to hear curse words anyway, so we're focusing on teaching her when, where, and how to use them appropriately instead of pretending they don't exist." She eyed the cabinets again.

"And I can't think of a more appropriate circumstance than this one, frankly."

I huffed. "They looked so good in the pictures online. Kind of... industrial loft meets 1950s retro. They were supposed to make me smile every time I looked at them—"

"Said every homeowner who ended up on Zillow Gone Wild." Tam crossed to the pizza box I'd propped atop a bunch of paint cans on the dining room table and helped herself to a slice. "I know I live in a Colonial in the suburbs, but I want my whole house to look like a dingy '70s cabaret! I'll smile every time I see the stripper pole in the corner and the leopard-shag carpet running up the wall!"

Against my will, I snorted. "Seriously, though, shouldn't my house reflect... well, me?"

"Sure. Right now, it's giving... *I'm totally conflicted and not sure what I want to be.*" Tam eyed me as she chewed her pizza, then said in a gentler tone, "Was that your goal?"

The weight of always feeling slightly out of step with everyone else made my shoulders tight.

Rolling my eyes, I retrieved an open bottle of wine and a glass from the laundry room that also served as my temporary wine cellar. "You want?" I asked Tam, lifting the bottle. "I can open a fresh bottle."

She shook her head, so I poured the remaining half bottle into my own glass.

"Delaney." Tam used her sister voice again. "Why not find something that reflects your style but also works with the house?"

I shook my head in disgust. "You sound like Brewer. He said the same thing after the vanity incident."

"So why didn't you listen, *especially* after the vanity incident? I know you're stubborn. It's part of your charm.

But I've never known you to be stubborn to the point of..." She wrinkled her nose at the cabinets. "Madness."

"Because he's bossy. He never explains his reasoning; he just acts like he knows best all the time, and I'm supposed to automatically trust him. And he gets this expression like..." I gave Tam a disparaging eyebrow lift. "His jaw gets all tight, and his eyes go all crinkly at the corners, and... he doesn't listen."

That look made me want to strangle him... and also kiss him until both of us forgot what we'd been talking about.

"So you decided you wouldn't listen to him?" Tam gave me a scathing look and tucked a caramel-colored curl behind her ear. "Sure. Great plan. That'll show him."

Unlike me, Tam had always moved through the world with easy confidence—whether on the hockey rink or in motherhood. Her entire being radiated a sense of belonging that I'd never quite managed to capture for myself.

I gulped at my wine. "You wouldn't understand, Tamsen. You get along with... people like that."

"People who know how to do their jobs?" she retorted. "And have tons of satisfied clients?"

"No! Big, beautiful, muscly..." Feeling my face heat, I stared into the depths of my wine. "Never mind."

The past week of cohabitation had been a special kind of torture. Brewer had been scrupulously polite, moving through the house like some kind of renovation ghost, materializing when I least expected him with tools in hand or, like this evening, coming out of the bathroom.

The image of him like that—water droplets sliding down his chest, towel knotted precariously low on his hips, body like a marble statue but so much warmer—flashed in my mind. His broad shoulders had tapered to a narrow waist, skin golden in the hallway light, dark hair curling damply at his nape. The brief glimpse had been enough to burn itself into my memory, and thinking of it now made my mouth go dry.

I took another gulp of wine.

Was it any wonder I'd taken to hiding in my office, emerging only when necessary... especially after what I'd heard through the wall that morning?

"Ahhh, I see." Tam moved her fussing daughter out of the sling and onto her shoulder. "This isn't about who's right. It's about you not feeling incompetent in front of someone you're attracted to."

"I'm not... That isn't..." I blew out a breath and motioned toward the cabinets. "I'm tired of looking at these things. Let's move to the living room, shall we? I'll even light a fire." I shot her a look before she could tease me again. "In the fireplace."

"That'll be a first," she murmured, following me out of the disaster kitchen.

I knelt in front of the fireplace and attempted to start a fire, following all the standard best-practice advice. I wadded newspaper into balls, arranged them under kindling with competent precision, and placed a few logs in a crisscross pattern on top.

But after three attempts to light it, I'd barely managed to make the paper catch before fizzling out, leaving the logs untouched.

"Here. Take your niece, and let me do it." Tam transferred Tierney to my arms. "Before people start talking about how you burned something else down."

I held the baby in the crook of my arm while Tam knelt and did something with the newspaper that made the logs catch in minutes.

"You make that look so simple," I said, mildly irritated.

"It is." She stood and dusted her hands. "When you have practice. Remember, the summer after Mom died, Dad tried teaching us survival skills? You sat on a log reading the fire-building manual out loud while Law and Wells and I had a competition to see who could build the biggest blaze—"

"And nearly set the woods on fire? Yeah." I rolled my eyes. "Ironic that everyone acts like I'm the fire hazard now."

"I was joking. Nobody around here actually thinks that," she scoffed, curling up on one end of the couch. "You said the camper fire was an accident, and from what I've heard, Brewer says the same."

"It was. A series of several accidents, actually—" I broke off when Tierney started to fuss.

"Hold her upright a little more," Tam advised, demonstrating the motion with her arms. "She's not a newborn potato anymore, and she needs more stimulation. She wants to see new stuff."

I shifted the baby, and she immediately quieted.

"You know," Tam went on, "you never actually explained what happened out at Brewer's camper. Or why you were even there."

I darted a look at her before focusing on the baby again. "Brewer's dog startled me," I admitted, ignoring the latter part of her question. "I tripped into the pole supporting his awning, which landed in his grill, and... well, things proceeded from there."

"Brewer's dog." Tam bit her lip, immediately understanding in a way hardly anyone else on Earth would.

"I wasn't afraid," I said quickly. I didn't look at Tam, in case she was giving me the soft, pitying frown that was the inverse of her sister look. "I was being... justifiably cautious.

Teeny's living here now, and I'm fine with it. Mostly. Brewer's been very good about keeping us separated."

"Does he know—?" She shook her head. "What am I saying? You can't talk to the man about cabinets. Of course you didn't tell him what happened with Gretzky."

"What, am I supposed to tell every new person I meet, 'Oh, hey, by the way, I got bitten by my family dog almost twenty years ago, and it turned into a whole thing that traumatized my entire family, so could you please disclose if you have any dogs or dog-related paraphernalia that might trigger me'?" I huffed. "No, thank you."

"Laney," Tam said in that gentle voice again.

"Anyway—"

"You know no one blamed you for what happened—"

"Anyway," I repeated, louder this time, before bouncing my niece a little bit. "Tierney says she's no longer interested in discussing this."

For a second, it seemed like Tam would argue, but finally, she sighed, allowing the subject change. "She seems fascinated by something on your bookcase," she offered.

"She does." I followed Tierney's gaze to one of the bookcases that flanked the fireplace. "Studies show babies like bright colors, right?" I picked up a small, intricately carved and painted wooden doll and held it closer so the baby could get a good look. "Is this what you see? Smart girl. This doll is from the Yanomami tribe in Brazil. I interviewed one of the tribal leaders a few years ago about deforestation policies and the impact on indigenous traditions. Can you say Ya-no-ma-mi?"

Tam laughed. "She can't even say Dada or Mama yet."

"My niece is brilliant, Tamsen," I informed her, "and you don't know what she's absorbing. It's never too early to instill in her an appreciation for cultural artifacts—"

Tierney seized the doll with both hands and clumsily directed it at her mouth.

"Yes, just look at her appreciating the culture!" Tam teased.

I removed the doll from the baby's grip, dropped a kiss on Tierney's forehead, and handed her back to Tam. "Never mind, Tierney. Ignore the haters."

Tam got the baby arranged on her lap and pulled up her shirt to feed her while I retrieved my wine.

"I meant to tell you... Samuel Purchase was asking about you today at Lyon's Imperial Market," Tam said.

I frowned as I sat on the far side of the couch. "Who?"

"Older guy?" Tam said. "Loves scarves? Has a yappy little dog called—?"

"Oh, Admiral Barkington?" I shuddered lightly. "Yeah, we've met."

She laughed softly. "Samuel said the Admiral was very taken with you. And since he's the editor of our local paper —Samuel, I mean, not the dog—he wondered if you'd be interested in writing for them occasionally."

I blinked at her in surprise. "Me? Writing for..."

"The *Gazette*," Tam supplied. "And yeah. Why not? Their money's as green as anyone else's, and it would help get you involved in the community, wouldn't it?"

"Maybe, but..." I frowned, trying to think of a way to explain it that she'd understand... and that wouldn't make me sound like an asshole. "It's like if Wells or Law decided to give up the NHL and play for a local rec team. My career might be taking a slight beating at the moment, but I don't think it's headed toward me covering the local Pumpkin Princess and the selection of apples at the grocery store either."

At least I sincerely hoped it wasn't. My career was an integral part of my identity.

Tam shrugged. "He said to hit him up if you were interested. But no pressure. If you're not into it, fair enough." After a pause, she asked, "Why is your career taking a beating?"

"*Ugh*. You remember me telling you about the Empire Ridge article I'm working on?"

"Sure. The David and Goliath one that Marjorie's all excited about."

"Yeah." I blew out a breath. "So, my whistleblower sent over some financials, which I've been trying to untangle. From everything I can see, Anthony Harmon had spent years trying to level up the family business he'd inherited—bigger jobs and bigger payouts, that kind of thing. So when this mega-huge company called Empire Ridge approached him about doing some work for them as a preferred vendor, it was a no-brainer, right?"

Tam nodded. "Unless there was a catch?"

"Exactly. I mean, Anthony admits himself that he should have known better. I guess this company had approached Anthony's father a bunch of times about buying some of Harmon's property, and Anthony's father had refused, claiming Empire was shady. Anthony thought his dad was just being shortsighted."

"Oooh." Tam rubbed Tierney's back. "Trust your parents, kids."

I snorted. "I guess. Anyway, Anthony hires more guys, takes out loans and buys equipment. Scales up the business, you know, since now he and Empire are best friends and he's got all this work coming in. But then Empire says, 'Since we're besties now, why don't you let us buy this piece of property from you for an obscene amount of money—'"

"Wait, the same land Anthony's father hadn't wanted to sell?" Tam demanded.

"Yep. Except now, Empire Ridge has Anthony over a barrel, don't they? If he tells his besties he's not interested in the land deal, are they gonna take away all his pretty contracts and leave him broke? Now, according to Anthony, he'd already started to suspect his dad had been right, so he tried to back out..."

Tam winced. "Didn't go well?"

"Nope. They came at him with both barrels," I confirmed. "They invited him to a meeting and made him an offer he couldn't refuse. 'Oooh, sorry, friend. See this map? We've bought all the property around you, and if you don't sell us your property, too, so we can build River Bend —that's the name of the housing development they built, worst name ever—we're gonna use our shady contacts and connections to get the town involved. See this firehouse here, on the land you currently own? The town wants that firehouse, and we're gonna get them to take your land by eminent domain. If they do, you'll walk away with a pittance *and* no contracts. Orrrr you sell it to us for way more than the land is worth, and you get to stay our bestie subcontractor, and we'll all be happy.' Can you guess what he did?"

She shook her head. "He sold the land."

"Ding ding ding. And Anthony got the money and contracts as promised. He claims he hated every minute of doing business with Empire Ridge since they insisted on cutting corners, but he was too cowed at that point to speak out. Says he just wanted to get the project over with." I took a sip of wine. "But then, as a parting shot, Empire Ridge pointed the finger at Anthony's company, accusing *them* of shoddy workmanship and using improper materials." I shook my head. "Poor guy can't get hired to screw in light-bulbs now."

"Fuck," Tam breathed. "I'm with Marjorie. This sounds like an important story to tell."

"Sure would be," I agreed, "if I had any proof besides Anthony's say-so. Anthony's financial records show Empire Ridge knew exactly what materials they were buying and approved them. Great. But what shows they bullied him? What shows he'd been manipulated from the start? What'll help sway public opinion, at least enough to let him rebuild his business? I feel like it exists, but..." I shook my head. "I can't figure it out."

Tam made a considering noise, then sighed. "I can't imagine what's distracting you. I mean, it's not like you're living in a construction zone, with a certain... big, beautiful, muscly person as your new roommate."

My stomach flipped, but the wine was already hitting me pleasantly and loosening my tongue. "Yeah," I said in a small voice. "There's that."

"So why not just jump him?"

I blinked, sure I'd heard wrong. "Jump Brewer? The man renovating my house? The man doing work for me? That's the very thing I want to avoid doing."

Lie.

"Okay, but wait. Let's talk this through. You said yourself that Brewer's beautiful. He's sweet—"

Regrettably true.

"—and he's totally your type. And yes, I agree that it's a little... something... that he's your contractor. But he's not your employee. There's not a consent issue—"

"Isn't there?" I said weakly.

"And if the two of you were getting along, I'd probably say to wait until the job is done to do the jumping, but since you've also said your attraction is making it hard for you to work and hard for you to communicate about the house—"

It was making many things *hard*.

"I don't think I actually said—"

"Why not get it out of your system so you can move on? Seems like if you want to get busy on that article, you and Brew need to get busy first." She bounced her eyebrows. "He's got some serious toppy energy. You're into that, right?"

I stared at Tam and then at the baby in horror. "Tamsen Marie Monroe. I will not discuss my sex life with my sister. Especially not while you're holding that precious, innocent—"

"Pfft. Tierney can't understand a word we're saying—"

"Nope." I shook my head. "Not happening. La la la la la. I refuse."

"Delaney—"

"Je refuse. Ich weigere mich," I insisted, pulling out every language I spoke even a little. "No acepto."

Tam laughed. "No fair. You know I only speak English!"

"I have Google Translate on my phone, too," I reminded her. "I can do this all night."

"Fine. If you won't talk to me about this, at least talk to Jasper. You guys are friends, right?"

"Of course. I like Jasper a lot." I grinned, remembering Jasper's text that afternoon, which had been a picture of Janice Plum's cornucopia bonnet, a bunch of laugh-cry emojis, and the words, "Delaney, what have you done?"

My smile faded quickly. "Jasper's busy, though. With Watt. Doing their couple stuff. I'm not bothering him with this nonsense." I gave her a stony glare. "Especially when it's a nonissue."

Something in my tone must have given me away because Tam's expression went all soft and sympathetic again. "You know you could have 'couple stuff,' too, right? If you'd let yourself."

"Oh, dear God. Can we go back to discussing my shitty cabinet choices? Please?" I demanded.

Tam rolled her eyes, but before she could speak, there was a soft knock at the front door, followed by my brother-in-law's voice. "Tam? Delaney?"

"In here!" I called. I grinned at Tam. "Saved."

"For now," she agreed reluctantly. "But I'll get you next time, my pretty."

"Phew." Lucas brushed snow off his coat and hat. "It's really coming down out there. We should probably get going—"

"Lucas!" I jumped up and gave him an effusive hug, heedless of the damp snow patches on his coat and hat. "You know, Tam and I were just talking about how you're my favorite family member and how I probably shouldn't spend any time alone with Tam anymore since she's so much nicer when you're around—"

"Ignore him, babe." Tam lifted her face so Lucas could drop a kiss on her lips. "Laney's trying to distract you from his latest renovation drama."

Lucas's eyes widened, and he looked around as if searching for visible signs of destruction before turning to me. "Delaney, man, tell me you didn't try to move another outlet—"

"No," I said stiffly as Tam cackled. "Nothing like that."

My traitorous sister stood, setting the baby on her shoulder, and motioned Lucas toward the kitchen. "See for yourself."

"Oh, new cabinets." Lucas stared at them and nodded

diplomatically, exactly as Tam had done. "They're very... ah. Very statement-making. Very you."

Tam and I exchanged a look, and she burst out laughing. "That's almost exactly what I said, babe." She kissed Lucas's cheek. "Married-people mind-meld nearly complete!"

Lucas gave her a look of warm amusement that said he didn't mind one bit.

"It's fine," I told him. "I've already admitted they're terrible. I just... don't know what to do about it, exactly. And your annoying wife was not helping."

"I think you do know what to do about it," Tam countered, bundling the baby into her car seat while Lucas collected the baby luggage they seemed to carry everywhere. "Think about what I said. About evvvverything." She wiggled her eyebrows. "And you'll figure it out."

"Stick to fire-building," I advised. I kissed her cheek and then leaned down to kiss Tierney's forehead. "And be safe."

"We will." She frowned as Lucas said goodbye and hauled the baby out to his car. "Is Brewer coming back tonight? Remember, we're just down the street if you need—"

"I'm fine." I waved a hand. "They're only predicting flurries."

I stood in the entryway until the taillights of their car disappeared down the driveway, then walked back to the living room. The refinished hardwood floors Brewer had insisted on gleamed in the firelight, but the recently repaired ceiling still needed paint. The bookcases were mostly filled with books and other treasures I'd collected, but the walls were bare. Half-finished, like everything else in my life.

With Tam gone, the house felt chillier, and the silence I

usually craved rang through the space and beat against my eardrums. A strange, hollow feeling expanded in my chest—not loneliness, definitely not, but... possibly something adjacent to it. For someone who treasured solitude, I was suddenly, acutely aware of being alone in this big, half-finished house.

Outside, snow was falling heavily, thick flakes visible even in the darkness. I checked the weather app on my phone, but it still assured me there'd be no accumulation.

I checked my texts. There was nothing from Brewer—which was fine. I mean, I wasn't sitting at home waiting for him... even if I happened to be sitting at home waiting for him. But I'd missed a message from Marjorie.

MARJORIE

Counterpoints is ready to commit if you can give me a firm deadline! Call me ASAP to coordinate.

My stomach knotted. I was no closer to finishing than I'd been when we'd last talked.

I closed her message and headed upstairs to change into pajamas... then I headed to the laundry room for a fresh bottle of sauv blanc.

As I opened the wine, I spotted Brewer's sweatshirt folded neatly on top of the dryer. I hesitated, running my fingers over the soft, worn fabric. Then, darting a glance around just to make sure no one was there to see, I brought it to my nose.

Under the clean laundry detergent fragrance was the distinct scent of sawdust and Brewer, a warm, masculine musk that made my pulse quicken. My mouth actually watered as I inhaled again, which was at least as ridiculous and embarrassing as my Pavlovian Dick Response. But just smelling Brewer's scent, even when he wasn't around—especially because he wasn't around—made my cheeks go hot.

I wanted more of it.

I darted another guilty glance toward the laundry room door, but I knew I'd have plenty of warning when Brewer came home—the rumble of his truck engine, the clomp of his boots. Besides, my short pajamas were the height of comfort but not the height of warmth, and with the snow falling, the temperature had dropped...

"Fuck it," I muttered, pulling the sweatshirt over my head.

It enveloped me completely, the sleeves extending past my fingers, the hem nearly to my thighs. It was the closest I'd let myself come to admitting what I really wanted—to be wrapped in Brewer's arms, surrounded by all that strength and warmth.

The thought was both terrifying and intoxicating, and my skin prickled with goose bumps that had nothing to do with cold or drafts.

I pushed the sleeves up to my elbows and grabbed the wine bottle.

I shut off all the lights and settled on the floor in front of the fire, leaning against the couch. The flames cast dancing shadows, and outside the window, the snow created a curtain of white against the black night.

Despite the house's emptiness, I wasn't truly alone. Brewer's presence lingered everywhere—in the tools spread around the kitchen, in the half-finished projects throughout the house, in the sweatshirt wrapped around me like a confession. Everything Tam had said echoed in my mind, impossible to dismiss when I was alone with my thoughts.

Maybe I was being stubborn about the wrong things.

Maybe there were things I wanted more than being right.

Maybe I should try jumping Br—

No. Nope.

I pulled out my Kindle, determined to distract myself with the hot alien romance I'd been reading, but even that betrayed me.

"The warrior's massive hands could span his captive's entire waist..." My skin flushed hot as I imagined Brewer's hands on a cabinet, adjusting a level.

"His rumbling voice sent shivers down Matteo's spine..." A corresponding shiver ran down my own spine, remembering Brewer's low growl of frustration when something wouldn't fit right.

I gave up and set the Kindle aside. I refilled my glass, let the wine settle warmly in my veins, and watched the snow as my thoughts drifted hazily.

The memory of that morning came back to me—because of course it did—with sudden, unwanted clarity.

I'd been half-awake, reaching for my glasses, when I'd heard a low creaking from the other side of the wall. At first, I'd thought Brewer was just shifting on his mattress or, I don't know, maybe doing push-ups.

But then a soft groan had escaped him—a sound so primal and unguarded it had sent electricity straight to my core—and I'd frozen in place, suddenly wide, *wide* awake.

His mattress had made soft, rhythmic shushing noises against the floor that came faster and more urgently. He'd let out a few stuttered breaths—*huh, huh, huh.* And I hadn't been able to stop myself from picturing Brewer—his powerful body tense, his head thrown back, that fucking jaw locked, one hand wrapped around himself, working urgently.

I'd had no idea if my imaginings were accurate, obvs, but let me tell you, no alien warrior could compare.

I'd covered my head with a pillow like a scandalized Victorian maiden, but it had been too late. My ears had already become totally attuned to his sounds and sought them out, even through the dense memory foam.

When he'd finally come with a muffled groan, I hadn't just heard it; it had vibrated through the wall and directly into my own balls. My body had thrummed with sympathetic arousal, my cock painfully hard under the sheets.

I hadn't been able to look Brewer in the eye all day, afraid he'd somehow know I'd heard him. Afraid he'd see how it had affected me. Afraid he'd know it was still affecting me now, hours later, the memory making my skin flush and my—

"Gahhhh!" I screamed—actually screamed—as something cold and wet pressed against my forearm.

I grabbed my phone and scrambled up onto the couch, wine flying from my glass and splashing across the floor. My heart hammered against my ribs, adrenaline surging through my body.

For one absurd, alcohol-fueled moment, I thought: *Alien abduction. This is how I die.*

But when my eyes finally focused through the darkness, the reality was ten times worse.

Brewer's enormous dog stood a foot away, her massive form outlined by the firelight. She watched me with her head tilted and her tail slowly wagging, like I was amusing.

I scrambled up onto the sofa, my heart slamming against my ribs. "Holy fuck! What are you doing down here?" I demanded.

She stood perfectly still, watching me for a long moment, then padded forward with the doll Tierney had been playing with earlier dangling from her mouth. Her massive paws made no sound on the hardwood. In the firelight, her dark eyes reflected golden sparks.

I pressed back into the cushions. "That's far enough!" I said firmly. "S-stop right there! No jumping."

Surprisingly, she listened. She took the doll and settled onto the hearth several feet away, still watching me.

"I forgot about your door-opening trick," I muttered. "How the fuck did I forget that?"

The fire crackled between us, and despite the distance I was maintaining, this was still the closest I'd been to a dog in years without panicking.

"Look," I said after our stare-down had gone on for a moment, "you seem... friendly. But the last dog I got friendly with seemed that way too." I rubbed absently at my forearm, where faint scars remained. "Until he bit me."

Teeny tilted her head, as if she was actually listening.

"And Tam might say what happened afterward wasn't my fault, but we all know it was, okay? It's Monroe family lore. I'm the reason we didn't have any more pets." I took another sip of wine. "See that? I can admit when I'm wrong. Just not to certain large, sexy, know-it-all contractors."

Teeny made a small whuffling sound.

"Yeah, you know exactly who I'm talking about." I laughed, the wine making everything seem funnier than it was. "He drives me crazy." I lowered my voice. "In all the ways."

Teeny shifted, stretching out on the hearth.

"Tam thinks I should jump him. Get it out of my system." I rolled my eyes. "Like the Pavlovian Dick Response isn't bad enough already, let's just make it worse! Can you imagine?"

The dog made a soft noise that almost sounded sympathetic.

"It's not like me," I confessed. "I mean, yes, my dick generally points the way to destruction. But, like, only temporarily, like a compass in a weird magnetic field. Take the last guy I dated..." I burped gently. "Big guy. Met him at the gym when he corrected my form. Muscles on muscles, you know the type?"

Teeny licked her lips.

I snorted. "You get me. For, like, a whole week last summer, I listened to Jared tell me about his macros and how, 'if it's not lifting, it's not a real workout.' I listened to him not listening to a fucking thing I said about my work or my opinions or my interests. But then reason and logic asserted themselves." I took a sip of wine and pointed my glass at her. "I remembered I'm a higher life form, not an amoeba with a dick. I remembered I deserve respect. And I kicked Jared to the curb, just like that."

Teeny lifted her head and growled low.

"Thank you. Yes, it was empowering. But now, with Brewer... Fuck, I don't even know. It feels like it's part of a —" I hiccuped. "—a larger problem. I had a whole life in New York before I moved here," I informed the dog. "An apartment, a favorite coffee place, a... a gym membership. And yeah, I didn't have tons of friends because I traveled so much, but I didn't care."

Teeny buried her head in her paws.

"Okay, maybe I cared somewhat. But it was my choice, and I knew why I was making it. Here in Copper County..." I sighed and shook my head, then whispered my deepest, darkest secret. "I don't know who I am here. I don't know what I'm doing. And I fucking hate that. Hate it," I repeated with drunken solemnity so the dog would know I meant it. "I feel like I'm standing on a prissy... a pressy... a precipice, and the ground might fall away. I don't know how to get back to where I was. To who I am."

Teeny slow-blinked as my admission hung in the air between us. It was heavier than I'd expected, but it was the most honest thing I'd said out loud in months... even to myself.

In the city, I'd been Delaney Monroe, award-winning journalist. Here, I was Tam's brother, the one who'd burned down a camper, couldn't build a fire, and fought with his contractor over cabinets that looked like shit and wouldn't fucking stay closed.

The identity I'd built my entire life around was slipping through my fingers like sand.

Outside, the wind howled, making the windows rattle. Both Teeny and I cocked our heads toward the sound.

"Just the storm," I assured her, though my pulse quickened. "Anyway, 'nough of that, huh?"

Draining the last of my wine, I set the glass aside and, to my own surprise, slid down to lie on my stomach on the floor. Still a safe distance from Teeny, but no longer cowering against the cushions.

"You're not s'posed to be down here," I said softly, watching the firelight play across her fur. "But I won't tell Brewer if you don't."

She looked at me with eyes that seemed to see right through me and gave her doll—I mean, *my* doll—a lick.

I chuckled lightly. "Hey, I don't recall giving you permission to touch that," I said, nodding at it. "But God, you've got pretty eyes, don't you?"

The more I looked at her, the less overtly threatening she seemed.

"You're actually kind of beautiful," I admitted, my voice

dropping to nearly a whisper. "Terrifyingly beautiful. I wish you and I could be... friends."

We couldn't, of course. This whole situation would be very different if I was thinking clearly. But for now—

Boots clomped heavily down the hall, and a body came skittering around the corner.

"Delaney," a familiar voice growled.

I twisted and sat up, almost knocking over the half-empty wine bottle in the process.

Brewer filled the doorway so completely his shoulders nearly touched both sides. Melting snowflakes sparkled in his dark hair and clung to the scruff along his jaw. His eyes were shiny and a little unfocused, his cheeks pink.

Even from across the room, I could see the way his chest rose and fell as his breath came faster than normal, like he'd rushed to get here. But his urgency seemed to have vanished because his whole body locked as he stared at the scene before him—me sprawled on the floor in his sweatshirt and my pajama shorts, his dog on the hearth.

"Hey. Hi. Hello. I, uh... I didn't know you were coming home so early." My voice was embarrassingly high, and I was pretty sure I was blushing, though hopefully he couldn't see it.

How much had he overheard? What would he think about the sweatshirt? *Distract, distract, distract.*

I cleared my throat. "Your... your dog opened the kitchen door and broke into the house," I accused, feeling only a little bit guilty for throwing Teeny under the bus. "A-and stole my doll. And I..."

I trailed off in confusion as Brewer took a step closer, his eyes never leaving my face.

I'd been expecting him to get annoyed. I didn't want to

provoke him, exactly, but our confrontations were familiar. Solid ground I could stand on.

The look in his eyes wasn't anger, though.

It was intent, yes. And it was hot—hot like boiling lava, hot enough to burn right through me—but it didn't look like Brewer wanted to fight. It almost looked like he wanted to... to...

I swallowed hard, nearly choking on my own saliva.

Shit. I'd had too much to drink, hadn't I?

I had. I must have.

I was incredibly, ridiculously drunk on a bottle of wine, and I'd been reading that romance novel, and I was having some sort of waking dream. Something like a fantasy but more.

That would explain why it looked like Brewer's glittering eyes had fallen to half-mast and why he appeared to be moving across the living room toward me with that focused, lazy grace—*stalking*, my brain supplied, *he's stalking*.

It would also explain why, despite my heart going a million miles an hour, I didn't jump to my feet to present a bigger target—rookie self-defense—but stayed exactly where I was.

Teeny got to her feet as if to greet Brewer, then quickly sat back on her haunches, but I was only vaguely aware of her movements because the dog was no longer the biggest predator in the room.

Brewer was the one I was focused on. The one I found myself tilting my head back to look at.

Good Lord, he was big.

Good fucking Lord, he was sexy.

My breath caught. My stomach swooped. My body hummed with awareness. I felt the urge to casually pinch myself, but... fuck, did I really want to wake up when Brewer was looking at me like this? Like he... *wanted* me?

"Delaney," Brewer growled again, right in front of me now. The word was a question.

I licked my lips. "Y-yes?"

He bent down, grabbed my hand, and pulled me to my feet.

My toes curled into the hardwood floor, and I sucked in an unsteady breath of Brewer, laced with the tangy scent of beer. Suddenly, the precipice I'd feared was *right there*, so much closer than I'd realized. And as Brewer pulled me against him, I felt the very ground beneath me start to crumble.

But did I run? Or fight? Did I move a fucking muscle or say a word to save myself? Nope.

I leaned against his warm chest and gave myself over to it.

And, I realized, this—*this*—was exactly what I'd been afraid of. Not that I'd fall, but that, like an idiot, I would jump.

But in that moment, with Brewer's eyes holding mine, I couldn't remember a single reason why I shouldn't.

CHAPTER SIX

THE SECOND DELANEY tipped his face up toward mine and whispered, "Y-yes?" I was gone.

I didn't think. I didn't hesitate. I took his lips with mine.

His mouth was warm, pliant, wine-sweet, and when he sighed into me, it wrecked me completely. Weeks—months —of tension, of low-key wanting to strangle him and high-key wanting my hands on him, unspooled in a flashfire. I groaned as I wrapped one arm around his waist and hauled him closer.

Delaney made a surprised, eager sound and pushed onto his toes, hands curling into my shirt like he couldn't get close enough. His body melted against mine, all silk and heat under my sweatshirt. His lips clung to mine like a promise.

Fuck, he tasted good.

Delaney kissed like he argued—instinctively, no holds barred. There was nothing tentative in it, no trace of hesitance. Just heat and need and hunger. His mouth moved under mine eagerly, and every sweep of his tongue sent a jolt down my spine.

My fingers slid beneath the hem of my sweatshirt he wore, finding the smooth, warm skin of his hip as I backed him toward the couch. I was desperate to get my hands on more of him, to feel more of his skin and hear whatever ridiculous noise he might make if I bit—

Without warning, something in the house gave a loud mechanical *pop* and cut off with a dying wheeze. All the white-noise electrical whirring of a home with electricity ceased. And the room was abruptly, eerily quiet.

We jumped apart like guilty teenagers, panting and wide-eyed.

"The, uh... That was... " I ran a hand over my kiss-bruised mouth. "Storm knocked the power out, I think."

Delaney made a huffing sound—a laugh, but not—and straightened his shoulders. "Yes. Right. Good... good observation." He glanced around the firelit room, his eyes darting from the couch to the windows to the bookcases—anywhere but at me. "That was unexpected."

He probably meant the electricity, but my face went hot anyway.

What the fuck had possessed me? I had no business kissing my client like that. Jesus, I had no business kissing *anyone* like that—no warning, no preamble, like I wanted nothing more than to crawl into Delaney's mouth and write my name there, to brand him from the inside.

I sure as fuck had no business wanting to do it again. Immediately.

My brain knew better, but the beer buzz running through me made everything seem... looser.

Possible.

Down boy.

"I've had beer," I said stupidly. "Three? Four? Not... not too many. But I didn't have dinner, so they hit me hard.

Hard-ish. And Reed—you know Reed Sunday?—was at the Hive, and he offered to drive me home, so."

"Uh-huh. Uh-huh." Delaney nodded almost compulsively. "Smart thinking. The not-driving part, I mean. And that explains the, ah, the lack of truck noise." His nostrils flared. "I'd *expected* some truck noise."

"Oh..." I wrinkled my nose. He sounded angry about that, and I wasn't sure how to respond. "Sorry?"

As he waved away my apology, his ping-ponging gaze found the wine bottle he'd left on the floor. He grabbed it by the neck and set it on the mantel. "Actually, I was drinking, too. God, yes. *Super* drinking! Wine, though, not beer. And I... I can't even remember if I ate, that's how tipsy *I* am." He forced a laugh. "Definitely... definitely feeling the effects."

I nodded, not surprised and only slightly disappointed. Delaney had to be a little buzzed, kissing me back the way he had. And I'd tasted the wine on his tongue—

Not thinking about his tongue.

I cleared my throat. "I guess Hen was right, huh? He predicted we'd get at least a foot. *Never bet against the leg*," I quoted.

Delaney scowled fiercely, a perfect blend of disbelief and exasperation, like he took Hen's leg as a personal affront.

"What century is this?" he demanded, though the word came out more like *shenshury*. "Have people in Copper County never heard of science?"

"They have..." I remembered my cousin and Kel's definition of science, and despite everything, I grinned. "In a manner of speaking. I heard Hen say it's about a microclimate in the area and a drop in barometric pressure affecting him."

"Oh. Well. That's..." He gazed out the window thoughtfully for a moment, then scowled more fiercely. "Fucking annoying."

My laughter erupted unexpectedly. "It's annoying because there might actually *be* a scientific explanation?"

"I meant it's annoying because I still haven't bought a fucking shovel." He shot me a sidelong glance. The light from the flames reflected in his glasses. "But yeah, that too. It's annoying, having to reshuffle the way you think about things."

It was hard not to find Delaney adorable at the moment... because of the beer, naturally.

His hair stood up in places where my fingers had slid through it, his lips still slightly swollen from our kiss, and something about the disheveled, firelit version of him made my chest tighten.

Belatedly, I nodded, and my tongue darted out to lick my lips. "Or," I suggested, "you could just not think. For tonight. I mean, since you've been drinking. Probably not the best time to... think."

Not about Copper County. Not about our kiss. Not about how he looked with my shirt hanging down his thighs—

"Yeah," Delaney said finally. He blinked like he was trying to bring me into better focus. "I agree."

I was so distracted by all the things I wasn't supposed to be thinking of it took me a second to remember what the fuck we'd been saying. When I did, I nodded again.

I'd become a throat-clearing bobblehead.

"Good." I rubbed at the back of my neck, feeling the full weight of the awkward tension between us. "Should I—? I mean, I should probably take Teeny upstairs for the night." I shifted a thumb toward the garage, like Delaney might have forgotten where I was staying.

Teeny, who'd stretched out in front of one of the bookcases flanking the fireplace, heard her name and lifted her head inquisitively.

Delaney chafed his arms. "But... if the power's out, the heat won't work, right? Won't she be cold?"

My eyebrows rose. He was right, of course, and I should have thought of that. *Would* have, if I hadn't been so backfooted. But since when did he care about my dog's comfort?

His jaw set stubbornly. "What? I'm not an asshole. I feel for other creatures, Brewer, even if I don't entirely trust them. Besides, we reached a... a detente." He darted a glance at Teeny. "Tell him."

Teeny panted happily, big eyes fixed on Delaney with unconcealed adoration. Her tongue lolled out of her mouth, and though I couldn't see it, I knew a small pile of drool was collecting on the floor.

"So all I'm saying," Delaney continued, not looking at me, "is that if you—and Teeny, obviously—wanted to stay here, by the fire, with me, that would be... that would be acceptable."

I took a deep breath. It hadn't just been for Teeny's sake that I'd wanted to retreat upstairs. Like a genie that had escaped its bottle, the sexual energy between Delaney and me was harder to push down now that it had had a taste of freedom, and every goddamn time Delaney moved, I had to suck in a breath as pure want surged under my skin.

But Delaney was right; with no electricity, the boiler wouldn't be working. There was no need to start the generator now. Not when we didn't know how long the power would be out and when the fireplace could keep this room comfortable. It was the practical solution. The reasonable choice.

Besides which, Hayes's voice was still in my head, accusing me of retreating when things became difficult.

"Okay," I said at length. "Let's grab some blankets and things. I'll get the sleeping bag I've been using. You can get... whatever you need."

I was already walking toward the kitchen and turning on my phone's flashlight by the time I finished speaking. Cold had seeped into the breezeway, and I slowed my steps, hoping the chill would help me calm the fuck down. The beer had given me a nice buzz—that wasn't a total lie—but kissing Delaney had given me an even stronger one.

I misjudged the distance to the doorframe and bumped my shoulder against it, cursing under my breath. Then I pressed the heel of my hand against the front of my jeans, willing my body to cooperate. The last thing I needed was to return with an obvious hard-on.

When I returned to the living room, Teeny was still sitting in the spot she'd claimed, apparently content to observe the weird humans from a distance. Delaney had pulled the pillows off the sofa and sat on the floor with his knees pulled up to his chest. It appeared he'd fetched a fresh bottle of wine and a glass for me.

"You think we need more to drink?" I asked casually as I squatted down to stoke the fire. Though the flames were crackling warm and steady, my pulse was definitely not.

No looking at his legs. No remembering how he tasted.

"I figured more wine would help with all the not-thinking I'm doing," he joked, his voice rougher than usual. "Unless you can think of a... different way to distract me?"

"What?" I twisted around so quickly I nearly face-planted.

Delaney's eyes widened. "No! No, no," he stammered. "I meant distract me with your talents." His eyes widened impossibly further. "Not *those* talents! I meant dancing! Or singing! Or... magic tricks!"

It was one of the strange truths of my interactions with Delaney that sometimes the more upset he got, the more calm I became. Seeing him now, flushed and mortified, I felt warmth surge through my chest.

"Don't know any magic tricks," I said easily. I plunked myself down beside him—close enough to see him in the dim light, not close enough that we were touching—and stretched my legs out toward the fire. "And I don't sing or dance."

"Lies." He looked away quickly and took a deep drink of wine.

I laughed and picked up the second glass he'd poured. "Nope. I suppose I've been known to chicken-dance at the occasional wedding, but you'd have to get me a lot drunker or really make it worth my while if you wanted me to demonstrate."

Delaney darted a look at me. "I meant singing. I heard you sing. The other day at the camper."

"Oh." There were a lot of memories his words might have conjured. Shitty, scary ones of the camper burning.

Instead, my brain summoned a memory of Delaney's finger jabbing my chest, the heat of his touch lingering long after he pulled away, and I had to shift positions to hide my reaction.

"That's..." I blinked as the full meaning of his words actually made it through my muddled brain. "Wait, what did you hear?"

A slow smile spread across his face. "You. Singing 'Defying Gravity.' Pretty convincingly, too."

"You..." I swallowed. "You were pretty angry, so you might have misheard..."

"Lies," he said again softly.

My face went hot.

It wasn't that I was embarrassed about liking what I liked or that I purposely kept it a secret. I didn't. I just... rarely shared much about myself. Rarely felt close enough to anyone to share. Hell, Reed had known me a lot longer than Delaney had, and he didn't have a clue.

"I sort of wondered," he continued, "if it was a hallucination brought on by smoke inhalation, but your face right now confirms it."

I ran a hand over my face like I could rearrange whatever he saw there. "Great."

Delaney's answering laughter was warm, not mocking. He shifted his body so that instead of facing the fire, he was now facing me. The movement made his knee brush against my thigh. The contact, small as it was, sent electricity up my leg. "Okay, I have a distraction idea. Ready?"

I shot him a look. He was smiling, his posture relaxed, and I wondered for a second if that strange inverse effect worked both ways—like the more off-balance I was, the more he chilled out.

"Ready for what?" I demanded. "I'm not singing for you, so get that idea right out of your head."

"Not that." His smile widened. "I think we should play a game. My very first editor used to say that you can get to know anyone by asking them five good questions. So let's test the theory. Answer honestly and fully, or..." He shook his glass slightly. "Drink."

"A drinking game?" The idea felt... dangerous. Though, honestly, any damn thing that kept Delaney in proximity felt dangerous at the moment.

Which was, as a voice in my head that sounded like

Hayes and Kel mashed together pointed out, just another form of deflection.

"Or," Delaney said, smile fading, "I guess we should probably talk about the renovation, huh?" He darted a glance toward the darkened kitchen, where the red cabinet monstrosities were hanging.

"No," I said quickly. The only thing worse than thinking about kissing Delaney was arguing with him, which was how we'd inevitably end up. "I declare a renovation ceasefire for the rest of the night. Let's..." I blew out a breath. "Let's play your drinking game. But I'll go first."

Delaney waved a hand like he couldn't care less. "G'head." But I noticed a distinct tension in him that said he wasn't as cool about it as he wanted to appear.

All the questions I wanted answered swirled in my head—*Why are you so defensive all the time? Why are you so pigheaded? Have you thought about kissing me before now? Do you want to kiss me again?*—but of course, I wouldn't ask any of those.

What finally popped out surprised us both. "Where's the best place you ever traveled?"

Delaney's eyes lit up as he considered my question, like I'd handed him an unexpected gift.

"Oh, Peru," he said with zero hesitation. "A tiny, *tiny* village called Huacahuasi in the Andes. I went there for a story about illegal logging, and I ended up staying for almost three weeks."

"*You?* Lived in a remote mountain village for three weeks?"

I couldn't picture it. As far as I knew, they didn't do silky pajamas or sticky notes on Tupperware there.

"To be fair, it was supposed to be three *days*, but shit

happened. As usual." He rolled his eyes. "Got to Lima fine. Met the guide I'd arranged to take me into the mountains. But his truck broke down two hours' hike from the village. No cell service, so he hiked me up to the village, told me he'd be back as soon as he could, then hiked back down the mountain to see about his truck. The first day, I fell in an irrigation ditch and broke my glasses—"

"Holy shit, Delaney. Seriously?"

He scowled. "Yes, seriously. This is my job, Brewer. I do whatever I have to do to get the job done."

"No, I know. I—" I shook my head. I didn't know how to explain that I was both impressed against my will and weirdly, retroactively protective. The thought of him alone and vulnerable made something fierce stir in my chest, not because I didn't think he could handle it—obviously, he had —but that he'd *had* to. "Sorry, continue. Still waiting to hear how this becomes your *favorite* place."

"Because it was beautiful, once I got over that first hiccup and let myself notice. Mountains rising up all around, mist rolling through in the morning. Green, green, green everywhere. And the people there were amazing. They fixed my glasses, found me a place to sleep, gave me info for my story..." His face took on an abstracted look. "Every night, the village would gather after dinner, and the adults would talk as the kids ran around. I didn't speak the local language, but most people spoke some Spanish, and I can smile and nod with the best of them." His smile was soft and... something else that I didn't fully understand. Wistful, maybe? "It was nice. For a little while."

"Wow," I said inadequately.

When his eyes focused on me again, he looked faintly embarrassed. "Don't get me wrong, I practically wept with joy when the guide came back and took me to a hotel with hot water and electricity and cell signal. Obviously."

"Obviously," I echoed. I sipped my wine, still trying to parse that soft smile.

"Now." Delaney's smile took on a distinct edge. "My turn."

I knew exactly where this was going. "Yes, fine, I was singing 'Defying Gravity.' It's my favorite song from my favorite musical." I paused and considered. "One of my favorites."

"*One* of?" His eyes widened. "You're a closet musical theater junkie? Have you always been?"

"Not closeted," I said firmly. "About anything. Not talking about things isn't the same as keeping a secret."

Delaney gave me a speculative look. "Isn't it?"

"No. And no, I wasn't always into it, but I dated a guy who thought I needed more culture in my life. He took me to see *Phantom*." I shrugged. "Turned out I liked the culture better than the guy."

Delaney's eyes, shiny with alcohol and excitement, narrowed. "Best *Hamilton* song?"

"Huh?"

"It's a simple question, Brewer." He pushed his glasses up his nose and said loftily, "If you really *are* a musical theater junkie."

Once again, startled laughter escaped me. "Uh. I don't know if I have one. 'Quiet Uptown,' I guess—"

"Hmm. *Wrong*. I mean, technically, it's an opinion question." He grinned. "But the correct answer is 'Wait for It.' If you're a true fan."

"Ah." I nodded soberly. "Noted. Thank you for correcting me. So, what's *your* favorite musical, then, true fan?"

"Pfft." He waved a hand with tipsy carelessness, and his fingers brushed my arm. "*Hadestown*."

This was such a random conversation. There was no reason my heart should be racing. No reason why I'd moved so close to Delaney that even in the low light, I could count the freckles dusting his nose, could see the faint stubble on his jaw, could almost taste the wine on his breath.

"Original cast of *Hadestown* or current?" I demanded.

Delaney's eyes lit. "Eva Noblezada *was* Eurydice, so." He folded his arms across his chest, as though daring me to argue, but his grin was downright infectious. "Why *Wicked*?"

"Because... because I like that Elphaba figures out who she was supposed to be all along, I guess? And also because Jonathan Bailey as Fiyero in the movie is a fucking wet dream."

The minute the words were out, I realized I should not have been talking about wet dreams with Delaney.

Not ever, but especially not now, when we were sitting so close together, cocooned by the snow and the firelight, trying so hard to not-think.

I sat upright and pretended to check on Teeny, who was fast asleep. "So, did I pass?"

"You... yes. You did." Delaney stared down at his glass for a long moment. "You're full of surprises, Brewer."

I could say the same about him, and I wasn't sure if that was a good thing.

This teasing, intimate version of Delaney wasn't new, exactly, but I'd only ever caught glimpses of it before. Seeing it now made it even harder to remember why I was not-thinking.

"So... next question? Or do our musical questions

count? I figure you've got a complex system of rules you haven't fully informed me of yet," I teased.

He shoved my knee. "Shut up," he said without heat. "Yes, fine. Ask your second question."

"Why'd you move to Copper County?" I asked. "For Tam and the baby, I know. But that's a big change to make for your niece."

Delaney's head snapped up, and he glared at me, twice as hot as the fire. "Hold up, we're getting personal now?"

"Weren't we before?" I shot back.

"I mean... no? You were supposed to ask my favorite author or ice cream flavor, and I'd tell you Gabriel Garcia Marquez and Coffee Coffee Buzz Buzz!" He slammed back a gulp of wine. "Fuck's sake, Brewer."

"Explain the rules beforehand, Delaney," I mocked. "Or suffer the consequences."

But when Delaney ran a frustrated hand through his hair, the movement caused the too-big sweatshirt to slip down over his collarbone, and that sliver of skin became the whole focus of my consciousness... which felt a whole lot like *me* suffering the consequences.

"I guess..." Delaney licked his lips. "Can we blame it on an early midlife crisis?"

"Full and honest or drink," I reminded him.

He gave me a glare that wasn't nearly as searing as usual, either because the wine made it hard to focus or because he didn't seem to notice that his glasses had slid down his nose again and he literally couldn't see me. The urge to reach out and push them back up for him was almost overwhelming.

So fucking cute.

"That *is* an honest answer," he argued. "But if you need

the full version..." He sighed. "You know how I visited Tam last fall when she was on bed rest?"

I nodded. Everyone in Copper County knew about Tam's pregnancy complications and that all of her brothers had come, at one point or another, to check on her. Delaney was the only one who'd stayed.

His fingers toyed with the hem of his shorts. "So, we were sitting in her sunroom one day. A bunch of people had come over to bring her baked goods, and I was stuffing my face. Tam was sprawled on her chaise, laughing her ass off at something—probably me. Then she stopped laughing suddenly and looked at me and said, 'Delaney, you need to promise you'll visit more when the baby's here. I want my daughter to know her uncle. Fuck, I wish you assholes lived closer.' Meaning me and our brothers, you know?"

Delaney darted a glance at me like he wasn't sure I was still paying attention.

As though I could possibly pay attention to anything else.

"Yeah. I got that," I said roughly.

"Anyway, I don't know what came over me—this is the early midlife crisis part—but we both got all emotional and sappy after that." He pulled the sweatshirt cuffs over his fingers. "Tam can at least blame the pregnancy hormones, but I have no excuse. I remember thinking how *pretty* and *colorful* the trees by the lake were, and how the air smelled like woodsmoke, and how fucking delicious the muffins I was eating were. And next thing I know, I opened my stupid mouth and said, 'I'll move here!'" He rolled his eyes. "Like an idiot."

"I don't think that's idiotic," I said. "I think it's sweet."

It was also surprising. God knew I was no stranger to impulsive decisions—after the dustup with my father, I'd walked away from my job at my grandfather's company with no plan whatsoever—but impulsive wasn't on my top ten words to describe Delaney.

"Sweet," Delaney scoffed, "is generally a euphemism for idiotic. Did I consider logistics of traveling for work or whether I'd even like this place permanently?" He shook his head. "I made the least logical decision ever 'cause I was all up in my feels." He shot me a look and muttered, his voice so low I almost missed it, "Not the only time I've done that."

I wondered if he was talking about the kiss, or the camper fire, or something else entirely. Maybe impulsive *should* be in my top ten Delaney words.

But to me, the decision to stay here didn't seem illogical. Especially not after hearing the Peru story and seeing how his face had softened when he spoke of the community there and their little rituals. The realization that Delaney Monroe—prickly, perfectionist Delaney—might be lonelier than he let on made something in my chest ache.

"Maybe you wanted connection," I suggested. "Community."

Delaney wrinkled his nose, then shook his head. "Nah. Doesn't sound like me."

I pressed my lips together to hold back my grin, but I was pretty sure I couldn't hide the warmth in my eyes. "Do you regret it?"

Though it was hard to tell in the dim light, I'd swear he blushed. His eyes held mine for a beat too long, and the air between us thickened.

"I..." He looked away. "I don't know. Ask me again after the renovation is done," he said with some of his usual asperity.

Delaney set down his wine and stretched his arms high, like he was loosening his muscles, the movement causing my sweatshirt to ride up his thighs. Then he relaxed and fixed me with a steady look. "My turn." He rubbed his hands together. "What to ask, what to ask…"

"Fuck," I muttered. Just to throw him off, I said, "I knew I was gay when I was thirteen. I don't know how many guys I've slept with—not because there's a lot, just because I don't keep count. My mom died seven years ago. My hero was my grandfather, who taught me all about building and carpentry. I'm not close with my family, except my cousin Hayes, who's like an annoying little brother. I didn't go to college. I have a teacup collection, which was actually my grandmother's that I inherited, but I guess they're mine now, so… whatever. Hawaii is the best place I ever traveled. And you already know about the musicals." I dusted my hands together. "There. Now, go ahead and ask me about authors and ice cream."

Delaney laughed out loud. "Oh my God. You're adorable."

"Me?" I blinked. "That's a new one."

"Is it?" He bit his lip and directed an incredibly distracting look at my chest. "Maybe you only let the adorable show when you're drunk and the power's out."

I swallowed hard. I was pretty sure it had more to do with him than the alcohol or the electricity.

Before I could think up an easy response, Delaney spoke again.

"Tell me about *her*." He nodded toward Teeny. "Specifically, why'd you acquire a dog the size of a small horse when you lived in a camper and why'd you saddle her with such a lame name? I mean, seriously, Teeny? 'Cause she's enormous? You couldn't at least go for, like, Biggie Smalls or something?"

I felt the smile spreading across my face. Whether he

knew it or not—and I was pretty sure he did, which meant I owed him one—he'd given me an easy out. A gimme.

I shifted my position, stretching my legs out and leaning my weight on one arm, which brought me close enough that our shoulders touched. Delaney didn't move away.

"I didn't acquire her on purpose. I was doing a kitchen renovation for an elderly couple, the Harrisons, a few years ago. They'd gotten her when she was first weaned and named her Queenie."

From her spot by the fire, Teeny recognized her name, lifted her head, and looked around sleepily.

Delaney didn't move or flinch, except to clench his fingers around his bent knees. I lifted my own hand to reach out and take his—

You were doing so well, Brewer.

—but stopped myself at the last minute.

"The Harrisons weren't able to take care of her properly. By the time I met them, her fur was all matted, and she was underweight—"

"Wait." Delaney's brow furrowed. "They neglected her?"

"No. Not intentionally. They loved her. But I think they didn't know what they were in for, having a Newfoundland. Mr. Harrison had Parkinson's, and Mrs. Harrison couldn't handle walking or grooming a big dog, especially not a giant, excitable puppy. I found out pretty quickly they were renovating because they were planning to sell the house and move to an assisted-living place—"

"Ugh." He stared at the dog, who'd gone back to sleep. "I know it's not their fault, but it wasn't hers either. And that was her home, too!"

Delaney might not like my dog, but he seemed ready to

fight for her. *And* to make sure she got Kitchen-Couriered dog biscuits while he did it.

My stomach twisted and flipped, sending more alcohol sloshing through my system, and I had to take a deep breath before I could continue.

"It, ah, it worked out okay. For both of us. Teeny needed more than they could provide, and..." I hesitated, the alcohol making me more honest than I might have been otherwise, "well, I needed a best friend, I guess."

Delaney's expression softened. "So you say. But best friends don't take away a noble name like Queenie—a name that evokes both Beyoncé *and* Freddie Mercury—"

I did reach out then, because I couldn't help it, and gently pinched Delaney's lips closed. His eyes widened, and his breath caught.

"D'you want the full and honest answer or not?" I demanded softly.

He nodded once.

I removed my hand, but not before my thumb traced the curve of his bottom lip. His skin was impossibly soft, and the small contact sent heat coursing through me.

I tangled my fingers in my own shirt before I could remember all the other things I could do with them and continued. "The very first thing I did was bring her to a groomer, who had to shave her in a few spots to get rid of the mats. Mats hurt," I explained. "So it needed to be done. But it was a rough morning for the girl." I directed my gaze to Teeny. "When they were done and brought me back to see her, she was curled up on a pile of blankets, shivering and shorn. And she made the most forlorn sound. Like she was crying—"

"Oh, don't." Delaney pressed a hand to his throat, his eyes large and liquid. "I can't take it."

"And all I could think was that life had done her wrong. So I got her out to the car, and I turned on my usual playlist, and what do you think was the first song that came on?" I hummed a few bars of "I Dreamed a Dream."

Delaney stared at me blankly for a moment, like the wine was making his brain buffer. Then suddenly, his jaw dropped. "You named your dog... *this* dog... after Fantine from *Les Mis*."

"Yep. And called her Teeny 'cause it's close to Queenie, and I didn't want her to be confused." I smiled smugly. "Still think it's a terrible name?"

Delaney burst into laughter—the kind of laughter that consumed his whole body and bled the tension from his shoulders. The kind I couldn't help joining in on.

He leaned forward, one hand landing on my thigh to steady himself. "If you gave me," he said, wiping his eyes, "one hundred guesses, I would never have guessed that, but it's so, so perfect." He grinned at Teeny. "For both of you."

Delaney's smile was a beautiful thing. So beautiful I wanted to kiss him again.

But that wasn't what this game was about.

This was about... about...

Fuck, I couldn't remember anymore. Not with his hand on my leg and the alcohol making my thoughts move like molasses.

I stopped laughing, gulped my drink, and said quickly, "My turn. Why don't you like Teeny?"

Delaney's entire body stiffened in an instant. His hand jerked away from my thigh, and he gave me a look of reproach, probably for killing the lighthearted mood. "I don't *dislike* her. Jesus. It's not *personal*."

He blew out a breath, seeming to consciously relax himself. "I'm cautious around dogs, that's all. We had a dog when I was a kid. A golden named Gretzky." He cut his eyes to me. "Named for the hockey player."

"Right," I agreed. I wasn't sure what I'd expected him to say, but it wasn't this.

"It's a silly story, actually. With no real explanation. I was just reading in the backyard when I was... ten, maybe? Sometime after my mom died. And Gretzky... He bit me." The last words sounded as sad and betrayed as if all the intervening years hadn't happened.

Delaney rubbed his arm absently, and when he spoke again, he sounded clinical, almost detached. "I guess that just happens sometimes. And it wasn't serious. Four puncture marks. But there was a lot of blood, and the babysitter freaked out and called an ambulance, and afterward..." His eyelashes fluttered. "Like I said, I became cautious."

Delaney made it sound like it was a deep, dark confession, not a normal reaction to a traumatic incident.

I reached over and gently touched his arm where he'd been rubbing, the spot where I imagined faint scars might be. "Of course you were scared. Anyone would be," I said.

Delaney's eyes locked on my hand, then lifted to meet mine. Something passed between us before he quickly looked away.

He shook his head. "I don't know about that. And the, ah... the caution got worse over time instead of better. My brothers would corner me on the sofa and do *supervised cuddles* with the dog to remind me I didn't need to be scared, but that made it worse. I started having nightmares. And I just kept thinking that I didn't know why I'd made him bite me the first time, so I didn't know how to... how to avoid a repeat. You know? How to trust that I wouldn't get bitten again."

My fingers tightened around his arm protectively. My

other hand clenched into a fist. "Didn't anyone realize you needed to see a therapist?" I nearly growled. "Fuck, Delaney—"

"My mom was a therapist, actually. If she'd been alive..." He shrugged. "Anyway, my dad was way more pragmatic. He sent Gretzky to live with his sister in Vermont. No dog, no problem."

I felt those words like a sock to the gut. "Except it doesn't work like that."

"Well... to be fair, it's rarely been an issue. I mostly avoid dogs, and everything's fine. Except, you know, recently. But I'm going to work on it." He turned his head to look at me. "Really. It's not *her* fault." He tilted his chin toward Teeny.

"No," I agreed, "but you don't need to rush it." I realized my hand was still on his arm and reluctantly withdrew it. "I wish I'd known—I wish I'd *asked*—about this before now. That's on me—"

"It's not—"

"I'll make sure to lock the kitchen door from now on so she can't get in here. Or we can go and stay with my cousin—"

"Brewer," Delaney interrupted. He looked almost angry. "I said I'm going to work on it."

"Yeah, but—"

"I didn't ask you to move out, and I didn't ask you to keep the door locked." He forced out a breath. "I can handle it, okay? I'm a capable person."

I raised my hands in surrender, shifting back slightly to look at him. I had no idea how the mood had shifted so thoroughly, so quickly.

"I didn't say you couldn't." Delaney was one of the most

capable people I'd ever met... except when it came to relocating power outlets. "I just—"

"I do not need you and your large muscles protecting me from your dog or my stupid cabinet choices or... or anything."

My eyes widened. "Whoa. Back up. My large—?" I glanced down at myself, then back to him. I shook my head trying to stay focused, though that was nearly impossible since I wasn't sure what was happening here. "I thought we weren't talking about the cabinets."

He blew out a breath. "Yes. We are. I'm hereby ending the renovation ceasefire."

"Delaney—"

"Look, I know your feelings on those cabinets, okay? You made it pretty clear when you canceled the order without even discussing it with me—"

"Because I knew you had your heart set on those, but I wanted to show you I could do something custom that you might like just as much, and then—"

"And then I insisted on these because there was no way my bossy contractor could possibly know better than me—"

"I wasn't being bossy," I interrupted. "Or... shit, if I was, I didn't mean to be. I was doing my job, trying to make your style work with the house, and—"

"I know. I *know*," Delaney said. "It's like with the damn dog. I just don't know how to trust that—" He broke off and shook his head.

"I guess I should have explained better," I admitted. "And not expected you to... what'd you call it? Fling trust around like Mardi Gras beads?" I took a deep breath.

"Anyway, what I'm trying to say is—"

"—I'm sorry," we said together.

We stared at each other in surprise.

"You are?" I demanded. "Why?"

"For insisting on these cabinets and being dead wrong? I appreciate you trying, but they look awful, Brewer," Delaney said in a small voice. "Just like you said they would."

"You... you hate them?" I said, scared to hope that we might have gotten on the same page finally.

He glared up at me from beneath his lashes. "You sound way too fucking cheerful about that."

I laughed. "I'm not! I... fuck. Maybe I am, kind of," I said. "I thought you were going to insist, and I wasn't sure how to handle it. I'm relieved."

"Insist? After seeing that?" Delaney shook his head. "I can't do it, even though I've exploded my own budget and my timeline."

"Well..." I frowned. "I can't do anything with the upper cabinets that I already hung. But Hen might be able to help us return the base cabinets and get your money back. And I can still make you custom ones, if you want. It might take a little longer, but I'll show you the designs and the materials. I'll make sure you like them."

He nodded tightly. "I... I would appreciate that."

I felt a smile spread across my face. I was relieved about the cabinets, yes, but this felt bigger than that.

"You won't regret it," I told him.

Delaney huffed out a laugh. "Unlike those?" He jerked a thumb toward the kitchen. "I don't even want to fucking look at them again. They're like... they're like the scarlet letter of cabinets. A giant red A for Asshole."

I snort-laughed, and a moment later, so did he.

"God, I wish we could rip them out right now," he confessed. "Just so I don't have to look at them again."

I stopped laughing abruptly as an idea formed, an idea

that would distract me from my... distraction and hopefully help Delaney work out his frustration. I pushed to my feet and held out a hand. "Come with me."

"What?" He looked up at me in confusion, but after a moment's hesitation, he grasped my hand and let me pull him to his feet.

We stood there for a heartbeat, nearly chest to chest. Then I stepped back, still holding his hand, and led him toward the kitchen.

The room was shadowy and dark, illuminated only by the glow from my phone's flashlight. Delaney's shoulder pressed against mine as we surveyed the red monstrosities hanging on the wall.

"Wait here," I said. I jogged out to the garage, the cold air a brief shock against my heated skin, and returned moments later with a sledgehammer, two pairs of safety goggles, and a battery-powered work light that cast the kitchen in a stark, dramatic glow.

"Holy shit. You're going to rip them out now?" Delaney's eyes were wide, a mixture of shock and something that looked like excitement on his face. "*Right* now?"

"No. Of course not." I moved behind him, close enough that my chest pressed against his back, and put the safety goggles on over his glasses, securing the elastic around the back of his head. Then I took his hand in mine and wrapped his fingers around the wooden handle.

I leaned down and spoke directly in his ear, my lips nearly brushing his skin. "You are."

I felt him move against me, his breath catching audibly. His head turned, bringing our faces so close I could feel the heat radiating from his skin.

"Me and tools..." He bit his lip. "Remember what happened last time? This... this is probably a terrible idea."

"Maybe," I agreed, my voice low and rough. "Or maybe you should stop thinking about all the last times and concentrate on *this* time." I moved my hands to rest lightly on his hips. "Because I guarantee it'll feel phenomenal. Trust me, Delaney."

Delaney laughed, a breathless sound that sent heat racing through me. "Fuck it," he whispered, eyes gleaming. "Okay."

CHAPTER SEVEN

DELANEY

Brewer's solid chest pressed against my back as he guided my hands on the sledgehammer, and his hips aligned with mine in a way that was highly, highly distracting.

"There's no trick to this," he murmured, and though his deep voice was soothing, his warm breath against my neck was the opposite. "There's no trick to it. Just lift the hammer and smack the fuck out of the cabinets, yeah?"

"Yeah. Yes. I can do that." My voice came out breathless and tipsy, a little from the wine and mostly from Brewer.

"I know you can." He gave me a gentle push forward, breaking our connection.

The sledgehammer was lighter than I expected as I lifted it, and I felt a grin spread across my face. I channeled all my frustration through my arms and into the steel head... and whacked the first shiny, red cabinet door. The impact sent a satisfying jolt up my arms as the door crumpled, hinges tearing loose from the cabinet frame.

It was messy and gratuitously destructive...

And I let out a whoop of triumph that echoed through the darkened kitchen.

"Hell yeah!" Brewer encouraged from behind me, his voice warm with amusement. "Hit it again. Hit it like it insulted your journalism degree! Hit it like it just told you that Hen's achy elbow predicted a hurricane!"

Laughing giddily, I repositioned my hands on the wooden handle and squared my feet, which were just a little unsteady.

I wasn't drunk, exactly. Not drunk enough to make any truly terrible decisions, anyway... At least, none worse than the ones I'd already made tonight, like kissing my contractor senseless or confessing my deepest insecurities to his *dog*.

I swung again, catching the upper corner of the same cabinet, and this time, the entire unit ripped away from the wall, taking a small square of plaster with it. It crashed to the drop cloth with a magnificent clatter that had me grinning like a maniac.

"God, that feels good," I panted, surprised by how much I meant it. My heart hammered in my chest, exhilaration coursing through me. "I'm gonna keep going!"

I darted a look over my shoulder to gauge Brewer's reaction, but he just nodded, his arms folded over his chest and his too-handsome face wearing that tip-tilted smile that made my stomach whirl. So I took aim at the next cabinet, swinging harder as memories of Brewer's beer-flavored kiss fueled my mini-demolition spree.

Smash. The cabinet door folded, its hinges surrendering with a satisfying shriek. *Crack.* Another swing, another section of red metal folding like tissue paper.

With each impact, I felt a rush of something wild and unfamiliar—a reckless kind of freedom I hardly ever allowed myself. Brewer's presence behind me made it worse... or maybe better, depending on how you looked at it. I was still standing on a precipice, about to tip into the unknown, but knowing he was right there made the edge less terrifying.

I took another swing, and another, watching as metal bent and wood splintered. My arms burned with the effort, but I couldn't stop myself. And with each impact, I mentally cataloged the mistakes the stupid, shiny cabinet represented.

The relationships where I'd been too much or too little. Every time I'd been too stubborn to admit I was wrong. The way I'd waltzed into Copper County, thinking I could just plant myself and grow. Even this new, annoying uncertainty that I didn't know who I was or what the right next step was.

Every whack was liberating as fuck. Enough to make me wish I could deal with all my problems that way.

But with all that heady, happy freedom pulsing through me, I may have forgotten a few crucial things.

Like that my hands were sweaty from all the exertion and that a sledgehammer—no matter how light it might feel with adrenaline coursing through my system—was, by its very nature, really fucking heavy.

Like that Newton's Law of Physics was a *law* for a reason.

Like that the universe tended toward entropy and destruction.

Worst of all, I forgot that I could not, under any circumstances, be trusted around tools or even those who used them.

I swung once more, bracing myself from a distance since I knew the cabinet would fall... but this time, instead of connecting with the cabinet, the whole fucking sledgehammer flew out of my grasp. It sailed through the open air and hit the exact spot where the first cabinet had been with a sickening crunch. Then it just... lodged there.

"Oh," I managed, blowing out a breath. "Shit. For a second there, I thought I—"

The wall trembled—literally trembled, like an ancient god had awakened—and a rain of plaster dust crumbled to the floor, leaving behind an opening at least a foot tall and more than a foot wide. The sledgehammer tipped and fell to the ground somewhere inside the hole with a metallic *clunk*.

"—destroyed the wall," I finished in a whisper. "Fuck."

This pattern was becoming very familiar in recent months. I tried moving an outlet and flooded my living room. I started writing the story Marjorie said would be my best yet and sputtered out halfway through. I went to express my outrage to my contractor and burned his freaking camper down. I ordered a vanity I loved and somehow neglected to calculate the depth of the thing. I enjoyed a moment of freedom and... *this*.

How could one person be wrong so often?

Behind me, Brewer burst into laughter. He gripped my arms and shook me lightly. "Holy shit! *Shit*. I mean, I figured you were pretty strong, but that was... beyond."

I ripped off my goggles and whirled to face him, dislodging his hands and nearly sliding on the plaster dust in my socks. "Brewer! Did you not see the part where I *broke the wall*?"

"Uh, yeah." The work light and the wine made his blue eyes shine like summer lake water. "Kinda hard to miss. But we knew there'd be some damage. Sledgehammers, not known for their precision, right? So, tomorrow morning, I might grumble 'cause it'll be a pain to repair the wall. But it *can* be repaired, like most things can."

Brewer's eyes got those crinkles at the corners. "And for *tonight*... well. That was cathartic, right? And it was fucking hot."

I stared at him. I was breathing hard, and not just from all the whacking.

I mean, I figured you were pretty strong...

That was... beyond...

And it was fucking hot...

"Brewer." My voice cracked slightly, and Brewer's smile slid into concern.

"Whoa. Are you okay?"

I looked at him, at the dust in his hair and the warmth in his eyes, and felt something inside me shift irrevocably.

"No," I said, reaching for his shirt.

I pulled Brewer against me with the kind of desperate strength that lets mothers lift cars. He made a surprised sound that transformed into a groan as our mouths crashed together.

That first touch unleashed a torrent of heat that melted through me like wildfire, turning every one of my bones to liquid. His mouth opened against mine, hot and eager, and the taste of him was more intoxicating than anything I'd drunk all night. I sucked his bottom lip between my teeth and was rewarded with a shaky exhale that ghosted across my cheek.

I twisted my fingers into his hair, needing *more* and *harder*, but his hands caught my hips, fingers digging into my flesh.

"Delaney," he growled. The word vibrated through my chest.

"Please, Brewer?" I said. For once, I had no idea what I was asking for. No opinions. No thoughts. No demands. No need to be in control. No need for anything but him.

"Living room," he gasped after a piece of plaster crumbled to the floor behind me.

I pushed against his chest with my free hand, walking him backward through the kitchen doorway, our bodies glued together. The cool plaster dust on my hand left ghostly prints on his shirt, marking him as mine, if only for tonight.

"Delaney," Brewer said again. His eyes were dark and heavy-lidded. "Are you sure—"

I silenced him with another kiss, deeper this time, my tongue sliding against his. My hand still gripped his hair like a lifeline.

We stumbled into the living room, nearly tripping over the pillows I'd laid on the floor earlier. From her spot near the hearth, Teeny lifted her head, then huffed and curled back into a ball, apparently unimpressed by our display.

I pushed Brewer down onto the couch, the momentum carrying me forward until I straddled his lap, my knees bracketing his thighs. His calloused hands slid beneath my —his—sweatshirt, leaving trails of fire everywhere he touched.

"God, you feel—" he murmured against my neck, his stubble scraping deliciously against my skin. "I've wanted this."

The confession hit me like another kind of sledgehammer.

"You..." I gasped as he sucked on my collarbone. "You thought about this? With... me?"

My stomach was tight with need, and my heart thundered with nerves. Was this just the heat of the moment, or was it possible Brewer had actually been attracted to me?

"You fucking kidding?" he huffed without taking his mouth off my skin. "Can't fucking function around here. All those legs and those fucking glasses always slipping down your nose."

Brewer's hands moved down to my hips, fingers digging in as he pulled me down against his hard length. As soon as our cocks touched, I couldn't help but grind down into him. "W-what did you w-want?" I asked, desperate to find out what he'd meant by "wanting this" but also desperate to feel his hands and mouth on me.

My brain felt like it was both electric static sparking all over the place and gooey sludge locking up every available oxygen molecule and brain cell. But I needed to know what the hell he'd meant. Because there was no way my sexy contractor had actually meant he—

"Wanted you naked under me," he breathed hot against my skin. "Wanted to see your cheeks turn all splotchy and your eyes roll up. Wanted to know what it would take to make you shut up, stop thinking, and just fucking *feel*."

"Uh," I said stupidly as he continued to torment me with his roaming mouth and hands. "Well... *Oh*."

His hands moved down over my silk-clad ass and squeezed. "Wanted to feel this ass," he murmured as his nose pressed up under my chin. He took his time sucking the skin there before pulling back and meeting my eyes. His were dark with need, and his nose was slightly red from my stubble. "Wanted to make you come, Delaney."

I lurched down to kiss him on the mouth again, grinding our cocks while sneaking a hand between us to feel the length of him through the denim of his jeans. "Fuck," I whimpered before pressing my lips together to keep from begging him to fuck me. Was that rude? To ask your contractor to fuck you after one or two maybe-alcohol-induced kisses? It seemed like it was.

But then I remembered he'd offered to make me come.

That had actually happened. "Yes," I said quickly. "Yes, please."

The edges of his lips turned up. "You gonna let me take care of you?"

His wording took me aback. Take *care* of me? I did not need a man to *take care* of me. I didn't need taking care of, period. I needed an orgasm.

"Pants off," I said, asserting a little control. I tried climbing off him but tipped over and fell forward between Brewer and the sofa cushions instead, letting out a little *oof*.

His smile faded. "Y'okay?"

"*Pfft*. Pants off. I'm... supervising. From here."

Brewer stood up like he was no longer as drunk as other people in the room and started to make a big production of taking off his jeans. The knowing quirk of his brow might have annoyed me if I hadn't been so distracted by his little striptease.

"Faster," I urged, moving to the edge of the sofa without realizing what I was doing. "Oh, never mind. Here. I'll do it." I reached out to shimmy his jeans past his hips, watching with rapt attention as the thick outline of his erection was revealed under the cotton fabric of his underwear.

Brewer's fingers tangled in my hair. "You look like Teeny when I finish a steak and offer her the bone," he murmured.

I glanced up at him before settling my eyes back on his package as I stroked it appreciatively. "I will not dignify that with the expected bone joke. Nor will I be compared to a feral beast."

His fingers moved through my hair more gently. "Thank you for telling me about the dog thing," he said softly. "I didn't know."

I shook my head. Nobody wanted to talk about childhood trauma right now, and I had a pretty good idea of one way to stop the conversation, a way I considered a win-win for all of the people in the room. "I want to suck you off."

My fingers continued to explore the size and shape of his cock as I leaned in and rubbed the edge of my jaw across its hard length. He smelled so damned good.

Brewer's thick, muscled ass tightened, pushing his dick against my face as I continued to tease him. His eyes darkened further. "Delaney," he warned, voice like bourbon over gravel.

Dampness bloomed on the cotton in front of me, the scent of his precum making me dizzy. "Brew," I breathed, still nearly face-first in his groin. "I want—"

With one hand still in my hair, he used the other to pull down his boxer briefs, nudging me back a little until his stiff cock fell forward against my cheek. "You want?" he asked, looking unsure, like he was suddenly worried he was crossing a line.

I met his eyes and confessed. "Yes. I want. I've wanted you for a while."

THE SIGHT of Delaney Monroe on his knees for me had both sobered me and made me feel ten times more intoxicated than I'd felt coming home from the bar.

But hearing him say he'd wanted this? Wanted me?

It was enough to make me want to grab the man up by the armpits and toss him face-first onto the nearest bed before sliding between his cheeks and feeling him from the inside out.

Right now, though, I wasn't moving from this spot. Not with this gorgeous, fastidious man willing to put his mouth on me. My chest heaved with disbelief. Was this really happening?

I closed my eyes and tried not to question it because I knew if I did, I'd have to stop this. It was wrong. Delaney was my client. My business...

"Fuck, yes," I groaned as Delaney's hot mouth engulfed my cock. His hair was messy and eyes bright as he peered up at me. Watching his lips stretch around my shaft made my balls ache. "Feels amazing."

Delaney blinked, the edges of his lips quirking up in an adorably tipsy way. "You like this?"

I ran my fingers through his hair. "Smug bastard." I grinned down at him. "What's that quote you have framed in your office?"

He knew I remembered the quote. We'd talked about it before. "What you plant now, you will harvest later." Delaney had pointed it out in one of our discussions about painting his office woodwork.

It was attributed to Og Mandino, some salesperson or other, but Delaney had mentioned appreciating how it could also refer to following breadcrumbs of a good story while doing research.

Delaney leaned down and suckled at my crown, his tongue paying particular attention to just the right spot under the edge before he pulled off again and grinned up at me. "Are you planning on harvesting in my face?"

I tightened my grip in his hair and held his head in place as I leaned down and kissed him hard. "Shimmy off those silky things, Farmer Del. I want to suck your cock."

Within moments, we were head-to-dick on the floor in front of the fire, sucking and stroking each other into a frenzy.

Delaney pulled off my cock with a gasp. "Motivation beats talent. I a-applaud your diligent efforts."

It was a reference to another one of the damned self-help quotes hung on his office wall, a quote I may have argued against under my breath a time or two in the past few weeks of trying to convince my prickly client that I had both motivation *and* talent.

Which only motivated me to prove it to him now.

I pinched his ass, enjoying his laughing yelp. "Talent's

gonna make you come," I grumbled before leaning down to pull one of his balls into my mouth.

Delaney's slender fingers dug into the back of my thighs as he groaned and arched into me. "Please, Brewer. Fuck, please. *So good.*"

Instead of letting him come, I punished the snark by pulling off and dropping barely there, open-mouthed kisses along his inner thigh before finally licking and sucking a bruise into the tender skin there.

"*Brewer!*" he cried, pulling off my own cock. "Fuck, please. Make me come." He moved his warm, wet lips along my shaft, nearly causing my brain to short-circuit.

If there was something consistent about Delaney Monroe, it was his need to prove himself right, to make sure no one thought he was deficient in any way. He'd be damned if he'd lose a contest or come up short in anyone's opinion.

So he sucked my cock like he was being interviewed for a permanent position.

And fuck if I didn't want him to get the job.

"Just like that," I murmured.

The whimpered sound that replaced his begging triggered my orgasm just as his hot spunk painted the side of my cheek. It was quick and dirty and absolutely fucking amazing.

We lay in a sweaty, gasping heap while Teeny's rhythmic snores continued on in the background and the fire popped and crackled. I pressed my lips against the thin skin over his hip bone, inhaling his warm, musky scent as I teased him with my tongue.

Delaney's hands moved slowly up and down the back of my leg as we caught our breath, and my heart rate returned to a semi-normal level. "I don't want to move," he said softly.

"Mm," I agreed, moving to nibble the soft, fleshy skin of his inner thigh.

"And, really. We shouldn't," he continued, moving so I could get better access. "The power is still out, and that attic space has to be frigid. It would be irresponsible for you to take yoursel—er... dog up there. And my bedroom gets drafty at the best of times. I believe I've mentioned that to you. We're much better off here in front of the fire."

"Mmhm," I murmured, smiling against his skin. He definitely had mentioned it to me, which was why I'd replaced the weather stripping around the windows and bled the radiator in his room. It was snug as it could be now, but I appreciated the lie nonetheless.

"Besides," he continued in a breathy voice while allowing me to widen his legs even further so I could move my lips down the inside of one thigh. "Y-you had a lot to drink tonight. Someone should keep an eye on... *ohh!*"

I pulled the skin on the inside of his knee into my mouth and scraped my teeth across it, enjoying the sight of his toes spreading apart. "*Nnn-hnnn,*" he encouraged. "Thass'alright."

My hand wrapped around his narrow foot. I dug my thumb into his arch and rubbed. "Yeah?"

"S-studies show foot massage reduces pain in patients recovering from cervical spine surgery," he babbled. "S'good."

"Interesting," I said, turning so I could see his face. "You have spinal surgery lately?"

Delaney was pink-cheeked and golden in the firelight. His eyes were soft and glassy as he gazed at me in a way that tightened my stomach and made me wonder if he'd even heard my words.

His plump lips were too tempting to ignore, so I moved

around and stretched over him, leaning down to kiss his mouth.

For some reason, the combination of the storm, the power outage, and the alcohol had shifted our reality. It had made this feel like a time out of time. Like it didn't count.

Like it was allowed.

I shoved the idea aside and focused on taking as much of him as I could before morning arrived, and I could no longer ignore why this was such a bad idea.

We spent another hour kissing and exploring each other's bodies lazily in front of the fire until we finally took a break to clean up a bit, yank a few clothes back on, and urge Teeny out for a final pee.

When I opened the door to a blustery shock of frigid air, Delaney yelped and scurried under the blankets.

Thankfully, Teeny made it quick, and we returned to the warmth of the fire within minutes, where I enjoyed torturing Delaney with my cold hands.

"You're a monster," he hissed as I ran my hands up under his/my sweatshirt.

"You're actively snuggling me," I pointed out, pulling him closer. "Hard to take your complaints seriously."

He burrowed his nose into my neck. "How are you simultaneously a furnace and an ice block?" he grumbled.

We teased each other for a few more minutes, and a few minutes after that, we were naked again, humping each other like animals coming out of winter with a single-minded determination to propagate the earth.

"We shouldn't be doing this," I confessed as I took us both in hand. Our cocks were wet from the aborted blowjob he'd started before I'd yanked him up and kissed the fuck out of him, rutting against him with a wet, slippery desperation.

"Dare you to stop," Delaney challenged with broken breath. "But also don't. Fuck, Brewer, oh God, that feels…"

The next sound out of him was my name on a gasp as he came hot against my fingers and cock. I stroked him through it, thrusting up into my own grip so I could feel the added heat and slide. Watching his ruddy tip disappear into my fist was erotic as fuck.

But it was the glazed look in his eyes and the still-wet spike of his eyelashes from choking on my cock that finally pushed me over the edge.

This time, Delaney was too fucked out to do more than offer me a sleepy slur of agreement when I told him to stay there while I cleaned up and fetched him a warm wash-cloth. By the time I got back to the fire, he was dead asleep with his arm stretched out and the barest edge of one fingertip resting on the hair at the end of Teeny's tail.

The sight of his little stealthy attempt at overcoming his fear made my chest ache. Maybe I didn't give Delaney Monroe enough credit. The man I'd thought was a fussy know-it-all might just be hiding a tender heart after all.

I leaned down with the cloth and cleaned him up before repositioning his head on a pillow and lying down next to him. Once I'd settled next to him and pulled up the blan-kets, I couldn't help but stare at his face in the golden light from the fire.

He was so beautiful… sensitive and reactive in all the best ways. But he was still my client.

This was a royally bad idea. A mistake of gargantuan proportions.

And when morning came, I remembered why.

In front of many, *many* witnesses.

CHAPTER NINE

KAK-WEEEEE! KAK-WEEEE!

My eyes shot open at an unholy sound piercing the peaceful cocoon of sleep... and piercing my eardrums in the process. For a single, disorienting moment, I had no idea where I was, only that I was warm... and naked... and wrapped in blankets on a hard surface that was definitely not my bed.

"What the fu—" I started, then froze as my elbow connected with something solid—humanly solid—beside me.

Brewer. The sledgehammer. The wall. The kiss. The... everything else.

KAK-WEEEE!

"What the—?" Brewer mumbled, his voice thick with sleep. When he rolled over, the sleeping bag slid down to reveal his bare chest, and the sight made saliva pool in my mouth. His dark hair stood up in approximately seventeen different directions, and there was a suck-bruise on his shoulder that might or might not carry the DNA of a local journalist.

He looked just as good in the cold light of morning as he had in the glow of the firelight, which seemed unfair on a fundamental level.

"Hey." He smiled warmly at me for a moment, then frowned. "Is something on fire?"

"Doorbell," I croaked, tearing my gaze away. "Someone's at the door."

As if on cue, the bell rang again, followed by sharp rapping on the door. "Delaney? Brewer? Are you in there?" a woman's voice called from outside.

Eyes wide and head throbbing, I caught bits and pieces of several voices having a lower, more muffled conversation.

"No way anybody'd sleep through that racket—"

"Brew's not answering his phone, but Reed said—"

"The power's back, so maybe they're—"

"...ain't leavin' 'til I give 'em croissants—"

"And poor Delaney, without a shovel!" the woman wailed.

Oh. My. God.

I scrabbled around on the floor for my glasses, nearly face-planting when the blanket tangled around my ankles. "People," I whisper-hissed, shoving the glasses on my nose. "Multiple people! There are multiple people outside my house, Brewer!"

Brewer, who'd risen with considerably more grace, simply stretched and yawned. The sight of his naked body —all of it, because apparently, morning was his, er, *happiest* and most *confident* time—momentarily short-circuited my panic.

"Relax," he said, reaching for his jeans. "It's probably just some neighbors checking on you because of the power outage and snow." He nodded toward the window where the morning sun glinted off at least a foot of pristine white stuff.

Hen's leg, it seemed, had been vindicated.

"*Just* neighbors?" I dived for my pajama shorts. "Just *neighbors* who are about to find us naked? Together? With —" I gestured wildly at the rumpled sleeping bag, the haphazard pile of pillows, and the empty wine bottles that clearly told the tale of our night together.

A face appeared at the window, and I yelped, diving behind the couch like a cartoon character.

"Put on some clothes!" I whisper-shouted to Brewer, who was moving with infuriating calm as he stepped into his jeans.

"What do you think I'm doing?" The thread of amusement in his voice said he was enjoying my panic way too much.

I crawled across the floor, grabbing whatever clothes I could find—which happened to be my pajama shorts and Brewer's sweatshirt. I yanked the shirt over my head just as the doorbell rang again.

"I'll take Teeny out the back for a bathroom break," Brewer said. A glance over my shoulder showed he was mercifully now wearing his jeans and henley from last night. "*You* handle the welcoming committee."

He whistled softly, and Teeny, who'd been watching our frantic dressing routine with judgment in her doggy eyes, rose and padded after him.

"Thanks a lot!" I called after him. My head throbbed harder as I stumbled to the door, trying to finger-comb my hair into something that didn't scream *I've just been thoroughly ravished by a hot contractor.*

I pulled the door open, wincing at the blast of cold air—

and found myself face-to-face with what appeared to be the entire winter sports section of an REI catalog.

"Delaney! Finally!" Janice Plum cried, her cornucopia hat now replaced with an aggressively pink ski cap with a pom-pom the size of a cantaloupe. "Thank goodness you're alright! We were so worried when you didn't answer the door."

Behind her stood Hen in a blinding blue parka, along with Brewer's cousin Hayes and my Kitchen Couriers delivery guy, who wore matching neon green snowsuits that made them look like human highlighters.

"You were?" I shivered and rubbed my bare legs together. "Sorry, did I miss a memo about a neighborhood... snow ritual or something?"

"Silly Delaney. We're here to THWAC you!" Janice declared, throwing her arms wide with such enthusiasm that her pom-pom nearly took out Hen's eye.

"*Thwack* me?" The morning sun reflecting off approximately three trillion snowflakes made my eyes water, and for half a second, I felt like I had, indeed, been thwacked. Hard. Either that, or I was still asleep and having some kind of strange wine-induced nightmare.

"T-H-W-A-C," Hayes supplied. "As in, The Helpful Wintertime Association of Coppertians."

Hen shrugged and muttered, "Janice came up with the name."

"We shovel snow for folks who can't do it themselves for whatever reason," Kel said proudly. "And for people who, like, don't have shovels." He gave me a sympathetic look.

"Oh. Well. That's... that's very nice." I said. But I wasn't sure what to say after that. Was I supposed to pay them? Or invite them inside for refreshments I didn't have? Or, fuck, offer to *help* them with my nonexistent shovel? I fussed awkwardly with the cuffs of my sweatshirt.

Hayes caught the motion and gave my shirt an up-down look, and then his whole face brightened. "Nice outfit," he said.

I glanced down and realized that my chest was emblazoned with "Portland Builders Convention 2018."

My face went nuclear. "Oh, this? This is... I, ah..." I folded my arms over my chest as though I could belatedly stop them from noticing. "Funny story, actually."

"Really? I love a funny story." Hayes grinned.

"Heh. Yeah. Maybe Brewer could help you tell it?" Kel's shit-eating grin was the mirror of Hayes's. "We tried calling his phone like fifty times—"

"We were asleep until two minutes ago!" Their grins widened, and I felt my face go impossibly hotter. "I mean, *I* was asleep, and *he* was asleep. Independently. Just two people... sleeping. And then he had to take Teeny out—"

Hen's eyebrows went up.

"I assume," I added quickly. "Though I would obviously have no way of knowing."

Hayes nodded. "Since you were sleeping independently."

Kel snorted into his glove.

"Well!" Janice chirped, completely oblivious to the subtext. "We brought provisions!" She held up a large thermos. "I made coffee! And Hen got you something at the bakery—"

"Strawberry croissants," Hen said gruffly, holding up a small plastic container. He didn't quite meet my eyes. "Heard you like 'em."

I blinked, even more overwhelmed by this gesture than by the arrival of a brigade of snow warriors...

Which was the only excuse for my delayed reaction—and failure to block the doorway with my body—when the THWAC crew cheerfully pushed past me into the house.

"We were at the Hive when Brew left last night," Kel announced, unzipping the top of his suit. "Man, he couldn't get out of there fast enough once he saw how heavy the snow was. Reed said Brew was super worried about getting back to you."

"Getting back to *me*?" I repeated, my hungover brain processing this information with the speed of cold molasses.

Hayes nodded, stripping down the top of his own snow-suit with the same practiced efficiency to reveal a thermal undershirt below. "Yeah, once he realized how bad the storm was getting, he was like, 'Gotta get home to Delaney!' We teased him, but he just got all serious."

"That's not... We don't... Wait, really?"

"Kitchen's this way, eh?" Hen interrupted, saving me from having to form a coherent sentence. He was already halfway down the hall, carrying the croissants.

"No, hang on, don't—" I lunged after him, but it was too late.

"Holy crap!" Hen's exclamation echoed through the house. "What happened here?"

The rest of the THWAC crew converged on the kitchen like vultures to roadkill, and I had no choice but to follow, my stomach sinking.

In the harsh morning light, the destruction looked even worse. The demolished cabinets littered the floor, and the gaping hole in the wall seemed even larger. Plaster dust coated every surface, undisturbed except for two sets of footprints and—oh God—what were clearly handprints on the wall, marking the spot where I'd jumped Brewer.

"Whoa," Hayes breathed, eyes as wide as dinner plates. "Who did this?"

I cleared my throat. "I did. It's kind of hard to explain. It was an accident, sort of. I—"

"Dude!" Kel said, peering at the hole with the enthusiasm of a kid at a science museum. "You straight-up murdered your kitchen!"

"Did you and Brew have some kind of fight?" Janice asked, concern pinching her features beneath that ridiculous hat. "Was this like..." She lowered her voice. "The camper?"

"No!" I said, too quickly and too loudly, making my own head throb. "No, we just decided, um, that the cabinets weren't working. It was a spur-of-the-moment renovation decision." I spoke with as much dignity as I could muster while wearing another man's sweatshirt and sporting sex hair.

Hayes snorted. "Yeah, I bet there was a lot of *renovation* happening."

I was saved from responding—or possibly committing murder; the jury was still out—by the back door opening and Brewer entering with Teeny. He'd added a flannel over his henley and boots on his feet, making him look irritatingly put together... while I still resembled something the dog had played with and then abandoned.

"Morning, everyone," he said casually, as if finding the house invaded by Coppertians was a normal weekday event. "I see you've discovered our midnight redesign."

"*Your* redesign?" Hen asked thoughtfully, eyebrows climbing his forehead. "This was you?"

"Sure. Both of us, really. It's Delaney's house, after all." Brewer moved to stand beside me—close enough to present a united front but with a careful inch of space between us. "And we should probably get back to it."

"But..." Janice brandished her thermos again. "We brought provisions."

"And Hen plowed your driveway, but we need to finish clearing a path to the porch," Kel argued.

"Plus, I thought maybe Kel and I could stick around and clear a spot where we could take Teeny out to run around without getting too snowy," Hayes said. "From a distance," he amended with an eye roll when Brewer and Kel both gave him concerned looks. "I do remember that I'm allergic."

Brewer's face softened. "I appreciate the thought. But I —*we*," he said with a nod at me, "can handle the rest of the snow removal later. Right now, Delaney and I have to clean up our mess."

I forced a smile despite my nagging hangover headache. "We do," I agreed.

More than one, in fact, if you counted what happened last night... which made the kitchen seem like the easier prospect by far.

Hayes smirked. "Which mess are we talking, cousin?" he asked, as if reading my mind. "This—" He nodded at the mangled cabinets. "—or the one in the living room?"

I choked on air, my cheeks burning hotter than the fire that had warmed our naked bodies just hours ago.

Shit. Of course he'd seen that.

Brewer's expression didn't change, but something in his eyes cooled several degrees.

"Hayes," he said, and just that—his cousin's name, in a tone that could have frozen boiling water—made Hayes's smirk falter. "You can catch up with my dog later. Right now, my priority is handling this renovation and ensuring there's no structural damage to the wall," Brewer went on in a measured, professional voice.

As if choreographed, the others turned as one to examine the hole I'd made.

And when their backs were turned, Brewer caught my eye and gave me the briefest, smallest wink.

My heart pounded like I'd just finished the treadmill sprints at Barry's Bootcamp.

"Huh," Hen said, turning back to us with an approving smile. "Pretty deep space you uncovered, boys. Looks like it was a jam cupboard, once upon a time."

I tried to focus on the conversation and not the possible interpretations of that wink. "Jam cupboard?" I repeated. "What's a jam cupboard?"

"Just exactly what it sounds like." Hen stroked his mustache. "Lotsa houses around here have these odd little nooks and crannies that were once used for storage. In more recent years, some folks walled 'em off 'cause they decided they'd rather have a nice long, unbroken run of cabinets and countertops." He shrugged. "But I always did love a jam cupboard, myself."

"Hey, look! There's stuff in here. Old newspapers, looks like," Kel said excitedly.

Janice clasped her thermos to her chest excitedly. "Oh, this could be just like that *National Treasure* movie! Brewer, we can—"

"I promise you, Janice," Brewer said in that same no-nonsense voice. "I've found plenty of hidden nooks over the years, and not one of them has led to a secret underground city made of gold. If this one does, the Council for Historical Happenings will be the first folks we call."

Janice sighed dejectedly. "I suppose you're right. As usual."

I snorted and tried to cover it with a cough, but the amused look Brewer shot me said he wasn't fooled.

"There are lots of Coppertians out there who need THWAC's help this morning," Janice reminded her crew. "We have a sacred duty. But first..." She brandished the thermos yet again. "Coffee?"

I desperately wanted coffee, but I was even more desperate to talk to Brewer and figure out what was going on.

"We should let you..." I began, trying to think of a way to say, "Get the hell out," without sounding rude.

"Yes," Brewer said, heading for the laundry room and the cups there. "I'd love some."

Five minutes later, I stood against the wall, nursing my coffee, as Brewer efficiently managed the THWAC invasion.

He ate a croissant and drank coffee but managed to politely evade all their questions about our plans for the kitchen by asking them about the origins of THWAC and volunteering his services for the next storm.

When Janice offered to help him find a new camper, Brewer redirected her, and soon she was talking about some art exhibition she was setting up.

When Hayes asked him over to play video games—after making a snarky comment about the dusty handprint on my/Brewer's sweatshirt perfectly placed over my ass—Brewer somehow steered the conversation into a discussion of the tournament Hayes and Kel were having without committing to playing video games one way or the other.

He was so freaking *good* at handling them—at being firm but kind, friendly but not too friendly—I wondered if they even realized how little information he gave them.

And I wondered *why*.

Twenty minutes later, he had them all bundled back into their rainbow snow gear and stood beside me at the door, waving them off to tackle other unsuspecting driveways. As the door closed behind them, I let out a breath I felt like I'd been holding since the doorbell first rang.

"Well," I said, turning to him, "I guess we should probably—"

But Brewer was already moving back toward the kitchen.

"Get this cleaned up?" he called over his shoulder. "On it. You probably have your own work to do, huh?"

I frowned. "Yes. Always. But I can help you first," I said, trailing behind him. "I was the one who caused the damage, after all—"

Brewer stopped and turned, forcing me to stop, too. "Hauling out cabinets is a one-man job." He gave me a stilted smile. "Why don't you grab a shower? Not sure when the power came back, but I'll bet the water heater's kicked back on, too."

This felt like a dismissal, and it stung more than it should have.

"Sure," I said, striving for the same casual tone. "Sounds good."

I stood in the shower a few minutes later, letting the hot water pour over me, trying to make sense of what had just happened.

Last night, Brewer and I had shared something incredible. Something that had felt passionate, and raw, and honest, and, well, *profound*, not that I'd spit that sort of purple prose out loud. I felt like I'd been swept off the precipice I'd been clinging to and into something new. Something Brewer and I might explore together.

But the distance Brewer had put between us after everyone left had made it clear that I was flying solo.

"Good job," I muttered to my dick while scrubbing shampoo through my hair with more force than necessary. "You've picked another winner."

After dressing in jeans and a sweater, I headed straight to my office rather than the kitchen. I couldn't face Brewer while my head was still spinning. I needed to ground myself in something familiar, something that was entirely mine.

Work. I would focus on *work.*

I opened my laptop and pulled up the Empire Ridge files. I'd been digging into this story for weeks, but in the past few days, I'd stalled. Some evidence was there, as I'd told Tam, but not nearly enough to make a compelling case, an *award-winning* case.

I'd conducted interviews with Anthony's second-in-command, as well as a couple of other people who'd been friends with Anthony for years and, predictably, corroborated his story. I'd contacted the people at Empire Ridge for a comment, and they'd referred me to their website, where I'd found lots of glamour shots of the cookie-cutter River Bend housing development and a single press release denying all knowledge of the incident.

In other words, nothing helpful at all.

I went to close the website when an aerial map of the development caught my eye, and I clicked to enlarge it. The development was divided into several smaller cul-de-sacs interspersed with pools, tennis courts, a clubhouse, an elementary school, and even a community theater. I wondered which part of the property had been Anthony's property, so I looked for the firehouse... but I didn't see it.

Confused, I pulled up the website for Southbourne,

New York—the town where the development had been built —to find the address of the new firehouse, but their website was so outdated I gave up in disgust. I emailed Anthony Harmon, asking if he could point me in the right direction.

Then I reviewed the notes I'd made for the seventeenth time, hoping some fresh line of inquiry would pop out at me.

Spoiler: it didn't.

A knock on my open office door a moment later startled me more than it should have. I glanced up to find Brewer leaning against the doorjamb. At some point, he'd changed into different clothes—a dark green henley hugged his broad shoulders this time, and his jeans clung to his thighs in all the best ways.

He looked unfairly good for a man who'd spent the night on a hardwood floor.

"Hey," Brewer said in that same professional, neutral tone from before. "Didn't mean to interrupt."

"You're not." I closed my computer. "You're saving me from chucking this laptop out the window."

He chuckled, low and intimate... or maybe that was just how I *wanted* to hear it.

"Story not going well, I take it? Not easy making things fair and right?" His tone was teasing but surprisingly sincere.

Or maybe not so surprisingly, after our conversation last night.

"It's not." I pushed up my glasses and rubbed my eyes. Some of us were not meant to sleep on floors, and it showed. "I'd really appreciate it if the bad guys could just twirl their mustaches, or wear T-shirts that say 'Bad Guy,' and/or have little manifestos on their websites about being bad. Who can I send a strongly worded letter to about this?"

Brewer laughed. "If it was that easy to tell who the bad guy was, wouldn't you be out of a job? Or were you thinking of taking up sledgehammering professionally?"

I laughed, too—which I hadn't thought was possible, given how frustrated I was. Then I adjusted my glasses. "Did you need something?"

"If you've got a minute. I finished cleaning up and started looking at the jam cupboard... and I think we might have a mystery on our hands." He bounced his eyebrows.

I sat back in my chair. "What kind of mystery?"

"The mysterious kind. Come see," he said, tilting his head toward the kitchen.

Curiosity piqued, I followed him down the hall.

The space had been mostly cleared of debris, the cabinets Hen had authorized us to return were stacked neatly, and the hole in the wall was more defined now, like Brewer had removed the loose plaster around the edges.

I moved closer, peering into the opening.

At first, all I could see was what the others had seen—bare wood, dust, and scraps of yellowed newspaper. But as my eyes adjusted, I saw that at the back of the visible space, there appeared to be a set of shelves holding several flat parcels.

"Oh my gosh. What are those?" I demanded, pointing.

"If I knew, it wouldn't be a mystery, would it?" Brewer shrugged. "I didn't want to look any further without you."

I turned to face him. "That might just be the nicest thing you've ever said to me, Brewer," I said seriously.

He snorted. "Yeah, well. I swear to Christ, whatever they are better not lead us on some Nicolas Cage treasure hunt—"

"Aw, Brewer." I looked up at him with a lazy smile. "If Janice could hear you now, she'd be crushed."

Brewer's grin hit fast and crooked, like he hadn't meant to let it loose, and the air between us tightened, humming with something that felt a lot like inevitability—

Or maybe not so inevitable since a second later, Brewer stepped back.

"We should... get to work widening the opening," he told the floor. "Take off the rest of the plaster in this section so you can see what's in there."

I folded my arms over my chest and nodded. "Weren't we going to have to do that anyway? I mean, we uncovered a jam cupboard. We can't just cover it up again."

Brewer darted a look at me, his lips tilting up in that hooked smile. "Well, we could. Jam cupboard's just another word for a plain, old pantry, so if you'd rather have counter space than storage—"

"*Bup bup bup.* Did you just insult my jam cupboard by calling it a pantry?" I demanded. "My vintage, hidden, ye oldey-fashionedey jam cupboard?"

He shook his head, still smiling. "Right. I'll grab my tools."

"The sledgehammer?" I asked hopefully.

"Not unless you feel the need to hit things again," he called, already heading for the garage.

Frankly, when Brewer had refused to look at me, I'd felt very much like hitting something.

But when he came back with a pry bar, he also handed me a pair of work gloves and showed me how to remove sections of the plaster without damaging whatever might be behind it, which was almost—but not quite—as good.

Our hands brushed occasionally, sending jolts of awareness through me that I tried desperately to ignore. After about twenty minutes, the opening was wide enough for me to step inside.

"Wow," I said when I did. Brewer was partly correct—the space we unearthed was basically a dusty closet paneled in rough wood and with shelves hung at regular intervals along one side, but it was not a "plain old" anything. The space smelled like cedar chips, and on the shelves sat at least a dozen stacked rectangular packages wrapped in butcher paper. Scrolls of tightly wrapped papers stood in one corner, too.

I gently pulled the top package off the stack, brought it out to the kitchen, and set it on the floor to open it.

"Is that...?" Brewer's voice trailed off.

"A painting," I finished, turning it toward the light.

The unframed canvas was small—maybe eight by ten inches—but exquisitely detailed. It was a landscape of Copper Lake in the fall, when the maple and oak trees were lit up in crimson, amber, and gold. At the water's edge, a woman stood in profile, gazing out over the water with a secret smile on her face. A long-forgotten breeze caught at her burgundy dress and sent strands of dark hair curling like ribbons toward the water.

"E. Winters," Brewer read. "1977."

"It's beautiful," I said. "Grab another."

The second canvas showed a different view of the lake. In this one, it was clearly winter since all the trees were bare, and early morning light bathed everything in a crystalline glow. In the background, the Observatory House—the Copper County landmark where Theo and Bennett lived—was in the early stages of construction, with scaffolding visible on one side. In the foreground, the same dark-haired woman, this time in a navy blue coat, stood with her back toward the artist, one red-gloved hand shielding her eyes as she looked toward the rising sun.

All in all, there were more than a dozen paintings, most

of the lake or the woods surrounding it. All of them were signed E. Winters and dated from 1970 to 1983. All of them featured the same woman.

"Who is the woman in the pictures?" I wondered.

"And who's E. Winters?" Brewer asked. "And why were they hidden away?"

Our shoulders nearly touched as Brewer crouched beside me on the plywood floor and we leaned over the paintings. The bergamot-and-Brewer scent was more powerful than ever, but I fought the Pavlovian Dick Response with all my might.

I forced a laugh. "Good God. We actually found a treasure," I muttered. "Does this mean I have to call Janice for real?"

Brewer laughed, too. "Probably. And you could ask Samuel Purchase."

I turned my head and frowned. "The guy from the *Gazette?* The guy with... Admiral Barkington?"

Brewer nodded. "Sam knows a *lot* about the history of the area. Really smart guy. Funny, too. I redid his bathroom a couple years back, and we've had dinner together a few times." Brewer's mouth quirked into a half smile. "Apparently, the Admiral insisted."

"Oh. Well. That's... that's great for you." I sat back on the floor, fighting an unexpected twinge of something like jealousy. If I recalled correctly, Samuel was pushing retirement age, but maybe that was Brewer's *thing.* "And for him."

"What's that mean?" Brewer asked, catching my expression.

"Nothing," I said quickly. "Just... you seem to know everyone in town pretty well."

"Not *well.*" He shrugged. "But when you've lived here a

few years, you can't *not* get to know most of them, at least a little. They won't let you," he joked darkly.

I nodded, striving for Brewer's casual tone. "And do you make it a habit of getting to know all your clients... thoroughly?"

The moment the words left my mouth, I regretted them. Brewer's eyes widened slightly before his expression shuttered.

"No," he said firmly. "I fucking do *not*. This job's a first for me in that regard."

Our eyes locked, and I saw nothing but sincerity in his gaze.

My shoulders slumped. "Brewer," I began. "Look, about last night—"

He shifted, twisting on his boots. "Delaney, last night was..." He shook his head and smiled slightly. "I don't have to tell you how good it was. You were there." He ran a hand over his stubbled jaw. "But this... you and me... it's a bad idea. I'm your contractor, and you're my client. And if people in town found out we slept together—which they would, since lots of 'em already suspect it—then I become known as the guy who sleeps with his clients instead of the man who does the best restorations in the area."

"Okay, but—"

"I've got a job to finish," he continued, holding up a hand to keep me from interrupting. "And I want—*need*—to do it well. Barnum Restorations is my life, Delaney. It's what I love and how I honor everything my grandfather taught me about this work."

"Your grandfather?" I frowned. "Did he start Barnum Restorations? I didn't realize it was a family business."

Brewer shook his head. "It's not. I told you last night I don't have much to do with my family aside from Hayes.

My father…" He hesitated. "He's not a good man. He gave away something that was mine, and I've never forgiven him for it. But my grandfather… *he* was amazing. He taught me restoration work by letting me help him restore his own house one room at a time. And he taught me about the importance of integrity. He used to say, 'A craftsman leaves two things behind, Brewer. The work of his hands and the weight of his reputation. We're only as good as the promises we keep.'"

I leaned back, watching as he ran a hand through his hair, his massive shoulders tense under his T-shirt. A traitorous part of my brain couldn't help but remember how those shoulders had felt under my palms last night, solid and warm.

But I also recognized how important this was to him.

"That's beautiful," I said softly.

"It's *true*," Brewer corrected. "The houses I work on aren't just jobs to me. They're… promises." His voice softened. "I promised you a renovation, Delaney. Not complications."

I swallowed. "And last night was a… a complication." I tried to keep the hurt from my voice but failed, and my chest tightened with embarrassment.

Of course Brewer was being pragmatic about this. I should do the same.

Brewer's eyes met mine, and something in them made my breath catch. "Last night wasn't a complication, Delaney, it was a goddamn hurricane. And I…" He leaned forward, resting his elbows on his knees. "Fuck. Hayes is right. I don't know how to talk about this stuff."

"About complications?"

"About… feelings." He looked up. "About… starting something with you."

"Oh." The single syllable escaped me like it had been punched from my lungs.

The very idea of "starting something" with Brewer was knee-knockingly terrifying. All wrong for the life I led. For the person I'd always thought I was. My track record with relationships was objectively terrible, and the common denominator was me.

Besides, what kind of *something* were we even talking about?

"Oh?" he repeated wryly. "That's profound. Aren't you the one of us who's supposed to be brilliant with words?"

I nodded, then shook my head, then nodded again. "I am, but I'm not... I don't..." I looked away, pressing my lips together, and admitted, "I'm starting to think I might be better at telling other people's stories than my own."

He laughed out loud. "Well, then... sounds like we're both in over our heads, baby."

I laughed, too, though it came out a little shaky. I couldn't remember anyone calling me *baby* before. I sure as fuck couldn't remember wanting them to. "So... what do we do now?" I asked softly.

"Now..." He shrugged. "I finish your renovation. You finish your article and solve our Jam Cupboard Mystery." Brewer gave me a half smile. He lifted one huge hand to my face and brushed something—plaster dust, probably—off my cheek with the gentlest caress. Then he adjusted my glasses. "And then you go to your next big story, and I go to Reed and Chris's kitchen renovation."

I wanted to argue, to push, to demand more... but I could tell he'd made up his mind. The rejection was sharp and brutal.

"Right," I said. I cleared my throat. "Yes. Good. Because I *do* have a very important trip to Costa Rica coming up. Tourists are disappearing, and I need to find out why."

"Sounds exciting," Brewer said easily.

"It is. It *is* exciting," I insisted. "Very. My career and my reputation are very important to me, too, you know."

He nodded. "So, then... friends, sort of?"

I smiled. "Friends, sort of," I echoed, the word feeling hollow in my mouth.

After all, what else could we be?

I had a mystery to solve, an article to write, and a whole fucking life to figure out... and Brewer had promises to keep.

But first, it seemed like the hurricane wasn't done with either one of us.

CHAPTER TEN

BREWER

I KNEW Watt's snowblower was wrecked the moment I turned it on and heard a grinding sound, followed by a clunk that rippled through the machine like it was having a heart attack.

"Jesus." I flipped the switch off, then crouched down to peer under the housing. "What the hell did Jasper do to this thing?"

"I told him not to try clearing slush with it." Watt Bartlett handed me a crescent wrench from the tool kit we'd spread on his garage floor. "But he was trying to surprise me, and... Well. Surprise."

I snorted. "You let the California boy loose on the wet New York snow? Recipe for disaster." I accepted the wrench, but my mind wasn't fully on the conversation or the repair. Or my unexpected reputation for being the town's "Snowblower Expert" after I'd accidentally fixed one for the Ross family two winters ago. Instead, my thoughts kept bouncing around like a pinball, replaying the events of the last couple of days.

Delaney's face in the firelight. The jam cupboard

discovery. The way Delaney's naked body had felt against mine. The hurt in his eyes when I'd explained why we couldn't be more than contractor and client.

"Hey. Earth to Brewer." Watt crouched beside me and waved one large glove in my face. "You still with me?"

"Sorry." I blinked. "What were you saying?"

"Asked if you need the Phillips head."

"Oh. Yeah, thanks." I accepted the screwdriver and started removing the housing plate, trying to focus.

This was why I was here. Because Watt had called explaining in a slightly desperate tone that they'd only had the snowblower a month, and Jasper had tried to be helpful, and now there was something smoking and stuck, and could I please save them from having to buy a new one?

Of course I'd said yes. I liked being helpful. I liked fixing things.

I also liked not spending my afternoon coming up with reasons to casually stroll past Delaney's office and then physically forcing myself not to act on them.

"Shit," I muttered when the plate came off, revealing the damage inside. "It looks like he sucked up a chunk of wet cardboard?"

Watt sighed. "Don't ask your teenager to take out the recycling when he's talking to a guy he might or might not have a crush on. Lesson learned."

I put down my tools and began carefully extracting soggy, shredded cardboard from the blades. The work was delicate enough that my full concentration was required, which was a blessing. The problem was simple, finite, and solvable.

Unlike certain other situations.

The sound of the back door opening distracted me.

"Babe?" Jasper called. "Did Brew rescue our poor snowblower? Are we gonna play that game where you teach me a lesson because I've been a naughty— Oh. Um. Hi, Brewer."

"Hey," I replied without looking up. "Rescue is under-way. And then you and Watt can get back to whatever the fuck you—"

For some reason, I glanced up at that moment, right as Watt stepped over to greet his partner with a kiss that was on the heated side of casual. It wasn't super risqué, but I found myself unable to look away until the moment had passed.

"I made muffins, if you guys are hungry," Jasper announced after clearing his throat. He poked Watt lightly in the ribs. "Those chocolate protein ones your kid likes to eat by the dozen."

Watt grinned, "He has good taste. I'd love one."

"For a muffin, I might just save this snowblower," I agreed.

Laughing, Jasper went back inside and returned a moment later with the snacks and coffee. As we ate, Jasper and Watt stood side by side, teasing each other over random stuff, like who ate muffins the most tidily and whether Jasper was, as he claimed, better at "summer chores" than Watt.

The two men were always competitive—anyone who'd ever attended one of their regular "cook-offs" knew they'd throw down over literally anything—but their rivalry was never mean-spirited. It was pretty clear that when they'd gotten together a few months back, twenty years after what-ever had ended their childhood friendship, they hadn't been messing around. No trial period, no let's-see-where-this-goes. They were a unit, solid and unbreakable, and that made them surprisingly easy to be around.

"Anyway. I'll let you guys get back to it," Jasper said.

"You're a miracle worker, Brewer." He gave Watt's arm a brief squeeze, then disappeared back into the house, whistling cheerfully.

Watt watched him go with an expression that spoke volumes.

"You've got it bad," I teased, turning back to the snowblower.

"Shut it." There was no heat in Watt's words, though, and he was smiling as he knelt back down to hold the flashlight for me.

We worked in companionable silence for a few minutes as I extracted the last of the cardboard and began to reassemble the housing. But my mind kept circling back to the way Watt had looked at Jasper.

It had been similar to the expression Delaney wore when he was deeply interested in something—a kind of open, unguarded focus that seemed to exclude everything else.

"So. I heard you and Delaney had a pretty epic night the other night," Watt teased.

The wrench I was holding slipped, smashing my thumb against the metal housing.

"*Fuck!*" I shook out my hand and narrowed my eyes at Watt. "Who said that? Was it Hayes? Because he has no idea what he's talking about, okay? Delaney is my client. Cli. Ent. And no matter what the gossips in this town say, I—"

"Brewer." Watt stared at me, looking utterly confused. "Chill. I heard you knocked down a wall that revealed some hidden paintings or something."

"Oh." My face went hot. "*That.* Yeah. We... we did."

Watt's gaze took in my flushed cheeks and my stammering. He looked away, but not before I caught a glimpse of his smile.

"Huh. So what do you know about the paintings? Are they worthwhile?"

I shrugged. "I don't know much of anything. Delaney's looking into it, I think. His house, his mystery. And it's not like he'd tell me since I'm just his contractor and he's my client."

"Yeah," Watt said mildly. "So you said. Client, client, client." He lifted his gaze to mine. "I can't imagine why anyone would think otherwise."

I ducked my head to hide the fact that my face was getting redder. "They wouldn't. Or they *shouldn't*. You know how town gossip is."

"Sure do." He nodded. "I remember when Jasper and I were getting together, the whole town was discussing it."

I scowled. I was pretty sure he'd purposely picked the one example of town gossip being accurate. "This isn't like that," I insisted.

"No, of course not." Watt overturned a five-gallon bucket and sat on it so he could hold the flashlight steadier. "I get it."

"I mean, people would have to be crazy to think there could be anything between me and... and *Delaney*," I scoffed.

Watt frowned. "Hey. I think Delaney's great. He's a little... intense, but he's been a good friend to Jasper. You could do a fuck of a lot worse," he said in a tone of mild reproach.

Was the man insane?

"Of course there's nothing wrong with Delaney," I said, staring at Watt. "I just meant he and I are totally different people. He's a... a brainiac who travels constantly for work—

like, apparently, he's off to Costa Rica for some big story soon." I rolled my eyes. "And he's prickly."

"Ah—" Watt began.

"And he quotes things," I continued. "Every five minutes, he's telling me *studies have shown, Brewer.*" I snorted, imagining Delaney pushing up his glasses while he said it. "And he speaks, like, four languages—I've heard him on the phone. And... Jesus, did I mention the prickly thing? Because he *really* is. And not in a cute hedgehog way. In an 'I will shank you with my spikes if I feel vulnerable' way."

Watt poked his tongue against the inside of his cheek. "Whereas *you* are very easy to get to know and definitely don't put up walls to deflect people."

"I'm not—" I started to argue, then caught Watt's amused expression and sighed. "Okay, yeah. It's been pointed out to me recently that I might have a small problem with that. But that's just another reason why there's absolutely nothing between Delaney and me."

"Because you're both polar opposites and too much alike." Watt nodded. "Got it."

I blew out a breath. "I'm just saying, if you overhear anyone gossiping about me and Delaney, please set them right, okay? Last thing I need is Copper County thinking I sleep with my clients."

Watt's eyebrows shot up. "Clients, plural? Delaney's one client."

"One too many," I insisted. "It's called *professionalism.* It's called... keeping my promises."

He ran a hand over his beard thoughtfully. "Damn. You must really like him, huh? A man only makes this many excuses when he's in the throes of some powerful feelings. Trust me, I know."

My hands stilled for a moment. I hadn't allowed myself

to think about me and Delaney in quite those terms. Attraction? Sure. Chemistry? Fuck, yes. But powerful feelings? That was ridiculous.

"No," I lied. "We barely know each other. We had kind of a rocky start to his reno, but we're finally getting along. So just... just leave it, okay?"

Watt held up his hands in a gesture of surrender, but there was a knowing look in his eyes I didn't appreciate.

We worked in silence for a few more minutes until the snowblower was reassembled, looking no worse for its cardboard consumption.

"There. That should do it," I said, brushing off my hands and standing up. "Just make sure Jasper knows to avoid the recycling."

"I'll make sure he knows." Watt grinned. "Thanks, Brew. Seriously. I owe you."

"Nah. No big," I said, tucking my tools back in their bag.

We walked toward my truck in easy silence, and I climbed in. But just as I was about to shut the door, Watt grabbed the edge and held it open.

"You, ah..." He cleared his throat and rubbed the back of his neck uncertainly. "You know people around here like you, right?"

I gaped at him. "Huh?"

"Just... the stuff you said before." Watt lifted a hand in the direction of the snowblower. "People don't recommend you for renovations just because of your professionalism. They do it because you're good at what you do and because you're a nice guy who rescues snowblowers from soggy cereal boxes."

"Oh-kay?" I frowned, not sure what he was getting at or

why he was making both of us uncomfortable by starting us down this road at all. "Thanks?"

He blew out a breath. "What I'm trying to say is you're allowed to have a life, Brew. You can be human. You can sleep with a client. You can be a little cocky, like Reed. Or see the entire world through the lens of *John Ruffian: Pretender*, like Chris. You can wear a fucking cornucopia on your head, if that floats your boat."

I snorted, thinking of Janice.

"Just... be you, Brewer. And fuck anyone who's not cool with that." Watt nodded to himself. "Okay?"

"Okay." To my surprise, I found myself fighting a smile. "Thanks, Dad."

Watt's cheeks went nearly as red as mine, but he grinned. "Fuck off."

"No, seriously, is this the kind of talk you give Derry?" I wondered. "Or Jasper when he's *naughty*? Because, if so, ten out of ten—"

"Goodbye, Brewer." Watt slammed the door.

I started the engine and rolled down the window. "Hey, Watt," I called when he was halfway back to the house. "Thank you."

He turned his head to give me a wry smile and a wave.

As I drove off, though, I found my own smile fading. Something about Watt's awkward sincerity hit me hard. And as I made my way down the lake road to Delaney's place, I found myself thinking about friendship and honesty...

And about the prickly man who'd looked at me in the firelight with such raw honesty on his face, it had terrified me.

CHAPTER ELEVEN

DELANEY

"Stop pacing, for the love of God," Tam said without looking up from the cheese she was grating.

"Pfft. I'm not *pacing*. I'm walking. There's a difference. Tell your mommy that the brain can be affected by a lack of proper oxygenation during periods of reduced mobility," I instructed my niece as we made another circuit from the kitchen, through the dining room, and into the living room of Tam and Lucas's home.

Tierney, settled against my shoulder like an adorable, drooling sack of potatoes, made a gurgling sound I chose to interpret as agreement.

"See?" I demanded of Tam. "She says she'd walk if she could, but while she's still working on pesky things like controlling her limbs, she has Uncle Delaney to walk for her. *She* understands that development of balance and spatial awareness in infants is directly correlated with exposure to varied positional changes, and studies show that—"

"Laney, I agree that Li'l T is brilliant," my brother Lawson said from the kitchen table, where he was mowing through a bag of plantain chips while drinking his second beer. "But please let her roll over before you have her start quoting studies at me."

I shot him a withering look. "Your understanding of child development rivals your understanding of proper nutrition, Lawson. And her name is Tierney. Tier. Ney. She's not one of your locker room buds."

Lawson snorted, but the sound lacked his usual energy, and he didn't clap back at all.

In truth, my NHL-star brother looked like someone had used his face as a hockey puck—dark circles under his eyes, shoulders slumped, his left arm held against his body in the careful way that suggested his shoulder had been lightly maimed during his last game but he didn't want to acknowledge it.

The oven timer dinged, and Tam moved to the oven to take the foil off her lasagna. The rich scent of tomato sauce, melted cheese, and garlic bread filled the air.

"Should you even be here right now?" I demanded of Lawson, studying his exhausted face. "Don't the Monarchs want their new defenseman to stay in Ontario, where they can keep an eye on him?"

Lawson rolled his eyes. "I escaped custody for the night. Long-ass drive, but worth it for Tam's lasagna."

"All for the lasagna," Tam agreed. "Definitely nothing to do with avoiding his new coach."

"Hey! I didn't say anything about my coach," Lawson protested—weakly, in my opinion. "He's fine. Everyone's fine. It's just... different. That's how it goes when you're traded. Takes a while to find your place."

"Hmm." I kept my eyes on him as I made another circuit of the dining room.

Lawson huffed. "Anyway, I didn't come here to talk hockey. I came to see my li'l... *niece*—" He raised an eyebrow at me. "—and to catch up with everyone. So give me the Copper County goss. How's that former-model friend of yours settling in?"

"You mean Jasper," I supplied. "He's doing well."

"Good! Good. And, ah..." He snapped his fingers. "The sweet guy with the glasses, what's his name?"

"Chris Sunday?" Tam guessed. "He seems fine."

"Great. That's great. And how's, um... how's Oliver Castillo doing? Is he dating anyone, or...?"

I wrinkled my nose at Tam. "Who's Oliver?"

"Physical therapist, friend of Watt's," Tam said. "You've probably met him and don't remember." She flipped a dish towel over her shoulder and gave Lawson a curious look. "I'm not sure how Law knows him, though."

"I don't *know* him." Lawson suddenly seemed very invested in reading the label on the plantain chips—and not a moment too late since he'd eaten enough sodium for ten men. "I just vaguely remembered meeting him at the bar when I was here over Thanksgiving, that's all. He seemed cool."

Tam and I exchanged a look.

"Nope. Put that expression away, Tamsen. It was a simple question. If you wanna play detective, let's turn our attention to the giant, *pacing* elephant in the room." Lawson waved a hand at me.

I stopped pacing—I mean, *walking*—just long enough to glare at him.

Tam snorted and did turn her attention to me... just as the asshole formerly known as my brother had *known* she would when he'd thrown me under the bus.

"Law's right. You have been walking rather aggressively. What's on your mind, Laney?"

The answer to that question was as simple as it was mortifying.

Brewer.

Specifically, Brewer's eye crinkles. Brewer's laugh. Brewer's jaw. Brewer's chest. Brewer's mouth on mine. Brewer's big hand, which could wield a hammer with force but could also hold a fussy, flowered teacup or fix my glasses with such gentleness. The little frown on Brewer's face when he needed to jot down a measurement and tried patting down the front pockets of his work shirt, the area around his band saw, and the space behind his ear before finding the pencil clamped between his teeth. Brewer's deep voice as he reminded me that he'd *promised you a renovation, Delaney. Not complications.*

I nearly tripped on a corner of the rug as I rounded from the living room to the dining room.

"Nothing," I said firmly. "Nope. Not a single thing."

"Nothing? Really? That's interesting," my brother teased. "Because if *I'd* just found a treasure trove of artwork in my wall, that might be on *my* mind."

"Don't be pedantic," I told him, walking faster. "Obviously, I've thought about it. I simply meant it's not 'on my mind' in a negative way. Google says there was a pretty prolific artist called E. Winters, but their styles are totally different." I shrugged. "So I texted Samuel Purchase to see if he knew anything, and Janice recommended an art appraiser, who's coming by next week—"

"Wait, you told Janice? On purpose?" Tam demanded. For Lawson's benefit, she added, "Janice Plum's one of the biggest gossips in town."

"Why not?" I lifted my chin in challenge without slowing down. "Brewer basically promised we would, and

Janice knows a lot about history. She was *very* excited when she saw the canvases—"

"She came to your house?" Tam's eyes were wide. "You invited her inside?"

"She's not a vampire, Tamsen. And yes. Several people stopped by, actually," I said with dignity. "All of them were excited, too. It's been kind of... fun, figuring out the mystery. I'm not *stressed* about it."

"I have got to see these paintings," Tam muttered. She folded her arms and watched me walk by. "So is it the Empire Ridge story that's bugging you, then?"

"Oooh, I remember you mentioning this in the sibling chat. Corruption and shit, right?" Lawson said. "That'd bug the fuck out of me."

He wasn't wrong. But when Marjorie had called today and begged for an update, the only thing I'd been able to tell her was that Anthony Harmon had emailed me back about the firehouse... and told me there *wasn't* one.

Mr. Monroe,

As you've discovered, there's no firehouse on the property Empire Ridge acquired from us.

After threatening us with eminent domain, they apparently changed their minds about how the land would be used... or, more likely, never planned to build the firehouse at all.

I wish I had copies of the plans they presented us during the meeting, if only to show their pattern of lies and manipulations, but obviously, they were too smart to provide me with any. The company that did all the site analyses and infrastructure planning for River

Bend—Cornerstone Development Solutions—claims to have no knowledge of this "second set" of plans.

Once again, I have no proof aside from my word.

A. Harmon.

"It's frustrating," I agreed. "Every line of inquiry has been a dead end, and I'm all out of ideas. But I'm sticking with it. I'm not too stressed."

When I passed through the kitchen the next time, Tam was leaning against the counter, watching me. "Why not ask Marjorie to hire you a research assistant? Maybe someone else will have a fresh perspective."

I considered this for a moment. "That's actually a really good idea."

"Right? And then you can start prepping for your next story at the vacation resort in Costa Rica." She wiggled her eyebrows. "It's a hard knock life, bro."

"Oh, fuck me. You're going to Costa Rica for *work*?" Lawson shook his head in disgust. "'Become a hockey player, Lawson,' they said. 'It'll be so much fun,' they said. Nobody mentioned how few tropical destinations would be involved. You have the best job, Delaney."

I frowned and paused. "You think?"

"Shit, yeah. The freedom to decide what you write about and *where*?" He waved a hand, indicating Tam's house, the lake, and possibly all of Copper County. "Pretty fucking sweet."

He was right, of course. I just hadn't expected *him* to say it. For as long as I could remember, I'd assumed my siblings felt sorry for me. The runt who couldn't keep up. The one who'd never mastered sports. The oddball who'd chosen words over physicality.

But seeing the fatigue in Lawson's eyes, thinking about how he'd been traded to a new team without so much as a by-your-leave…

"I'm really lucky," I agreed as I resumed my walk.

"Hmm." Tam tapped her lip. "So if you're not upset about the paintings, and you seem to be taking your frustration about your article in stride—"

I knew where she was going with this and began shaking my head immediately. "Stop. I have no comment on this matter."

"—then I can only think of one other reason why you're stomping around my house so energetically that my kid's gonna need a FitBit before she can walk."

"La la la la. Can't hear you," I insisted as I passed through the living room.

"Tell us about your contractor, Laney!" she singsonged. "Did you jump him?"

"Can't we talk about Lawson and *Oliver* again," I demanded desperately. "Sounds like there's a heck of a story there, huh?"

Predictably, they ignored me. And when I passed the kitchen table again, Lawson was leaning back in his chair, rubbing his salty fingers together gleefully. "Laney *jumped* his contractor? Our little Laney? Fuck yeah!"

"Fuck *no*," I huffed, pushing my glasses up. "And I'm not *little*. I am a man of average size and weight—"

"So, I don't know if Laney actually jumped him yet," Tam was already saying. "But Brewer is gorgeous, Law. Like, *so* jumpable. He's got dreamy eyes and shoulders like *whoa*. So I advised jumping him—"

"Tamsen Marie! You are a married woman!" I stopped directly in front of her and clutched the baby tighter. "Leave Brewer's shoulders alone."

"—but thinking about it later," she went on, "I'm not sure that was *good* advice."

"You're not?" Lawson and I said together.

"Well, I don't know Brewer all that well," Tam told Lawson. "The guy hardly ever talks—"

"That's not true. He talks plenty," I informed her. "*Plenty.*"

"And he's bossy—" Tam went on.

"No," I muttered. "Not anymore."

"And..." Tam sighed. "You know how stubborn Delaney can be, Law. How he likes to argue for the sake of arguing when he's feeling vulnerable—"

"I do not!" I argued... stubbornly.

"So, as you can imagine, he and Brewer do *not* get along." Tam shook her head sadly.

"We do! We're being very polite." I wondered if I sounded as miserable about this as I felt. I'd preferred our arguments to the way Brewer and I had orbited around each other this morning before he got called to Watt's, not touching and only talking when necessary.

"Even though Brewer's hot, I'm just not sure he and Delaney would really be compatible in a... *jumping* scenario, if you know what I mean," Tam finished.

"Excuse you, we were absolutely compatible!" I said hotly. "We were fire! We *jumped* literally all night!"

The kitchen was silent for a long moment but for the hum of the refrigerator. Then, a slow smile spread across Tam's face.

I lifted my chin. "I hate you," I said as I resumed my steady, measured, *non-pacing* walk. "Both of you. I do not appreciate being managed."

"It was either that or get you liquored up, if we wanted

you to be honest," Tam said apologetically. "So... what happened?"

I blew out a breath. "If you must know, Brewer and I hooked up. During the storm, the night before last. And that information stays in this room, do you hear?" I shot both my siblings a glare that said I meant it.

Tam nodded.

"Dude, I don't share your business. Besides, who'm I gonna tell?" Lawson demanded.

I huffed out a breath. "I know, but it's not just *my* business. Brewer wants to maintain his professional reputation and doesn't want the town to know he hooked up with a client. Especially since it was only a onetime thing. A bad idea. A... a complication." This time, I was sure my unhappiness was audible.

"Did *Brewer* say that?" Tam's chin jutted out mulishly, and her eyes narrowed. "About *you*?"

"Huh. Where's this guy live again?" Lawson asked with deceptive calm. "And how big is he, exactly?"

I gave a half laugh. "Don't even *think* about beating him up, Law."

"Who said anything about beating him up?" Lawson blinked innocently. "I'm a pacifist, bruh. I just wanted to have a pleasant chat with him. That's all."

I shook my head. "Like you had a *chat* with Marc Broder after he checked me too hard during practice when we were twelve? You threatened to run over him with a Zamboni."

"Hey. That was Tamsen," Lawson insisted, pointing a finger at her.

This was unfortunately true.

"And when Martin Phillipowski called me a pansy-assed

nerd and you *chatted* with him, and the next day, he acted like he was too scared to speak in my presence? Was that Tam, too? Or when Dad got rid of Gretzky because I couldn't handle my fear, and you all told me it was fine, even though I know you cried over it?" I shook my head. "I'm not weak. I don't require anyone's protection or pity. I can take care of myself."

"Who said you were weak?" Lawson scoffed. "And who pities you, Mr. I'm Flying To Costa Rica, Hold My Calls? Jesus, Laney. Us being protective doesn't mean we think you're incapable. It means we fucking love you." He crumpled the empty chip bag. "Asshole."

My shoulders loosened and fell. "Anyway, it doesn't matter. Because I... I agree with Brewer. It was a... a one-night storm-induced moment of insanity. But he and I are very different people with wildly different lives. We have nothing in common."

Except musicals.

And wine.

And jam-cupboard mysteries.

And firelight chats.

And sledgehammers.

And the new cabinets he'd begun designing, after getting my input on the sketches and the specific materials I wanted.

And the way he made me feel strong and competent and understood. Like I *fit*.

"It's simpler this way," I said with finality. I continued bouncing Tierney, though the urge to walk had mostly faded.

Tam and Lawson both watched me for a long moment. Lawson's look was mostly sympathetic, like he understood my feelings all too well.

Tam's look was more calculating. "I'm sure you're right," she began.

"Oh, God." I rolled my eyes. She didn't sound sure at all.

"But hear me out. If you *did* want something to happen..."

"Tam. I don't!"

"If you *did*... Brewer won't always be your contractor," she pointed out. "So *maybe* you could find a way to let him know you'd *maybe* be open to the possibility of a repeat, if he was *maybe* interested. Then you could sort of... keep it casual and see where things go."

I shot her a look. "Aren't you the woman who forbade your siblings to use hookup apps within a ten-mile radius of Copper County so the gossips wouldn't hound you for details? And now you *want* me to hook up with Brewer?"

She shrugged. "What I want is for you to be happy, Delaney." She motioned to Lawson. "That's all either of us wants."

The timer on the stove went off again, and everyone—including the baby—raised their heads.

"Speak for yourself," Lawson joked, standing up and heading to the drawer to grab some potholders. "I want *lasagna.*"

I laughed.

Tam squawked and attacked Lawson with her dish towel when he tried to sneak a taste of the molten hot lasagna after she told him to "Wait for Lucas to get home for dinner, you barbarian."

And thankfully—very thankfully—the moment passed.

But as I walked up my driveway later, past the piles of neatly shoveled snow, I kept thinking about Brewer—I mean, *obviously*—and about what Tam had said, too.

It was exhausting, pretending that I didn't want him, that I wasn't thinking about him all the time, and that the "bad idea" of starting something with Brewer didn't feel like the best idea I'd heard of in a really long time.

So what I needed to do was convince Brewer somehow. Provide him with a compelling argument—the best one of my career—that it was worth exploring what was between us, at least temporarily.

No matter how hard I tried, though, I couldn't think of a compelling reason to convince him to ignore his damned principles and touch me again.

Until twenty-four hours later when the idea finally came to me.

CHAPTER TWELVE

BREWER

Two days after the storm, I still couldn't get the taste of Delaney Monroe out of my mouth.

I ran my palm over the smooth poplar board I'd been sanding for his kitchen cabinets, checking for imperfections. Like the knots in the wood, my thoughts kept circling back to the same spot no matter how much I tried to smooth them away—Delaney on his knees in front of me, his glasses askew and his blue eyes looking up, determined and hungry.

Christ.

I adjusted myself in my jeans and focused on the cabinet design I'd sketched out with Delaney's input—one that would blend the industrial feel he wanted with the home's traditional character. Reclaimed metal hardware he'd sourced on the warm wood I'd suggested, with glass panels on the upper cabinets to make the space look light and airy. His style, my craftsmanship. Nothing either of us could have come up with on our own.

The normalcy of the work was grounding. Simple. Unlike the shit my brain *wanted* to stew over, like the way Delaney's hands had moved over my body, and the way he'd said my name when he came, and how badly I wanted to do it all again.

"Fuck," I muttered under my breath.

After I'd gotten back from Watt's yesterday, things with Delaney had been... awkward. I'd wanted to get back to some level of normalcy, which meant no casual touching. No lingering looks. Instead, with the exception of working on the cabinets or the day-to-day business of living together, we'd tiptoed around each other literally and figuratively, careful with our movements and even more careful with our words... which was the opposite of normal for Delaney and me.

When I thought about it—which I'd done pretty much from the moment Delaney had fled to Tam's house for dinner—he and I had never had an easygoing, polite relationship.

Delaney had a million opinions and would argue passionately about each and every one. I *didn't* usually have opinions to volunteer, and even when I did, it was rare that I let myself care enough to fight over them. But it was different with Delaney.

He was so damn determined not to compromise who he was or what he wanted, he might as well have the words "Take Me As I Am, Bitches" tattooed on his forehead. And yeah, that meant our conversations were often heated. But seeing him be so open and honest made *me* want to speak up more. To figure out my own opinions and express them. To care about things enough to fight about them... and for them. To be known... at least by Delaney.

But all the reasons I'd given Delaney for why it was a terrible idea for us to take things further were still there. His job. My job. Our very different lives—

KAK-WEEEE!

The doorbell rang for the fourth fucking time that morning, jarring me from my thoughts.

And for the fourth time, I reminded myself that I'd agreed to this... sort of.

When Delaney mentioned yesterday that he planned to share our find with Janice, I'd known what would happen—the news would travel around Copper County at twice the speed of sound, and the entire town would *need* to see "Delaney's jam cupboard paintings" for themselves. But seeing Delaney so excited, I hadn't protested.

Now, it wasn't even noon, and we—well, *Delaney*—had already had six visitors today alone.

From the living room, I heard Delaney's voice bright with enthusiasm as he explained the composition of one of the lake paintings to whoever had arrived. The sound of him happy like that did something to my chest that I didn't want to examine too closely.

I turned back to my work, only to hear approaching footsteps.

"And *this* is where we found them!" Delaney's voice grew louder as he led whoever-it-was toward the kitchen. "In a vintage jam cupboard that's been hidden in the wall for decades! Can you believe it?"

I glanced up to see Delaney's sister holding Tierney against her chest. Her eyes darted between me and her brother with obvious interest.

"Hey, Brewer," she said with a knowing smile. "I heard you and Delaney made some... amazing discoveries the other night."

Clearly, Tam had gone to the Watt Bartlett School of Double Entendres.

"Tam. Good to see you." I glanced at the baby. "And Tierney. She's growing fast, huh?"

"Like a weed," Tam agreed. "So... any idea who E. Winters might be?"

"Not me," I answered, "but I'm sure someone will. And since half the town's come by to see the paintings—"

"Not that many," Delaney protested. "Like, half a dozen." He paused. "Or possibly a dozen and a half."

"Delaney told Janice," Tam said, shaking her head. "He should've known better."

"It was really just members of the Council for Historical Happenings," Delaney continued. "As well as a few other... key stakeholders."

"Key stakeholders," I repeated, fighting a smile. "Like when Constantine Bloom brought his kids by for a field trip yesterday?"

"His children were sweet and respectful," Delaney argued. "I think it's commendable that he values education." He shot Tam a look. "I bet *he* understands the importance of walking to the development of the newborn brain."

"And when Janice brought Angela Ross to see them this morning, was *that* educational, too?" I wondered, unable to keep from teasing him.

"No." Delaney lifted his chin haughtily. "If you *must* know, that visit wasn't about the paintings at all. Angela came to renew her invitation for me to join her book club." He considered, then added, "And *then* she saw the paintings."

"Her book club," Tam repeated. "I thought you told her you didn't have time the first time she asked."

"I... I did," he admitted. "Who wants to read because they *have* to when there are too few hours in the day to read what you *want* to? But Janice happened to see the book I'd left open on my tablet when she was here earlier, and it turns out that's the exact book they're reading this month, so…" He shrugged. "I said I'd swing by the Books n' More next Wednesday."

"Oooh," Tam said eagerly. She did an unconscious little bounce-and-swing move that was putting the baby to sleep. "What's the book? Maybe I've read it, too! I've been thinking I need to get out more. Postpartum life, you know?"

"Oh. Um." Delaney cleared his throat and looked away, but I'd swear he was blushing. "I don't think you've read this one, Tam."

Tam's eyes narrowed. "How do you know?"

"I just… I don't think…"

"If *you* enjoyed it, why wouldn't *I* enjoy it?" she demanded in a whisper, probably out of deference to her sleeping daughter. "I do have brain cells. And I know you think you're the only intellectual in the family—"

Delaney whirled around in shock. "What? No, I don't."

"—but I do read from time to time. Actual books, with no pictures in them. And I do have a shiny college degree I got all on my own."

"I know!"

"And just because I know how to play hockey and light a fire in your fireplace, that doesn't mean I don't enjoy reading and discussing literature, just like *you* being a smarty-pants, big-deal, traveling journalist doesn't mean you don't enjoy sledgehammering the fuck out of your *kitchen*," she finished in a whisper-yell. "Tell him, Brewer."

Eyes wide, I lifted my hands. "Whoa," I said. "I don't think—"

Delaney looked from me to her, then ran a frustrated hand over his head. "This is like me not understanding you guys being so overprotective, isn't it?" He tugged the hair at his crown. "Tam, I know how smart you are. If anything, I'm jealous of *you* and how good you are at freaking *everything*. At how easily people take to you." He put a cautious hand on her arm and gave her a teasing smile. "It's tough being 'Tam Monroe's brother, the one who doesn't play hockey.'"

"Probably about as tough as it is being Delaney Monroe's jock sister," she challenged, raising an eyebrow. But then she shook her head. "Don't mind me, Laney. I'm worried because Law seems unhappy with his new team, and I'm literally fizzing with postpartum hormones, and... as much as I *adore* my daughter, I'm bored as fuck, being stuck at home, mostly alone, thanks to the weather." She sniffed. "So... what's the book?"

Delaney pressed his lips together. His cheeks turned red, and he darted an almost guilty look at me. Then he mumbled, "Timdbythekurkinwrlrd."

Tam and I exchanged a glance. I shrugged.

"Could you repeat—" Tam began.

Delaney blew out a breath. "I said, *Tamed by the Kraken Warlord*. Okay? It's a profound emotional journey about a headstrong young man who accidentally finds himself imprisoned on a planet ruled by Krakenpeople. It's a metaphor for our society, Tamsen, illuminating the challenges of—"

"Oh, Laney." Tam's eyes danced. "Does the young man have sex with the kraken warlord?"

Though his cheeks were still pink, Delaney raised his chin once again. "Irrelevant. You can't dismiss a book simply because—"

KAK-WEEEE!

Delaney's ridiculous doorbell sounded again, making me and Tam jump and Tierney start to fuss.

"Delaney, what is that sound?" Tam demanded. "It sounds like someone's strangling a muppet."

"I was thinking *deranged cuckoo*," Delaney said. "But I dunno. It's kind of growing on me."

"If you could keep the parade of visitors out of the kitchen while I'm sanding, that'd be helpful," I called, only half-serious, as he headed for the front hall.

Delaney turned in the doorway. Our eyes met, and for a moment, I was back on the living room floor, his body under mine, his plaster handprints all over me.

"Okay." His voice was rough, like he'd gotten caught in the same memory. "Yeah."

The doorbell rang again, and Delaney turned back to answer it.

"Well," Tam said, inspecting the cabinet sketches I'd taped to the wall. "I'm glad to see you and my brother are getting along better."

"Of course." I shrugged, feeling my face heat. "We had some differences of opinion in the beginning, but I think we've realized we're on the same side now."

She laughed. "That's huge. Delaney's the most stubborn person I know, but that means he's also the most loyal. If Delaney's on your side—"

She broke off as a man's voice came floating down the hall.

"This is *just* like Season 2, Episode 9 of *John Ruffian: Pretender!*" Chris Sunday said excitedly. "You know the one where John pretends to be an art authenticator to expose a gallery owner who's selling forgeries, only to discover the cache of real paintings in the secret compartment behind the bookcase?"

"Chris... I have no idea what you're talking about," Delaney said. "I've never seen *John Ruffian*."

Tam snickered. "Oh, he's in for it now," she said under her breath.

"Ohmigosh, Delaney! Okay, as soon as I set down this tray, I'm emailing you an episode order because if you watch the episodes chronologically, you'll miss the—oh!" Chris paused in the hallway, a small platter in his hands. When he caught sight of me and Tam, he grinned brightly. "Hey, guys!" He glanced down at Tierney, who was blinking sleepy blue eyes, and his whole face softened. "Hey, sweet girl."

"Hey, Chris," Tam said warmly. "You wanna hold her for a bit?"

"Heck yes!" He glanced down at the platter and then looked around at the utter lack of flat surfaces on which to set it. "Er... trade you?"

"Is that one of your winter charcuteries with the honey-comb?" Tam demanded. "Because if so, that's a fair trade."

Chris laughed. He handed Delaney the plate, practically ran to the bathroom to wash his hands, then took the baby and settled her against his chest with a murmured "Theeere we go, sweet potato. You're okay."

Delaney and I exchanged an amused glance... then he bit his lip and looked away.

"The, um... the paintings are in the living room," Delaney said. "If you wanted to look."

"I do! But... I'm really interested in the jam cupboard, to be honest." Chris pushed up his glasses, which were a little larger than Delaney's. He peered into the opening Delaney and I had created and took a deep breath. "Oh, man! It smells like cedar and lavender from a hundred years ago, doesn't it?"

"I thought the same thing," Delaney agreed.

"Reed and I haven't found anything this cool during our renovation yet. But maybe you'll be our lucky charm when you do the kitchen, huh, Brewer?" He turned his guileless blue eyes on me. "Still thinking you can get started in a few weeks?"

"Around that," I agreed easily, though the reminder that this project would be over soon made me uneasy.

I'd be moving out, even if it meant renting a place for a while since I wouldn't stay here once the renovation was done.

Would I be glad I'd dodged a complication bullet? Or would I regret the missed opportunity?

Or would I bite the bullet and try something reckless and ill-advised, like asking the man out?

"I'll be able to give you a more exact date once I get these cabinets done," I told Chris, nodding at the boards I'd been sanding.

Delaney gave me a guilty look. "We should probably get out of the kitchen and let Brewer get back to work," he told Chris and Tam, making me wish I hadn't complained earlier.

They filed into the living room, but even after they were gone, my attention kept drifting back to them. To Chris, who was crooning at the baby. To Tam eating honeycomb and teasing him about being a baby whisperer. But mostly, as usual, to Delaney, who sounded more relaxed and happy than I'd ever heard him.

Being alone had been my happiest state for so long it was strange to find myself wishing I was in the other room with them.

By four o'clock, the stream of visitors had dried up, and everyone had left. Despite the interruptions, I'd made good progress on the cabinets, and just before retreating to his office for a call with his editor, Delaney had promised no more "tours" until tomorrow. So I was surprised when the doorbell rang again, startling me just as I was putting away my tools.

Since I could still hear Delaney talking, I answered the door myself.

"Brewer, my dude!" Kel wore his Kitchen Couriers hat with a lime-green parka, a pair of sandals over thick socks, and a bright grin. "How's one half of the Dynamic Duo of Demolition?" He added in a conspiratorial tone, "That's what me and Hayes decided to call you."

I rolled my eyes. "Kel, if you're here to see the paintings—"

"Nah, man. Janice said Delaney put out the word. No more coming by and interrupting you 'cause you need to finish your job quick," he recited. "So I'm here in a strictly professional capacity." He picked up an enormous white Courier bag he'd set by his feet and extended it with a flourish. "Burger Barn order for Delaney."

"Oh." I frowned. It wasn't a surprise that Delaney had ordered dinner, but usually, he asked if I wanted anything. Then again, I imagined he was done with socializing for the day... and possibly done with *me*.

"I'll give it to him," I said, taking the bag.

"Kel?" Delaney emerged from his office wearing a pair of soft cotton pants and a V-neck sweater, his glasses askew like he'd been toying with them. "Hey. You're early. I thought I scheduled you for five."

"Tryna keep my best tipper happy." Kel grinned. "Especially when he's the guy who got our service area extended."

"You're... pleased about that?" Delaney demanded.

"Shit, yeah. Doubled my tips. And our manager read one of your letters out loud at our last staff meeting. He said it was the most passionate plea for food delivery he's ever seen." He lowered his voice and added, "I cried."

Delaney looked embarrassed. "Well. That's... good. I guess." He looked at the bag in my hand. "Everything in there?"

Kel's chest puffed up. "Dude. I don't make mistakes." He winked again. "If you get the urge to *pound* anything tonight to see if you can find any more, ah, hidden treasures... remember safety first."

"Bye, Kel," I said, swinging the door closed, but not before we heard Kel chuckle as he walked away.

Once he was gone, Delaney and I stared at each other for a beat too long. He looked good—really good, even better than usual. More mouthwatering than whatever was in the delivery bag.

Belatedly, I held the bag out to him. "Your dinner. I'm guessing you want to have a quiet night." I summoned a smile. "I'm done for the day, so I'm gonna grab a shower, walk Teeny, and head to the Bar and Grill so you can have the house to yourself."

"No, wait." Delaney's hand shot out and covered mine on the bag. I had the impression of his smooth fingers against mine for just a second, and then he blushed and snatched his hand back like he'd been burned. "I got food for you, too. It's not... I mean... You said we were friends, sort of, so I thought..."

"Okay," I blurted, not letting myself think too much about it.

"But obviously, if you'd rather go out, that's—"

"Delaney," I reminded him softly, as I so often did. "I said *okay*. Just let me shower and see to Teeny first."

"You, ah..." He blew out a soft breath and didn't quite meet my eyes. "You can bring her, too, if you want."

"Yeah?" Delaney's "detente" with Teeny had extended to us all sleeping in the living room, but I hadn't wanted to push the issue, so I'd continued to keep her upstairs for the most part.

"I said I'd work on it." His eyes met mine. "I keep promises, too."

My heart rate ticked up, but I forced myself to nod easily. "We'll be back in a minute, then."

Teeny's excitement when I led her into the office a half hour later was off the charts. Unfortunately, so was mine, especially when I saw that Delaney had moved his laptop, cleared off his desk, and set up our takeout containers like a little picnic. He'd even fetched us soda from the fridge in the laundry room.

"Sit," I told Teeny, pointing to a spot by Delaney's visitor chair.

Delaney pointed to a white paper bag on the desk. "Looks like they misdelivered me dog biscuits again," he said with a put-upon sigh. "Not sure how that keeps happening. But since they're here, you, ah... might as well give them to her, I guess."

"Misdelivered?" I peered at Delaney over his desk. "But Kel doesn't make mistakes."

Delaney opened his mouth, then closed it again, a flush rising up his neck to his cheeks.

"You know what I think?" I went on. "I think you're secretly in love with my dog, and you're trying to win her affection with dog biscuits."

"Yes." He rubbed his hands on his pants nervously. "You caught me, Brewer. This heart-pounding terror is all an elaborate ruse."

I shrugged. "I think you can want something and fear it at the same time. Right?"

Delaney's eyes met mine, and then he looked away. "Right," he said softly.

I grabbed the bag off the desk and held out a biscuit, not to Teeny but to Delaney. "Go on, then. Give her a treat."

Delaney blinked at me. "What, like... put my hand close to her mouth?"

I shrugged. "You said you're working on it. No risk, no reward, right?"

He studied me for a long moment. "Yeah," he said with a strange intensity to his voice. "Yeah, I guess you're right." He took the biscuit from me with the tips of his fingers. "Teeny? Come here, girl."

"Gentle," I warned her since the way she normally ate treats—or anything at all, really—made it seem like she'd never seen food in her entire life.

Teeny approached Delaney slowly, like she had some strange, innate canine sense that she needed to not make any sudden motions. Then she sat with her tail swishing lazily against the area rug beneath Delaney's desk.

Delaney's arm shook a bit, and Teeny sniffed the biscuit gingerly, as though she'd never seen one before.

I rolled my eyes. The two of them were ridiculous. And kind of adorable.

Teeny took the treat gently from his fingers, her tongue barely brushing his skin.

Delaney exhaled a shaky breath. "Huh. That wasn't so bad."

"See?" I said. "Progress." I could hear the pride in my own voice and wondered when I'd started caring so much about Delaney conquering his fears.

"Speaking of progress," he said, wiping his hand on a napkin before picking up his burger, "how's the kitchen coming? I know we turned your workspace into Grand Central Station."

"It wasn't that bad." I took a fry from my own container.

"Things are coming along. I got most of the base cabinet frames built, and Hen said I can return the red cabinets Monday, which will give me more space to move around in there." I wiped my mouth on a napkin. "What about you? Any progress on your article?"

"Nope." Delaney grimaced. "I took a side quest and looked into our Jam Cupboard Mystery instead." He licked a bit of sauce from the corner of his lips. "I googled E. Winters yesterday and found an artist with the same name." He unlocked his phone and began typing. "A pretty prolific mid-century painter who had a couple showings at the Met. I'm not sure if it's *our* E. Winters, though. Does this look similar-ish to the paintings we found?"

He turned his phone and scrolled up and down, displaying some paintings of urban scenes. A taxicab in the rain with faceless pedestrians hurrying by. A park with the Empire State Building in the distance.

I squinted at the images for a minute, then shook my head. "I can't say. Those are pretty, but they don't reach out and grab me like the ones we found. Maybe because the subjects are so different?"

"Maybe, yeah." He frowned at his phone, then turned it off and set it down. "We'll have to wait for the appraiser to come by next week to know for sure. And I'm meeting with Samuel Purchase tomorrow."

"I bet he'll know something," I said. "I think he grew up in Copper County. Have you done a record search on the previous owners of the house? I'm more curious how the paintings got there than who painted them."

"I haven't pulled any records yet, but I will. Janice did say the house was vacant for a while before the owners put it on the market last fall, though, so who knows how long the paintings were there."

I took a quick sip of soda. "That tracks. It was vacant when I came to town. I do know it's a 1932 Arts and Crafts bungalow designed by Everett H. Lowell, but I don't think that helps answer these questions."

Delaney laughed. "No... but it actually brings up several more." When his eyes sparkled behind his glasses, it was really fucking hard to look away. "Not just a theater nerd but an architecture nerd, huh, Brewer Barnum?"

"No." I shifted uncomfortably on my chair. "I mean, not architecture in general. I do love Craftsman-style houses, though."

"Yeah? Why's that?" Delaney munched a french fry, but the look in his eyes left no doubt that he was focused on my answer. That he genuinely wanted to know.

And to my own surprise, I found myself answering, explaining the various houses I'd worked on with my grandfather growing up and how something about the intentionality of the Craftsman style spoke to me.

When I mentioned that the use of local stone in his fireplace designs was one of Everett Lowell's hallmarks, Delaney's eyes widened. He'd written a piece on sustainable building materials, he said, and he jumped in to explain how similar techniques were being revived in modern eco-architecture.

He wasn't just humoring me; he was genuinely engaged, making me draw connections I'd never considered, which, in turn, made me want to share even more.

Before I knew it, Teeny yawned dramatically, drawing both our attention, and when I glanced at the clock on Delaney's bookcase, I saw that hours had passed.

"Well," I said with true regret. I'd probably spoken more words tonight than I had all week, and I still could have talked to Delaney for another few hours and not felt the time. "I guess we should go to bed."

The word *bed* hung in the air, charged with meaning.

"I meant me and Teeny," I added quickly. "Obviously."

"Obviously," Delaney echoed.

We cleaned up his office, then walked down the hallway together, stopping at the foot of the stairs, where we'd go our separate ways.

"Thanks," I blurted. "For the dinner and the conversation. I figured you'd be tapped out after so many visiting Coppertians."

"Nah. This was the best part of my day." Delaney flushed, as if realizing he'd said too much. "Because of Teeny, I mean. Conquering my fears and all." He bent down to give the dog's head a cautious pat, and Teeny panted happily.

Jealous of my damned dog.

"Well." I rubbed the back of my neck, suddenly feeling awkward. "Good night, then, I guess."

"Yeah," Delaney replied. "Good night."

Neither of us moved.

The air between us crackled with tension. His eyes dropped to my chest for a split second, then back up. I swallowed hard, remembering how his fingers had caressed the very spot he'd just been looking at.

How his lips had felt under mine.

How his body had responded to my touch.

With significant effort, I took a step back. "Come on, Teeny," I called, my voice embarrassingly hoarse.

As Delaney watched us go, I'd swear there was disappointment in his eyes.

In the attic, I stripped off my jeans and stretched out on my air mattress while Teeny settled onto her bed and immediately began snoring. But tired as I was, I couldn't sleep.

I'd made the right call, leaving Delaney tonight. I knew I had. I needed to focus on work, to finish the renovation, and then to move on. It was a solid plan.

Unfortunately, my body disagreed vehemently, still thrumming with *want* from that charged moment in the hallway—hell, from every fucking moment we'd spent together in the past few months.

Acting on that want the other night had only made the wanting worse... which was why I would not be doing that again.

I flopped to my back, propping one hand behind my head, and stared at the shadowy beams in the ceiling. From the other side of the wall, I heard water running through the pipes as Delaney got ready for bed, and then silence.

I closed my eyes, willing sleep to come, but just as I started to drift off, a faint noise jerked me back to wakefulness.

A moan. Soft but unmistakable.

I froze, straining to hear. Was Delaney having a nightmare? Should I check on him?

Another moan, slightly louder. Followed by the rhythmic creak of his bed.

Oh.

Oh, fuck.

Heat rushed through my body. Delaney wasn't having a nightmare. He was... I swallowed so hard it echoed through the quiet attic.

Next door, the sounds continued, growing more distinct. The cadence of creaking quickened, punctuated by small, helpless noises that went straight to my groin. Without conscious thought, my own hand drifted down, pushing aside the waistband of my underwear and wrapping around my rapidly filling cock.

Maybe Delaney had the right idea. Being around him all day had me in a constant state of pent-up arousal, and I hadn't jacked off since the day of the storm, when I'd taken care of my morning wood while imagining Delaney on the other side of the wall—

I sat bolt upright, mind racing.

Holy shit, had *he* heard *me?*

I hadn't realized how thin the walls were until this moment, and while I couldn't remember how loud I'd been that morning, I knew I hadn't been silent. So if Delaney had heard me, and he was making this much noise now...

He *wanted* me to hear him.

He was fucking *provoking* me.

As I sat there stunned, another low moan came through the wall, this one louder and more desperate. "*Brewer! Fuck. Yesssss.*"

My body responded instantly, blood rushing south so fast I felt light-headed. I could picture him perfectly—head thrown back against the pillows, one hand working beneath the sheets, the other perhaps pinching a nipple or splayed across his stomach. That visual, paired with his voice calling my name, sent a jolt of pure lust through me that was almost painful in its intensity.

I was out of bed and down the attic stairs before I could think better of it, moving on instinct and raw need. I moved through the house and up the inside stairs like a lightning strike. Then I paused outside his door, my hands braced on the cool wood of the jamb, giving myself one last chance to turn back.

The sounds continued, growing more urgent. My cock pulsed in my underwear, straining against the fabric as I listened to Delaney's quickening breaths, the occasional creak of the bed springs, the unmistakable slick sounds of his hand working himself faster.

A guttural moan filtered through the door. "God, Brewer, please…"

Those words, the plea in his voice, shattered the last of my restraint.

I knocked once, then opened the door without waiting for a response.

The room was dimly lit by a bedside lamp, casting everything in a warm golden glow. Delaney lay on his back naked, one hand working beneath the sheet. He stilled when he saw me. Glasses off, his blue eyes were wide and unfocused, his chest rising and falling rapidly.

"Need help with that?" I asked, my voice low and rough.

For a heartbeat, he just stared at me. Then, slowly, he nodded.

I crossed the room in three strides, yanking my shirt over my head as I went. The sheets were cool against my heated skin as I climbed up and straddled him.

Delaney jackknifed up and reached for me immediately, greedy hands skimming over my chest, my shoulders, my back. "Oh, fuck yes."

My own hands were just as greedy, tracing up his arms and over his collarbone, then up to cup his face.

"You knew I could hear you," I murmured.

His eyes met mine. "Yes." No apology, no embarrassment—just uncompromising Delaney honesty.

"You were trying to get me in here? Despite all the complications?"

"No risk," he said, quoting my earlier words, "no

reward." Then his fingers tangled in my hair as he pulled my mouth to his.

The kiss was hot and demanding. Pure hunger. I nipped at his lower lip, then soothed the sting with my tongue. He made a desperate sound in the back of his throat and arched against me, pushing his dick against mine with only the smooth sheet between us. I spread my legs, bracketing his thighs with mine, and groaned at how fucking good it felt.

Delaney's fingers slid into my underwear and then down, pulling me closer. "I want to feel you," he whispered, pushing at the waistband. "All of you."

I stood and quickly shed my underwear, then pulled back the sheet covering him. Then I paused for a moment to drink him in—the lean lines of his body, the flush spreading across his chest, the way his lips were already swollen from our kisses. "You are so fucking beautiful."

He gave me a crooked smile. "Not like you."

Not like me, I wanted to tell him, but like *himself*, which was infinitely better. But when I lowered myself down so we were pressed together, chest-to chest and dick-to-dick, I found I couldn't speak. My breath caught, and a broken moan escaped me.

Delaney's hands found my ass, urging me to put more of my weight on him, and I was helpless to resist. I rocked against him experimentally, the friction sending sparks of pleasure up my spine.

His legs twined around mine. "More," he begged.

I complied, setting a rhythm that had us both panting. He lifted one leg to wrap around my waist, changing the angle and increasing the pressure in a way that made my vision blur.

"Fuck, Brewer," he gasped, his hips rising to meet each thrust. "Just like that."

I buried my face in the curve of his neck, breathing in the scent of him—clean skin with the faint, floral smell of his soap. His hands roamed my back, my shoulders, my arms, like he couldn't get enough of touching me.

The pace quickened, our bodies sliding together with increasing urgency. I felt the familiar tightening at the base of my spine, the gathering heat that signaled I was close.

"I'm not going to last," I warned, my voice strained.

"Me neither," Delaney admitted, his breath hot against my ear. "Don't stop."

As if I could. As if anything in the world could make me stop when he was underneath me like this, moving with me, saying my name like a prayer.

His soft hand slid between our bodies, wrapping around both of us. The added sensation was almost too much. I cursed, my hips stuttering as I fought to maintain the rhythm.

"Come with me," he urged, his grip tightening.

It was his voice that pushed me over the edge—that command all wrapped up in a plea. I came with a shudder that racked my entire body, Delaney following moments later, his release spilling hot against my hand and his belly.

For a long moment, we lay there, tangled together and breathing hard. I shifted to the side slightly, not wanting to crush him with my weight, then rolled toward the edge of the bed. He made a small sound of protest, his arms tightening around me as if to keep me close.

"Don't go," he murmured, his voice already sleepy.

"Just getting a towel," I assured him. I cleaned up in his bathroom and brought back a damp cloth for him, too.

"You can stay," he said hesitantly. "If you want."

After a moment—more like a millisecond—of deliberation, I climbed back on the bed and pulled Delaney against me, resting my head on his pillow and draping my arm over his waist. I was pretty sure I wasn't imagining the way Delaney's whole body relaxed when I did.

We lay in silence for a minute while Delaney traced lazy patterns over my chest, his touch light but deliberate. "Should I apologize?" he asked softly.

I knew what he meant, but I couldn't help snorting. "For being so fucking sexy I literally ran through the house to get to you?" I pretended to think about it. "Actually, maybe you should. There were a *lot* of stairs."

He laughed, the sound light and happy as he cuddled against my chest. "Next time I want you, I'll just use a sledgehammer and save you the trip," he said, motioning toward the wall.

Next time.

I waited for the urge to pull back and put distance between us to grip me... but the feeling never came. Instead, a kind of contentment spread over me and settled. The die had been cast, the decision made. However long this physical connection between us lasted, however messy it would be when it ended, I was in it now.

And with Delaney in my arms, it was impossible to regret it.

As we lapsed into comfortable silence, his fingers continued their idle exploration of my skin, and I found myself relaxing into his touch, taking a true deep breath for the first time in days.

I cleared my throat. "I think I might owe *you* an apology," I said. "I pulled away the last couple days. Which is kind of my go-to, if you listen to Hayes."

"I get why you did." Delaney lifted his head. "You care about your professional reputation. Nobody understands that more than I do..." He rolled his eyes. "Even if I happen to be doing a shit job of focusing on my own career this week." His gaze softened. "The complications are real. I just... wanted you too much to stay away."

The honesty and vulnerability in his voice made my chest tight, so I leaned up to kiss him, hard and messy, pulling his lower lip between my teeth.

"Same," I admitted a few breathless moments later. "I want you, Delaney. That was never in question."

Delaney settled himself against me with a sigh. "Maybe we should—"

"Tell me about the article you're supposed to be writing," I blurted, changing the subject before I could say anything more revealing. "No breakthroughs, you said? No mustache-twirling bad guys revealing themselves?"

"Shockingly, no." His nose wrinkled adorably. "I can't remember how much I told you, but the goal of the article is to expose this really shitty housing developer, Empire Ridge. I have evidence that shows they've done a bunch of shady stuff, but what I really want is to prove—" He frowned up at me. "Hey, you okay? You just got all tense."

"Did I? Sorry," I said, forcing myself to relax. "I recognized the name. Empire Ridge."

"Oh my God." Delaney threw a leg over me and twisted up to prop his chin on my chest. "I'm such an idiot. I can't believe I didn't ask my *renovation specialist* if he knew the fucking *huge* construction company that's headquartered, like, two hours from here!" He rolled his eyes. "Have you worked with them? Or do you know anyone who has, who'd want to go on the record for my article?"

I took a deep breath... then hesitated. It was on the tip of my tongue to tell Delaney the whole truth right then—that Empire Ridge had bought my grandfather's house and destroyed it, just as surely as my father had destroyed my grandfather's company, that I hated everything they stood for—but I couldn't.

Here in Delaney's bed, in his arms, I was *happy*. Delaney was, too, I thought. Dredging up ghosts of the past wasn't how I wanted to spend this night.

"I've never worked with them," I answered honestly. "I've heard of people who have and regretted it."

Delaney nodded and settled himself against me again. "Truth," he said. "They're sharks who've fucked over a lot of people."

"Which is why," I couldn't resist adding, "only unscrupulous people get involved with them in the first place."

"Or desperate people. Either way..." Delaney yawned hugely. "This story's going nowhere, which means I'm not leaving for Costa Rica anytime soon."

Costa Rica. Right. *Fuck*.

I tightened my arm around him, suddenly afraid of how easily I could get used to this—to having him beside me, in bed and in life.

I wanted to build things that lasted. That was who I was at my core. And Delaney...

Delaney was a hurricane, just as I'd told him. He'd moved to Copper County on impulse, he'd blown things into chaos, and soon he'd move on, first to Costa Rica and then to wherever his next story led. Hurricanes didn't stick around long.

"You okay?" Delaney asked again, his voice thick and drowsy.

"Yeah," I lied. "Fine. Just tired."

He hummed in acknowledgment, his breathing already evening out as sleep claimed him, but I lay awake a while longer, listening to the steady rhythm of his heartbeat against my chest.

I knew whatever Delaney and I had was temporary. It couldn't be serious, and it would be foolish to let myself believe it could. But as Delaney shifted in his sleep, his body instinctively seeking mine, I wondered if I had any choice in the matter.

Because the truth was, it wasn't just physical like I'd tried so hard to convince myself.

I couldn't remember a time when I'd felt as content, as calm, and as purely *myself* as I did curled up against this man who was my opposite in every way but had somehow burrowed past all my defenses.

My last thought before sleep claimed me was that I was going to enjoy this ride for as long as it lasted, even knowing the tracks might run out long before I was ready.

After all, hurricanes were known for leaving devastation behind.

CHAPTER THIRTEEN

DELANEY

I'D ALWAYS BEEN a one-obsession-at-a-time guy; ask anyone. I'd date one person—usually the worst possible person—until I realized I was super unhappy, and then I'd move on. I'd throw myself into a story, chase it to the ends of the Earth, then move on to the next. A serial obsession monogamist, if you will.

But as I strolled down Weaver Street in O'Leary on Wednesday morning with a wrapped painting under my arm, I found myself obsessing over not one but *three* different things because, apparently, I was becoming an overachiever.

First was the obsession I was calling *E. Winters and the Jam Cupboard Mystery*—which, yes, sounded like the title of a lesser-known Hardy Boys book, but I was going with it.

Second, the Empire Ridge story, aka *The Avery Decker Award-Winner Delaney Never Finished.*

And third, *The Case of the Extremely Hot Contractor Whose Talented Hands and Mouth Should Come With a Warning Label.* I was still workshopping this title.

Of the three, though, there was only one that was truly consuming my brain every waking moment.

Brewer Barnum, with his crinkle-cornered eyes, big, comfortable chest, and tip-tilted smile had hijacked my brain... and he made me feel so very *good*, I wasn't even mad about it.

I'd told myself, when I woke up this morning still cuddled in Brewer's arms, not to get too used to it. We were "friends, sort of" but now... possibly with benefits. A contractor and client who'd shared a bed on occasion. Simple biology mixed with proximity—the baking soda volcano of relationships—that would soon fizzle out. I'd recounted to myself, ad nauseam, all the reasons why that was all it could be.

But by the time I left the house a few hours later, I'd had to stop lying to myself.

I could pretend it was casual all I wanted, but I practically vibrated when Brewer walked into a room, purred when he smiled, and had stared at the precise angle of his jaw so long I could sculpt it out of clay in the dark, though I was barely capable of drawing stick figures. None of that felt casual.

Yes, that was scary as fuck, thank you for asking.

And no, I had no idea what I was going to do about it. The man wasn't exactly open with his emotions, and it was too soon to bring it up.

Or maybe I was too scared.

I reached the *Gazette* office and paused outside, willing my body to settle down. Samuel had asked if I could meet him here to talk about the paintings, and I really didn't need to walk in sporting a semi because I'd been thinking about Brewer and his jaw.

Get it together, Monroe.

The bell above the door jingled as I stepped inside, and I was immediately enveloped by the scent of ink and old paper, though I was pretty sure they didn't actually print newspapers here. Something about the space felt immediately comfortable—three battered wooden desks set in a row, each stacked high with folders and notes; a century-old printing press displayed in the corner; a wall of framed front pages marking historic moments in Copper County's history.

It was cute, in a wholesome way.

Charming, if you liked that sort of thing.

And to my surprise, I kind of did.

But no sooner had my shoulders relaxed than I spotted Samuel's tiny terror curled in his doggy bed by the desk. Admiral Barkington lifted his head to fix me with beady eyes and let out a sharp yip.

"Don't mind him, Delaney," said the older man rising from behind the desk. "Admiral Barkington thinks he's the welcoming committee. We're both happy to see you again."

I recognized Samuel Purchase from our brief encounter at O'Leary Hardware a week and a half ago, and I extended a hand in greeting while keeping a careful distance from the Admiral.

"Mr. Purchase," I said. "Hi. Thanks for making time to see me on such short notice—"

"Samuel, please." He shook my hand briefly, then waved me to a chair in front of my desk. "And don't thank me. Everyone's been talking about the treasures you uncovered for days now, and I've been dying to see them for myself. I was nearly giddy when I got your text."

I laughed as I set the painting on the desk, and he immediately started to unwrap it. "I'm afraid I don't know for sure who the artist is or how they came to paint so many scenes around Copper County. I have an appointment with an art appraiser who'll hopefully tell me more. But I was mostly wondering if you could tell me why they would've been hidden in my wall—"

Samuel's breath caught as the final bit of wrapping fell away and he took in the lakeside autumn scene. "Elizabeth Winters," he said softly. "My God."

"You recognize the artist?" I asked in surprise.

He glanced up at me distractedly, like he'd momentarily forgotten I was there. "Hmm? Oh, yes, these are Elizabeth Winters's work—E. Winters, as she was professionally known."

"Really? Because I saw some E. Winters paintings online, and they were..." I hesitated. "Different."

Samuel smiled and sat back in his chair, though his eyes kept returning to the painting. "Yes, Elizabeth was best known for her urban landscapes. Street scenes, crowded cafes, subway platforms. Very bright and energetic. Lots of faceless people—"

"Yes!" I sat forward eagerly. "That's exactly what I thought."

He nodded absently. "The work she did in Copper County was quite different. More... personal. Not as well-known, I don't think... but that might be because she gave so much of it away." He smiled. "For example, I have a portrait at home that she painted of me, aged seven, eating an apple with no front teeth."

"Wait, you knew her?" I demanded. "Personally?"

"I did. I imagine most folks around here knew Elizabeth —at least, folks of a certain age." Samuel gave me a wink and ran a hand over his thinning gray hair. "She was a Coppertian, after all."

I stared at him, stunned. "*Was* she?"

"Yes, of course. She owned your house once upon a time," he said, seeming bemused. "You didn't know?"

I shook my head, but of course, it made perfect sense. So many of the paintings of Copper Lake looked like they could have been painted in my backyard… because they had.

"I didn't know a single thing about my house when I bought it," I admitted. "Except that it was close to Tam's house, and it felt… happy."

It felt like a silly thing to say about an inanimate object, but Samuel simply nodded. "I always thought so, too. My mother and Elizabeth were friends, so I spent quite a bit of time there as a boy. Elizabeth and Jean were Copper-plates back then—summer residents," he explained, "but they moved here full-time in… oh, '76 or thereabouts? When I was in high school, anyway. Jean taught English at the high school."

"Jean?"

"Jean Soler." Samuel tapped the edge of the canvas gently. "Elizabeth's partner."

I stared at the woman in the painting. At her secret smile. At how the light seemed to caress her. At how she radiated off the canvas, though I couldn't have picked out one remarkable thing in her figure or her features that made her beautiful.

Elizabeth had painted Jean in a way that rendered the stunning lake, the vibrant trees, and the expansive sky as mere backdrop for Jean's heartbreaking loveliness.

"When you say partner," I asked softly, sure I already knew the answer, "you mean…?"

He smiled. "I mean they were very much in love, yes." He sat back, steepling his fingers, and his face took on an abstracted look. "If I recall correctly, Elizabeth was already a fairly established artist when they met. Jean was a writer—brilliant woman, worked for several magazines. They collaborated on a project, don't ask me what, and... sparks flew." His smile softened. "And kept flying, as long as I knew them."

"And... and people here were okay with that?" I demanded. "Two women, in the seventies?"

Samuel tilted his head from side to side. "There might've been some folks who muttered behind their hands. But most folks just saw two women who made each other happy. Small towns can be surprising that way, Delaney. We know each other too well to waste our energy on hate."

"Huh. The rest of the world wasn't like that then. Hell, it's not like that now in lots of places."

"True." He pursed his lips. "Which might explain why these paintings were hidden, I suppose. I never knew Elizabeth painted Jean like this. I imagine she kept those paintings close to her heart. I did hear that when Jean died in the nineties, Elizabeth changed. Retreated from everything, even her art." He shrugged. "She might've hidden these away, not knowing there'd come a time when their life together would be viewed as anything but scandalous."

My chest tightened as I studied the painting again. "That's really tragic," I said softly. "Because this is beautiful."

"*They* were beautiful," he said. "I remember thinking so, even when I was a kid. And they set a high bar for love, let me tell you. I spent years searching for a relationship like theirs. A true partnership."

"Did you find it?" I asked, noting the gold band on his finger.

Samuel smiled, turning the ring thoughtfully. "I did.

But I had to come full circle to find it. Isn't that always the way?"

I shook my head. "I don't follow."

"I grew up here, but I couldn't wait to leave. Real life happened in big cities, I thought. So I became a reporter for the *Boston Globe*. Spent fifteen years there, covering everything from city politics to international crises."

"Impressive," I said, meaning it. "So why'd you come back?"

"My mother got sick. Cancer," he said simply. "I took leave and came back here to help care for her, thinking I'd stay a few months. Then I met her doctor, Marcus, and we've been together ever since." He laughed out loud. "Dear God. The expression on your face, Delaney."

"Sorry! Sorry," I said. "It's just very..." I hesitated. "Hallmark movie?"

"Yes, so my niece tells me," he said wryly. "And yet..."

"But didn't you miss it?" I demanded. "I mean, I'm sure Marcus was worth it, but wasn't it kind of a letdown, covering the annual town spelling bee and whatnot, when you could've been covering so many bigger stories?"

Samuel's eyes twinkled. "That's the secret no one tells you, Delaney. The stories aren't bigger in the city, just louder. Here, I know the people I'm writing about intimately. I know their *whole* story, not just the newsworthy moments. I still do cover big stories, just... from a narrower perspective." When he leaned back this time, his chair creaked. "I find it more fulfilling, honestly."

"I... I suppose," I said, not entirely convinced.

He shrugged. "Not for everyone, for sure. But if you ever decide you're interested, let me know. The *Gazette* could use someone with your talent, whether it's telling

Elizabeth and Jean's story—" He nodded down at the painting. "—or something else entirely."

"I don't..." I started to decline automatically, but something made me hesitate. "I mean, I've got an assignment already and another in Costa Rica waiting in the wings, so I appreciate the offer, but..."

Samuel nodded, unbothered. "Beautiful thing about Copper County," he said, rewrapping the painting carefully, "is that it'll still be here. Door's open, if and when you're ready."

From his bed, the Admiral gave a halfhearted *yip*, and I startled.

"The Admiral agrees," Samuel said with a wink.

I thanked him and left, the wrapped painting tucked securely under my arm, but the drive back to my house was filled with thoughts of Elizabeth and Jean, of hidden love and hidden art, and of a community that had quietly accepted what the larger world would not.

By the time I got home, I was practically buzzing with excitement to share everything I'd learned with Brewer. I burst through the door, calling his name.

"Kitchen!" he called back.

I rounded the corner to find him kneeling on the floor, hands coated in sawdust like giant powdered donuts, frowning fiercely as he checked the level on one of the cabinet bases he'd built.

I grinned automatically.

But then Brewer glanced up, and his whole face lit, like just the sight of me made him *glad*, and that made my stomach tremble.

"Hey," he said, setting down his tools and standing. "How'd it go with Samuel?"

I opened my mouth, then closed it again. The way

Brewer looked at me—like I was remarkable, like my presence was important—felt dangerous.

"Good," I managed to say. "Very good." I set the painting down on the workbench Brewer had set up and jammed my hands in my pockets so I wouldn't reach for him. That was boyfriend behavior, not... whatever it was we had right now. "Guess who accidentally bought the house once owned by E. Winters, well-known artist and former resident of Copper County?"

Brewer's grin widened. "No kidding?"

"Honest truth. And the woman in all the paintings? Her *partner*, Jean." His excitement amped my own exponentially, and suddenly, I couldn't stop the flow of words, yanking my hands out of my pockets and gesturing excitedly. "They lived here together for *decades*. Samuel said they couldn't be open about their relationship in the larger world, but here in Copper County, people accepted them."

"Wow." Brewer's eyes never left my face. He leaned against the cabinet he'd been working on and wiped his hands on a rag distractedly, seeming content to watch me bounce around the kitchen like a kid hopped up on sugar.

"Samuel thinks Elizabeth hid the paintings after Jean died in the early nineties. She probably never imagined there'd be a time when their story could be told openly." I paused, suddenly feeling emotional. "It's sad, you know? That she felt she had to hide her best work. The paintings that probably meant the most to her."

Brewer pushed off from the counter and moved closer, lifting a hand to push my hair off my forehead.

I froze.

"You had some sawdust," he murmured.

My heart hammered wildly. *Brewer* was covered in

sawdust. I hadn't touched a single thing since entering the kitchen. There was no way...

I swallowed hard and nodded. "Sawdust," I whispered. "Thanks."

"You know," he said without moving away. "I think it's pretty lucky that those paintings were found by a man who wants to make sure everyone has a voice and likes to make things fair and right."

Something warm and sweet unfurled in my chest. "Yeah?"

"Yeah." His deep voice held utter conviction. "You'll make sure their story gets told, Delaney."

I sucked in a breath and looked away. Brewer's faith in me meant something. Way more than it should for a friend... sort of. Even one with benefits.

"Thank you," I said, feeling some kind of way. I stuck my hands back in my pockets before I did something incredibly stupid, like grab Brewer's beautiful face, kiss the ever-living shit out of him, and tell him to mate me like one of the Krakenpeople. "So... dinner tonight?"

"Okay."

"Or not," I added. "I mean, you're not *required* to eat dinner with me every night just because you're staying—"

"Delaney," Brewer called from mere inches away.

I looked up and met his big blue eyes. "Yeah?"

"I said... *okay*." He smiled. "Dinner sounds good."

And it was...

But what happened after that was even better.

CHAPTER FOURTEEN

I sucked at keeping my distance from Delaney.

This was especially true when the man was bent over, perfect ass showcased in faded jeans, reaching for the pipe connection under the sink cabinet I'd pointed out thirty seconds ago.

Christ, how was any red-blooded man supposed to maintain professional boundaries when faced with that view?

Then again, my plan to stay professional had basically crumbled when I'd heard him through the wall last night, moaning my name. And when he'd returned from meeting Samuel Purchase, flushed with excitement about a long-lost love story?

Moth, meet fucking flame.

Watching Delaney's eyes light up as he shared the discovery about his house's previous owners had done something to me I couldn't explain. His whole face transformed when he talked about things that mattered to him, and knowing how quick he was to care about women he'd never met had pulled me in even deeper.

Our conversation had continued over a sandwich dinner, Delaney getting choked up about Elizabeth hiding her paintings, me finding any excuse I could to touch him or breathe his air because I wanted to be as close to him as possible.

The strength of my reaction scared the fuck out of me. It felt like Delaney wasn't just breaking through my walls; he was making me want to disassemble them myself, brick by brick.

"What am I looking for here, Brewer?"

I snapped my head up and squinted at Delaney. While staring at his ass was an incredible way to spend an evening, it wasn't conducive to high brain function. "Hmm?"

Delaney shook a wrench at me. "Do I want this dealie or the other thingamajig?"

Right. *Plumbing.* We were working on the pipes under the freshly installed sink cabinet in the kitchen. Because, scared as fuck or not, I hadn't been ready for good night, so when we'd finished dinner, I'd blurted out an offer to teach him about plumbing.

Because nothing said *distance* like seeing Delaney on his knees, head in the cabinet, presenting his tight ass to me, right? Nothing said *control* like watching his pants slide down his hip bones inch by inch as he shimmied around. Nothing said *resistance* like hearing him breathlessly mutter, "Jesus, you're so tight," to a particularly stubborn piece of PVC or growl, "That's right, you fucking stay where I put you," to the P-trap that had slipped out of alignment.

It was the most porn-tastic scenario I'd ever witnessed in real life, starring the most gorgeous man I'd ever met, and if I hadn't already known I had a knack for unintentional self-torture, plumbing with Delaney would've been all the proof I needed.

Still, the man was so damn enthusiastic, it almost —*almost*—made the torture worthwhile.

"Okay, first off," I said mock-severely, crouching by his hip, "they aren't 'dealies' or 'thingamajigs.' Respect your tools, Monroe." After a pause, I picked up a wrench and added, "You want this doohickey here, with the open end."

"Doohickey. Got it." Blue eyes twinkled under his glasses. "Thank you for teaching me your language, Brewer. If I'm ever off on assignment and find myself stranded in a remote mountain Home Depot, I'll be able to communicate."

I snorted. "Yes, you'll stun them with your understanding of P-trap assemblies and instantly be accepted as one of them."

"New life goal." Delaney's answering grin was infectious. "Now, get under here with me and tell me what to do with these nuts."

Jesus Christ. If I continued down this path of "enjoying the ride while it lasted," I'd be riding this fucker straight to hell.

But because I still hadn't learned my lesson, I obeyed and slid to the floor beside him.

"These," I said, picking up a metal fitting, "are hex nuts. They secure the pipe connections. You tighten them with the wrench I just gave you."

"How tight do I want my nuts?" he asked, all innocence.

I rolled my eyes. "Not so tight they crack, but tighter than you can get them with, ah... with just your fingers." I took a deep breath and inhaled Delaney's sexy bodywash and fabric-softener scent. "You kind of have to go by... feel."

"Huh. Will you show me?" Delaney's voice was lower than it had been a moment before.

I swallowed and reached for his hand, wrapping it around the wrench and guiding it to the connection. "Like this," I murmured, demonstrating the proper pressure. "You feel that resistance?"

His breath caught. "Y-yeah."

"That's where you stop." My voice sounded like it had been dragged over gravel.

Delaney was silent for a beat too long. Then... "But what if I want to keep going?" he whispered.

When I turned my head, our faces were inches apart.

"Delaney," I said softly, half warning, half plea.

His gaze dropped to my mouth, and he sighed.

"I think," he said slowly, setting the wrench down with a soft clink, "I might be done with the home improvement portion of the evening."

"Yeah?" I managed. My heart hammered so freaking hard I was sure he could hear it. "What do you want to do now?"

"Well. That kinda depends on you." Delaney's lips quirked. "You said you wanted to be professional, but last night, I... well, *wasn't*." His eyes met mine, frank and honest. "I want you, Brewer. But I don't want to keep pushing you. I don't want to get my way because *I'm* convinced I'm right, and I disregard what you want. I don't want our hooking up, or whatever you call it, to be something that happens because I'm relentless, and you get swept along—"

I surged forward, capturing his mouth with mine, unable to wait another fucking second.

I couldn't remember the last time someone I cared about had prioritized my comfort like that, and the fact that stubborn, headstrong, fucking gorgeous Delaney *had* undid me completely.

The kiss was deep and hungry from the first touch, my tongue sliding against his with an urgency that made him gasp. His hands immediately clutched at my shoulders, pulling me closer even as I pressed him against the side of the cabinet and explored his mouth.

Fuck, I loved the taste of him. I could get drunk on the little moans he let slip.

My thumbs slid against his stubbled jaw as I angled his head, taking our kiss deeper. *This* was Delaney, I thought—rough and soft, prickly and pliant, hot and sweet.

"For the record?" I said, interspersing each word with kisses. "It's not just you, Delaney. I want you, too. As much of you as I can have."

Before it ends, I thought but didn't say.

Because I refused to dwell on something that fucking depressing, I moved my leg over Delaney's, fitting us together from chest to thigh, until the press of our bodies made the thought spin right out of my head.

Delaney's answering smile was incendiary... and worth every wall I'd let down to get us here. "Then have me." He gripped my hair in both his hands again and pulled me into another kiss.

We kissed like we were starving for each other because, even after just a few hours apart, we were.

We scrambled out from the awkward cabinet space, hands already reaching for each other before we were even fully upright. I backed him against the temporary workbench I'd set up, lifting him to sit on it and then stepping between his spread thighs. His arms wrapped around my neck as he pulled me to him once again, but this time, his mouth skated along my cheek, his tongue licking at the edge of my chin.

My cock pulsed in my jeans.

"Fucking love your jaw," Delaney murmured. "Your chest. *God.*"

My *jaw?* The very idea would have made me laugh if the press of his thighs against the outside of mine hadn't stolen all my breath.

"I've been wanting to do this all night," he confessed, the words skating over my damp skin and raising goose bumps. "Watching you work, seeing you in your element… it's ridiculously hot."

"Yeah? Hex nuts do it for you?" I slid my hands up his thighs, squeezing gently.

"Shut up." Delaney nipped at my lower lip. "You know what I mean."

I did. I knew *exactly* what he meant. Because watching him try to figure out plumbing, his brow furrowed in concentration, had nearly driven me out of my mind.

"Too many clothes," Delaney complained, his fingers making quick work of the buttons on my shirt before working at my belt.

"Agreed," I growled. My hands found the hem of his T-shirt, pulling it up and over his head. Delaney shivered, but I was already pulling his chest against mine and slotting my mouth back over his, warming him inside and out.

When the kiss broke, I'd somehow laid Delaney out on the drop cloth beside the cabinets. The thin cloth barely cushioned the hardwood floor, but he didn't seem to care.

His hair was mussed, his cheeks flushed, his lips swollen from my kisses, his glasses slightly askew.

I hovered over him, drinking in the sight.

"Brewer," he said hoarsely, his hands roaming across my shoulders and down my arms like he couldn't get enough.

"God, you're beautiful," I murmured.

"Says the man who looks like he walked out of a lumberjack fantasy," he shot back.

Laughing, I lowered myself to kiss him again. Everything about Delaney was addictive—his sweet taste, his clean scent, the needy sounds he made when I kissed my way down his neck.

"Brewer," he gasped as I found a particularly sensitive spot below his ear. "I want you to fuck me."

The words hit me in the solar plexus, and I sucked in a breath. "Yeah," I managed. "Yes. Fuck yes."

"Upstairs," Delaney instructed. He pushed at my shoulders. "Please, Brewer."

I knew he was right—we had no supplies down here, so if I kept him pinned to the floor, this night would end with a very satisfying frot and not with me inside him the way I wanted to be—but it was hard to make myself move. I kept going back for another drugging kiss, and another...

"Brewer!" he demanded breathlessly. He gripped my hair and pulled me back, pausing only to bite my bottom lip gently. "This is not like the cabinets."

I frowned, trying to make sense of his words while also trying to kiss him again. "Huh?

"I know exactly what I want *and* what I need," he informed me. "Are you going to make sure I get it?"

Well, when he put it like that...

We barely made it up the stairs, stopping every few steps to kiss, to shed my jeans so Delaney could run his hands over my ass, to grab him by the shoulders, pin him against the wall, and suck a bruise into his collarbone.

By the time we reached his bedroom, we'd both lost our

pants and stumbled through the doorway in just our underwear.

I backed Delaney toward the bed, my mouth never leaving his, until his knees hit the edge and we tumbled onto the duvet together. He reached for his nightstand drawer, producing lube and a condom, tossing them beside us on the mattress.

"How do you want this?" I trailed my mouth down his chest and across his stomach, feeling him tremble beneath my touch.

"Just like this," Delaney said promptly, pulling me up to face him. "I want to see you. I want to feel your eyes on me."

That might have been the hottest thing I'd ever heard.

I nodded jerkily as I reached for the lube. "I'll make it good for you," I promised. "I'll take it slow—"

"You better not," he said breathlessly. "Don't you dare hold back. I can take anything you give me."

"Anything?" I challenged. "Then let me take care of you."

I took my time prepping Delaney, every touch deliberate, every kiss soft and slow, trying to show him without words how very all in I was.

My hands roamed over his chest and legs, feeling him relax under my touch. Patience was thin on the ground, but I'd had enough of him by now to know I didn't want to rush it. Delaney was meant for savoring tonight, not scarfing him down in one quick bite.

When I finally moved my hand between his legs, he was biting out curses, challenging me with dares, and pretty much trying everything to get me to go faster.

"Your begging just makes me want to slow down, Monroe," I teased as I gently smoothed a finger against his entrance, circling slowly until I felt him open up for me.

His breath hitched as I slid my finger inside of him. Delaney tensed... then his whole body melted into my touch.

I moved slowly, memorizing his face, learning what made his eyes roll back in pleasure and what made his lips part in a silent gasp.

"That's it," I murmured, adding a second finger and scissoring gently. His back arched, and a broken moan escaped his lips. I moved up and kissed his shoulder, whispering words of encouragement into his salty skin. His body responded, relaxing further, and I slid a third finger into the heat of him.

Delaney writhed on the bed, hands gripping the sheets, hips moving in sync with my fingers. His cock was rock hard, leaking against his stomach, and his breath came in pants. "Touch me," he begged. "Brewer—"

"Not yet, baby. Fuck, you're doing so well. You feel incredible."

His slim body shuddered in response—whether from my words, or my fingers, or both—and he whimpered softly. I could feel him clenching around my fingers, his body eager for more.

And Jesus fuck, so was I.

I slowly withdrew my fingers, rolled on a condom with lightning speed, and slathered more lube over myself. I positioned myself at his entrance, taking one second to appreciate the heat radiating from him... then I pushed inside.

"Oh my fuck. Fuck. *Fuck*." Delaney threw his head back, pushing into the mattress and arching his body as I filled him slowly and relentlessly.

When I finally bottomed out, I had to pause, letting us both adjust to the intensity of the moment.

Being this close to Delaney was overwhelming. I could

feel his heartbeat against my chest, the rise and fall of his breath syncing with mine.

Delaney, who was usually so prickly and opinionated, looked utterly undone beneath me, and I felt something fundamental shift inside me.

This was Delaney without his armor, without his need to control everything, proving that vulnerability didn't equal weakness.

And it was the most breathtaking sight I'd ever seen.

His eyes fluttered open, meeting mine. A soft, almost shy smile played on his lips. "Brewer," he murmured, his voice barely audible. *"Brewer."*

The way he said my name sent a jolt straight to my cock. I could already feel the heat building in my balls, the tension coiling in my gut. I began to move, each thrust deliberate and deep, hitting that spot inside him that made him gasp and writhe.

"Fuck, Delaney," I panted against his neck. "You feel amazing."

"Don't stop," he panted, his body tensing beneath me. "Oh God, right fucking there."

I had no intention of stopping. Not when his body was taking me so perfectly, not when every thrust brought those incredible sounds from his throat, not when I could feel him tightening around me as he got closer to the edge.

His cock throbbed between us, leaking and desperate for release. I reached down, wrapping my hand around him, stroking him in time with my thrusts.

His eyes squeezed shut, his mouth fell open…

"Come for me, Delaney," I growled low. "Let me feel you come on my cock."

His body convulsed around me, his cock pulsing in my hand as he came, hot and hard, and the sight and feel of his release pushed me over the edge. My balls tightened, and with a groan, I came, shuddering hard, whispering Delaney's name like a promise.

We collapsed together, our bodies slick with sweat. Every limb felt numb from exertion and the strength of my orgasm, but Delaney's arms and legs wrapped around me, holding me in place, as though he didn't want us to separate just yet.

I understood the feeling.

Neither did I.

Eventually, though, I did roll to the side, disposing of the condom and returning with a warm cloth to clean us. When we'd finished and I got back into bed, Delaney immediately turned to face me.

"Fuck, Brewer..." he started, then stopped like all words had failed him.

I chuckled, still boneless and breathless, and flopped onto my back. "Better than plumbing?"

He grinned. "Possibly, just the *tiniest* bit better," he said with a return of his usual snark. "But we might have to practice more for me to really be sure."

"Couldn't agree more. Once you pick out a replacement vanity for the downstairs bath, you can do all the piping yourself. Plenty of practice—"

Delaney poked my ribs, and I laughed before grabbing his hand and pressing a kiss to his lips.

"That is *not* the kind of practice I meant, Brewer." He propped himself up on one elbow. "I meant sex. With you."

"I know." I pushed back a lock of hair that had fallen over his forehead—which was becoming my favorite new hobby. "And yes, there'll be plenty of opportunities for that, too. I want to keep doing this. You and me. I can't seem to stop myself."

Delaney looked at me for a long moment, then settled himself against my side with a little huff that made me laugh. "Good."

We fell silent, the easy comfort between us both surprising and... not.

It felt natural to be here with him, holding him, our bodies still humming with aftershocks of pleasure.

It wasn't until the night deepened around us that reality began to seep back in.

Delaney had a life waiting for him outside Copper County. A career that would take him to Costa Rica and beyond. A plan for his future that likely didn't include a small-town contractor with a complicated past who both wanted to build things that lasted... and also hadn't let himself put down roots.

But even knowing all that—even being fucking terrified of that—I still couldn't bring myself to walk away from him again. Not when he fit so perfectly against me. Not when being with him made me feel more like myself than I had in years.

I'd compared him to a hurricane, and I'd meant it. But I was beginning to realize that some storms changed your landscape forever.

So, no, I wouldn't give up Delaney.

Not yet.

Not until I had to.

Not until he made me.

And maybe, a voice in my brain whispered, not even then.

CHAPTER FIFTEEN

DELANEY

When I pulled my little Audi into a spot on Weaver Street Monday morning, Marjorie had been chattering at me through my car's speaker for five full minutes.

"And Amber dug up some really interesting background info, not on Harmon specifically but on his company—"

"Sorry, Marjorie," I interrupted as I shifted into park. "I've gotta go. I'll read her email when I get home."

"And when will that be?" she demanded. "Delaney, do you want to finish writing this story or not?"

"Did your research assistant find proof that Empire Ridge set up Anthony Harmon?" I demanded.

Marjorie was silent for a moment. "Well, no, but—"

"Then, I can't finish, can I?" I replied.

"Delaney—"

I grimaced. I could hear the frustration in her voice, and I knew whatever she said next would involve Costa Rica, my schedule, and something along the lines of "what the fuck is going on with you this week?"

I also knew—or was, like, *ninety-five percent sure* I knew

—how I'd respond, but I wasn't quite ready to have that conversation yet.

Especially not when my sister was waiting for me at the bakery down the street.

"Talk soon, Marjorie," I said, and then I disconnected and stepped out onto the sidewalk.

The truth was, very little had changed for me in the past week... at least on the surface. I still lived in my mostly renovated house on the shores of Copper Lake, was still trying to write my Empire Ridge article, was still talking to various Coppertians to learn as much as I could about E. Winters and her Jean. But below the surface, the tectonic plates of my life had rearranged themselves completely.

I'd gone to book club last Wednesday—*me*, voluntarily mingling with Coppertians!— and loved it. I'd petted Teeny twice without having heart palpitations. And I'd spent every night with Brewer—sometimes having deep discussions, often laughing while we ate pizza, and always curled up, cum-drunk and satisfied, when we finally fell asleep.

The night Brewer had run across my house to "catch" me jerking off, something had shifted. While we hadn't had any kind of formal discussion about our... well, whatever you wanted to call it, neither one of us was trying to maintain any kind of professional distance anymore. And with every day that passed, with every stolen kiss and slow, eye-crinkling smile, it was harder to remember why the fuck I'd want to.

I'd started feeling something suspiciously, dangerously, like happiness... and I really, really hoped Brewer was feeling it, too.

If you'd told me two months ago—two *weeks* ago—that I could feel this way, I'd have called you a dirty liar. But it turned out when a person stopped clinging to the precipice of their old life and fully embraced the unknown, he discovered all sorts of things he'd been missing out on.

Take, for example, jam cupboards.

Heat swept through me so suddenly I nearly stumbled on a crack in the sidewalk as I remembered last night. One minute, I'd been standing in the kitchen peering into the jam cupboard, admiring the way Brewer had cleaned and oiled all the wooden shelves and added trim pieces around the opening. The next, Brewer's big hands had yanked me into the cedar-scented space, and I'd found myself backed against the shelves with six-plus feet of very hot, very hard man caging me in.

"I've wanted to try something since we uncovered this spot," he'd murmured.

"Oh?" I'd managed to ask, my voice already embarrassingly breathy. "What?"

"To see exactly how much you can fit in here."

"Don't you... don't you need a measuring tape for that?" I'd stammered as his tongue and teeth worked their way up my neck.

"Nah. For a project like this, I prefer to measure in Delaneys." Brewer had spread my arms wide like he was checking my wing span. He'd wrapped my left hand around the edge of a shelf and my right around the trim work he'd just installed.

"Perfect fit," he'd growled.

Then his mouth on mine had been hot and demanding, and his hands—God, those hands—had made quick work of my belt, sliding my pants and underwear to my knees. Brewer had dropped to his knees, too, right there in the half-hidden cupboard, and used his tongue to draw a moan from me that might've startled the loons on Copper Lake.

He'd swallowed me down in one smooth motion, his

hand cupping and rolling my balls in a way that had my eyes crossing. And then I'd felt his finger pressing, circling, teasing my rim, not quite pushing in but promising more.

I'd come embarrassingly fast, my body racked with shudders as Brewer swallowed every drop. Then he'd tucked me back in, kissed me softly with a mouth that tasted like me, set his perfect, *perfect* jaw, and gone right back to the trim work like he hadn't just performed the hottest sex act of my life.

Jam cupboards were the best thing *ever*.

In fact, I was pretty sure—*ninety-five* percent sure, as I said—that I never wanted to be without a jam cupboard again.

But it was ridiculous to consider changing your life for a jam cupboard.

Irresponsible, really.

Wasn't it?

I was still considering that question when I stepped into the warm, fragrant interior of Fanaille and spotted Tam at a corner table, a steaming mug in front of her and a croissant already half-demolished.

"Finally," she said, pushing a second mug toward me as I sat down. "Your coffee's getting cold."

"Sorry," I said automatically, though my mind was still half back at the house. "Traffic."

She snorted. "In O'Leary? You mean three cars at the four-way stop?"

I took a sip of coffee and refocused on my sister. She looked good—her caramel-colored hair was pulled back in a ponytail, her cheeks had a healthy glow, and for the first time in weeks, the purple shadows under her eyes had faded.

"No Li'l T?" I asked.

Tam grinned. "Nope. She's with her daddy. Lucas and I figured out this amazing system where I get two hours a day, three times a week, to be by myself. Just Tam. Which makes it *so* much more fun when I get to go home and be Mama again." She sighed happily.

"Good," I said sincerely. "Because I like 'just Tam.'"

"That's also why I'm joining book club," she went on, taking another bite of croissant. "Oh, speaking of! I've been reading the kraken book, and oh my *God*. It's like *War and Peace* but with tentacles and love!"

I nodded absently, but my thoughts had already drifted back to Brewer.

To the way his voice dipped low when he said my name

"Delaney?" Tam waved a hand in front of my face. "Hey. You were a million miles away. Oooh! Were you thinking about tentacles?"

"What? No! Jesus. If you must know, I was thinking about..." I thrust out my chin. "Jam cupboards."

I told myself this wasn't a lie.

"Jam cupboards," she repeated slowly, her brow furrowing. "What about them?"

"Well..." I felt my cheeks heat. "How they're awesome? And special? And I've never had one before, but now that I do, I..." I swallowed, feeling ridiculously vulnerable. "I really love—I mean, *like* it. A lot. And I might want to, um.... keep it?"

Tam's eyes lit with understanding and excitement. "Oh, Delaney! You and Brew? That's..."

I darted a glance around the half-full bakery and gave her a warning look.

She cleared her throat and pressed her lips together. "I mean, yes. I can definitely see the appeal of a... jam cupboard. They're sweet, and helpful, and... so *broad*."

Remembering Tam's comment about Brewer's shoulders the other day, I narrowed my eyes.

"That's kind of the problem, though. Every time I look at... my jam cupboard... I feel safe and comfortable and happy. But..." I blew out a breath. "How do I know if I'm even a jam cupboard *person* when I've lived my whole life without knowing a jam cupboard like this one existed? What if I renovate my whole life because I want to... to keep this jam cupboard and then regret it?"

"Aw, Laney—"

"You know me, Tam. I've had bad luck with... cupboards in general."

"Haven't we all?"

"So how do I know that my feelings for my jam cupboard won't wear off? How does someone know if they want to have a jam cupboard permanently?"

"I mean, first things first, talk to the jam cupboard—" Tam broke off, shaking her head. "What the fuck am I even saying right now?"

"Tam, please?"

"Fine, fine." She waved a hand. "You picked this metaphor, let's roll with it. Get on the same page as your jam cupboard, step one. And then, stop thinking so hard about what you thought your... kitchen?... would look like. Could you imagine choosing a jam-cupboard-less life? Would you be happy knowing your jam cupboard was *right there*, but you never tore down the wall to find it?"

"I..." I tore my croissant into small pieces. "I'm thinking of telling Marjorie I don't want to go to Costa Rica," I admitted. "That maybe I don't want to travel at all for a little while."

Tam received this shocking revelation with a quiet nod.

"Did you hear me?" I demanded. "I said I might stop traveling."

"I heard." She shrugged. "When you moved here and bought a house, I figured it meant you were ready to slow down for a season."

I blinked. "No. I hadn't even considered that."

"No?" She chewed her croissant. "You just moved to a small town two hours from the closest airport and bought a property that requires maintenance? You don't think maybe you knew, subconsciously, that you needed a change?"

I frowned.

"You know, I never thought I'd be as happy as I am here," she went on. "I made fun of Lucas for years when he suggested moving closer to his family. But from the day I arrived, this place felt right. And that wasn't *just* because I love Lucas, even though he was the catalyst that made me move here. It was that... I could breathe here. That my thoughts could stretch out." She made a gesture with her hands. "That probably makes no sense."

I considered this for a moment. "The first few months I lived here, I felt like I'd found myself on the edge of a cliff, and I was clinging on for dear life. But then, suddenly..." I shrugged.

"You needed something to help you let go, long enough for your head to catch up to your heart," she finished. Her eyes took on a teasing glint. "A good jam cupboard will do that for you."

"Oh my God," I groaned. "I changed my mind. Call him Brewer."

"But where's the fun in that?" She nudged my foot under the table. "Though it's nice to see you admitting that you're falling head over heels for the guy. It's been obvious since the camper fire incident, you know."

"Nuh-uh," I said like the little kid I sometimes became around my siblings. "We didn't even like each other then. We fought all the time. He thought I was ridiculous and stubborn, and I thought he was bossy and arrogant—"

"And incredibly gorgeous, with really good shoulders?" Tam suggested slyly.

"Enough with his shoulders!" I protested. Then I sighed. "Yeah, essentially."

We finished our coffee, Tam gleefully extracting details about my relationship—shit, *was* it a relationship? It felt like I needed Brewer's buy-in before I could call it that.

By the time we got up to leave, I felt lighter than I had in days.

"Thanks for listening to me ramble," I told her as we pushed open the door and stepped out into the cool morning air.

"That's what siblings are for," she said, adjusting her purse strap. "That, and occasional free babysitting once my baby sleeps through the night."

"You're a mercenary woman, Tamsen Marie."

"Facts are facts, Delaney Patrick. See you at book club? I'm calling it right now—Commander Xorleth's mating bite makes his human grow tentacles."

I snorted. "I'll be there," I promised. And realizing that I actually *would* be able to be there, not just occasionally, at least for the next little while, brought a rush of relief.

Tam shook her head and waved, heading toward her car while I turned to walk back to mine.

"Delaney!"

I jolted as Janice Plum suddenly appeared from behind a decorative tree. I was starting to think she lived there.

"Janice," I said, recovering my composure. "Love the hoop skirt."

And she was, indeed, wearing a voluminous blue-and-cream hoop skirt that clashed completely with the produce-aisle cornucopia atop her head.

"You like it?" She twirled, the skirt swishing around her.

"You're a vision," I assured her.

"Aw. You're nearly as sweet as Brewer," she said, ducking her head. "Oh, speaking of! You two should come to the Historical Happenings candle-dipping event Sunday! I'm calling it 'Dip Your Wick with Janice.' Catchy, right? Just like you told me." She beamed. "I've already had five people sign up!"

Dear God.

I opened my mouth, hesitated, then closed it again. "I... will not be there," I said firmly. "But I hope it all goes well. See you at book club?"

I made it back to my car, feeling strangely at peace despite the prospect of facing Marjorie again. But when I turned the key in the ignition, my phone rang once more.

"Delaney," Marjorie began before I could say *hello*. "You didn't call me back."

"Because I'm not home yet. I'll read the email, I promise. This story is important to me."

There was a beat of silence.

"That's actually what I wanted to talk to you about. Delaney," she began slowly, reasonably. "You know there comes a certain point where we maybe have to admit that we haven't found a smoking gun because there *isn't* one. Right? While she was doing research on Harmon's company, Amber talked to quite a few of his former associates. None of them wanted to go on the record with a character reference. The opposite, in fact. He's known as being *very* ambitious and a bit... ruthless."

I frowned. "So?"

"So... maybe it's okay to walk back our goal from full redemption. Or maybe it's time to put a pin in this story and move on. The Costa Rica story—"

"Marjorie." I took a deep breath, considered for a moment, and realized I had no doubts. "I'm not taking the Costa Rica story."

This time, the silence lasted longer than a moment. "I don't understand," she finally said.

I ran my thumbnail over the logo on my steering wheel. "Look, I'm not saying I never want to travel again, but for the next little while, I'd like to stick close to home. To Copper County."

"But... but *why?*" she demanded. "I feel like there's a story here, Delaney Monroe."

"You could say that. *My* story." I laughed and counted out a twenty-word recap on my fingers. "I finally feel like I'm *who* I should be and *where* I should be, so I'm staying." I grinned, though she couldn't see me. "And Brewer's hot."

She sighed. "Yeah, I'm definitely going to need the full story."

"And you'll get it," I promised. "Along with a proposal for a new story about hidden artwork and true love. But for now, I'm going to focus on Empire Ridge. I'll read through Amber's email and give you an assessment by the end of the week."

"Fine," she said, resigned. "If you change your mind about Costa Rica—"

"You'll be the first to know."

Driving up to my house that afternoon, I found myself smiling at the very sight of it. The midafternoon sunlight glinted off the snow in the front yard, and the renovated porch looked sturdy and welcoming. Tam had been onto something with her visualization exercise. Just seeing the house made me feel settled in a way that surprised me. This house, this town, this life... it had all snuck up on me when I wasn't looking.

I rushed inside, eager for Brewer to be the first person I told about my revelations.

"I'm home!" I called excitedly.

"Delaney, come see this!" Brewer called back.

I found him in the kitchen, tightening the hinges on a cabinet he'd been installing—an upper cabinet with a glass-fronted door that made the kitchen feel larger and brighter. Through the glass panel, I spotted a familiar cup.

"What do you think?" he asked. He followed my gaze and explained, "Oh. Just using that to check the height of the shelves. Wanted to make sure your stuff fit comfortably."

Something about seeing that teacup—*his* teacup—sitting in my cabinet made a lump rise in my throat. It looked right there. Like it belonged. Like I wanted to make *Brewer's* dishes *my* dishes...

Which was a thought so sappy and ridiculous I found myself blushing.

"Looks perfect," I said, my voice coming out rough. "Perfect."

"Yeah." Brewer gave me a tip-tilted smile. "So, how was your morning?"

"Eventful." I took a deep breath. "I almost don't know where to begin. I had a convo with Marjorie, and I met Tam for coffee—she's doing amazing, and I talked to Janice." I briefly recounted Janice's historical hoop skirt ensemble. "We were invited to *dip our wicks with Janice* this Sunday, by the way—"

Brewer's eyes widened, and I burst out laughing.

"I told her I was busy," I said saucily. "But obviously, you'll need to make your own decisions."

I expected a smart-assed reply, but instead, Brewer's face softened. He reached out a hand to brush my hair back —a little motion he'd been doing compulsively and which I really loved. "I like seeing you like this," he said.

I shook my head. "Like I've been mildly traumatized by a woman in a hoop skirt?"

"Excited." His voice was warm and affectionate. "Happy. No sledgehammer required."

"Not today," I agreed. I leaned back against the wall, and Brewer moved with me. "But possibly tomorrow. I contain multitudes, Brewer."

"I'm discovering that," he murmured, bracing a hand on the wall beside my head. "You're like a million hidden jam cupboards, aren't you, Delaney Monroe?"

Brewer had no idea my stupid metaphor was a thing, but my heart did some complicated gymnastics anyway.

"I changed my mind," I whispered. "*That* might be the nicest thing you've ever said to me."

When Brewer kissed me, I could taste his smile, and it felt like coming home. The kiss was slow, thorough. A leisurely exploration rather than a desperate rush. His hand came up to cradle my jaw, thumb stroking my cheek in a gesture so tender it made my chest ache.

I sank into the kiss, my hands finding the solid warmth of his waist and slipping under his T-shirt to touch bare skin. He made a soft sound of approval against my mouth, pressing closer until I was pinned between his body and the wall.

We were both breathing hard when we finally broke apart, but Brewer didn't move away. Instead, he rested his forehead against mine, his eyes closed.

"You know the art appraiser will be here soon," I reminded him, though I made no move to push him away.

He huffed a laugh. "Always so responsible."

"Me?" I snorted. "Uh, no. That's definitely your role in this... this *partnership*, Mr. Promises-Kept."

Brewer's blue eyes opened, warm and amused. "Then why am I seriously considering taking you upstairs and making us both very, very late for that appointment?"

Heat pooled in my stomach at his words. "Tempting," I admitted. "But I really want to know what he thinks of the paintings. Maybe later we could..." My heart pounded, too fast and off-kilter. "Talk and stuff."

Brewer sighed dramatically, then pressed one more quick kiss to my lips before stepping back. "Yeah. Art first, debauchery later."

"Deal."

Dr. Richard Chen arrived precisely on time, his enthusiasm evident from the moment he laid eyes on the paintings spread out in the living room.

"Elizabeth Winters," he confirmed immediately, his eyes lighting up behind wire-rimmed glasses. "This is extraordinary."

I looked at Brewer, who'd followed me to the living room, and we shared a smile. Though I had zero reason to doubt Samuel, the validation was kind of a thrill.

Dr. Chen carefully examined the first painting without touching it. "Elizabeth Winters was quite prolific in her urban era, but I've always been a fan of her later work. The so-called 'Lake Period.' As far as I know, there are only about a dozen pieces from that time. She seemed to have become somewhat less productive."

Remembering what Samuel had told me, I offered, "Or perhaps she simply gave the paintings away."

Dr. Chen seemed startled. "I hadn't considered... possibly, yes. Either way, this is a significant discovery you've made, Mr. Monroe. I can't wait to tell my colleagues about it."

"And Mr. Barnum." I caught Brewer's arm and dragged him forward. "It was his discovery, too."

Brewer shook his head. "Not really."

"I assure you," I told him, "I wouldn't have broken down walls without you."

"You might, though," Brewer said under his breath as Dr. Chen went back to his examination. "Next time you decided to move an outlet."

I was surprised to find myself laughing at his teasing. But with Brewer, I didn't feel judged for what I wasn't good at but liked for what I was.

"What do you think we should do with them?" I asked later, when Dr. Chen finished.

"Well," Dr. Chen said, "these paintings should be cleaned and properly preserved, certainly. I'd be happy to connect you with a conservation specialist. After that... I suppose you'll have to decide what you want to do next."

I nodded.

"For insurance purposes, I'd conservatively appraise this collection at between $800,000 and $950,000. The museum-quality pieces alone—" He gestured to some of the larger canvases. "—might each command $60,000 to $75,000 at auction. But I must emphasize the historical and cultural significance of the complete collection far exceeds its monetary value. These works document not only an artist's private vision but, from everything you've told me, a hidden chapter of LGBTQ+ history. As a complete narrative collection, they could potentially fetch well over a million dollars if sold to the right institution or collector."

Beside me, Brewer's jaw dropped, and I knew mine did the same.

After Dr. Chen left, promising to email a formal appraisal, Brewer and I stood in the living room, staring at the paintings.

"A million dollars." I grinned up at him. "Guess you can get a fancy camper now, huh? What would you do with half a million?"

Something flickered across Brewer's face—discomfort, maybe, or surprise—and his smile tightened at the corners. "I wouldn't. I like a pretty simple life, Delaney. No need to split your imaginary money with me."

I frowned, confused by his reaction. "That's not—"

"I think the paintings should go to a museum," Brewer interrupted, taking a small step back. "I mean, if you wanted my input, I think that's where they belong. People should see them."

"Actually..." I smiled. "That's a great idea. I want everyone to be able to see them, too."

But the easy mood from earlier had suddenly evaporated.

"The Copper County Historical Society would be a good option. Or a bigger museum in the city." Brewer rubbed the back of his neck, still looking uncomfortable. Then, as if catching himself, he relaxed his shoulders and moved back toward me. "But there's no rush to decide. There's, uh... time." He slipped his arm around my waist, though the gesture felt slightly forced.

His sudden awkwardness sent an unexpected pang through me, especially after his strange reaction to the money talk.

I wanted that time. Badly. But it was occurring to me that, as much as I felt like I'd gotten to know Brewer through our late-night conversations, and as desperately as I wanted to know *everything* about him, there was a lot he wasn't telling me.

Brewer must have noticed something in my expression because he frowned down at me. "What's wrong? Did something happen with Marjorie? Is she changing the timeline for... for Costa Rica?"

"Sort of. Not exactly. I..."

My stomach fluttered with nerves. What would Brewer say if I told him I was planning to stop traveling? Would he immediately feel weird about it, like it was putting too much pressure on our quasi... whatever this was? The happy confidence I'd felt all morning seemed to have vanished without a trace, and I needed to find it again.

"Are you free for dinner?" I blurted. "Maybe we could go out, just the two of us. Get something to eat and talk."

Brewer winced, and I realized exactly what I'd asked. For Brewer to be seen with me in public—something that wouldn't be regarded as "professional" in the eyes of the town gossips.

Sure enough, he shook his head regretfully. "I can't tonight. I promised Hayes I'd see him. It's been almost two weeks, and... well, he moved to Copper County for me, so I try to catch up with him once a week or so."

"He did?" I found myself genuinely interested, not just relieved by the change of subject. Every time Brewer shared something about himself—a small fact, a piece of his history —it felt like being given a rare gift. "You guys are really close, huh?"

"He's like a little brother—in all the good and bad ways." Brewer huffed out a laugh, his eyes soft. "I don't have a lot of family, and when I went no-contact with my dad, I lost half of what I did have. Hayes stuck by me." He made a face. "Even if he *does* keep trying to get me to reconsider that now."

I felt a strange prickle at the back of my neck. The way Brewer talked about his father made me wonder just how deep that estrangement went—and what had caused it.

"Fuck that," I said. "I mean, if Hayes knows how strongly you feel, and he believed what you did was right..."

"He knows. Mostly," Brewer corrected, his jaw tightening. "He knows the facts. But I don't talk about it much. There's no reason to, really. Sometimes it's okay to walk away and protect your peace."

There was a story there—a bigger story than the brief outline he'd given me that night by the fire. But I didn't push.

Instead, I asked, "But if you told Hayes that, if he understood how strongly you feel about it and why, he'd stop trying to get you to reconsider. Wouldn't he? Wouldn't it be better to have the conversation, to talk about it even if it's hard, so that he could understand you better? And know what you want?" I attempted a smile. "Everyone deserves to have their story told, but that means you kinda have to *tell* it."

Brewer looked at me for a long moment. "Yeah," he said finally. "You're right. That's smart advice, Delaney."

"Ha. Well. I have my moments," I joked, but a twist of uncertainty snaked its way through me. If Brewer was this guarded with his own cousin, how much was he keeping from me? How badly was I deluding myself, thinking we'd gotten closer over the past week?

He tilted his head and studied me. "You want to talk about your Marjorie situation? I can bang together a cabinet out of scrap lumber, and we can get the sledgehammer if you need it after all. Or I could get your personal Kitchen

Courier to bring you some strawberry croissants. Somebody once told me they were *medicinal*."

The smile that spread across my face was so big it practically hurt my cheeks. Despite my sudden unease, I couldn't help responding to Brewer's warmth. A wave of affection had me stepping into him, wrapping my arms around his waist, and burying my head in that glorious chest.

"Hey, hey." He wrapped his arms around me instantly. "It's gonna be okay." He tilted my chin up. "I believe that, Delaney, 'cause I believe in *you*. Whatever it is, you'll figure it out, and I'll help you if I can."

I took a deep breath. That didn't sound like the talk of a man who was totally against the idea of a relationship, did it?

"The thing with Marjorie—well, part of it, anyway—is that the article I'm writing isn't going well, like I told you. Marjorie said I might need to accept that it never will. But I don't know. Part of me worries I'm just being stubborn, and the other part of me feels like I need to keep going. I don't want Empire Ridge to get away with their shit, and I want to get justice for the people they've hurt—"

Brewer's face went still for just a fraction of a second—so briefly, I might have imagined it—before he smiled.

"Well, I *like* how stubborn you are," he said, his voice warm despite the flicker I'd noticed. "I mean, it drives me crazy when it's in reference to the forty-seven bathroom vanities you keep saying aren't perfect—" He grinned. "—but I respect it. You don't compromise your principles. You do what you say you will. So if you feel like you want to let it go, then let it go. But if you want to get justice... stick to your guns, no matter what. Trust yourself."

"Wow." I studied him, wondering if the momentary

tension in his face had been my imagination. "Thank you." I leaned up and pressed a quick kiss to his lips. "And regarding the rest of the Marjorie stuff, can we talk tomorrow?"

"Of course." His mouth quirked up at the corner. "Whatever you want."

I felt my face flush. What *did* I want from Brewer, exactly? I was starting to think it was... everything.

He pressed a soft kiss to my temple, then went back to his cabinets, leaving me feeling both hopeful and increasingly unsettled.

The rest of the day passed in a kind of pleasant haze. Brewer grilled steaks for an early dinner—not shirtless, alas —then stood beside me in the kitchen afterward, watching Teeny play in the yard through the window, the snow glinting in the setting sun. Brewer's arm was warm around my shoulders, and I found myself leaning into him automatically, like my body had already learned this was where it belonged.

He sighed. "Kinda wish I hadn't promised Hayes I'd stop by, to be honest. Video games are so not my thing."

I pulled back just far enough to give him a look. "Did you tell Hayes *that?*" I asked. "Have you ever revealed your deep, dark love of musicals? Maybe he and Kel would watch *Wicked* with you."

Brewer snorted. "Can you imagine?"

"Actually, yes," I said seriously. "I can't tell you how many things I 'couldn't imagine' that have actually happened to me in the last few months. It's this place, man. Weird shit happens in Copper County. Anything is possible. Just talk to him. About everything."

He frowned, and I wondered if I'd overstepped. How

much did I really know about his relationship with Hayes? About any part of his life before we met?

"No risk, no reward?" I asked softly, pushing up to press a kiss to that hard jaw I loved—*liked*—so much.

Brewer's lips found mine in a kiss that was achingly tender. When he finally pulled away, his eyes were dark with promise, and I'd forgotten how breathing worked. "See you tonight? Might be late."

"Come to my bed," I whispered. "I'll be the one with the kraken warlord."

The way his eyes crinkled made me forget everything else. "Then maybe I should leave you to his watery depths," he teased.

I shrugged. "Warlords are overrated. I'd rather be ravished by a man with a tool belt riding nice and low. Pretty sure 'Sledgehammer My Heart' is next month's selection, now that I think of it. Contractor romance is an underserved niche."

My cheeks burned with embarrassment as I realized that I'd inadvertently used the words "heart" and "romance" as if... well, as if I had expectations of him.

I held my breath in fear I'd made things awkward again, but he snorted with laughter.

"You could do serious damage to someone's heart with that thing, Monroe," he said, snickering through a final kiss to my forehead.

I watched him walk away with a strange mix of emotions—relief, longing, hope... but also a growing sense that Brewer and I needed to have a talk. To get on the same page about our... whatever we were doing here.

After the door closed behind him, I headed to my office to tackle the emails from Marjorie's assistant. I needed to find something to break this Empire Ridge story... or decide it wasn't breakable and set it aside once and for all.

But when I opened my inbox for the first time all day, I found it overflowing with messages.

I sighed. Amber had dug up building permits, tax records, and zoning applications for days, sending me a separate email about every single detail, no matter how unimportant.

After scanning through some zoning applications that seemed to make no sense, I clicked into one labeled Property Sale. The first and only attachment was a deed of transfer, dated eight years ago last June.

"Between Anthony Harmon," I read aloud. "As trustee of the Belles Pivoines Trust, in regards to a property at 19 Halifax Street in Southbourne, New York. And Empire Ridge Development Corporation... *huh*."

Anthony hadn't mentioned that the land he'd sold to Empire Ridge had been in a trust, rather than outright owned by him or Harmon Construction. This wasn't a big deal, necessarily—it was most likely a family trust—but something about it niggled at me.

I scrolled to the next page of the document. "Being a parcel of land with residential dwelling and improvements thereon," I murmured. "Containing 4.75 acres, more or less."

I was surprised to discover it was a residence. Anthony had made it sound like unimproved land, not a house. Had he inherited it from his father the same way he'd inherited Harmon Construction? Was it a family home or investment property? None of that mattered, necessarily... except somehow it *did*, for reasons I couldn't quite put my finger on.

That same gut instinct kept me from picking up the

phone to call or email Anthony to get easy answers to those questions. I needed more information first, at the very least a reason for caring one way or the other. It seemed to me selling a home someone might have lived in was an even more egregious result of Empire's strong-arm tactics.

Googling the property yielded no further results, and a street view map gave me none of the information I wanted. I emailed Amber and asked her to get me whatever information she could find on the background of the property.

My phone vibrated on my desk, startling me, but warmth spread through me when I saw the message on the screen.

BREWER

Hayes says hi. Might crash here tonight. FYI, we're watching Wicked and he loves it. Who knew?

Teeny will be fine until tomorrow after all that playing. Will you be okay on your own?

I was glad Brewer wasn't there to see the goofy grin on my face because I was pretty sure if he saw it, he'd know...

I blew out a breath. He'd know I had feelings for him. Strong feelings. Feelings I couldn't hold back. Feelings I hoped like hell he reciprocated.

I really needed to talk to my jam cupboard, as Tam had said.

I typed out a message. *Hey, when you get home—*

But before I could send it, another message from Brewer appeared.

BREWER

FYI, I'm taking your advice and talking to
Hayes about other stuff too. You were right.
Thank you, Delaney. xx

My chest melted into goo, looking at those little x's, hearing Brewer sound so happy—like opening up to Hayes was as cathartic for him as sledgehammering had been for me.

I immediately deleted what I'd written.

I was the one who wanted answers, who wanted facts, who wanted to know in plain English how Brewer felt and where he thought this—*us*—might be heading.

But Brewer needed time with his cousin tonight, which meant I needed to chill. My feelings would keep until the morning.

I'll be fine. Sleep well. We'll talk tomorrow.

I closed my laptop and pushed away from my desk, suddenly exhausted. I stopped to check the lock on the front door, grab a glass of water, and shut out the lights in the dining area. It was funny how quickly I'd gotten used to having Brewer as part of my nighttime routine and how empty the house felt without him.

Then I walked into the living room, headed for the stairs, and saw a pair of giant eyes lurking in the shadows near the bookcase.

I paused with my hand on the banister.

"Fantine Barnum," I scolded. "We are going to talk about this habit of yours, young lady. You can't just come in here and accost me with those eyes whenever you want. There are rules, and without rules, there's chaos."

Teeny lowered her head to rest on her paws.

"You miss Brewer, huh?" I murmured.

Her tail thumped the floor.

"Yeah." I sighed. "I feel that." After a brief hesitation, I surprised myself by waving a hand and saying, "Come on, then. Keep me company tonight."

She followed me upstairs eagerly, nails clicking softly on the hardwood. When we reached my bedroom, I pointed to the rug next to my bed.

"You sleep *there*," I told her firmly. "My bed's a hard limit."

Teeny seemed to accept this. She kept those irresistible pleading eyes safely holstered, circled three times, then settled with a contented sigh in the spot I'd indicated.

I watched her for a moment before climbing into bed, surprisingly comforted by her presence. I was tired but also wired, thinking of all the things I wanted to tell Brewer.

For some reason, I felt nervous, which was unlike my usual fired-up, confrontational style.

I blew out a breath, reminding myself that Brewer and I had come a long way in a few short weeks, and the change had begun when I'd started being honest with him, even about the things that made me nervous.

So tomorrow, I'd tell Brewer how I felt about him and find out if he felt the same way.

Now that I'd admitted to myself I was all in on having a jam cupboard, it was time to get the jam cupboard on... board.

Because this house and the life I was building in it weren't just another stop on my journey anymore. They were my home.

And so was Brewer.

CHAPTER SIXTEEN

IT WAS SOMETIME after midnight when I slipped into Delaney's darkened house, drawn like a compass finding north to the man sleeping inside it.

Opening up to Hayes tonight had been cathartic. For years, I'd avoided discussing my father—what for, when it changed nothing?—but I'd known for a while that my silence had put Hayes in a tough position, and I'd owed him an explanation.

To my surprise, though, once I'd started talking, a torrent of words had tumbled out. About our family business. About my father's years-long push to grow Harmon Construction—supposedly for *my* sake—while ignoring my ideas and suggestions and then my increasingly angry objections and warnings. About how selling our grandfather's house hadn't been my father's only betrayal, just the worst... and the last.

Hayes had truly listened. He'd understood. And then we'd ended the night watching *Wicked*.

But when it came time to sack out on their sofa, I'd changed my mind. I'd missed Delaney. Missed his laughter and his kisses and the soft weight of him beside me as he drifted into sleep. I hadn't even cared when Hayes teased me for wanting to "get back to Hot Delaney."

I simply hadn't been able to stay away.

At the base of the stairs, I met Teeny coming down —*had Delaney actually let her sleep with him?* The thought made warmth bloom in my chest—and I let her outside briefly. I voiced no objection when she curled up by the radiator in the living room as I made my way upstairs.

I stood in the doorway of Delaney's bedroom, watching moonlight spill through the curtains and land in silver puddles on his sleeping form. His dark hair was tousled against the pillow, his face relaxed and peaceful, but one of his arms was stretched out across the empty space beside him as if searching for something.

As if searching for *me*.

I undressed quietly and slid between the cool sheets, trying not to wake him, but when the mattress dipped, Delaney stirred and turned instinctively toward me.

"Brew?" he murmured, opening his eyes a fraction. His sleepy smile sent heat rushing through my body. "Thought y'were at Hayes's."

"I was. But I needed to come home."

Home. The word settled over us like a thick blanket.

When had Delaney become that for me? Sometime between our wine-drunk confessions and our Jam Cupboard Mystery revelations, between apology croissants and accidental dog biscuits, between learning how much he cared about making the world fair and right... and watching him try to make things right *for me.*

I brushed that lock of hair off Delaney's forehead, and his breath caught. Our eyes met in the darkness. Without a word, he slid closer and rested his hand over my thundering heart.

From one beat to the next, our lips crashed against each other, desire and tenderness tangled together. Delaney's mouth opened beneath mine, and I groaned, tasting minty toothpaste and desire.

"Need you," I growled, my hand sliding down to find Delaney's cock, which was already half-hard beneath his sexy, silky shorts.

Delaney arched against me, gasping. "Fuck, Brew—"

Our clothes vanished between more desperate kisses. My mouth blazed a trail down Delaney's neck, chest, and his lean stomach. Then I took him in my mouth, swallowing him deep and relishing the cry that tore from his throat.

Delaney's fingers twisted in my hair, pulling me up for a bruising kiss. "Inside me. Please."

Our bodies aligned with practiced ease. I could count on two hands the number of times we'd done this—fuck, the number of *days* we'd been doing this—but it already felt familiar and perfect. When I pushed inside, Delaney's eyelashes fluttered, but his eyes stayed locked on mine, vulnerable and burning with an emotion I was scared to label out loud.

It looked like adoration. Like *trust*. Finally.

We moved together in perfect rhythm, pleasure building between us like a gathering storm. The way I felt for him was beyond lust, beyond need.

I pulled back out almost all the way and held there for a breath before pushing back in. Delaney's head twisted, his neck arching as his mouth opened on a silent scream.

"Look at me," I commanded, voice wrecked. "Be with me. Stay with me."

"With you." With his eyes on mine, those words

thrummed with power. Like a promise. Like a vow. "Brewer."

His legs wrapped tighter around my waist, pulling me deeper.

When we came—when the storm finally broke—we came together, my hand wrapped around Delaney's cock and the rhythmic pulsing of his channel pulling me head-first into my own orgasm.

After, when we lay tangled in sweat-dampened sheets with Delaney's head on my chest, too tired and sated to move for the moment, words hovered on my lips, begging to be spoken.

Words about falling. About staying. About fitting together like dovetail joints in a way that couldn't be pulled apart.

I wanted to give them all to him.

But already Delaney was yawning, his body going lax and heavy against mine in sleep, so I decided they'd keep until the morning.

I pulled Delaney's plush duvet over us and held him tighter.

And just as I drifted off to sleep, I heard Delaney whisper against my skin, "I'm so glad you came home."

The next thing I knew, weak morning light was filtering through Delaney's bedroom and assaulting my eyelids. I had no idea how long I'd slept or what time it was—I was pretty sure my phone was on the floor somewhere along with my pants—but I felt like I'd slept hard... and apparently without moving a muscle since Delaney was still in my arms.

He wasn't asleep, though. The moment he realized I was awake, clear blue eyes flashed to me, and he gave me a shy smile.

"Good morning," he whispered. "I—"

I wrapped my fingers around the back of his neck and pulled him up to kiss him thoroughly, until those eyes I loved went hazy and his lips were shiny red.

"Now it's a good morning," I said with satisfaction.

Delaney shook his head as if to clear it. "Wow. You should go see Hayes more often if this is what happens."

I laughed. "It was a good night," I admitted. "There were... many revelations."

"Oh?" Delaney's eyebrows went up, but he didn't press, though I could tell he was curious.

To my own surprise, I was eager to tell him.

"Hayes asked me straight off if I'd rather watch a movie or play his zombie game. So I said, 'Hey, have you ever watched *Wicked*? It's really good.' And then I took a deep breath and said, 'I really love musicals.'"

"And he was supportive?"

I rolled my eyes. "The little shit pretended to be all serious. He grabbed my hand and said, 'Thank you for telling me, Brewer. I'm so proud of you.' Apparently, Hayes heard me singing show tunes in the shower."

Delaney pressed his lips together, but his eyes were filled with mirth.

"Go on and laugh," I told him. "Apparently, I'm an open book after all."

"Not true." Delaney sounded serious, but he dropped an affectionate kiss to my chest. "Then what happened?"

"Then... we watched *Wicked*. Twice. And he and Kel loved it. Kel said, 'Fuck, bro, Jonathan Bailey is a *snack*.'"

I laughed, and so did Delaney.

"Hayes was stunned. 'But, Kels, you're straight.'" I did my best impression of Hayes's pearl-clutching shock. "And then... I left." I looked down at him. "It's way more comfortable here."

"Comfortable, huh?" His hand drifted down my happy trail, and he grinned mischievously. "Did *Wicked* get you excited? Be honest. It was Fiyero's tight pants and boots, right?"

I laughed, stretching back into the mattress and propping my free arm behind my head. Delaney's fingers were teasing me gently—too gently—stroking down my hip and thigh as far as he could go before making their way back up, bypassing my morning wood. It was the best kind of torture.

"Honestly," I said once I remembered what the fuck we were talking about. "I'm more into the tousled hair and the vest." I shrugged. "The vest does things to me."

Delaney's hand paused its exploration.

"I have a vest," he whispered. "In fact, several vests. Vests for literal *days*."

"Is that right?" I grinned down at him and found his eyes hot, half-lidded, and focused on my jaw. "Lucky me, huh?"

Just when I thought I couldn't be any more captivated by Delaney, the man blushed.

I grabbed him, rolled him to his back, and kissed him soundly.

"Fuck, you're gorgeous," I said, propping myself on an elbow some long minutes later. "I love being with you like this."

"Me too," he said softly. He blinked up at me, trying to focus without his glasses. "I would—*will*—really miss this, if —I mean, *when*—you get a new camper."

"Yeah," I agreed.

Though by that point, Delaney would be in Costa Rica, probably.

I didn't know exactly how his job worked—was he *always* gone for weeks or months? How long would he spend in Copper County between assignments? Would he want to be with me when he was here? Would a relationship hold him back from achieving his ambitions?

The questions were complicated, painful, *risky*. Emotions that usually made me disengage before I risked too much of myself, back away slowly before I got hurt. But I knew instinctively that I was in too deep with Delaney already.

It was time to stop dancing around what was happening between us. To be brave and name it. To ask what Delaney wanted and be honest about what I could accept.

"Delaney, there's something I need to tell you—" I blurted.

"Brewer, we need to talk—" Delaney began at the exact same time.

He burst out laughing, and I did, too.

"You first," he said. "Please."

"Okay," I agreed since I needed to rip the Band-Aid off anyway. I took a deep breath. "Being around you makes me want to be more open and honest than I've been in a long time. Which is why I need to tell you..." I swallowed, my tongue suddenly too thick for my mouth. *Come on, Brewer. For the love of fuck.* "What I'm trying to say is—"

KAK-WEEEE!

The doorbell's unholy shriek sliced through the morning stillness.

Delaney and I jumped.

"No," Delaney said firmly. His teeth set, and his eyes narrowed. "Absolutely not. *Je refuse.* Continue, Brewer. Please."

"Right." I let out a shaky laugh. "Okay. What I want you to know is—"

KAK-WEEEE!

Delaney closed his eyes. "I take back every single nice thing I have accidentally and erroneously begun to think about this town," he bit out. "I swear to God, Brewer, if someone is ringing our bell to invite me to a butter-churning workshop, or to reenact a human sundial, or—"

"They're probably looking to see the paintings," I said reasonably.

Delaney inhaled through his nose.

KAK-WEEEE! KAK-WEEEE!

Downstairs, Teeny let out an inquisitive bark, just in case the whole fucking town hadn't heard the bell.

"Forces are conspiring against us," he whisper-moaned.

Despite myself, I laughed and pressed a kiss to his cheek.

"Go let Teeny out," I said. "I'll get rid of them. Meet back here. Yeah?"

I grabbed my jeans and T-shirt off the floor and pulled them on as I ran, which meant I was halfway down the stairs when I realized I'd grabbed Delaney's shirt.

KAK-WEEEE!

Fuck.

I pulled the shirt on anyway, though it was ridiculously tight around the shoulders.

"Coming!" I shouted. "Jesus Christ." I threw open the door.

"Oh, thank fuck, Brew!" Kel stood on the front porch wearing his trademark Kitchen Couriers uniform and year-round Birkenstocks. But today, he was wide-eyed, and his hair stood on end—like a cartoon character who'd caught the end of a live wire. "I need to talk to you. Like, *now.*"

"What the fuck?" I demanded. "Is everything okay? Is it Hayes?"

"*Yes!*" Kel pushed a hand through his hair. "Yes, it's Hayes. My dude, I haven't slept. I can't eat. I can't even drink coffee without puking, and you know I can't survive without caffeine." He held out a hand to show me how it trembled.

"Kel," I demanded. "What happened to Hayes?"

"Oh, man." He ran both hands over his face. "He's just... *ugh*. He's *perfect*."

I blinked at him. "He... what?"

Kel shook his head. "I just... I woke up early this morning, and Hayes was laying there next to me, sleeping, and I just... I couldn't..."

His eyes met mine, and then he stopped and cocked his head as if actually seeing me for the first time.

"Brewer, my dude, what are you wearing?"

I glanced down at myself. Delaney's U Conn T-shirt was stretched so tight across my chest, the outline of my nipples was clearly visible in the cold air, and so short it might as well have been Bear Chest night at the Hive.

I hunched my shoulders. "Who cares? Answer me, Kel! Is Hayes okay? Is he sick? Is he injured?"

Kel wrinkled his nose. "What? No! He's completely fine."

"Thank fuck," I breathed. Then I shot him an angry glare. "Then why the hell are you ringing the bell like that this early?"

"Because I need to talk to you, man—"

"Brewer?"

I turned to see Teeny and Delaney standing behind me in the hallway. Delaney had pulled my sweatshirt on over his sleep shorts again. His glasses were slightly askew, and his feet were bare.

Every cell of my body screamed *fuck yes*.

"Oh. Hey, Kel," Delaney said uncertainly. "Everything okay?"

"Yeah," I said.

"No," Kel insisted.

An icy breeze blew through the open door, and Delaney shivered. Without a thought, I pulled him against my side and dropped an arm over his shoulders. For a second, Delaney relaxed against me.

"Ohhh." Kel's eyes widened, and he pointed a finger between the two of us. "Shit. You two were 'sleeping independently' again, weren't you?"

Delaney reacted instantly, stepping away from me with a guilty, apologetic look.

"Stop it right now," he told Kel defiantly. "Whatever you're thinking, you're wrong. I was cold, and Brewer was being... courteous. That's all. We have a professional, client-contractor relationship because Brewer is a professional... *professional*."

If I hadn't already known I'd fallen hard for Delaney Monroe, I would have known it then, watching him stare Kel down with fire in his eyes in order to protect my reputation... all the while, draped in my Portland Builders Con sweatshirt and sporting unmistakable sex hair.

Suddenly, all my questions about the future didn't seem insurmountable. We'd figure it out.

I had no idea what Kel meant by "sleeping independently," but that didn't matter either. I pulled Delaney against me again, ignoring his halfhearted protest.

"We sleep dependently," I told Kel. "Very dependently."

Delaney blinked up at me from behind his glasses. "We do?" he whispered.

"Don't we?" I challenged.

Delaney took a deep, shuddering breath. "We do," he agreed.

I grinned, and then, without looking away from Delaney, I reached out and pushed the door closed. "Talk later, Kel," I called. "Delaney and I are busy now."

"No! Wait!" Kel knocked the door open again. "Brew. Brew-man. Brewski. I *really* need to talk to you. I have a situation. Like, a Code Red Emergency, Houston We Have a Problem, Fire in the Hole situation—"

"Kel," I began.

"*Please*, Brewer. I'll owe you one. I'll owe you a million—"

I started to refuse again, but Delaney put a reassuring hand on my chest and gave me a wink before stepping away. "Come on in, Kel," he said. "I'll make coffee. Brewer and I will talk later."

Because those last words sounded like a promise, I nodded once.

"Fine, then," I told my cousin's friend. "Talk."

"I..." Kel's phone pinged. "Shit. I'm on the clock. I have another order to courier. Could you..." His expression turned pleading. "Could you come with me in the Courier-Mobile?"

Delaney covered his mouth to hide his smile.

I sighed. "Fine. I'll grab my shoes."

"And, like, maybe a shirt that doesn't give *Winnie the Pooh*?" Kel suggested. He shrugged sheepishly. "Kitchen Couriers has standards, man."

This time, Delaney didn't try to contain his laughter.

"I had a plan," I told him as he followed me up the

stairs. I sounded a little petulant because I was. "A plan where you and I had a long, serious talk. Because I have things I want to say to you."

Delaney bit his lip and nodded. "I have things I want to tell you, too."

I grabbed the shirt I'd worn last night from the chair, exchanged it for Delaney's, and continued. "A plan where I showed you the lube I hid in the jam cupboard."

"Oh, fuck," he breathed. "Jam cupboards really *are* the best thing ever."

I shoved my feet into my boots and stood quickly, backing Delaney against his bedroom wall. "A plan that did not involve my cousin's best friend."

"Fuck. Changed my mind," Delaney said, only half teasing. "Sorry, Kel. We need to execute Brewer's plan."

I laughed. "Oh, we're still executing the plan," I promised, kissing him until he was breathless. "We're just reconfiguring it slightly. A tiny tweak to the blueprints. The architect never has to know." I pressed a final swift peck to his lips. "Be home as soon as I can, baby."

Leaving Delaney slumped against the wall, looking gratifyingly slack-jawed and distracted, I grabbed my jacket and went back downstairs.

"This better be good," I told Kel as he backed down Delaney's driveway.

Kel gripped the steering wheel so tightly his knuckles whitened. "It's not good, man. It's... fuck. It's awful. It might literally be the end of the world as we know it. Well, as *I* know it."

"What is it?"

"Okay, so... you remember last night when we were all watching *Wicked*?"

I stared at him. Of all the places I'd thought this conversation might be going...

"Yeah?"

"And Hayes..." Kel chuckled, but it sounded almost pained. "He sang along with 'Dancing Through Life' the second time we watched it and was up on the sofa, doing all the moves?"

I frowned and nodded.

"Well." Kel braked at the three-way stop sign and leaned forward to bang his head gently on the steering wheel. "I think I might be in love with your cousin."

I dropped my chin to my chest. "This was your emergency, huh?"

He whirled to face me, his face stricken. "Obviously! Dude. *Brewer*. What the fuck am I supposed to do now?"

I patted his shoulder. "Keep driving, Kel. Let's get you some coffee."

Kel drove us to Fanaille, where he needed to wait for his next order because, as the server told us apologetically, "We've had a run on honey buns this morning, and Cal's making more."

I ordered us each a coffee while Kel found a table.

"We're best friends," Kel said, picking up his tale before I'd had a chance to drop my ass into the chair. "Closer than brothers. I don't have a single thought I don't share with him. When I think it, *boom*, Hayes knows it. One time, he went to the bathroom when we were at the diner, and I noticed this whirly pattern on the tabletop that looked like a monkey carrying a sword while riding an elephant, and I texted a pic to him while he was peeing just 'cause I knew he'd laugh. You feel me?"

"That's... slightly disturbing. On many levels. But sweet," I added quickly.

I couldn't really relate since I'd never experienced the need to share everything with someone... But then again, I realized I was mentally cataloguing this whole conversation so I could share it with Delaney later, so maybe I had.

"I feel you," I assured him.

"Right, so then you get the problem." Kel looked more serious than I'd ever seen him. "I can't just, just... *feel* this..." He motioned vaguely at his chest. "...and not tell him. If I tried to keep a secret, he'd know."

"So..." I tried to be as gentle as I could. "Why not tell him?"

"Tell him?" Kel gaped at me. "Just drop a bomb of unrequited feelings into the tranquil waters of our best-friendship and see what happens? Dude." He shook his head. "What if he doesn't feel the same? What if he feels bad for me, and we try... something... and it doesn't work out? I can't lose him."

"Yeah," I said heavily. "I definitely feel *that*." I took a sip of coffee. "But—and I can't believe I'm saying this—you can't go through life expecting people will let you down. Someone smart recently reminded me: no risk, no reward."

"That how you started sleeping dependently with Hot Delaney?" he asked.

"We're still not calling him Hot Delaney, Kel," I said with narrowed eyes. "And... yeah, kind of. We're still figuring things out. His job, my bullshit. It's complicated. But I guess the risk of not trying feels scarier than the risk of trying." I swirled my coffee a bit to cool it. "You know, Hayes looks at you the way you look at him."

Kel frowned. "Uh, not helpful, Brew. Until, like, twelve hours ago, I looked at him as a bro and thought I was straight."

I ran a hand over my mouth. "Or maybe you've felt this

way for a while, and you only just let yourself realize it twelve hours ago?" I smiled, realizing this applied to me and Delaney, too. "You're not freaking out about being bi, right?"

Kel gave me a scathing look. "Be pretty stupid if I was, since my best friend's bi, Brewer."

I nodded. "For what it's worth, while we were watching the movie the second time, Hayes wasn't watching the screen. He was pretty much watching *you*."

"Wait, really?" Kel frowned.

"He loves you," I said. "You know that. So talk to him, Kel. Take it from someone who's spent too long not being open with people. And trust that he'll stick with you, no matter what. He's as loyal as they come, and he has a giant heart. But you already know that."

"Yeah, okay," Kel said. He stared at the wall dreamily. "I just need to figure out exactly how to tell him. It needs to be perfect."

By the time Kel stood to collect his order a few minutes later, I was beyond ready to get home and talk to Delaney.

So much so that when Reed approached me with a friendly smile and a lead on a new camper for my land—" my friend Bob and his wife are looking to upsize, and he'll give you a sweet deal"—I thanked him but barely glanced at the contact info he gave me.

Frankly, I wasn't sure living so far outside of town was what I wanted anymore. I thought I might prefer living closer to Hayes and Kel. And Reed.

And, most of all, Delaney.

If only people around here would leave us alone long enough for me to tell him so.

CHAPTER SEVENTEEN

WHILE BREWER DRAGGED Kel out of the house by the elbow, I made my way downstairs in a dreamlike state. Think treacly-sweet Disney princess twirling through the forest... mixed with a dash of Wile E. Coyote after the anvil fell on his head.

I realized in a distant sort of way that this was concerning, or should be. I'd never in my life exhibited any kind of mushy, lovestruck behavior and would have been highly annoyed had anyone suggested I was even capable of it.

But it turned out, being kissed senseless by the man you had strong feelings for after hearing him declare to a known gossip that you slept *dependently* had a remarkably settling effect on a person.

Ten out of ten, strong recommend.

I couldn't even work myself up to more than a mild annoyance about Kel's emergency preventing me and Brewer from having our talk... and our jam cupboard reckoning. After the way he'd made love to me last night, after everything we'd *almost* said this morning, I was confident

Brewer and I were building a future on an unshakable foundation.

Silly me.

After I grabbed some coffee from the kitchen and fed Brewer's dog, I opened my laptop, more determined than ever to finish Empire Ridge one way or another and put it to bed once and for all. I was surprised to find a new email from Amber at the top of my inbox.

"Well, well. Harmon Construction—Background Photos," I murmured to Teeny, who'd flopped on the floor at my feet, apparently deciding we were best friends now. "Amber's been a busy woman overnight."

Curious, I opened the attachment.

The first shot was a black-and-white photo of a tall, smiling, broad-shouldered man in work clothes and a diminutive woman with a bouffant hairstyle, standing in front of a Queen Anne Victorian with a sagging front porch. The caption read: *Harmon Construction Founder Barney Harmon and his wife, Elsie Brewer, outside the family home, 19 Halifax St, Southbourne, 1963.*

The man's smile beamed with so much pride I wanted to smile back... but found I couldn't.

The Halifax Street property Anthony had sold to Empire Ridge *had* been his family home, the one he seemed to have grown up in.

My brain kicked into gear, trying to find the angles here. Why hadn't Anthony mentioned that? Anthony's goal in getting me to write this article was to make himself a sympathetic figure—the little guy corrupted by the big, evil corporation. So why withhold information that supported this claim? It was so counterproductive it had honestly never occurred to me to go looking for this kind of thing.

I quickly reopened the email from last night and

perused the deed of transfer again. Belles Pivoines Trust had owned the property. Why did that name seem familiar? I'd need to go through Anthony's financials again and see if it had been there. But who'd put the property in trust—Anthony or Barney? Who'd been the beneficiary? Why hadn't I explored any of this before?

Frustrated now, I shot off an email to Amber asking if she could find any information about the trust in the heaps of research we now had.

Then I flipped back to the Background Photos email and kept scrolling, looking for answers.

The next items in the document were snippets from newspaper announcements, and I wondered idly if Southbourne's library had digitized their old newspapers.

Announcement of Marriage: Mr and Mrs James Brewer are pleased to announce the marriage of their daughter Elsie to Barney Harmon of Southbourne.

I frowned at the clipping for a moment—Elsie *Brewer?* —before shaking my head at my own foolishness. This was one of those weird synchronicity things. Think of Brewer, find all the Brewers.

The two next clippings announced the arrivals of Elsie and Barney's children, B. Anthony Harmon and Catherine Harmon.

And the one after that—

My breath caught as my eyes landed on an obituary from ten years ago.

SOUTHBOURNE, NY - Barnum "Barney" Harmon, 87, beloved craftsman and founder of Harmon Construction, passed away peacefully...

Born February 3, 1930, to William and Martha Harmon, Barney founded Harmon Construction in 1962...

He was preceded in death by his wife, Elsie Brewer Harmon. He is survived by his son, Brewer Anthony Harmon, daughter Catherine Harmon Lovatt, and grandsons Brewer Harmon and Hayes Lovatt, all of Southbourne...

Shock turned my fingers ice-cold, and the edges of my vision went black.

Hand shaking, I somehow kept scrolling, wanting to find something—anything—that showed it was all a misunderstanding.

But the next image was of a short piece from the *Southbourne Courier*. The headline read: "Father-Son Team Expanding Family Legacy." Below was a photo of two men in tool belts standing side by side, grinning at the camera: an older man with graying hair I recognized as Anthony... and a younger man with a happy tip-tilted smile.

"Brewer," I whisper-moaned to the empty room. "Oh, fuck."

I pushed my chair back from the desk, and Teeny lifted her head in concern.

How was it possible I was writing an article about Brewer's father? More to the point, how was it possible that I hadn't *known* all these weeks?

My brain started putting pieces together, trying to make it make sense. Coincidences like this were practically impossible, weren't they? So had Brewer known I was writing an article about his father and then decided to—?

No. I dismissed the idea as quickly as it formed. *I had*

approached Brewer about the renovations because he'd been recommended, and I'd hired him well before I'd ever heard of Anthony Harmon.

Besides, Brewer wasn't a liar. He wasn't.

I thought about calling Brewer right away, but I needed to get a little clearer on the details. He was estranged from his father, and his father was Anthony Harmon, the man I was trying to *defend* in my article.

Before I talked to him about it, I needed to get the facts straight in my head.

In a daze—*not* the Disney princess kind anymore—I scooted my chair back toward the computer and kept scrolling. The article detailed how Tony Harmon and his son Brewer were expanding the family business, honoring Barney's legacy of quality craftsmanship while taking on larger projects.

Two years later, there was another small newsprint clipping stating that the historic Harmon family home had been sold to Empire Ridge Development Corporation for an undisclosed amount. Plans were underway for a new housing development.

Brewer's words rushed back to me. The stories of him helping his grandfather renovate his house. And then, from that night, we unearthed Elizabeth Winters's paintings: *I'm not close to my family aside from Hayes. My father gave away something that was mine, and I've never forgiven him for it.*

Jesus Christ. Was it possible he was talking about the house?

What if the grandfather who'd loved him and taught him so much wanted Brewer to have his house? And Anthony had sold it before Brewer had a chance to inherit it.

And then they'd razed it to the ground.

My breath caught in my lungs.

If so, this wasn't just a story about corporate corruption, about fighting for the little guy. It was a story about Brewer.

And Brewer hadn't shared it with me.

When we'd been tangled in my sheets, talking about Empire Ridge, I'd asked if Brewer knew anyone who'd had dealings with them. He'd said he had... but he hadn't explained it had been someone in his own *family*. Brewer had stiffened physically and emotionally. He'd pulled back —his default response when he felt vulnerable. He hadn't let me in.

Which begged the question, how much did I still not know about this man who'd somehow become the center of my universe?

The idea that the man who'd told me from the beginning to *trust me, Delaney* might not trust *me* burned in my chest.

I wanted to call him, right that fucking minute, to confront him and demand to know what the fuck was going on.

But just as my anger caught fire, a tidal wave of sympathy and indignation on Brewer's behalf broke over me and snuffed it out.

What must it have been like for Brewer—having his own father sell his grandfather's house to a big developer? The place must've been full of memories, presumably happy ones in which his grandfather had given him a love for craftsmanship. To watch his father hand over his grandfather's legacy to Empire Ridge must have felt like a betrayal.

Christ, no wonder Brewer had built his walls so high.

No wonder he kept people at arm's length and pulled back when he felt vulnerable.

When the person who's supposed to protect you betrayed you like that, how did you ever trust anyone again?

It made my chest physically ache to think about how it must have been—might still be—for Brewer. The man who measured things in Delaneys, who sang Broadway show tunes while grilling steak, who'd crafted parts of my house with those talented hands... had lost his *own* home. And he'd carried that wound alone.

Did Brewer have the same facts his father had given me? Had Brewer chosen not to believe his father? Did he know something I didn't?

If I was able to prove the case I'd been trying to prove, would that matter to him? Would it *help*?

I rolled my eyes at myself. Why the fuck was I sitting here and wondering what Brewer would want... when I could just *call Brewer*?

He hadn't talked to me about his family, and I didn't want to push him, but at the very least, I needed to tell Brewer the article I was writing was about his father. Now that I'd discovered the connection, I couldn't and wouldn't keep it a secret.

I scrambled for my phone and dialed Brewer's number expectantly.

A second later, the muffled sound of Brewer's ringtone came from upstairs.

"Fuck," I groaned, knocking my head on the desk. "He left his fucking phone? Now what?"

I briefly considered calling Kel, but... whatever he had going on seemed like a true emergency. This... wasn't. Technically. No matter how hard my heart was beating.

I'd wait for him to come home so we could discuss this

in person, with context and care. Because he wasn't a fucking source for an article; he was *Brewer*.

The man I was falling for.

And while we were talking, I was going to tell him that, too. Tell him about my feelings, no matter what his reaction was.

Then, if I was very, very lucky, we'd get to the part of the day with the jam closet because Brewer had promised we'd execute his plan—

I froze in my seat, hearing Brewer's deep, woodsmoke voice in my head. *We're just reconfiguring it slightly. A tiny tweak to the blueprints. The architect never has to know.*

"The architect never has to know," I told the dog, recalling the words Brewer had spoken. "The architect never has to know!"

Teeny lifted her head curiously.

All this time, I'd been lamenting the fact that Anthony Harmon couldn't *prove* he'd seen a second, detailed set of official site plans that Empire had used to manipulate him, that Cornerstone Development insisted didn't exist. But what if they'd used a *different* company to develop those plans?

I pulled out a notebook and began googling urban planners in Upstate New York, then contacting all the likely candidates. It was on my third phone call that I finally got a hit.

With shaking fingers, I typed out a text to Brewer.

> Hey! Hope things are okay with Kel. Got a lead on my story and I need to check it out. I'll tell you all about it later. Be back by dinner.

Then I said goodbye to Teeny, grabbed my keys, and ran out the door.

Because there wasn't a question in my mind that *Brewer* was my priority here. Brewer was the person I wanted to make things fair and right for.

I didn't know if getting this evidence would fix things for the man I cared about, but I was damn well going to try.

CHAPTER EIGHTEEN

BREWER

W~HEN~ K~EL~ finally pulled into Delaney's driveway, my knee was jumping, and my brain was buzzing.

I'd only been away from Delaney for a couple of hours, but it felt like years. I wanted to touch him. To kiss him. To ask him if he could see us building a future together. To promise him I was done holding back.

I was as excited as a kid on Christmas morning *and* as nervous as a student rolling into finals without cracking a book. The very large coffee I'd consumed hadn't helped matters.

Neither did seeing an empty parking spot at the end of the driveway where Delaney's Audi had been.

"Shit," I muttered.

"Problem?" Kel asked.

I shook my head. "Looks like Delaney's out. He and I were going to talk when I got home. Maybe he's at Tam's."

I reached into my pocket for my phone to see if he'd messaged me, only to realize I didn't have my phone on me at all. It was probably sitting upstairs on the floor of Delaney's room, where I'd undressed last night.

"Fuck." I dragged both hands through my hair.

"I mean… you'll talk later, right?" Kel said reasonably. He studied my face like he didn't understand my overreaction. "It's not like he's left town."

"Of course not." I scowled, too amped up to appreciate reason and platitudes. But honesty compelled me to admit. "Not yet anyway. He's going to Costa Rica soon."

Kel's eyebrows winged up. "Yeah? Dang. I was hoping he'd stick around more, now that you two are… sleeping dependently."

"His career is part of who he is," I said hotly. I realized I sounded more like Delaney at his most prickly than like any version of myself. "He makes the world a better place by making sure everyone's story gets told." I shook my head. "I'd *never* want him to give that up."

"Well, yeah, but I don't think he'd wanna give up spending time with you either, so." Kel gave a good-natured shrug.

"We'll see. That's one of the things we were starting to discuss this morning—" I clamped my mouth shut.

"Ah, shit, bro." Kel made a face. "And then I interrupted? My bad. Tell Hot Delaney I'm sorry, and I'll bring you guys some chocolate cake later. My treat."

"It's okay, Kel." I patted his shoulder. "Everything will work out."

"Risk and reward," Kel said sagely. "You're walking the walk, and I dig that, Brew. It's, like, inspiring."

I laughed. I wasn't sure I was walking the walk, but I was trying. And I'd feel a fuck of a lot better once Delaney and I could talk.

Sure enough, after Teeny greeted me at the door with a tail wag so hard her whole body wiggled, I found my phone on Delaney's floor and saw a missed call *and* a text message from him.

DELANEY

> Hey! Hope things are okay with Kel. Got a
> lead on my story. I'll tell you all about it
> later. Be back by dinner.

I blew out a breath. It was ridiculous to feel this disappointed about a short delay. Delaney had a job to do... and so did I.

Teeny had trailed me upstairs and laid herself out on the floor in front of me like a large, fluffy rug. Some of the tension left my shoulders as I knelt to rub her belly.

"Delaney left you loose in the house, huh? Your detente has turned into a full-on love affair?" She panted excitedly. "Same, girl. Same."

I spent the rest of the day distracting myself with work, putting the finishing touches on Delaney's kitchen cabinets. They looked amazing. Next week, I'd install the countertop, paint the walls, and declare this room done.

But there were other projects I could imagine taking on around here. Delaney needed more bookshelves in his office and maybe a deck overlooking the lake for summer evenings. Some finials for the jam cupboard that Delaney could hold on to when I fucked him in there.

I caught myself mid-thought and smiled. I was planning a future here, with him. Setting down roots.

When the sun began to dip lower in the sky, I cleaned up my workspace and sent Delaney a text:

> Did the lead pan out? Where did you have
> to go? Ordering dinner to be delivered in
> an hour.

I scheduled the food and began cleaning up my tools.

When the food arrived and Delaney still hadn't texted, I felt the first stirring of nerves. We usually ate dinner by seven since most restaurants around here closed early. Had his car broken down? Had he gotten a flat tire?

But I put the food in the oven to keep warm and told myself Delaney hated when people were overprotective.

Still, I couldn't resist calling him. His phone clicked to voicemail immediately, so I sent another text.

> Dinner's here. ETA?

I decided maybe Kel had the right idea about making things "perfect" for when I dropped my "feelings bomb." I found a clean drop cloth I could use as a table covering, liberated some candles from the drawer in the laundry room, and after pacing in front of the windows—no sign of headlights—with Teeny tracing my steps, I took my supplies to Delaney's office to set them up.

He'd set up picnics on his desk often in the past couple of weeks since it was the only flat surface in the house, and I knew how he cleaned off his desk. Since he seemed to have taken his laptop, the only thing that needed to be moved was his notebook.

But before I could spread out my drop-cloth table cover, I noticed a business card on his desk where his notebook had been.

Without thinking, I picked it up.

B. Anthony Harmon, Harmon Construction

The world seemed to tilt sideways for a second.

"What the fuck?" I asked the empty room. Why did Delaney have my father's card?

My first thought was that he'd come here. That Hayes had refused to act as the go-between any longer, and my father, never one to take no for an answer, had decided to track me down and have his say... which was enraging.

But then I caught sight of the notes scrawled on the pad in my hand.

The top line read: *Empire Ridge — second River Bend plans?*

Beneath that, the words *Cornerstone Development* and *Paradigm Urban Planning* had been scrawled and then crossed out.

On the final line, the words *Beatty Site Solutions* were circled twice.

I let the notebook, along with the candles and table-cloth, slide to the desk.

Of the notes written on the page, the only part I understood was the first line... and even then, I didn't understand.

Empire Ridge was the company Delaney was writing about. The one that had bought my grandfather's house back in Southbourne and destroyed it to build a housing development. River Bend was the name of that development.

But what the fuck did the rest of it mean?

My brain felt like sludge as I tried to process, but one thing came through loud and clear. Of all the shitty things Empire Ridge had done and all the people they'd hurt—which was a fucking large number, given their reputation—the person Delaney had been trying to make things fair and right for... was my father.

I blew out a breath and sank into Delaney's desk chair, my father's card still clutched between my fingers.

Teeny whined softly, sensing my distress, and came to rest her head on my knee.

Did Delaney know B. Anthony Harmon was my father?

If so, how long had he known?

For a fraction of a second, I wondered if he'd known all along—had been working for my father to bring me back into the family fold or something—but even stunned as I was, I knew Delaney would never do something like that.

My father had always been charming, convincing. He'd made people believe he was a power player or a poor, pitiful victim, depending on what suited his needs.

Delaney wasn't like that. He was honest to a fault.

Which meant Delaney had to have just made the connection today, in which case he might be hurt or upset that I hadn't shared...

I stopped suddenly with the realization he might not have made the connection yet at all. It was possible, given how long ago I'd left Harmon Construction and how thoroughly I'd cut my father out of my life since then. We didn't even have the same last name anymore.

Against my will, my brain served up our last conversation, the one I'd walked away from.

"You don't understand, Brew. Empire Ridge threatened me. They threatened us—"

"Bullshit. What did they threaten you with, Dad? Losing money? How much is your integrity worth? How much is mine worth? You might not give a shit about those things, but I do. You had no right to make this deal, to give away what was mine—"

"I didn't ask for your opinion on this deal because I didn't have to, son."

Remembering how helpless and frustrated I'd felt that day made me sick. I hadn't believed a single word my father had spoken, especially not excuses about supposed "threats" he'd used to justify his actions. It was just like my father to shift the blame.

Now, I couldn't help but wonder if he'd been honest for once. If the "threats" hadn't been to his bottom line but of actual physical harm.

Trying not to panic, I called Delaney again.

Voicemail.

Empire Ridge was dangerous—it was clear in the way they'd taken down Harmon Construction and other smaller companies. I'd never heard about them trying physical intimidation, but I wouldn't put it past them.

And now Delaney was out there somewhere, trying to find justice for one of the least deserving men on the planet. What if he was doing it by accusing—or *provoking*—Empire Ridge?

It hit me then just how stupid I'd been not to talk to Delaney about this sooner. As soon as I learned he was writing about Empire Ridge, for sure. I'd prioritized my own comfort. I'd needed to keep my walls up, to stop myself from getting hurt.

And now, Delaney could potentially be in danger.

My stomach churned. This was what happened when you let people in. When you let yourself love someone and that love made you tear your walls down.

I had half a mind to call Kel, apologize, and tell him that "no risk, no reward" was the stupidest Hallmark bullshit ever invented.

I tried calling Delaney again, but once again, fucking voicemail.

I was closer to panicking than I'd been in a long time, and a part of my brain knew I was being unreasonable—he was an *hour* late at most, he hadn't given a specific time in the first place, I had no evidence he was in danger—but I also knew it wasn't the facts that were making me panic.

It was the knowledge that I, a man who'd loved nothing more than solitude, who'd kept nearly every relationship in his life at a surface level for years because that was easier and safer, had somehow given my heart to another human being.

Delaney Monroe was right now walking around—Jesus, please let him be walking around—with *my* heart beating inside his chest right next to his own.

His hurts were my hurts. His frustrations were my frustrations. His sorrow was my sorrow.

How the fuck were you supposed to cope with that? How did you just accept that you were vulnerable, 24/7 for the rest of your life, and continue on drinking coffee and building cabinets and eating croissants?

Teeny whined softly, reminding me that while I was having an existential panic, she probably needed to pee.

I grabbed my coat.

Standing in the backyard, I tried to calm down and breathe, but I couldn't. Now that my walls had crumbled, I didn't know how to compartmentalize. I felt like a tiny boat lost in a sea of emotions—bobbing on tides of fear and anger, nearly swamped by waves of love.

The night was cold but clear—not a single cloud to be found—and through the spindly winter tree branches, moonlight glittered on the snowy lake. Above, a billion tiny stars spilled across the inky blue sky in random, patternless splotches that humans had spent centuries trying to neatly organize into pictures so they could find some sense of order and meaning in them. So they could feel like they were in control.

But as my dog turned herself into a snow angel in the

lingering patches of icy snow, I finally managed a deep breath and remembered something Bennett Graham, the owner of the Observatory House across the lake, had said to me once.

"The most important thing to know about stars, Brew, is that they shine brighter when you're stargazing with someone you love."

At the time, I'd thought he was a total sap—frankly, I still thought that, and so did anyone who'd ever seen him with Theo—but now I wondered if maybe he had it right.

There were a lot of things in the universe you couldn't control. Stars. Fathers. Random, ridiculous camper fires. A world that could be so callous about your love you needed to hide the evidence away in a jam cupboard for decades.

But building walls to protect yourself didn't stop you from being hurt. It sure as fuck wouldn't make the world more fair and right.

All it got you was a solitary life in a camper without the brave, prickly man you loved.

And that was no kind of life for me. Not anymore.

Not when Delaney's triumphs could be my triumphs, and his joys could be my joys.

"Teeny," I called. "Get over here. We're going to find Delaney."

I would call his sister, the police, and my father, in that order. I'd drive to Southbourne and take the town apart brick by brick if I had to.

And then I'd tell the man I loved that I fucking *loved* him, because the fear of being honest was nothing in comparison to the fear of living without him.

But it turned out I didn't have to search for Delaney, because the moment I walked inside, a key turned in the front door.

Delaney was home.

CHAPTER NINETEEN

DELANEY

The ride home from Southbourne had been torture.

A small part of me had been relieved because I'd finally cracked the fucking case. But now that I had proof that, yes, Anthony Harmon had been strong-armed by Empire Ridge, it was cold comfort. Because I'd also learned that, in the process of selling his parents' house, he'd also stolen the one thing Brewer loved most in this world.

His grandfather's house and the legacy he'd been so proud of.

My heart broke for him. I could finally see all of the pieces, and I had to be honest, it left me reeling. Tam was right. Maybe I did always want to find heroes and villains. I wanted so badly to defend the Davids of the world from the Goliaths that I completely lost sight of the fact some people were just... Anthonys.

Typical greed. Simple manipulation to feed big egos. And in this case, wanting to have your cake and eat it, too.

I let out a long breath and cursed myself for also failing to steal my phone charger back from my sister. Because after all of the navigation, calling, and note-taking today, my phone was deader than dead, and I was unable to reassure Brewer, Tam, or anyone that I was finally on my way home.

Maybe it was for the best.

Brewer was going to be so upset with me when he realized I'd come this close to writing an article spinning his father as a victim when the truth was, his father was neither hero nor villain. He was simply an ass.

Halfway to Southbourne, I'd heard back from Amber, who'd managed to track down the trust beneficiaries for Belles Pivoines Trust.

"There's only one, Delaney," she'd said. "Brewer Harmon."

As soon as she'd said it, my brain had belatedly served up the reason the name of the trust had sounded so familiar. I'd seen it printed in small letters on the underside of every teacup in Brewer's grandmother's collection.

Belles Pivoines. A symbol of the family legacy Brewer clung to with both hands and his full heart.

I groaned into the dark night. Today was supposed to be the day I told him how much I cared about him. That I wanted a future with him.

That he was mine and I was his.

But now... would he even listen? Would he want a future with someone who was so incredibly naive that I fell for the lies his father had told me?

Not lies, maybe, but half-truths and spin.

Something a good journalist should have recognized.

When I finally pulled into the driveway and saw my house—every window spilling over with golden light, that big red pickup truck parked in front of the garage—my shoulders hiked up even higher.

I loved him.

I loved him so much I wanted to cry. Because this news

was going to crush him, and I wanted to be the one to comfort him when it happened.

Of course, I wouldn't publish the article now, not if it would cause him any harm. But the mere fact I'd spent the past four months sympathizing with the man who'd seemingly been an innocent victim of big bad Empire Ridge was probably enough to make Brewer second-guess his decision to trust me.

And trust was everything to him.

I didn't walk up the front path; I slunk.

Despite taking my time unlocking the door, it flew out of my hands the moment I pushed it. Six feet of Brewer, wearing his heavy jacket and a face like a storm cloud, greeted me.

"Oh!" I pushed up my glasses and laughed a little nervously before I dropped my laptop bag to the floor. "You startled me. Hi. I'm sorry I'm—*mmmph!*"

Brewer's strong arms came around me, lifting me entirely off my feet. Then his lips met mine with bruising force, and he kissed the living shit out of me.

It took me half a second to react, but once I did, I wrapped my arms around his neck and kissed him back. Emotions crashed together in my head and heart, but one thing I knew.

I would take every single fucking thing I could get from him that he was willing to give me.

I noticed every detail. Brewer's lips were cold, but his mouth was hot and hard and tasted like the gum he chewed when he was nervous. His hands clutched the back of my coat like it had personally offended him. And the breaths punching out of him were ragged and fast, as if he'd run to the door from somewhere far away.

I was back on my feet before I could fully process the change in altitude.

"Where have you been?" he demanded, stepping away.

Disoriented, I stammered, "I texted you. Earlier, I mean. I... I caught a lead, which led to like four other leads, although I only actually followed one—"

"Christ, Delaney! That was hours ago! It's almost nine." Brewer stuffed his hands in his coat pocket. "I had no idea where you were."

I blinked. It had been a long time since I'd had a curfew or someone who expected me to check in. I felt like I should have been annoyed by this on some level, like I was when my siblings were overprotective. But I wasn't.

At all.

In fact, it felt pretty fucking amazing.

"My phone," I blurted stupidly. "It died. I was recording interviews all afternoon. I didn't realize you'd worry, and—" I bit my lip, then I launched myself back into Brewer's arms because there everything made sense.

Brewer kissed me back for half a second, like he couldn't resist, then he broke the kiss.

"I *was* worried," he growled. "Fuck."

"I..." I needed to tell him everything. Now.

But when he dragged a hand through his hair and stepped toward the open door, something stopped me. I noticed his coat and the fact that Teeny was sitting on the entry mat rather than curled up in a warm spot somewhere, like she'd been ready to go out.

Had Brewer been... leaving? Was he so upset he needed to go rebuild his walls again?

Fuck.

"I was in Southbourne," I blurted. "I'm writing an article about your father!" Why did I sound unhinged?

Maybe because I felt unhinged, like a door swinging wildly open and begging this man to walk out of it.

In the sudden silence, I heard the heat kick on and was vaguely aware of Teeny nudging the door closed with her nose.

I stared at Brewer, waiting for his shock, but it never came. His only reaction was the tightening of his magnificent jaw.

"Yeah," he said at length. "I figured that out."

Brewer tilted his head toward the open door to my office. The lamp on my desk was lit and the little pad where I took notes had been moved off to one side. "Found a business card with my father's name on it."

My palms began to sweat. If only I could have called up some of the anger that had motivated me to stomp across Brewer's land and accost him just a few weeks ago. Unfortunately, my anger well was dry.

Besides, this was too important to hide behind my anger.

I licked my lips. "Brewer, I swear I had no idea he was your father until this morning. He approached me last fall with his story, and I believed everything he said—that Empire Ridge showed him site plans that included a firehouse, threatened to basically have the town seize his property if he didn't sell it to them—and..."

I didn't know how to tell him the next part. I wasn't sure how much of this story he already knew and how it played into his relationship with his father. "And today I proved it, Brewer. They really did blackmail him into selling the house."

"Delaney—"

"No, listen, please! I found a man named Walter Beatty, a site planner who did all the fake plans for Empire. He showed me all of them. Your father wasn't the only victim of this scheme."

Brewer folded his arms, and his nostrils flared. "Which is exactly why I was worried about you!"

I'd already opened my mouth to keep talking. To tell him that I was handing over all the information about this to Marjorie on Monday and getting myself as far away from the story as possible. But as soon as his words registered, I clacked my teeth together in surprise.

"Worried? About me? I thought you were worried I was on the road late without calling."

He yanked me back into his arms and held on tightly. "Empire Ridge aren't good people, Delaney. I was worried you were meeting up with them alone or confronting them about something my father had talked you into."

Emotion and exhaustion clashed inside of me, making my knees weak. "Are you mad at me?" I asked in a small voice. "Because I didn't know."

Brewer pulled back just enough to cup my face in his big hands. His eyes were so damned soft, so... loving, I nearly wept.

"I'm mad at your sister for stealing your phone charger. When I called her asking if she'd heard from you, she admitted she'd taken it and suggested maybe you just had a dead battery. I'm buying ten charging cables and a portable phone battery for your damned car and your damned travel bags. If you're ever trapped in a damned Peruvian ditch again, I need you to be able to tell me you're okay, dammit."

I blinked at him. "That's a lot of damns."

He leaned in and kissed me hard, hard enough to bruise my lips and sting my face with his late-night stubble. "I love you, Delaney, Jesus." His voice was gruff and nearly broken.

I gripped his shirt collar with my fingers so he couldn't pull another inch away from me. "You do?"

He clenched his jaw. "Fuck. Yes. So fucking much. And if you don't feel the same way, too fucking bad because I—"

I lurched up and kissed him before crawling up his huge body and clinging onto him with my arms and legs. "I love you," I said in a giddy voice before repeating it. "I love you so much. I love you more. More than you could ever love me."

"'S not a competition, baby," he said with a laugh against my lips.

"Studies show competition in relationships is healthy," I murmured, sneaking baby kisses along the jaw I loved so much.

"You're making that up."

"I was so afraid I was going to lose you," I admitted in a whisper.

His arms tightened more around me before he moved us to the living room and dropped onto the sofa. "Delaney, you'd have to do more than write an article about an asshole to lose me. You'd have to do something egregious like..." He mock-glared at me. "Order red metal fucking cabinets for an unplumb wall again."

I hugged his neck and buried my face in it, inhaling his familiar scent. The scent of home. "Never. I promise. All my cabinets will be handcrafted from now on. By my..." I hesitated.

The deep rumble of his laugh vibrated through both of us. "Say it."

I shook my head, hiding my grin in his skin.

"Your boyfriend, Delaney. Say it," he teased again.

"I'm not writing the story," I said, ruining the mood. It needed to be done. Brewer needed to know everything I'd found out. "It's a shitty story, first of all. Turns out your father was a selfish ass, just like you said."

Brewer nodded. "You should have learned that from me, babe. I'm sorry I wasn't more open with you about my family situation. The stuff with my dad, with the family business... all of it. I finally talked to Hayes about everything, but I never talked to you. I'm sorry."

I ran my fingers along his neck and jaw before glancing up at him. "Will you tell me now?"

As he spoke, I settled comfortably against him on the sofa. Teeny snuffled softly by the fireplace, and the moon slowly rose through the window. The comforting rumble in Brewer's voice would have put me to sleep if he hadn't been telling me such an interesting and enraging story about his father's greed.

By the time he got to the end of it, I was on the edge of the sofa, fists tight and jaw even tighter.

"I'm taking him down," I gritted out. "Fuck that motherfucker."

Somehow, Brewer's eyes danced, and he seemed completely at ease. "No you're not. You're going to write the story, baby. And you're going to do an incredible job."

I crossed my arms in front of my chest. "Fuck that."

He gently pulled my arms away and guided me back into his embrace. "If by 'that,' you mean 'me,' then I say we have a jam cupboard to visit."

I stared at him, incredulous. How could he not... wait.

"A jam cupboard, you say? Tell me more."

He stood up and pulled me up next to him before kissing me and yanking me toward the kitchen. "Did you know there's such a thing as a Temptation Box? Janice Plum told me it used to hold alcohol during the temperance movement, but I think it would make the perfect hiding place for a bottle of lube."

I snorted. "A historic lube bin for teetotalers? I'm never missing one of Janice Plum's Historic whatever-the-fuck meetings again."

He turned to face me and leaned down to throw me over his shoulder with a laugh. "Maybe the wick-dipping wasn't what we thought it was."

We were halfway to a glorious jam cupboard rendezvous when a shrill sound split the night.

KAK-WEEE!

"Oh fuck," Brewer said. "That's probably Kel bringing me chocolate cake. And before you ask, it's a long story. Ignore it."

Easiest decision I ever made.

CHAPTER TWENTY

BREWER

THE STEADY HUM of voices in the grand entry of the old library was punctuated by the clicking sound of Tam's high heels as she walked quickly to keep up with me.

"He's so excited," she said. "And don't tell him I told you this, but he's nervous, too. Palmer Kellogg is here from the *New York Times*. He's been the art editor there for years. It's a big deal."

My eyes traced through the crowd in search of Delaney. What Tam didn't know was that I already knew he was nervous as hell. And I'd spent a good two hours earlier this afternoon trying to fuck it out of him.

"He'll do fine," I said, finally spotting him in a cluster of Coppertians standing next to his favorite E. Winters painting.

"It was generous of you to take time out of your work-week to fix the display," Tam continued, beaming at the way the art exhibition had come together. "The new lighting you installed looks amazing."

It did. Especially because it lit up the man of the hour like he was a golden statue of love personified. His face was warmly lit as he gestured wildly around at several of his favorite pieces. Janice Plum looked on with rapt attention, clasping some kind of basket purse close to her chest. She'd claimed it was "representative of" a Passamaquoddy basket purse "from the same era as Elizabeth and Jean's dear, brave love," but I'd already heard Tam refer to it being a popular mini picnic hamper on sale at Costco over in Piermonte.

"Gonna be a good night," I said to Tam before making a final beeline to Delaney. As soon as he saw me, his entire face lit up in a way that never failed to make my heart rate skyrocket.

"Here he is now," Delaney said, eyes bright. "Brewer upgraded the display lighting for the entire exhibit. He volunteered for hours to make sure that everyone had a chance to see E. Winters's work displayed as wonderfully as possible. Do you know there is a lighting quantity index for museum-level art displays? A study done at the National Museum of San Matteo in Pisa, Italy, showed that..."

As he continued to explain museum lighting theories to Janice, Hen Lattimer, Angela Ross, and a few people I didn't know, I realized how often Delaney's excitement and urge to connect with others was mistaken for intellectual snobbery or, more simply put, his being a know-it-all.

When we'd first met, I'd been put off by his constant quoting of "studies" because I'd thought he only used them to argue with me. But now that I knew him better, and I was aware of—and the lucky recipient of—his huge heart, I saw it more clearly.

He wanted others to experience the varied and rich world the way he did. If he learned something interesting that could improve someone's experience, he wanted to share it.

I leaned over and pressed a kiss to his temple. "I love

you so much," I murmured too softly for anyone but him to hear.

The resulting splotchy pink that crept up his neck made me want to say many other things to him, too, just to see the red streak further down into his collar. But we were interrupted by my cousin.

"Hayes," Delaney said. "Have you seen the lighting Brewer installed? He used energy-efficient—"

"Don't care," Hayes grumbled before ignoring Delaney and glancing at me. "Can I crash in the attic for a while?"

I frowned at him. "What's wrong with your place?" A quick glance around the room revealed his bestie was missing. "Where's Kel?"

Guilt swamped me. I'd meant to follow up with either or both of them to see if they'd worked out Kel's recent revelation, but then everything had happened with my father and Empire Ridge, prepping for the exhibition and settling into Delaney's place for real, and I'd completely lost track.

Hayes's shoulders were up around his ears. "He's being super weird and won't talk to me. I think... I think he's mad at me." He leaned in and lowered his voice until it sounded pitiful and small. "He's gone back to independent sleeping."

Delaney's eyes bounced to mine. I'd told him about Kel's visit, and we'd agreed to let Hayes and Kel sort things out for themselves. But now, I could see Delaney second-guessing our decision. He opened his mouth, no doubt to get involved, when I jumped in first.

"Talk to him, Hayes," I urged softly. "You love him. Tell him you're hurt and worried. Tell him you want to clear the air. Running away isn't going to solve anything."

Hayes's eyes bugged out. "You're telling me to stay and talk? That's rich. Never mind. I'll find my own place to stay." He turned to walk away, but Delaney caught his elbow.

"Wait. Of course you can stay with us. But I agree with Brewer. Staying with us will only draw this out. You would never tell one of us to leave without talking things through, would you?"

Poor Hayes looked miserable. "Fine. Fine. But give me the key to the attic anyway, just in case?"

I pulled out my keys and slid the right one off the ring to give to him. "Take an allergy pill if you head over there. I haven't had a chance to clean the dog hair out of that room yet."

He grumbled and started walking away, a dejected slump to his shoulders.

"Hayes," I called out. He stopped but didn't turn around. "I love you, bro. Come find me if you need me, okay?"

I saw the edge of his lip quirk up as he held up a two-fingered peace salute.

Delaney slipped his hand into mine. "Look at you all up in your feelings. My stoic contractor's come a long way from his grunting days."

I met his eyes and lowered my voice again. "Seem to recall myself grunting once or twice a couple hours ago, Monroe."

The red streaked down his neck into his collar. *Bingo.* "So you did," he said in a higher-pitched tone. "So you did. And I, for one, am in favor of it. Never had a problem to begin with, quite frankly. In fact, I think we could probably afford to take a quick grunting break right n—" His eyes bulged as a woman I didn't know stepped forward to greet us. "N-now, who's this? Marjorie? What the heck are you doing here?"

I glanced at the woman I'd heard so much about. The woman whose voice had risen loud enough through the phone I could hear it from the other room when Delaney had insisted he'd really meant it when he'd told her he was done traveling far from home in pursuit of a story.

"I came to bring you a framed copy of the story as well as a few messages thanking you for writing it and finally exposing Empire Ridge to the public. Mardison-Solvey was especially grateful since they were in the midst of a liability trial against Empire. And the Ghazali family was over the moon. Apparently, their daughter was on the verge of turning down an opportunity to study abroad because of money, and your article returned their confidence in the future of their plumbing business. Once you figure out the Beatty Site Solutions piece and found their other fake layouts, Empire was toast. Well done as usual, Delaney. You're my best *and* my favorite." She beamed at him.

You can't have him back, I wanted to blurt, but I kept my mouth shut. Delaney's journalism career remained just as important to him even though he'd changed directions with it and was focused on stories closer to home. Still, I couldn't help but worry I would lose him to the road one day, regardless of how many times he'd assured me he was mine for good.

Delaney's relaxed smile reassured me. "Nice try, Marjorie. I'm not covering the broken dam story."

"It's in upstate New York!" she squawked. "Only a few hours from here by car. I don't see why—"

Delaney gestured around us. "This is why. See that woman in the painting? Her story was never told. And I'm in the process of telling it."

"Why can't you do both?" she asked. "Keep the money

coming in while you work on the project of your heart. It's a common enough tactic for writers."

Delaney shook his head. "I don't need the money coming in. I landed me a sugar daddy."

I barked out a laugh, drawing attention from several Coppertians nearby. "Hardly," I said. My arm snuck around his back and pulled him closer. "Although I wouldn't be opposed to sharing anything I have with you. It's not much in the end. My most recent client only paid me in sexual favors."

Marjorie's eyes lit with humor while other people's eyes bulged in shock, not because of what I'd revealed—Delaney's and my relationship was old news in O'Leary and Copper County—but because I'd been so casual about speaking of it publicly.

Delaney laughed up at me. "That's not true. I paid you in cash money until you began refusing it. Then I had to get creative." He lifted an eyebrow, reminding me of the "creative" things we'd done to each other the night I'd refused to take his final renovation payment. We'd spent hours closed inside the jam cupboard while I thrust many, many lessons about gratitude into him, and he'd sucked his frustration out of me.

"Creative," I said, clearing my throat. "Yes." Later, I might mention to him that *creative* was a near anagram for *erotic cave*. But there was only so far I would go right now in revealing our personal life in public.

While Delaney insisted jam cupboards didn't need to be secret, they sure as hell needed to be private, especially on the odd Friday night.

I straightened my expression and offered a polite smile to Marjorie. "Has Delaney told you about the artist behind the exhibition tonight? About his discovery?"

"*Our* discovery," Delaney said, repeating a common refrain with a glare in my direction.

"Right. *Our* discovery," I said softly. I leaned down and pressed a kiss to his cheek. "The first of many, hopefully."

He stumbled over his words a little when he began telling Majorie about E. Winters and the paintings in the jam cupboard but eventually got on a roll. People moved closer to listen to him talk about the amazing artist behind the paintings and the lifelong love she had for her partner, Jean.

As I watched him hold court and share his passion for the story, I saw part of him come alive in a way I'd rarely seen when we'd first met last year.

Tam moved back over to me, this time bouncing little Tierney on her hip. Lucas wandered off to look more closely at the painting that featured the half-built observatory. Theo and Bennett had camped out near that one to answer questions about the observatory to anyone who wanted to know more since they lived there now.

"He's in his element," Tam said, tilting her head at Delaney as he launched into a timeline of E. Winters's life in Copper County.

"Who would have thought?"

She laughed. "I knew he had it in him. The question was whether or not he'd let himself relax enough to realize it." She glanced up at me. "He's actually good with people. If he can get out of his own way and let go of his insecurity."

I nodded. "I used to think he was a snob," I admitted.

She laughed. "Oh, he is. Surely you've heard his lecture about why powdered tannins in wine are—"

"A structural shortcut," I finished the phrase with her with a chuckle. "Please don't let him hear you, or he'll start expounding on the use of Mega Purple in cheap domestic reds. Trust me, you do not want to get him started on Big Cab Sav."

She nudged me with her shoulder. "I have to hide my boxed wine in a container that says 'breast milk stuff' just to keep him from discovering it."

We watched him for a few more moments until Tam glanced at me out of the corner of her eye. "Everything okay with you and your dad? Delaney warned me not to bring it up, but I can't help but ask how you're doing with all of this? Are you mad Delaney still wrote the story?"

I took a deep breath and let it out. "Tam. I'm so fucking proud of Delaney I don't know how to put it into words. He worked his ass off getting to the absolute truth of the situation and then presented it from all sides. Like a good journalist should. I would have been angry if he'd sat on it, and I would have been disappointed if he'd written it the original way he'd intended. But I also know he never would have done either one. He's good at his job."

"The best," she said proudly.

I held out my index finger when Tierney reached for my necktie. Her tiny fist tightened around it. "As for my dad, things aren't okay, and that's okay. If that makes any sense. I finally met with him, after the story was published, and let him say everything he wanted to say. And then he let me say everything I needed to say. And nothing changed. As far as I'm concerned, we have closure. He's not happy about it, but that's not my problem. I suspect he was only trying to make nice with me to get me to come back to the family business and bring my trust money. And that's not happening."

Delaney threw his head back and laughed as Janice gestured with her wicker basket purse and nearly knocked the ladle out of a nearby punch bowl.

I glanced at Tam. "I'm using that money to help Delaney establish the permanent E. Winters collection in an art exhibition wing here in the library. Don't tell him, though. Right now, I'm still negotiating with the head of the town council to get approval on the expansion before pitching the idea to Delaney. I know he wants to set up a permanent collection, but he hasn't been able to find a place to properly care for it. With my trust fund, I can endow a foundation for local art like this here in town."

Tam's eyes filled as she looked at me. "That's amazing. He's going to freak out when you tell him. But he's also going to insist on helping pay for it."

I glanced back at the man I loved, holding court here in this quirky small town—a place neither of us thought we'd ever quite fit in. "I look forward to the negotiations with him. I'm sure we can get creative," I murmured.

And later that week, in the warm lighting of our jam cupboard, we got very, very creative indeed.

EPILOGUE
DELANEY

A year and a half later

"Delaney, get over here!" Brewer shouted from across the large new deck on the back of the house. "Cheese or no cheese on your burger?"

Hayes nudged me. "He's calling for you, bro. Tell him double cheese for me and my boo. Gracias."

"You tell him," I said before thinking up a reason to head back into the house. Unfortunately, Brewer caught me at the back door.

"Come with me," he growled, pulling me by the elbow toward the monstrosity he called a grill.

"Oh, no, thank you," I said airily. "Important things in the kitchen. Must fetch them. BRB, love."

"Delaney Patrick Monroe," he snapped. "Contrary to your belief, you are not a danger to those you love while in proximity to a grill. Get over here and handle my cheese."

"You make it sound dirty," I muttered, following obediently now that I was caught out. "And, look, any number of our friends and family could have helped you with your little cheese problem."

The deep rumble of his laugh helped mitigate my nerves as we approached the Master Grill Station Ten Thousand or whatever the hell this thing was called. "*You're* my little cheese problem. You offered for everyone to put in special cheese requests on their burgers and then left me to manage six variations of cheese options." He pointed to the tray with all of the gourmet slices on it. "Who wants what?"

I began to tick everyone's preferences off on my fingers. "Samuel wants Gouda, Oliver wants cheddar, Derry wants—"

"Numbers, babe. How many of each?"

I handed him the slices and watched as he tossed them onto the patties, as if being this close to an open flame was no big deal. Thankfully, Teeny sensed my nerves and appeared at my side as she always did.

"Hey, big girl," I murmured, tangling a hand into her fluffy ruff. "I know you asked for five slices of Kraft American, but this house has standards, remember? We talked about it. No more square cheese product. It's because we love you. Studies show—"

She cut me off with a little *woof* of complaint.

"Don't think she likes your studies, babe," Brewer said.

"She liked the one about treat frequency versus tail-wag intensity," I reminded him before turning to greet Chris and Reed Sunday. "Good God, is that a baby?" I blurted. "Your surrogate gave birth?"

Chris beamed at me, holding the blanket-wrapped raisin proudly. "Meet Andrew Dante Sunday. He's three weeks old today."

Reed's big hand splayed on Chris's lower back as he

smiled lovingly down at his little family. "How could you not have known? My brothers took out an ad in the *Gazette* and the Little Pippin Hollow newspaper. I'm surprised they didn't ask the *New York Times* to run an article about it."

Brewer leaned around me to gaze at the wrinkly newborn. The way his face softened made my nonexistent ovaries twitch a little. "Looks like a charcuterie specialist in the making. Well done, guys."

Chris teared up. "You think? Gosh, that would be amazing! He could work side by side with me and—"

"Already got him a Nerf gun," Reed cut in. "Proper weapons handling needs to start from the cradle. Ask any operative."

Chris frowned. "I don't think—"

Tam stood up and stretched her back, inadvertently thrusting her giant belly into the patio table. "Fuck me, I wish this one had a weapon so he could shoot his way out right now," she muttered. "Remind me never to gestate another boy. They're violent and mean."

Lucas walked up and handed her a cold glass of lemonade before kissing her on the lips. "Tierney was just this bad, and you know it. And not ten minutes ago, I saw her playing dainty teacups with the most beautiful set of—"

The clatter of grill tools followed us as Brewer and I bolted into the house. "I forgot to lock the cabinet," I cried over my shoulder. "I'm so sorry!"

"I locked it," he said, grabbing my hand as we skittered to a stop in the kitchen and found Derry Bartlett and Bennett Graham's niece—who were home from college for the summer—sitting on the ground playing with Tierney. In the toddler's chubby hand was a little plastic teacup that looked like it had come from a Disney playset.

"Oh." Brewer and I said at the same time. I glanced at

the glass-front cabinet that held Brewer's grandmother's teacups. The cabinet he'd lovingly crafted for me when we'd first gotten together. All of the teacups were safely tucked behind the glass, and the lock was clearly secure.

I blew out a breath. "You all okay in here?"

Derry's eyebrows dipped in confusion. "Yeah? Me and Vega are just keeping an eye on Tierney." He elbowed his friend. "Vega, do you know Delaney? He's Tam Monroe's brother. The one who found the paintings."

"Ohhh, right." Vega nodded. "Nice to meet you."

For a second, I was almost amused. I'd gone from being the non-hockey-playing camper-arsonist to the finder of hidden paintings? All in all, a sweet trade.

But it was much sweeter knowing I didn't really care anymore what other people called me. I was a brilliant journalist. I was a Coppertian. And I was Brewer Barnum's one true love.

"You too." I nodded. "Can I get you guys anything?"

Derry's face lit up. "I'm starving. Those burgers almost ready?"

Brewer's eyes bulged. "The burgers."

Just then, someone yelled, "Fire!"

The two of us took off running toward the deck. When we burst through the back door, Janice Plum was gesturing animatedly. "And then the big, sexy fire chief climbed up the tree, of course, and rescued the kitten shifter, if you can believe it? He got there just in time and foiled the arsonist. And the badger fire chief and kitten accountant professed their love, which was a very..." She sniffed. "Poignant moment, as you can imagine."

Angela Ross rolled her eyes. "As far as honey badger shifter romance goes."

I glanced over to the grill where Brewer was taking the

tools back from Bennett and thanking him profusely for saving the burgers.

My shoulders fell as I let out a breath. "Jesus."

Lawson winked at me. "Agreed. Who knew romance novels were so exciting? I think I'm going to need a permanent pass to your book club, brother of mine."

He sat on a comfortable chair off to the side of the deck with his leg propped up on a small table and his strappy brace covering the nasty scars from his recent knee surgery.

"You should retire and come book-club with me full-time," I urged. It wasn't the first time I'd suggested it. His body couldn't keep taking a beating year after year like this.

"Nah. Still got a little juice left in the tank. Hell, if I can find a personal PT to come work for me full-time, I might be able to make it through a few more seasons. But I like my visits to Copper County. Don't know if you know this, but the Kraken Warlord series got me through the stress of playoffs and my resulting surgery." He leaned forward to reach for Tierney when Derry brought her outside. "C'mere, Li'l T. Uncle Law needs someone to cuddle and show me her sparkly nail polish."

Tierney's face lit up when she heard the words sparkly nail polish, so I left the two of them and wandered over to the grill to help Brewer.

Once we'd served everyone and finally found our own spot on the steps down into the yard, Brewer watched as I took a huge bite of my burger.

"I want kids," he said.

I began choking and sputtering. The damned asshole only grinned. "You did that on purpose!" I accused after catching my breath and taking a healthy swallow of beer.

"Maybe. But it's still true."

I opened my mouth to say... well, I wasn't quite sure

what I was going to say—it wasn't that I didn't want a family because I did, I just wasn't sure if I was ready or not—when he held up a hand. "Now, before you quote studies at me or tell me I'm rushing you, I need you to know I'm not in a hurry. I guess I'm just... I'm happy, Delaney. And I want to share it. Grow it. Grow something with you."

Across the yard, Watt Bartlett was showing Jasper the ramp Brewer had built onto the dock so that Teeny could get herself out of the water without swimming all the way to shore. Jasper peered up at his husband with amused affection while Watt mimicked the way Teeny lumbered up the ramp and shook off the water as soon as she was almost all the way to the top.

I looked back at Brewer. "Maybe it's time I gave you your birthday present."

His eyebrows dipped. "You gave me a new air compressor for my birthday, which was three months ago, for what it's worth. Not to mention, you also gave me tickets to *Mamma Mia* and a trip to New York to see it."

For some reason, I was nervous. "Right. And I had this ready for you, too, but I knew you'd probably refuse it, and I can't... I don't..." I blew out a breath and met his eyes. "Please don't refuse it," I finished in a whisper before pulling out a worn piece of paper from my back pocket. I'd been carrying it around ever since I'd chickened out on his real birthday.

Brewer pulled the paper from my grip and unfolded it. I watched his expression carefully as he realized what he was looking at.

"This is a deed to your house."

"*Our* house," I corrected, nodding at the paper. "If... if you'll have it."

We both knew I wasn't just offering the deed to my

house. I was offering him my home, *our* home. A permanent place in my bed and in my life.

And in my heart.

Brewer's giant hand cupped the back of my head as he smiled softly down at me. "Of course I'll have it, love. Everything I hold most dear is in this house."

"Your teacups?" I teased.

He leaned in and kissed me long and hard before pulling back and meeting my eyes. "Nah. The kitchen cabinets. Oh, and the custom-designed vanity I made you that matched Theo's girthy one."

I remembered coming home from Lawson's playoff game in Toronto to find the vanity of my dreams installed in the downstairs bath, and the memory made me a little swoony.

Still, it didn't do to let one's boyfriend—even if they were a beloved, custom-cabinet-making boyfriend—get too complacent, so I pinched his side. "Asshole."

He kissed me again, his fingers tangling in my hair. When he pulled away this time, we were both breathing heavily. He grinned at me.

"Okay, fine. The best damned jam cupboard I could have ever found."

I crawled into his lap and straddled him, right there in front of everyone, and kissed him for all he was worth. Brewer's arms tightened around me as a small, familiar sound of surrender escaped his throat.

He was right. Jam cupboards were the absolute best.

And so was this life I'd found in Copper County. My big, beautiful, limitless life with Brewer Barnum, our historic home, plenty of friends and family, and possibly little bossy baby Brewers running around one day.

We weren't misfits anymore. We were exactly where we were meant to be.

Ready to find out what happens when Kel confesses his feelings to his best bro, Hayes? Find out now in The Level Up, *a* Misfits of Copper County *bonus story →* https://readerlinks.com/l/4731504

Haven't met Hen and the other members of the O'Leary-Copper County Council for Historical Happenings yet? Start your binge read of the Love In O'Leary series today with The Fall *→* https://readerlinks.com/l/1570174

ABOUT MAY ARCHER

May is an M/M author who lives in Boston. She spends her days planning vacations, mainlining diet soda, avoiding the gym, reading M/M romance, and when all other forms of procrastination fail, writing it.

Visit her website at mayarcher.com to sign up for her newsletter to hear about sales and upcoming releases, freebies and behind the scenes info and more! Or join her Facebook group, Club May!

facebook.com/may.archer.author

instagram.com/mayarcherauthor

amazon.com/May-Archer/e/B075JQVGLX

patreon.com/MayArcherRomance

bookbub.com/authors/may-archer

ALSO BY MAY ARCHER

Find me online → https://linktr.ee/mayarcherauthor

Love in O'Leary Series

Whispering Key Series

The Sunday Brothers Series

Copper County Series

The Way Home Series

Licking Thicket Series

(cowritten with Lucy Lennox)

Champion Security Series

(cowritten with Lucy Lennox)

Honeybridge Series

(cowritten with Lucy Lennox)

For a comprehensive list of titles, audio samples, freebies, suggested reading order, and more, visit my website at www.MayArcher.com!